# THE GIRLS TAKE CONTROL

Geoffrey Kiggundu

www.geoffreykiggundu.com
Tuundu Publishers
Milton, Ontario

ISBN: 978-0-9918487-3-7

TO MY SISTERS

I would like to thank the following people for their help with this novel:

My editor, Barbara Feldman. Barb, you have done it again! Thanks for your diligence, attention to lexical and structural details and for your prompt communication. My book launch team in Toronto—you know who you are—for your ongoing support.

# 1

# July 2013

"I THINK WE should take Hellen's concerns seriously and try to address them," Herbert said as he closed the front door after he and Leah had said goodbye to Hellen.

"Why should we?" Leah asked.

"As a business consultant, Hellen knows what she's talking about. We should heed her advice and close down the restaurant."

"No," Leah answered, sounding irritated. "We may not be making any money from the restaurant but I am not ready to close it down."

"Darling, it's not just that we are not making any money from the restaurant. I think we are losing money there and we will lose much more if we don't—"

"But you and I know that that restaurant is not just a business. It represents a lot more to my mother. It's her legacy. And I am determined to protect my mother's legacy at all costs."

"But darling, that's not enough to justify keeping the restaurant open. Besides, I will ask you the same question that Hellen asked. Do you really know what takes place at the restaurant since your mother stopped working there?"

Leah stood up, not answering Herbert's question. She was beginning to lose her temper. "I think it's time for dinner," she said, and left the living room.

"That restaurant is bleeding money," Herbert said while they were having dinner, "and the earlier we close it down the better."

"Babirye and Hellen behave very much like your mother," Leah answered, indirectly making it clear to Herbert that she did not want to discuss the restaurant any further. "They want to impose their views on others no matter the outcome."

"Listen, darling, the matter of the restaurant is up to us. I don't think Hellen is going to insist on closing down the restaurant or even follow up. I think her major concern now is going to be how to make her long-distance relationship work."

"Conrad will have to move to America eventually. For how long will Hellen be coming here to see him?" Leah asked as she put another piece of steak on Herbert's plate.

"We'll see."

Herbert realized that Leah was determined to keep the restaurant open. He decided not to bring up the topic again.

\* \* \*

"Do you guys know that Mom and Dad don't seem to be paying any attention to how their mothers' businesses are being run?" Hellen said to her sisters after they had finished dinner in Babirye's home one hour and a half after she had talked to her parents. While the three sisters were talking in the living room, Babirye's husband Brian, Nakato's husband Roland and Conrad were discussing English Premier League soccer in the dining room.

"They simply don't care," Babirye answered. "But what would you expect? They didn't build those businesses."

"You know what? I'm not gonna let that attitude continue. I'm gonna jump right in, even if it means closing down those businesses. Are either of you with me on this one?" Hellen said.

"Yes, you have my support," Nakato answered.

"You have my support, too," Babirye said.

"Cool. Stay tuned," Hellen said. "I'll think of what to do and I will let you guys know when I am ready."

A half an hour later, Babirye and her husband Brian said goodbye to Hellen while Conrad, Nakato and her husband Roland drove Hellen to the airport.

At the airport, when she finally had to say goodbye, Hellen hugged Conrad and cried briefly. She said that she would miss him. He said that he would miss her too. Conrad put on a brave face because he did not want his sister-in-law and her husband to see him crying but had he been alone, he would have cried. He waved vigorously a few minutes later as Hellen disappeared into the crowd of departing passengers.

❋ ❋ ❋

During the flight back to Boston, Hellen's thoughts drifted from Conrad to her grandmothers' businesses. She was certain that the family could not afford to continue operating the restaurant. She'd try to convince Leah to close it down. But even though she hadn't had a chance to analyze the accounts of Ruth's Classic Boutique, she thought it could thrive under better management.

Hellen thought that a brief written report might be the best way for her to share her first impressions of her grandmothers' two businesses with her parents. She switched her laptop on and began to type some notes about her observations.

Under the heading "Ruth's Classic Boutique," she wrote, "I had a one-hour-long conversation with Elsie, the acting general manager. She answered all my questions satisfactorily. I also chatted with the team of buyers. They seem to be on top of things. Although the boutique seemed to be understaffed, it was running well, but it was clear that Grandma's sudden departure left a void. Elsie said that she is supposed to be reporting to Dad, but Dad has visited the boutique only once in the last six months. Uncle Clement visits the boutique regularly and he always asks Elsie to give him cash. Elsie says that Clement has no clue how to run a business. She also said that the poor relationship between her and the other manager, Katana, is her biggest problem at the moment."

Hellen stopped typing and read her notes. *Perhaps I should have stayed a week longer with my hubby.* Images of Conrad's smiling face flashed in her mind. She missed him already. She clicked on a few of the wedding pictures that she had saved on the laptop.

The young man who was seated next to her glanced at them and shifted in his seat. Although she would have liked to play an entire slideshow of the pictures, she closed the file and resumed typing her notes.

Under the heading "Kyatelekera Restaurant," she wrote, "Uncle Sam is in charge of the restaurant, but it seems he is there only because he has no other alternative. He failed to answer any of the questions I asked him about the operations of the restaurant. When I visited, there were two customers chatting with Uncle Sam. Most probably they were our relatives. When they finished their lunch, they walked out without paying for their meals. I don't think there is any chance of turning Kyatelekera Restaurant around. When I asked Mom and Dad about the restaurant, they didn't provide any satisfactory answers. When I asked if they really knew what takes place at the restaurant, Mom simply laughed at the question and said that she was not ready to close it down."

Hellen paused to think. *Mom has gotten emotionally attached to the restaurant. My grandmothers worked hard to build their businesses but it's sad that Mom and Dad have neglected them. It's not very surprising, though. They don't care much about the family's wealth because they didn't accumulate it themselves. I've got to do something to reverse that situation.*

\* \* \*

When Hellen arrived at Logan International Airport, her friend and business partner Gwen was there to welcome her back and to drive her home. They hugged before Gwen put Hellen's suitcases into the trunk of her car.

"That was one amazing wedding, Hellen," Gwen said as she started the car. "You are now a wifey! How does it feel? How was Conrad when you left?"

"He was good, although it was clear that he didn't want me to leave—you know what I mean?" Hellen said. "Thanks for coming and for being there for me. I was glad you were there."

"I had a wonderful time. Wow! That was like a wedding of a superstar. You guys rocked it."

"Yeah, it's been a month full of fun."

"I can't believe you are a wifey now!"

"Yes, I am. And I feel great," Hellen answered.

"How will Conrad cope without you?"

"He's feeling lonely now. But I told him I'd be going back in four months or so to see him. And he was like, 'That's too long. How can I live that long without you?'" Hellen said, smiling.

"You do miss him, too."

"Of course. Poor man, he has never cooked a sensible meal in his life!"

"He can't cook?" Gwen asked, laughing.

"No, he can't. He eats out most of the time or he eats at his parents' home. Sometimes, his cousin who lives in the same neighbourhood cooks him some food. But he found out during the days I was there that she's been buying groceries too frequently and too expensively."

"Really?"

"Yeah, apparently Conrad's been feeding her family too, and he only found that out last week! Obviously the woman was angry with me because she has been doing it for years. He told her right there in front of me that she has been milking him and that she would not get a single *dollar* from him again." Hellen caught her mistake and laughed. "She would not get a single *shilling* from him again."

Gwen laughed too.

"The woman couldn't hide her annoyance with me. You know what I mean?"

Just then Hellen's cellphone rang. It was Conrad.

"Hey, I've arrived safely. I miss you," she said. "I am with Gwen and we are driving home now. Say hi to her," Hellen said, turning on the speaker.

"So what adjustments are you planning to make now that you've added another facet to your life?" Gwen asked after Hellen had ended the call.

"What was that? Facet? That's funny," Hellen said, laughing. "Of course the daily phone calls to Kampala will continue. I have to make the long-distance relationship work and I think that's gonna be kind of challenging."

When they arrived at Hellen's condo building, after Gwen helped Hellen to take her suitcases upstairs, they watched a slideshow of the wedding pictures for half an hour while they chatted. It was obvious that Hellen was tired after the long flight.

"I guess you need a nap," Gwen said as she rose. "We'll catch up tomorrow. Your lunch and dinner are in the oven and please call me if you need anything."

Hellen did not go to sleep right away. Instead, she went into her home office room and wrote a rough draft of the following month's to do list, including intervention in her grandmothers' businesses, pausing for a while to wonder whether she was taking on too much. *Doing all this and making a long-distance relationship work? Oh, well.* Walking out of the office, she dropped the notebook on the couch and went to the bedroom.

She felt an urge to call her husband but before she picked her phone to call, it rang and it was Conrad. They said that they missed each other and talked for ten minutes. Hellen wanted to talk longer but Conrad insisted she rest. Minutes later she fell into a deep sleep.

✳ ✳ ✳

Hellen and Gwen had a business meeting the following day. After Gwen presented a business status report, Hellen thanked her for "holding the fort" while she was away. They then chatted a little more about the wedding. Hellen brought up her grandmothers' businesses.

She explained the situation to Gwen. "Both my grandmothers owned businesses, one a restaurant and the other, a home furnishings boutique, which they built over decades. But my parents have neglected them and they are losing money. I want to stop the losses by closing them down." She paused. "Actually, the boutique seems to be doing well. It simply needs better management."

"Did you tell your parents what your thoughts are?" Gwen asked.

"Yeah, I did, but my mom was like, the restaurant is her mom's legacy and she was like, 'We can't close it down when my mother is still alive.' You know what I'm saying? Like, educated as she is, she doesn't realize that it no longer makes sense to continue running the business."

"So, have you thought of a specific action plan for both of the businesses? What will you do about them?" Gwen asked, in full business consultant mode.

"Before my sister Nakato talked to me about the businesses' performance—she is the one who asked me to go see for myself—I didn't know what was going on there. But now that I am aware, I want to stop the losses and I am ready to do all it takes."

"Let me know if you need my help."

"Yes, please help keep me accountable. Make sure that I call Mom and Dad next Wednesday to continue the discussion," Hellen said as she rose to prepare lunch.

Gwen set a reminder on her phone.

# 2

# **July 2013**

CONRAD RETURNED TO work two days after Hellen left, arriving early at his office. But he couldn't concentrate on his work. He couldn't get Hellen off his mind. He pictured her beautiful face. Her smile. Her deep, warm voice rang in his head. He recalled the wonderful month they'd spent together. He wondered how he was going to live without her.

That evening after work he met with his friends at the Sunset Pub. He had not gone there during the month that Hellen had been visiting and now felt less enthusiastic about going there. He went anyway simply because he did not want to completely stay away from his friends—for one thing, he needed their company, and, two, he didn't want them to think that Hellen was controlling him.

Now, a married man, Conrad felt a new sense of responsibility. During the following weeks, for the first time in eight years, on some evenings he went straight home from work. There he would spend most of the time thinking about Hellen. He would open a bottle of beer and sit to watch TV while waiting for Hellen's daily phone call.

"So, what are you having for dinner tonight?" Hellen would ask.

"I have no idea. I think I'll head out for a quick bite," Conrad would often answer.

They would stop the conversation so Conrad could go to have dinner and resumed it before he went to bed.

One evening, Hellen decided to challenge Conrad to cook. "I don't think it's a good idea for you to eat out every day. Why—"

"You know my problem, dear. I don't know how to cook," Conrad answered, laughing.

Hellen laughed too. "Guess what? I will help you. Check the pantry to see what ingredients you have in there," she said.

Conrad went to the kitchen. He opened a cupboard and told Hellen the foods that were there. He then opened the refrigerator and told her the foods that were there.

"Okay. So, do you want to eat pasta or rice?" Hellen asked.

"Rice. I don't like pasta," Conrad answered.

"And you have it in the house? Honey, you shouldn't buy stuff you don't like."

"It's you who bought the pasta while you were here."

Hellen gave instructions while Conrad followed along, to prepare his dinner. From that evening on, he would e-mail his meal preferences to Hellen and she would walk him through some simple recipes to prepare his meals.

But Conrad couldn't stand living far away from Hellen any longer. He felt lonely. When he went to visit his older brother Nathan one evening, he talked to him about it. Nathan tried to help him find a solution.

"Have you tried to convince her to live here with you?" Nathan asked.

"No, I haven't but I don't think she would accept that," Conrad answered. "She is a very independent woman."

"Did you discuss your living arrangements before the wedding?"

"Just a little bit. We fell in love and focused mainly on that," Conrad answered, laughing, and Nathan laughed too. "But now I am in a dilemma. On one hand, I wouldn't want to walk away from my job and my current life. On the other hand, I don't want to live alone anymore when I am married. I miss Hellen."

"You are thirty-two but you are behaving like a teenager in love. It's time to make some tough decisions, brother," Nathan said, tapping Conrad's shoulder. "What are you going to do?"

Conrad remained silent for a while. "I think I will join her in Boston. Leaving everything behind and starting over is a tough decision to make but I think I would do it for Hellen."

"Here's my suggestion. If you feel you can't live without Hellen, take a year off work and go test the waters first," Nathan said. "Don't jump in with both feet. And if it doesn't work out, you can return home and to your job."

"Thanks for the advice," Conrad said. "I think that's the wise thing to do."

❋ ❋ ❋

A week had passed since Hellen had returned to Boston, and she still hadn't called her parents to discuss her grandmothers' businesses. She knew that the conversations would get more uncomfortable the more she pushed her parents to act, more so because Leah did not want to close down the restaurant.

Now she'd been sitting on her bed for about five minutes with the cellphone in her hand but could not bring herself to call. *I am now married. I should be caring about my and my husband's interests—it's up to Mom and Dad to decide what to do with their mothers' businesses. And after all, my big sisters live in Kampala. It's they who should confront Mom and Dad, not me. I shouldn't be labeled the troublemaker.*

However, since Hellen had asked Gwen to remind her to call her parents she knew that Gwen would ask if she'd called. "If you want to succeed at anything, don't avoid the hard stuff, don't avoid the difficult conversations," Gwen and Hellen often told their clients. And Hellen knew that she had to follow this advice.

So she went to the living room, sat on the couch and called her parents. "Dad, I want to know the plans you guys have for the restaurant," Hellen said after the greetings.

Herbert had predicted to Leah that their daughter would probably not continue that particular conversation, so Hellen's question took him by surprise.

"Hellen, if you want to talk about the boutique, I am listening," Herbert answered. "But don't ask me about the restaurant. I don't know anything about it."

"You don't know anything about the restaurant? Are you serious, Dad? Have you guys made any decisions about those businesses since we talked?"

"Hellen, nothing has changed. Your mother wants to keep the restaurant open," Herbert said as he rose to answer a call on his second cellphone. "Hellen, can you call me back in five minutes?"

Hellen thought that her father was looking for a way to avoid her questions. When he ended the call, she called her sister Nakato. Hellen said that she was frustrated by the fact that their parents hadn't made any decisions about the businesses. Nakato said that she would talk to their grandmother Ruth for advice on the matter.

❋ ❋ ❋

When Leah returned home that evening, Herbert asked her about her mother. They discussed Merab's health for a few minutes before Herbert remembered Hellen's call. She had only asked about the restaurant. "Darling, Hellen called this afternoon..." He hesitated. *Should I bring up the topic of the restaurant again? Won't we end up arguing again?* "She wants to know what you are planning to do with the restaurant."

"The restaurant is on my mind and I will see what to do with it when I retire," Leah answered as she walked to the kitchen.

"How many things will you be doing when you retire? You plan to spend more time with your mother, you want to renovate her house, you want to upgrade the farm. Your list of things to do seems to be endless. Where will you get all the time?"

"I don't think time will be an issue when I no longer have to go to work," Leah said, turning to face Herbert.

"Listen, darling. You need to plan your activities—"

"No. Don't worry about my activities. When I am in retirement, I will have lots of time and I will handle things as they come," Leah said.

# 3

# August 2013

MERAB HAD EVENTUALLY stayed home, letting her nephew Sam Mukuye run her restaurant. At eighty-three years of age, she realized that she had been working for money for almost seventy years. At first she enjoyed her retirement and was happy to cook meals for her grandchildren and great-grandchildren whenever they visited. She also enjoyed telling folk tales to her great-grandchildren, Nakato's four-year-old son and Babirye's five-year-old twin sons.

On the one hand she soon enjoyed being Merab, the caring, loving mother, grandmother and great-grandmother. On the other hand she missed being Mufuzi, the hardworking, money-making early-rising businesswoman. She felt a struggle within that reminded her of the early days in Kalasa when she had been torn between wanting to run away to be free from Lutalo and wanting to stay in her marital home to be a wife. She felt nostalgic. *Oh, how I miss the good old days in Kalasa. I came to the city to make money. Now that I am no longer working, I should return.*

One evening she decided to talk to her daughter about it. "Leah, isn't it time for me to return to my original marital home? Now that I spend the day here, idle, I miss Kalasa."

"But Mother, I don't understand why you would leave this beautiful home that you built in the city to return to such a rural area, and to a home that you didn't build."

"Try to understand what I am going through," Merab replied. "Now that I am older, I have come to realize that the home in Kalasa means a lot more to me than this home. I want to return to Kalasa and I want to die there."

"Don't even think about it. It's far and if you moved there, I couldn't come to see you as regularly as I do here."

"Can I at least go there to visit?" Merab asked, her eyes glistening with tears. "I would like to look around, pick weeds around your father's tomb and reconnect with the village."

\* \* \*

Merab hadn't visited Kalasa in over a year. When she and Leah arrived there, she was impressed by how well Leah and her half-brother Roger had taken care of their late father's home. They had renovated the large house, reroofed it with tiles, and had installed solar lighting.

"Thank you for caring for this home, Leah," Merab said as she stood in the front yard to admire the new roof. "It means a lot to me."

"You are welcome, Mother. Roger and I take our responsibility for this home seriously."

Merab kept quiet for a few seconds. "Of course I would miss seeing you so often but I wouldn't miss the city if I lived here," she said.

While the workers took Leah on a tour around the farm, Merab sat on a mat in the living room. Several people came in to greet her but for about an hour she was left alone, reflecting. She recalled the first time she had set foot in the house as a young bride. *That was nearly seventy years ago.*

She got up and took a close look at the old photographs that were still hanging on the wall. In a group picture, taken on her wedding day, she saw her late aunties Abigail and Namagembe. She remembered how much both of them had cared for her during the early years of her marriage. She missed them. She sat back down and cried.

Then she went to the newly constructed outdoor kitchen, picked up a hoe and went to the backyard, to the family graveyard about a hundred metres from the house. She walked around, reading the tombstones, including those of her ex-sister wives. She dug the weeds around the tombs, starting with the area around Lutalo's tomb. Then she dug the weeds in the vacant area next to Lutalo's tomb that had been reserved for her. *This will be my final resting place.* She stood still for close to a minute, then cried again.

\* \* \*

A few weeks after the visit to Kalasa, it became more and more difficult for Merab to get out of bed in the morning. Although many people lived in her home, including her stepson seventy-year-old Kulumba, who had never permanently moved out, Merab felt lonely.

"I like that I no longer have to wake up early to go to work. But sometimes I feel guilty when I wake up late with nowhere to go and with nothing definite to do," Merab told Leah one evening.

"That's all right, Mother," Leah said. "You will get used to your new life soon. You should use this opportunity to rest."

"You don't know what I am going through. Now that I am old, do you know what goes through my mind while I am sitting at home doing nothing? It's like I am waiting to die. It is scary."

"Oh, don't think like that, Mother! Most likely you are lonely. I am planning to retire soon and I will be spending more time with you," Leah answered, trying to reassure Merab. But she was becoming concerned about her mother's health.

\* \* \*

Ruth had stopped working in her boutique so abruptly that her regular customers wondered why the energetic woman had disappeared all of a sudden. Her children thought that she was probably grieving the death of their father, and the end of their nearly sixty-year-old marriage. Even Ruth herself was often surprised by her unceremonious departure from the business that she had built over decades. But she knew that her archnemesis Clotilda had collapsed while touring her school's farm and she didn't want to suffer the same fate—to die at work.

Ruth started her day with simple physical exercises like stretching or walking inside the perimeter wall of her home or gardening in her backyard. She'd then read. After she'd retired, she spent a lot of time at home and often reflected upon her long life. She realized, at eighty-two, that other than the years she had been in school, she had been working for money for nearly sixty years.

She would go to see Merab most Tuesday afternoons, and both she and Merab looked forward to what Ruth called "indulgence afternoons." By the time Ruth arrived at Merab's home, Merab would have cooked a copious meal, usually *matooke* plantain with smoked beef or fresh tilapia, with a side of Ruth's favourite vegetables.

For that first Tuesday visit, Merab had been in the process of placing a tray with cutlery on it on a mat, ready to prepare lunch, when Ruth had arrived. Ruth had asked Merab why she sat on a mat when she had a beautiful dining table. "I have always sat on a mat to eat," Merab had answered.

"No, let the table serve its purpose," Ruth had said, helping Merab to lay the table. They had lunched there ever since.

After lunch, they would always sit to chat, their favourite topic their granddaughters and their families. In the evenings, they would take a leisurely walk around St. Peter's Primary School nearby—the school that Ruth had helped to build.

Sometimes Merab did not want to go for the walk but Ruth would persuade her. "We need to walk every day because it helps our old bones to remain active and agile," she'd say.

On Wednesday afternoons, Ruth would go to a market a half-hour's drive away from her home to talk to a group of women traders whose small businesses she had helped to organize and fund. She'd sit in one of their stalls, give them advice and answer questions about their businesses.

On Sunday after church services she would spend the afternoon in meetings at St. Mark's Church, which her parents and parents-in-law had helped to build.

* * *

On the Tuesday following Hellen's phone call to Herbert, Ruth went to see Merab as usual. After lunch, they went to the living room to chat. Ruth sat on the sofa and Merab picked a mat from a corner of the room.

"Why don't you sit on the sofa since you have one?" Ruth asked, laughing. "Some of you seem to think that the good things in your homes should be reserved for visitors but that should not be the case."

"It's hard to change a habit," Merab answered. "I have been sitting on a mat for my entire life and I am not about to change."

Later, when Ruth asked for drinking water and Merab rose to fetch some, she saw that Merab had trouble rising from the mat. Merab had to place one hand on the wall for support and then fold her legs slowly before getting up. "You are aging fast, my dear," Ruth said. "You can't get up from the mat without holding on to the wall?"

"No. I have pains all over my body. My back hurts. I have pain in the joints. Even my feet and fingers hurt," Merab answered. "Babirye brought me some medicine, which helps a little."

"What kind of medicine did she give you?"

"I'll show it to you," Merab said as she walked slowly to her bedroom, and after five minutes returned with a jar of water with two glasses on a tray and a plastic bag with four containers in it.

"Oh, these are food supplements. I take those too. They should help you," Ruth said. "Do you take them daily, as recommended?"

Merab laughed as she sat back down on the mat. "No. I take them some days... other days I forget to take them. They taste like herbs and I don't like herbs."

"Hey, these will help you. You shouldn't be lazy at this age. You've got to take your medicine. Remember our children, our grandchildren and their children still want us around. Don't neglect yourself," Ruth said as she opened the containers one by one and gave four pills, one from each container, to Merab. "Take some now."

"I like what you said about our family," Merab said after she had taken her supplements. "They still want—"

"Oh, yes. They still want us around. Doesn't it feel like we are living for them?" Ruth answered.

"Yes it does. Very much so."

Ruth sat back on the sofa. "Nakato came to see me last weekend. She told me that she and her sisters have realized that their parents are not paying enough attention to our businesses—actually, their parents' businesses—I gave the boutique to Herbert and I guess you gave the restaurant to Leah. So, the girls want to take over the businesses. And they might close down the restaurant."

"Oh, why would they close down the restaurant?" Merab asked, surprised.

"Apparently the restaurant is not doing well. Aren't you aware of that?"

"Yes, I am, but I didn't know it was so bad that they would consider closing it down. Leah was here yesterday. She didn't even talk about the restaurant."

"Leah is opposed to the idea, but Hellen insists that it should be closed down. Leah should listen to Hellen because her job is to help businesses in trouble," Ruth said. "She knows what she is talking about."

"But my nephew Sam is now working at the restaurant. He has no other job. If they find him another job, then they can close down the restaurant," Merab said.

# 4

# August 2013

GWEN HAD JUST finished dinner at her condo when the security office called, telling her that she had a visitor. It was her boyfriend, Lorenzo.

"Hey, buddy—what's up? Come upstairs," Gwen said.

"Gwen, why do you call me buddy?" Lorenzo asked as soon as he entered the apartment. Gwen could see that something was bothering him.

"Hey, what's wrong with 'buddy'? Couples have names for each other."

"I don't like it."

"Okay, I'll call you something else. Have a seat. Are you in a hurry?"

"I've come here twice to see you today but you weren't home!" Lorenzo's voice was getting louder. "Where the hell have you been?" he yelled.

"Where have I been? That's a strange question. Don't forget that some of us have to work."

"But you work from home—"

"Yeah, I work from home but you know that I do go out once in a while to meet with clients. And you know what? I have a life and I am not a prisoner in this apartment."

"I get that but it'd be nice if you told me when you won't be here, so I don't have to look for you," Lorenzo said, still standing by the door.

"It amazes me that you behave like we live in the nineteenth century. Why don't you call first before coming over?"

"Can't I come see you whenever I want?" Lorenzo asked, still angry. "Do I have to make a freaking appointment to see you?"

"Would you like to have dinner? I just had dinner," Gwen said, trying to cool his temper.

"No. I'm good," Lorenzo said and walked out without closing the door.

\* \* \*

That night Gwen had trouble falling asleep. She tossed and turned in bed, thinking about Lorenzo. He was a tall, handsome, outgoing and successful real estate agent, and many people loved him, including Gwen's mother. But he had a dark side that manifested itself in his relationship with Gwen. He seemed to want to control all her movements and to vet her friendships. Although she loved him, his behaviour made her doubt that their relationship would last. Twice, he had asked her to move in with him but she had refused to do so. *I need a break from him, even a short one. I need to go far away from him to teach him a lesson. And if he doesn't change his ways, I might end up dumping him.*

\* \* \*

"I am traveling for my vacation next month," Gwen told Hellen at the end of their weekly meeting in her apartment the following day. "Please schedule it in next month's calendar."

"Yeah, sure. How long will you be gone for?" Hellen asked.

"For three weeks at the beginning of the month. I am going to Kampala."

"To Kampala?" Hellen asked and laughed, thinking that Gwen was joking.

"Yeah, I am not kidding. I thought long and hard about it last night. I am going to Kampala for my vacation and to help you with your grandmothers' businesses."

"Come on now, Gwen. You don't have to do that! But thanks so much. What would I do without you?"

"And I'm guessing one of your sisters can provide accommodation for the three weeks."

"Sure," Hellen said, "but I think the most convenient place would be Grandma Ruth's home. But are you serious? You want to go—"

"You know me well, Hellen. I've decided to go to Kampala," Gwen said with a serious look, "and that's it."

"Okay, I will call Nakato tomorrow to make some arrangements for you. That will be so cool! And you know what? I think you can handle my parents better than me. You are calm and won't be involved in arguments, especially with my mom, who I think is just wasting the family's money on a poorly performing restaurant."

"Let's discuss my trip next week," Gwen said as she shut off her laptop.

"Yeah, I'll include it in next week's agenda. What do I need to think of to prepare for your mission?" Hellen asked, ready to type some notes on her laptop.

"Draft a job description to guide me on the mission and please include who I will meet and who I will interview, the worst- and best-case scenarios—you know, that kind of thing. And I guess we'll need to do a thorough analysis of both businesses before we make any recommendations."

✳ ✳ ✳

Hellen called Nakato the following day to discuss Gwen's planned visit, and told her that its main purpose would be to analyze and to help find solutions to their grandmothers' businesses' problems.

"Oh, that is a welcome gesture," Nakato said. "It will be very helpful. Did you ask her to come here to help with the businesses?"

"No. We were in a meeting yesterday and she surprised me by telling me that she was going to Kampala. She was like, 'I am going for vacation in Kampala.' And I was like, 'Are you serious?' And then she goes, 'Yeah I'm not kidding.'"

"I am very glad to hear that. She is a true friend. Are you going to pay for her—"

"No, she is funding it all on her own."

"That's so nice."

"Can you make arrangements for her accommodation at Grandma Ruth's home?" Hellen asked.

"What kind of arrangements" Nakato asked. "There are free rooms and free beds there. And Brandon is usually free. He can take Gwen places when she is not working."

"Do you think Mom and Dad will cooperate with Gwen? Otherwise I wouldn't want her to waste her time."

"Of course they will cooperate. I don't see why they wouldn't."

"Okay, cool," Hellen said. "Among other things, Gwen will need to study both businesses' accounts, so it will be helpful if you can get the accounts ready."

Nakato paused to think. "Okay, I think I can get them. I will follow up right away. Tell Gwen that we will be glad to see her."

\* \* \*

The following week, after their business meeting, Hellen and Gwen discussed Gwen's planned trip to Kampala, and Hellen told Gwen that Nakato was excited about her upcoming visit.

"So, you will live in my grandmother Ruth's home," Hellen told Gwen. "My brother Brandon and his girlfriend live there, too, and he can drive you wherever you need to go."

"Cool," Gwen answered. "Did you draft the job description for my mission?"

Hellen handed a one-page document to Gwen. "Here—you will make a thorough analysis of the two businesses and make some recommendations. But both my preliminary observations and my gut feeling tell me that the restaurant should be closed down for good."

"What are the worst- and best-case scenarios?"

"The worst case scenario would be my parents refusing to cooperate with you. The best case scenario would be that they cooperate fully and provide you with all the necessary information. But I don't see any real obstacles. Nakato tells me that Mom and Dad will cooperate with you. Perhaps one problem might be the absence of data. I don't know—especially for the restaurant—if the books are up-to-date enough, like, for you to make proper recommendations."

"What kind of report will I write?" Gwen asked.

"Well, they won't be paying us for your services. Why not just brief notes?"

"Yeah, I thought about that, but in case they have to make some tough decisions and to involve their lawyers and stuff, they might need a more detailed report…"

"Okay. Write a report, but don't make it very detailed. Of course, you will need some time off, too, to enjoy your vacation," Hellen said. "Take a week off to go see the mountain gorillas and the mountains in the western part of the country."

"Oh yeah, I would love that."

"Cool. I'll ask Brandon to book that for you."

"There are no reports due next month, but while I'm away you might handle a higher volume of calls and e-mails. Get prepared for that," Gwen said.

"Cool," Hellen said. "Looks like we've got everything covered."

The two partners high-fived and shut off their laptops.

That evening, Hellen e-mailed Gwen the notes she'd made about Kyatelekera Restaurant and Ruth's Classic Boutique. Gwen read through the notes and sat back to think. *But will the trip be about the businesses or about me? I need a break from Lorenzo. He's both a control freak and a jerk.*

Going away to Kampala for three weeks without telling Lorenzo would teach him a lesson, Gwen thought—he didn't have to know where she was every moment of the day. She sat at her computer, taking a half hour to compare fares and to buy her return air ticket to Kampala. After she completed the purchase she went to bed, falling into a deep sleep, the first time in the week since she'd started contemplating dumping Lorenzo.

# 5

# September 2013

WHEN GWEN ARRIVED at Entebbe International Airport, Brandon and his girlfriend Delilah were there waiting for her. They arrived at Ruth's home and Gwen chatted with Ruth briefly before she showered and napped for a few hours before lunch.

After lunch, Brandon suggested she go back to bed due to the jetlag. "No, I'm fine. I won't be sleeping much since I have a lot of work to do," Gwen answered.

"Oh, are you going to start working right away?" Brandon asked.

"Yeah, I get bored quickly when I am not working," she said. *I need to get Lorenzo off my mind, too.*

"Mummy and Daddy will be coming for dinner," Brandon said. "I guess you will have some questions for them."

"I'll be glad to chat with them," Gwen said. "Do you think they will talk freely about the businesses?"

"Yes. But Mummy doesn't want anyone to even mention that the restaurant is failing. But it *is* failing. Some of our relatives even eat there for free, thanks to Uncle Sam," Brandon said and laughed.

❇ ❇ ❇

Brandon and Delilah were not at home for dinner that evening, and Herbert asked Ruth about his son Brandon while they were waiting for Gwen to join them at the table. Ruth didn't know where he was, though. "He is a grown man. Should I be asking him to tell me whatever he is doing?"

"Mummy, you've spoiled my only son so much that he doesn't seem to be thinking about his future. Brandon has no job and therefore no secure future," Herbert said.

"My grandson is doing well," Ruth replied. "He is a talented and popular musician."

"He might be a popular musician but he needs to get a proper job. He can't go on relying on the fame that he got from one song three years ago."

"But he still makes money from that song," Ruth said, laughing. "And he tells me that he is collaborating with his friend Zoe to release a new album. Besides, other than the boutique, which I handed over to you, everything I own is Brandon's."

"What? Do you really mean that, Mummy?"

"Oh yes. Let me repeat. Everything I own is Brandon's. The keys to this house shall be handed to him the very day I pass on."

"That's all right, Mummy. Thank you," Herbert said and poured some fruit juice into a glass for himself.

With that statement, Ruth knew that Herbert had ended the conversation about Brandon. She continued. "What is really bothering me is that you have neglected your son. You haven't cared much about him."

"What do you mean, Mummy?" Herbert asked.

"Let me give you an example. Do you know what's going on in his love life?"

"No. Do I need to know? I know his girlfriend. What's her name? Delilah?"

"Is that all you know?"

"Yes, that's all. Why don't they get married?"

"Oh dear. It's such a question that you would ask Brandon. They are happy now and they are planning to get married, thanks to my intervention."

"Mummy, you always want credit for things. What did you do for them?"

"Thanks for asking," Ruth said as she moved the chair closer to the table. "Now let me tell you what I did. Delilah is a beautiful well-behaved young woman—I can never praise her enough. She and

Brandon met in the university. She was the closest friend he had when he was still a student, when he was walking everywhere with a guitar strapped to his shoulder. She provided emotional support to him when you sent him away from home. But when he became famous after he composed and released *Tobbanga Nkoko*, he tried to break up with her."

"I don't know that," Herbert said and rose to pull a chair out for Leah, who had come to the table with a bowl of salad.

Ruth continued. "Listen. That's not all. I fought for Delilah. I defended her. Whenever Brandon came here with a bunch of other girls, I did not let them enter my house. I chased them away."

"Mummy, you did what?" Herbert was smiling now.

"I chased them away—literally! One day he came here with a girl who had a disrespectful attitude. I chased her with a broom all the way to the gate. Brandon was very embarrassed but he got the message. I don't tolerate nonsense."

Leah and Herbert laughed.

"Mummy, you can still run?" Herbert asked.

"Yes. A little bit," Ruth said and she and Leah laughed.

"Really? I actually wonder why you decided to stop working when you are still energetic," Herbert said.

"Oh, dear. You wanted me to work till I dropped dead?"

"No, but I know that most people age quickly when they retire."

"Hey, aging is one thing I am fighting. I am going to remain active as long as I can. I probably wake up earlier than most of you to start my exercises, six days a week. I also keep my mind sharp by reading. I don't think there is a book in this house that I've not read. You should buy me more books whenever you travel."

"Good for you, Mummy. So Brandon and Delilah are planning to get married?" Herbert asked.

"Yes, next year," Ruth answered.

"How come I don't know anything about it?"

"It's because you have not befriended your son. You are only fond of your doctor daughters."

Herbert and Ruth continued arguing. Leah listened to them, without joining in the conversation, which only stopped when Gwen came to the table. Herbert welcomed Gwen warmly and introduced her to his wife.

"Gwen, we met during Hellen's wedding, didn't we?" Leah said.

"Yes," Gwen said, "and I am glad to see you again."

While they were having dinner, Gwen asked Ruth about the boutique. Ruth said that Herbert was in a better position to answer.

"You see, Mummy abandoned the boutique that she built over decades," Herbert explained. "I was actually shocked when she just woke up one day and decided she was not going to work—"

"Hey," Ruth cut her son off. "I didn't abandon the boutique—it was time for me to retire. What did you want me to do? Work till I dropped dead?"

"No, that's not what I wanted. It was okay for you to retire. There is no problem with that. The problem was that you didn't make any arrangements to hand it over. You just dumped the responsibility for your business on me without preparing—"

"Hey," Ruth said again. "It is not my business anymore—it is your business. I wonder whether you actually value it."

"Mummy, I value the business and I can't thank you enough for handing it over to me. But I was not ready for it. You know I am a macro-level kind of guy. I've never run a small business before."

"What? Oh dear. You call the most successful home furnishings shop in the city a small business? Do you know how much money I made from that shop over the years?"

"Yes, I know you made a lot of money but its revenue is small in comparison with the kind of revenues I handle in my job."

"Gwen, don't be bothered by how we talk to each other," Ruth said, laughing. "I taught my children from a young age to express themselves freely. What you have just witnessed are the fruits of my efforts."

※ ※ ※

"Herbert, so can I talk to you for a bit about the business, if you don't mind?" Gwen said after dinner.

"The boutique? Sure," Herbert said, picking up his glass of fruit juice. "Let's talk in the living room."

While they were waiting for Leah to join them, Herbert asked Gwen about Hellen and their business. Leah joined Herbert and Gwen in the living room after she and Ruth's maid Nabakka had cleared the table.

Herbert started the conversation. "Gwen would like to talk to us about Mummy's boutique. Sorry, *my* boutique," he told Leah.

"Actually, if you don't mind, we can discuss both businesses since you are both here," Gwen said.

"Sure," Herbert answered. "I hope we will have some satisfactory answers for you."

Leah remained silent.

"I am here on Hellen's behalf on a fact-finding mission. Any information that you provide will be appreciated," Gwen said.

"Yes, sure," Herbert answered.

"Can we discuss the boutique to begin?" Gwen said, taking her iPad out of her bag.

"Oh, the boutique? Discuss that while I make a cup of tea," Leah said and rose to go to the kitchen.

"So, how is the boutique doing?" Gwen asked Herbert.

"I don't go there often but my brother Clement does. He says that it is doing well," Herbert answered.

"Okay. But are you aware of its actual performance?"

"Yes, I have examined the books, and its performance is quite satisfactory, even though it could be better."

"From the discussions with your mom at dinner, it appeared to me that you are not really interested in the boutique."

"Let me be frank with you, Gwen. If I were to choose, I wouldn't choose to run the boutique or even to own it," Herbert said. "But, well, it is what it is. I have to take over from my mother and I am grateful for the fact that of all her three children, she entrusted her business to me. You know she worked hard to build that business."

Gwen began taking notes on the iPad. "What plans do you have for the boutique, now that you own it?"

"Plans?" Herbert was obviously unprepared for the question. He said nothing as Gwen waited with her stylus, ready to type notes onto her iPad. Finally, after about twenty seconds, he broke his silence. "I have never really given that question much thought, if any. I haven't made any plans for the boutique. The truth is, I haven't yet felt that the boutique belongs to me." Gwen typed more notes without responding. "But I am glad that Hellen has taken an interest in it. If she has some good ideas, they are welcome." He stopped there and watched Gwen for a few minutes as she typed her notes in silence.

Leah returned with a tray with a thermos and three cups and placed it on a coffee table before sitting next to Herbert on the sofa.

Gwen finished her typing. "Sorry," she said. "To begin with, I should have stated clearly the reason I am here. Hellen is concerned that the businesses, especially the restaurant, are losing money. She wants to correct the situation."

"Yes, she mentioned that to us and we understand her concern," Leah answered, rising to pour their tea.

"Fortunately, our job involves advising businesses. I volunteered to come on this fact-finding mission and hopefully I will come up with some useful recommendations at the end of it all," Gwen said.

"You are a friend, indeed. Thanks for doing that," Leah said without taking her eyes off the cups of tea.

"Yes, we are grateful for your generosity. Expect our full cooperation," Herbert said.

"Cool. So, about the boutique—what do you think you can do with it?" Gwen asked.

"I will keep it open," Herbert answered. "It is a profitable business, as you will see for yourself. I assume you are planning to visit the boutique?"

"Yes, a visit or two is on my agenda."

"Good, then will you please advise me how to best run it?"

"We'll see about that."

Ruth walked into the living room at that moment. "Oh, are you in a meeting? Sorry to interrupt—"

"You are welcome to join us," Gwen said, but Ruth walked back out of the room and to the kitchen.

"Do you have more questions for me?" Herbert asked.

"I will have more questions for you during the week," Gwen said. "Let's discuss the restaurant for now."

"Good. I'll let Leah answer your questions concerning the restaurant. She knows it better than I do," Herbert said and rose to go to the kitchen to talk to his mother.

"How is the restaurant doing?" Gwen asked Leah as soon as Herbert had walked out.

"The restaurant is not doing well, in terms of business," Leah answered as she picked a cup of tea off the tray. "Its performance has been declining since my mother stopped working there."

"Why do you think that is so?" Gwen asked, ready to take notes.

Leah paused for a few seconds. "My mother has been running that restaurant for many years, so obviously her departure affected its profitability."

"Do you know its actual performance?"

"No. Not really but I get regular reports from my cousin Sam who works there," Leah answered, wondering whether her answer sounded intelligent. She felt guilty for neglecting the restaurant. "He says that the income is dwindling," she added.

"Your mother is no longer there and no doubt, she had a personal brand. Do you think her departure led to a loss of business?" Gwen asked as she put some sugar in her cup and sipped her tea.

"Probably. When I go there, I do notice that there are fewer customers."

"Would you be interested to know the restaurant's actual performance?"

"Yes, of course. I also have plans for its future."

"Did you write those plans down including some concrete actions you will take?"

"No. Do I need to write them down?"

"Yes," Gwen said. "We always advise clients to write them down, take action and keep track of progress. What plans do you have?"

"I intend to keep the restaurant—"

"Intention is not a plan, Leah. A plan is a step by step roadmap, backed by concrete action—do you know what I'm saying?"

"I do know," Leah answered and laughed, "but I haven't really set aside time to put my thoughts on paper."

"Are you an entrepreneur?"

"Pardon me?"

"Let me rephrase the question. You say that your mother has been running the restaurant for many years. Do you think you have what it takes to build on to her success?"

"Yes, I think so," Leah said and sipped some tea.

"Do you know the factors that helped your mother to succeed?"

"Not really. I have never tried to find that out."

"Do you know what she did on a daily basis to keep her business thriving?"

"No," Leah said, laughing.

Gwen paused and took a sip of her tea before she spoke again. "You will need to make some deliberate efforts to learn the business if you are to turn it around. But Hellen is concerned about the restaurant's performance. Actually, her recommendation is to close it down." She watched Leah's reaction carefully.

"No. I will not close down the restaurant," Leah said firmly, her determination evident for the first time since they'd started the conversation.

"Why not?"

"To me that restaurant is not just a business. It is my mother's legacy. Like I said—"

"Sorry to interrupt, but your mother opened the restaurant to make money. Isn't that so? Or were there other reasons?"

"You are right. The purpose of opening the restaurant was to make money but over the years, the restaurant has come to represent more than just a business."

"To you, to your mother, or to your customers?"

Leah did not answer the question and Gwen did not insist on an answer.

"I understand your situation and I see this all the time in my job. People get emotionally attached to their businesses and to things in general. You know what I'm saying?"

Leah still remained silent.

"But what we advise in cases such as yours is to let the business go, once we establish that it's no longer serving its purpose, which is to make money."

Leah's silence made it clear to Gwen that her friend's mother did not want to close down the restaurant.

Herbert and Ruth returned to the living room, sitting together on one of the sofas to join Leah and Gwen in conversation.

"Thanks for answering my questions," Gwen said to them all, putting her iPad back into the bag. "I guess we'll chat a little more after I have visited both businesses."

# 6

# September 2013

NAKATO AND GWEN went to visit Kyatelekera Restaurant the following day. Sam Mukuye was there when they arrived. He welcomed them with a handshake and showed them to a table. When he asked whether they wanted to have breakfast "on him" Nakato said they'd already had breakfast. She introduced Gwen and said that Gwen was there to review the restaurant's performance.

Sam's smile disappeared. "Is it an audit?" he asked.

"No, it's not an audit," Nakato answered. "Gwen, please tell Uncle Sam what you have in mind."

"Basically, I am here to see how the business is performing and to make some recommendations. I will need about a week to do that," Gwen said, smiling to put Sam at ease.

"Did she talk to your mother first?" Sam asked Nakato.

"Yes, Mummy is aware that Gwen is visiting the restaurant."

"I was about to head out when you arrived," Sam said. He motioned for a young woman to come over. "This is Hagar. She can answer any questions that you might have." Then he left.

"Hello, Hagar, I am glad to meet you. I am Gwen," Gwen said as they shook hands.

Hagar returned to her work after the greetings. Nakato and Gwen chatted for a few more minutes before Nakato left.

Gwen remained seated at the table as she waited to talk to Hagar.

Hagar returned and asked, "Can I give you something to eat or drink?"

"Yes please. Can I have some water?" Gwen answered.

Gwen placed her iPad and a notebook on the table. Hagar placed a bottle of water on the table two minutes later. "Thank you. Hagar, can I talk to you briefly when you have a moment?" Gwen said.

"Just a moment please. I won't be long," Hagar said and went to a room at the back of the restaurant.

She returned a few minutes later after greeting two customers who had walked in.

"I would like to ask you a few questions about the restaurant—I want to have an idea what's going on here," Gwen said. "Oh, by the way, your job is safe, so no worries. I am not here to make a negative report or to jeopardize anybody." She smiled. "Hagar, how long have you worked here?"

"I have worked here for three years but the restaurant has changed so much since Mama Merab left," Hagar said.

Gwen sensed that either Hagar seemed unsure of herself or was uneasy. "How has it changed?" she asked.

Hagar paused for a few seconds, to think. "The atmosphere in the restaurant has changed. And the standards have fallen. There is no order. The truth is, nobody is in charge."

"But you are in charge. Aren't you the manager?"

"Yes, I am, but I was not hired formally. I am a chef by training. I simply took over the manager's role when it became clear to me that no one was in charge. The previous manager quit shortly after Mama Merab left."

"Please tell me more about the restaurant. How do you source the food?" Gwen asked as she typed some notes on her iPad.

"This is a farm-to-table restaurant. We receive some of the food fresh every morning. Various suppliers deliver it here."

"But I have noticed that you serve French fries, too."

"French fries? Oh, you mean chips? Yes. It's Sam who brought the deep fryer. We didn't serve chips before he joined us."

"What does Sam do? What's his role in the restaurant?"

"Sam's role is not clear even though we report to him. He came in one afternoon when Mama Merab was still here, then he returned the following morning, and then every other day until Mama Merab left unceremoniously."

Gwen was listening attentively as she typed more notes onto her iPad.

"And he owes a lot of money to the restaurant," Hagar said, and rose to go to the counter. She returned with a notebook, which she placed in front of Gwen. "Look, Sam owes close to two million shillings."

"How did this happen?" Gwen asked, scanning the page.

"He buys meals for friends and relatives, which, unfortunately, he doesn't pay for."

"Why don't you stop him? I mean, if he hasn't paid his previous bills, why do you go on giving him meals on credit?"

"I mentioned the problem to Leah but she said that she trusts him to pay. But he has never paid. Not even a single shilling," Hagar said with resignation in her voice, folding her hands.

"So should I take it that Sam has no job here?" Gwen asked.

"He is mainly involved with quality control."

"How does he do that?"

"We receive some supplies twice a week and Sam is the one who deals with the vendors. He checks the produce before we pay for it."

"I see," Gwen said as she typed more notes.

Hagar continued. "Otherwise, most of the time, he sits around to chat with friends and relatives. Sometimes I am forced to send his people away to create room for our paying customers."

"Thank you. I'll let you get back to work as I analyze this information," Gwen said, and took a sip of her water.

Gwen remained for two more hours, observing and typing notes. Several curious customers stopped by to greet her as they walked in and out of the restaurant. A young man entered and asked if he could sit to talk to her.

"Yeah, sure," Gwen said, smiling.

The young man introduced himself as Crescent and told her that he worked at the Fresh Foods Supermarket a few minutes away. Just then Brandon walked in and told Gwen that he was there to take her home.

"It was nice talking to you, Crescent," Gwen said as she shook hands with the young man, went to the counter to thank Hagar for her time and left with Brandon.

\* \* \*

That evening, Hellen called Gwen to ask how she was doing. Gwen said that she was enjoying her time away. "I think this is going to be an interesting working vacation," she said.

"What was the highlight of the day?" Hellen asked.

"I checked out the restaurant and met briefly with Sam. Your uncle Sam."

"Oh, great. How did that go?"

"He was great and enthusiastic at first. He seemed happy to see us and he even offered us breakfast. But when we told him why I was there, he changed right away. You know what I'm saying? And in my mind I'm like, dude, we need some answers here. He left but I stayed there and talked to the manager instead."

"Cool. I'm glad you've started well."

"Anyway, we'll see how it goes. I chatted with the manager and I think you are right. The restaurant is in pretty bad shape. I'll visit the boutique tomorrow."

Brandon delivered printed copies of the restaurant's accounting statements to Gwen that evening. She spent most of the evening in Ruth's library studying them.

# 7

# September 2013

WHEN GWEN VISITED Ruth's Classic Boutique, Nakato introduced her to Elsie, one of the managers, who was acting as the general manager. "I'll let you two chat and I'll be working at the clinic," Nakato said before she left, and asked Gwen to call Brandon when she was ready to be picked up.

Gwen complimented Elsie on the cleanliness and the general ambiance of the boutique, and then asked how many people worked there. Elsie said that there were sixty-two employees, three assistant managers and two managers.

"Who do you report to?" Gwen asked.

"I should be reporting to Aunt Ruth, the boutique's owner and managing director. But when her husband died, she did not return to work. She called one morning after she'd been away for about three weeks and asked me to contact her son Herbert with any questions," Elsie said. "Have you met Herbert?"

"Yes, I have," Gwen answered as she typed some notes on her iPad.

"But Herbert comes here very rarely. His brother Clement... have you met Clement?"

"No, I haven't."

"Anyway, Clement comes here and, should I say, simply comes to sit in the managing director's office. We argue over almost everything. He and I don't get along well although he gets along well with the other manager, Katana. But I won't bore you with the details," Elsie said and laughed. "Anyway, Clement has no clue how businesses are run and if I had not been here, probably this boutique wouldn't have continued running until now."

After a little more conversation with Elsie, Gwen walked around the store's floor, looking at the various items of merchandise. She also discreetly observed the customers who walked in and out of the store. She made mental note of a few things, like the customers' gender, what they bought, the interactions between the employees and the customers and the most popular products in the store.

After she'd made her observations, Gwen sat in Elsie's office to make her notes. She wrote down her observations about the layout of the boutique, the ambiance and the customers. She realized that she had not observed the employees well. She walked back onto the store floor and watched several employees as they worked, and she noted that one man kept mopping while several customers stood in line waiting to pay for their merchandise.

Brandon delivered the boutique's accounting statements to Gwen that evening. Gwen studied them and when Herbert met with her after dinner, she asked him more questions about the boutique.

※ ※ ※

The second time Gwen and Brandon went to Kyatelekera Restaurant, Sam Mukuye was there again, sitting idly in the restaurant, dressed in a suit. Gwen thought he looked ridiculous.

"Sam, can I talk to you when you have a moment?" Gwen asked soon after Brandon left.

"Sure," Sam said. He sat on a chair, facing Gwen, and he seemed friendlier than the first time they'd met.

Gwen told Sam the little information she had learned about the restaurant so far. Sam admitted that the restaurant's performance had declined since Merab's departure but that he was hopeful that the restaurant could be turned around.

"Sam, what would you do if they decided to close this restaurant down tomorrow?" Gwen asked.

"I don't think Leah will close this restaurant down. She is very attached to it. And there is still hope that we will turn it around," Sam answered.

"But you and I know that mere hope doesn't work in business. And if I were to give you my honest opinion, I'd tell you that there's no hope for this restaurant—the numbers don't add up. What were you doing before you took over the management?"

Sam smiled and adjusted his tie. "I was in a senior position in a public company before I was laid off. My friend, I am a distinguished environmentalist with lots of experience. Like Leah's mother-in-law Ruth, I am a graduate of the London School of Economics. I have a Ph.D.—"

"That's all right. Congratulations. But I think you need to use that knowledge to make some money elsewhere."

"I have good plans but I don't have money to fund them. You need money to make money, right?" Sam said and sat up straight with a serious look on his face.

"You need only the ability to earn money, and you have that ability. Can we sit down to figure out how we can get you started?"

"Young woman, you don't know what I am going through. I am old and I have a lot of responsibilities. What haven't I done to get back on my feet?"

"It has nothing to do with age. You have a sound mind and the ability to earn. And you want to improve your situation," Gwen said. "Don't you?" At that moment one of Sam's friends came into the restaurant, and so Sam excused himself, got up and went to the man's table to greet him. It took a while for Gwen to realize that he was now chatting with the other man and wouldn't be coming back. "Sam, can we continue our conversation on Wednesday?" she asked, and sat for another hour there, observing the goings-on inside the restaurant and making more notes.

Crescent, the young man who had introduced himself to Gwen the first time she had visited the restaurant returned, and again he was annoyed when, like the first time, Brandon walked in soon after to take her home.

Gwen worked that afternoon and into the evening to analyze her observations both at the restaurant and the boutique. She noticed that the work kept her busy and she was thinking less about Lorenzo. *I wish I could move to Kampala permanently. Life is a lot less stressful here*, she found herself thinking, and laughed.

\* \* \*

That evening shortly before evening prayers, Sam sat in his living room and reflected on his brief conversation with Gwen. *She is a very intelligent young woman. I think I should talk to her again. Perhaps she can give me some useful advice.*

And two days later, when Sam walked into the restaurant, Gwen was already sitting at a table, working on her laptop. "Good morning, Gwen," he said, and sat down across from her. "Sorry to interrupt your work, but can I talk to you for a few minutes?"

"Absolutely. What's up?" Gwen asked.

"Like I mentioned the last time I saw you, I lost my job when I was laid off. Right now I am stuck. Can you imagine my predicament at my age? I am almost sixty-two years old!"

"Have you thought of what to do to turn the situation around?"

"Of course I've thought about it—many times! But at the moment nothing seems to be working."

"Why is nothing working?" Gwen asked, shutting off the laptop to focus on what he was telling her.

"To begin with, I am very disappointed. When I was laid off, I invested most of my severance pay in a business that belongs to two of my nephews. But I've never received any return on my investment. I actually doubt that those two young men are trustworthy."

"What's your role in that business?"

"No. I am not involved in their business itself," Sam answered, his tone slightly irritated. "I am just waiting for a return on my investment."

"Is it a big company?"

"No, it is a small graphics company but they convinced me that it's very profitable."

"And you thought that you would earn a profit without getting your hands dirty? Did you really think that you would make money without getting involved in the business?"

"I thought it would work."

"Can you start all over again?"

"What do you mean by that?"

"Can you re-launch your career? You know what I'm saying? Can you, like, start afresh?"

"Start afresh?" Sam asked and laughed bitterly.

"Yes, you are sixty-one, but that's not so old that you can't start something meaningful in your life now. I've read about people who graduated from college at eighty-five."

"What can I do? I can't start looking for a job now. I'm not just old—I'm also probably overqualified for all the jobs out there."

"Who do you hang out with?"

"Pardon me?"

"Who are the people you spend most time with?" Gwen asked. Crescent, the young man who had talked to Gwen on her two previous visits to the restaurant had just walked in and was trying to draw her attention to him. Gwen ignored him, pushing back her hair, a more serious look on her face.

"Men from my church," Sam answered her question.

"You had professional contacts in your old job, didn't you?"

"Yes, I had many of them. But I haven't talked to most of them since I was laid off."

"Don't you need them now more than ever?"

"I think I do."

"Great. Can you think of a service that you can sell to them? For example, you can work as a consultant, right?"

"Of course I can become a consultant—and a very good one at that—but I would need quite a large sum of money to start, which I don't have," Sam said.

"What would you need money for?"

"I would need an office, probably to rent one. And I would need equipment."

"You could start small. Can't you work from your house?"

"I hadn't thought about that. Yes, I can probably work from my house."

"If you started with one or two clients and offered them exceptional services, they would help bring more clients to you." She looked at him seriously. "Do you think that is possible?"

"Can you help me?" Sam asked. "I think I would benefit from your guidance."

"Okay, if you would like to, I can support you along the way. Here is where you can begin," Gwen said. "Write down all the ideas for business that come to your mind. Just write. Don't think much about them or edit them. You'll make a short list later on. Then let's chat about that tomorrow."

Sam and Gwen spoke for close to an hour, ending their conversation only when Brandon came in. Crescent, having only walked in after he had seen Gwen and had ordered a cup of tea and a bun that he had not intended to buy, left the restaurant when Brandon sat down to join Gwen and Sam. He muttered something almost to himself but Gwen did not pay attention.

* * *

Brandon, his girlfriend Delilah and Gwen met Sam in Nakato's home for dinner the following day. After dinner, Gwen and Sam sat in the living room to talk. She asked to see the ideas that Sam had written down for his business.

"I am sorry to say but I didn't write anything," he said. "When I returned home yesterday evening, there were two couples waiting for me there. They are all going through various challenges and by the time they left, I had no energy left to do anything constructive."

"I understand, and good for you," Gwen answered, "but I don't get it. You found time to deal with other people's problems but failed to spare even a half an hour to think of strategies that could potentially bail you out?"

"You raise a valid point, that much I must admit. However, I am a leader—I always have been. And there are many people who depend on me for various things."

"That's okay. It's good to be dependable. It's good to be a giver. But, what you need to do now is to examine your life. Make a deliberate analysis of your life. Ask yourself, 'Can I truly afford, at this stage of my life, to help these people?' and other questions of that sort." Gwen looked at Sam intensely as he struggled with his response.

"The answer is 'no.' I can no longer afford to help these people but they've depended on me for a long time, even for money," he said. "It's difficult for me to let them down now."

"Guess what, Sam. With that kind of thinking you are prolonging your pain."

"That's true. But right now I don't know what to do. I am stuck. What does a man do when he reaches a stage where he can't even pay his own bills?"

"What do you say to yourself in these circumstances?" Gwen asked. "What—"

"What I say to myself? 'I am blessed, I am a winner.' You know I am a firm believer in God. I do whatever I can to remain positive."

"That's all good. However, do you simply think positively or do you do a realistic analysis of your situation in order to look for practical solutions?" Gwen smiled. "What practical steps are you taking to improve your situation and to solve your problems? Let's consider today, for example, Sam. How many phone calls have you made to your contacts to look for new opportunities?"

"My friend, it's obvious that you don't know this country. People will only care about you when you have money," Sam said. "Only when they expect to get something from you. People here—"

"Nice try, Sam, but you didn't answer my question."

"That's what I am trying to tell you. When I lost my job, all the people I thought were my friends disappeared."

"Did you expect them to come knocking on your door at home? Like, 'Hey Sam, here is an opportunity. Come take it'?"

"No," Sam answered and laughed.

"Then do something. Take action."

Sam remained silent for a while, thinking, and then grasped Gwen's hand and began shaking it vigorously. "Thank you, thank you," he said. "What you are telling me is very important." Gwen said nothing. "Actually, you have been here for two weeks—why didn't you tell me these things earlier?"

"You didn't ask," Gwen said. "I couldn't give you advice that you didn't ask for. Remember, I am a business consultant. I get paid for my advice."

"Oh, are you now asking me to pay you?" Sam asked and laughed.

"No. I am telling you that, as a professional, I don't give unsolicited advice."

"But I heard that you are leaving soon. I would have loved to talk to you longer," Sam said. "Surely I will benefit from your advice."

"I can call you once a week for nine months to check on your progress and keep you accountable if you want."

"Thank you. That will help me. But why for nine months only?" Sam asked, jokingly.

Gwen laughed. "I plan my activities and goals nine months out. I can squeeze a weekly chat with you in there."

"Thanks again."

"Okay, we've got ourselves a deal. It's a huge commitment on my part but I will call you every Monday evening for nine months to help you with accountability. It was nice talking to you, Sam," Gwen said as she picked up her handbag and joined Brandon and Delilah, who'd been waiting for her.

❋ ❋ ❋

Gwen was looking forward to four days of relaxation. She, Brandon and Delilah were travelling to western Uganda to see the Rwenzori Mountains and the mountain gorillas. They'd be returning to Kampala two days before Gwen's departure back to Boston and then Nakato, Babirye and Brian were going to join Gwen for a final dinner at Kyatelekera Restaurant before she flew home.

During the long drive, she sat in silence in the back seat to read her report about Hellen's grandmothers' businesses, but her thoughts kept drifting to Lorenzo. It bothered her that she hadn't made a final decision about him yet. *Should I give him a chance? Should I dump him?* She was still in doubt.

*  *  *

*It's gonna be a huge surprise for her*, Lorenzo thought as he collapsed on the bed in the Lake Victoria Hotel in Entebbe, forty-one kilometres from Kampala. A few phone calls to Conrad had helped him to set up his plan. *Yes, when I return to Boston, I'll be an engaged man.*

Waking up seven hours later, feeling well rested, he placed three suits on the bed and took time to choose the best one for the occasion. He wondered whether he should wear a tie or not and that decision took a few minutes, too. After he had dressed, he sprayed a bit of Gwen's favourite cologne on his earlobes, and checked himself in the mirror. His appearance impressed him.

Lorenzo took a taxi to Kampala before the evening rush hour, as Conrad had suggested, ready to surprise Gwen. *How romantic! Flying twenty-one hours to Africa to propose to my hot girlfriend!*

On the outside Gwen was a petite blonde with kind blue eyes, but on the inside she was a tough, decisive woman. Lorenzo did not know that about her yet, but he was about to find it out.

# 8

# September 2013

INSIDE KYATELEKERA RESTAURANT, Gwen was enjoying a delicious meal of *matooke* plantain, a bit of rice, chicken *luwombo*—stuffed chicken cooked in banana leaves—and a side of avocado and leafy greens. She was seated with her back to the entrance, with Nakato at her side and Babirye and her husband Brian opposite them. The four new friends chatted as they ate, and Gwen told them how much she had enjoyed her vacation in Kampala.

"But it wasn't a real vacation," Babirye said. "You have been working all the time and I don't think you feel rested."

Gwen smiled, but before she could respond, she noticed that Brian was looking past her toward the entrance, watching as a tall well-dressed young white man with a huge smile strode towards them. Within a few seconds he was at their table, tapping on Gwen's shoulder.

"What?" Gwen turned around and looked up. "Lorenzo? What the hell are you doing here?" Conrad was just behind Lorenzo. "Conrad, is it you who brought Lorenzo here? Oh, my gosh! Will someone please wake me up?"

"No, you're not dreaming. It's me. Hi, everyone," Lorenzo said as he shook hands with the dining party.

"What?" Gwen said again. "Guys, this is my boyfriend, Lorenzo."

"Will you please excuse us for a while?" Lorenzo said to the group as he held Gwen's hand.

They sat at the only empty table in the noisy restaurant, near the entrance.

"Are you freaking kidding me? How and when did you get here?" Gwen asked as she placed her two plates of food on the table in front of her.

"I arrived early this morning. Doing all this for you, baby," Lorenzo answered.

"What? I still can't believe it."

Lorenzo pulled a chair out of the table for Gwen to sit down. As soon as she'd sat down, Lorenzo fell to his knee. *Waste no time. This is gonna be awesome.* "Gwen Linda Lake, will you marry me?"

"What?" Gwen said as she shifted on the chair to move closer to Lorenzo. She put her hand across her mouth. And then she paused.

Lorenzo looked at her expectantly. The fifteen seconds before she spoke again seemed like an eternity to him. "No. Sorry, Lorenzo. Sorry, I can't marry you."

"What?" Lorenzo asked as he rose, stunned.

"I am sorry," Gwen said again.

"Gwen, are you heartless? Did I travel all this way, a half way across the world to be rejected? Why, why, Gwen? Why did you say no?" Lorenzo asked. He was crying.

"Do I have to explain my reasons?" Gwen asked.

Two diners at a table across the aisle were watching Gwen and Lorenzo's interaction closely.

Lorenzo rose and stood in front of Gwen, dazed. "Give me your final word and I'll be out of here," he said.

"The final word is 'no.' I am sorry."

Lorenzo stormed out of the restaurant and jumped into a nearby taxi. He had planned to go back to the hotel in Entebbe with Gwen by his side, newly engaged and happy. But now he was alone, rejected, in shock. He was furious.

Inside the restaurant, Gwen had stayed seated, deep in thought. On one hand she was relieved that she had dumped Lorenzo. *Sorry, but it was the right thing to do. He is a control freak.* But on the other hand, they'd been together for a while and she was going to miss him.

Nakato walked to her table and sat on a chair facing her. "Are you okay, Gwen?" she asked.

"Yeah, I'm good, but I just broke up with my boyfriend," Gwen said and laughed.

*　*　*

"Hey Gwen, what's going on? Aren't you supposed to be sleeping?" Hellen asked when she answered Gwen's phone call at 3 a.m. Kampala time.

"Lorenzo is here," Gwen said, sounding fully awake.

"What do you mean?"

"Lorenzo is here in Uganda. We were having dinner at the restaurant and Lorenzo walked in."

"What?"

"It was so unexpected—I was totally shocked. Anyway, he proposed—he proposed right there in the restaurant. Everybody was staring at us," Gwen said. "And I said no."

"You said no?" Hellen sounded incredulous.

"Yeah—it was spontaneous. I'd spent the past few days thinking about him but I hadn't decided what to do. And you know what? I don't want to spend the rest of my life in misery."

Hellen remained silent for a few seconds. "You know what? Lorenzo called me last week and asked me where you were. I innocently told him. Then he asked me for Conrad's phone number and I gave it to him, not knowing he had a grand plan," she said. "But I haven't heard from Conrad."

"He and Lorenzo came to the restaurant together," Gwen said.

"What?"

"Yeah," Gwen said. "When I said no, Lorenzo seemed devastated, I tell you—and mad as hell. He just stormed out of the restaurant. And before we left Conrad confessed that he'd helped him plan the trip and book a hotel in Entebbe."

"You are one tough cookie, Gwen. Anyway, you followed your heart. I hope you sleep well and I'll see you here tomorrow."

"I just hope we won't be on the same plane back to the States," Gwen said.

❈ ❈ ❈

While she was checking in at the airport, Gwen looked discreetly around to see if Lorenzo was there, and was relieved when she didn't see him. About fifteen minutes into the flight she tried to mentally review her mission to Kampala, but her own worries kept intruding on her thoughts. *Did I accomplish my mission? Yes, I carried out an analysis of the two businesses. I interviewed all the stakeholders. Lorenzo must be hurting now, poor man. It felt terrible to see him crying. Are my recommendations practical enough to help Hellen make lasting changes? He's mean and self-centred... I don't want to live the rest of my life in misery.*

Soon realizing that she was not in the right frame of mind to accomplish much of anything, she decided to watch a family drama, but after ten minutes of impatience with the film's complicated plot she switched to a comedy that was easier for the mood she was in. Her thoughts drifted from Lorenzo to her mother, to her work and back again. She slept little.

❈ ❈ ❈

"Do you know what's weird?" Gwen said as Hellen drove her back to her apartment from the airport. "After I said "no" to him, I thought I would be devastated because I really loved and cared for him." Gwen paused. "But I actually feel relieved."

"You know what? You guys were awesome together, and I felt bad when you told me what had happened. When Conrad called me this morning, I told him that I had been—"

"Conrad called? Did he say anything about Lorenzo?"

"Yeah. He did tell me that he helped Lorenzo to plan the surprise trip but he didn't see him after the proposal. He called him after you all left the restaurant but Lorenzo didn't pick up…. Anyway, back to what I was saying, I told Conrad that I had been looking forward to your wedding."

"Sorry, Hellen. I had to dump Lorenzo and I guess I'll have to find another guy and start all over again. Of course it won't be easy for me or for Lorenzo or for my mom, who really liked him."

"I am glad that you did what's right for you and that's what matters."

"When Lorenzo left the restaurant I was kind of confused. But Nakato talked to me, and she made me feel good about myself. I'm so grateful that she cared."

Hellen had prepared lunch in Gwen's apartment so they continued to chat while they ate. After lunch, Hellen left with a small package that Conrad had sent for her and some dried foodstuffs for her aunt Victoria, saying she would let Gwen rest.

But Gwen couldn't sleep. *It's kind of weird—I miss him. Oh, well. My emotions are still raw.*

※ ※ ※

The following day Hellen called Herbert, who asked her to thank Gwen for her kindness and help with the businesses.

"I will thank her on your behalf," Hellen said, "but Dad, please assure me that Gwen's recommendations will be considered. I don't want her time and effort to be wasted."

"Oh yes, we are grateful for her work and I promise we will do everything we can to follow up," Herbert said.

Hellen said that she could e-mail Gwen's report to Herbert, but he replied that there was no need to rush, that they could discuss the report in a few months' time, during Hellen's next visit to Kampala. He sounded unenthusiastic, and Hellen doubted that he and Leah would take any action to execute Gwen's recommendations.

※ ※ ※

Two days after he had returned from Kampala, Lorenzo called Gwen three times, but when she did not answer he lost his temper. *She doesn't care about me. And I don't think she will ever talk to me again.* He tried again the following day, and this time Gwen answered his call.

"Gwen, I am very happy to hear your voice again," Lorenzo said, truly happy. He could feel his heart beating faster.

"Hey, I am glad to hear yours too," Gwen said. But when Lorenzo responded with "Are you serious? Do you mean it?" Gwen was silent.

"This is killing me," he said. "I miss you, Gwen. Why did you dump me?"

"Lorenzo, sorry, but didn't you realize all along that things weren't going well between you and me?"

"I am sorry, too, but yeah. I didn't see that coming. Anyway, after these past couple days I thought you might reconsider. I can't live without you."

*Oh, oh. Now he is pretending to be polite.* "You'll get over it."

"I still can't believe that you said no to me. Now, seriously, are you dating some other guy?"

"No."

"But, Gwen, did you see the diamond ring I bought for you?"

"I saw the ring. Yeah, it's beautiful," she said. "But I am sorry I can't accept it."

"It is an expensive ring, too."

"I know—you can check with the store to see if you can take it back for a refund."

"I didn't think I would need to do that."

"Lorenzo, nothing we do in life is guaranteed to succeed. It's a risk you were willing to take. And you know what? Take the ring back."

"Yeah, there you go. Now you sound like your true self. You are so mean and cheap," Lorenzo yelled.

"Hey, listen, buddy. If you give me shit, I'll give you hell. Have a nice afternoon now and please don't call me again. I don't want to see you ever again," Gwen said and ended the call.

# 9

# October 2013

SAM MUKUYE THOUGHT that Gwen would forget about him once she had returned home and doubted that she'd follow up on her promise to help him. However, still he followed her advice to call his contacts, writing up a long list of people from whom he could ask for help with a job or for business. He dreaded calling people to ask for favours but he knew he had to do it, and decided he could call three people per day.

Some calls were answered with promises of help, other calls were answered with no promises, and some calls were not answered at all. He placed a checkmark by the names of all the people he had called, forgot about them, and then he moved on to the next ones on his list, but he soon lost hope.

Then three weeks after she had returned to Boston, Gwen called. "Hi, Sam. I am checking in as agreed, to know your progress," she said.

Sam was surprised that she had called. "Thank you, Gwen. But I haven't made any progress. Things are easier said than done. I don't even know where to begin."

"But have you done anything since we last talked?" Gwen asked.

"Yes. I have called many people, but—"

"That's good. Contacting people counts as progress. Tell me, what do you want?" Gwen said.

"What do you mean?" Sam asked, puzzled.

"What is your major goal?"

"I want to get my life in order. If you knew what I am going through, you would understand. My situation is bad and if my wife didn't have a job—"

"Okay, I get all that but how do you plan to do that, get your life in order?"

"I need an income. My major problem is I have no income."

"Sam, please get a notebook and a pen before we proceed."

"I have a pen and a sheet of paper right here at my table. I was writing something when you called."

"Cool. Please jot down some notes as we chat. Write down a number, an amount that you want in income. You don't have to do that right now but think and write it down this evening."

"My friend, I don't need to *write* the income. I need to *earn* it."

"I get that, but first things first. You've got to know what exactly you want. How much income do you need? Your previous salary? Half of your previous salary? A quarter? Think about the amount and write it down."

"Oh, it would be great if I earned my previous salary," Sam said enthusiastically.

"Great. Write down that amount, then. And why do you want to earn that income? You should also write the reason."

"My friend, when I stopped working, the bills didn't stop—"

"Yeah, I get it, you've got bills to pay. But I don't think paying bills is motivating enough. There's got to be better reasons than that."

"I know the amount," Sam said, ignoring Gwen's last comment.

"Cool. Write it down, and then write the things you can do to earn the money."

Sam laughed. "Writing alone won't help me."

"I get it, but you need to get into a habit of writing your goals and taking action on them. I'm not saying that when you write the amount you will earn it right away. You've got to take some action," Gwen said. "Things, which, when done every day, will accumulate to give you your desired income. You know what I mean?"

"I understand but I don't know how writing is going to help me."

"Writing gives you a visual reminder of your goals. And, make sure you have a written plan before you start your day, your week, your month and your year."

The conversation continued for half an hour with Sam doubting his abilities and Gwen asking him to persevere and to take action on his written goals. By the time the call ended, Sam had agreed to follow Gwen's advice even though he was not sure it would help him in solving his problems.

❉ ❉ ❉

After their last phone conversation ended in anger, Lorenzo continued to call Gwen for the next three weeks, at least ten times a day, but she did not answer any of his calls. Then, all of a sudden, he stopped calling.

Another man, Miguel, had been working for two years as a virtual assistant for Gwen and Hellen, who both found him polite, respectful and hardworking. Before she had made a final decision about her relationship with Lorenzo, Gwen had realized that Miguel was interested in her—a few months before she'd broken up with Lorenzo she'd noticed that he had checked her LinkedIn profile a few times, and had even sent her a few polite and personable non-work-related e-mails. But she was surprised when one evening, about two months after she had broken up with Lorenzo, Miguel called her, inviting her out for dinner.

She laughed. "Thanks for the invitation but I can't accept."

"Why not?" Miguel asked.

"I am still dealing with some personal stuff; I need some time for myself."

"There's no need to rush. I will wait," Miguel said.

# 10

# December 2013

LIKE THEY DID whenever they "needed some laughter," Nakato and Babirye went to see their grandmother Ruth at home. Ruth was seated at the dining table writing when the twins arrived.

"Grandma, are you writing letters?" Nakato asked as she and Babirye sat down at the table to greet their grandmother.

"No. I am writing notes in my diary," Ruth answered, waving the little book. Ruth loved to chat with her granddaughters and even though it annoyed Leah, who was a strong advocate for Luganda, their mother tongue, Ruth and her granddaughters spoke English whenever they chatted.

"Oh, you are still keeping a diary? Grandma, I thought you had stopped that when you retired," Babirye said.

"How could I stop? I have been writing in a diary at least once a day for over fifty years," Ruth answered.

"Fifty years?" the twins said in unison.

"Yes, I have many diaries in my bedroom. I can show you what I wrote the day you two were born."

After the greetings, Ruth went to the kitchen to prepare some tea, and brought cups, a thermos and some biscuits on a tray into the living room before she went to her bedroom. She returned with a bag full of diaries so that she and her granddaughters could peruse the diaries while they chatted.

"It seems you have enough material in here for an entire book," Nakato said, pointing to the full bag. "Have you ever thought of writing your autobiography? Many people in the city admire you, Grandma, and I think there is a lot for people to learn from you."

"Yes—oh, dear," Ruth said, laughing. "I have been thinking of writing a book for many years and started so many times but I have never completed even a single chapter."

She continued chatting with Babirye while Nakato perused the diaries in silence.

"Grandma, there is very good historical information in these diaries," Nakato said after about ten minutes of reading. "If you give me permission, I think I can write your biography using the diaries as material. Simply collect them all and give them to me for reference."

"Hey, if you are serious about it, of course I give you permission. I would be very glad if you wrote my biography," Ruth answered.

"Can you write a book from the diaries alone, Nakato?" Babirye asked.

"Yes, I think I can. Grandma can help to fill in the gaps. Grandma, can we chat sometime this month? I'd like to record some information from the horse's mouth," Nakato said, smiling.

"I am always here," Ruth answered. "Just come here and we will chat."

"By the way, Grandma, I've never mentioned this to you. That was a wonderful speech you gave at the party a few months ago," Babirye said. "Everyone was moved and some of my friends are still talking about it."

"Thank you, my dear. What did you find impressive about my speech?" Ruth asked as she poured more tea into her cup.

"The way you delivered it. You are a great public speaker, Grandma."

"Thank you."

"The speech itself was wonderful, too, but there was one thing I disagree with," Babirye added. "You seemed to be implying that things are easier for women these days, which in reality is not the case."

Her grandmother smiled. "But it *is* true—I know you still have some hardships, but your situation doesn't compare with what it was when I was a young woman your age. You have rights and freedoms now that we only dreamed of back then. Society is much kinder to women now than when I was young."

"Believe me, it is still a man's world," Babirye said. "In addition to that, we still face intense scrutiny, of the way we dress, the way we talk and the way we conduct ourselves. In many situations, life is not easy for a woman in this city."

"I know that, but—"

"You still face challenges with men even when you are accomplished professional women like us," Nakato said. "For example—and don't laugh, Grandma—last week, a man who all along I thought was decent brought his baby for a checkup at the clinic. While I was examining his child, he tried to invite me for what he called 'a fun evening out.' I felt totally disrespected!"

"Tell me about it," Ruth said, laughing. "I encountered such men on a regular basis at the boutique when I was still much younger than I am now. And I can't forget one really hilarious one." She rose to dramatize. "This fellow came in and asked me out. When I told him that I was not interested, he walked around the shop to admire the various items. Meanwhile, I watched him, amused. His trousers were worn out at the knees and it seems his shoes had never been polished. Oh, dear! Then, when he was done walking around, he returned to the counter where I was standing and asked me to give him money for his fare back home!"

"What?" Nakato said. She and Babirye were laughing so hard they had to wipe away tears.

They continued chatting over lunch. When they left Ruth gave her bagful of diaries to Nakato.

＊ ＊ ＊

"Would you be interested in joining me in writing Grandma's biography?" Nakato asked Babirye while they were driving home. "I think it will be easier if we write it together."

"I think so," her sister answered, sounding a little doubtful. "But when Mummy learns that we are writing Grandma Ruth's biography, she will want Grandma Merab's biography to be written too. Can we write both at the same time?"

"Yes, you are right. Mummy will ask us to write her mother's biography as well, and I think that would be the right thing to do because both our grandmothers are extraordinary women. So why don't we compile both biographies in one book?" Nakato said. "One problem, though—I doubt Grandma Merab has any diaries."

"You can interview her to get a firsthand account of her story. I think we can also ask Hellen to join us in the project."

\* \* \*

When Nakato called Hellen that evening, her sister told her that Gwen was fine, but still upset after breaking up with Lorenzo. Gwen had found Nakato friendly, kind and easy to talk to during her visit, Hellen said, and she'd probably be comfortable talking with her about her feelings and appreciate hearing her advice.

"By the way, Grandma Ruth showed me and Babirye some of her diaries this afternoon," Nakato said. "There's enough material there for a book. In fact, we thought it would be nice to write Grandma Merab's biography too—two books in one. Would you be interested in co-writing it?"

"Hell, yeah! That'd be a great book!" Hellen replied. "When do we begin?"

"I'll be interviewing both of them and can have the recordings and some notes ready in a month's time," Nakato said. "So let's say about a month from now?"

"Cool. That sounds like a good plan," Hellen said and changed the topic to Conrad.

\* \* \*

When the twins visited their parents the following day, Nakato excitedly announced their plan. Herbert said that it would be a great honour for both Ruth and Merab if their granddaughters wrote their biography, but Leah had some concerns.

"Have you thought of involving the grandsons or is it just the granddaughters?" she asked.

"Just Hellen and us. We won't involve any men," Babirye said.

"I think you should involve Spencer and Simon," Leah said. "Your aunt Kate won't be pleased if you write the book without involving her sons. She told me last month that she did not like the fact that you did not involve them in organizing your grandmothers' recent party."

"Let her complain but we can't get Simon and—"

"It would be good to involve Simon and Spencer," Nakato said, interrupting Babirye, "but I don't think they would have the level of commitment and focus that's needed to write a book."

Babirye laughed. "I can't picture Spencer sitting on a plane, on one of his numerous business trips, writing a chapter of a biography instead of balancing his books and making business projections."

"I can't either," Nakato said. "Simon could sit and focus to write but with all the hours he puts in at his clinic, I don't think he would find time—"

"What about Brandon?" Leah asked. "You girls exclude your brother from everything you do and I don't like that."

"Brandon?" Nakato and Babirye said in unison and laughed.

"The only thing that Brandon writes is music. And he hasn't released a single album since *Tobbanga Nkoko*," Babirye said.

"Actually, Mummy tells me that Brandon and his friend Zoe will be releasing an album soon," Herbert said.

"I am glad that you are planning to write a book," Leah said. "But make sure you involve the boys, even in a small way, like doing the research. I don't want Kate to feel that her sons don't matter in the family."

"Mummy, we can't involve any of them. They will delay the project and make us fail," Babirye said.

Leah didn't reply, and she did not pursue the matter any further.

❄ ❄ ❄

The following week, when Nakato went to Ruth's home for their first interview, she found Ruth in her living room, chatting with her longtime admirer, Cornelius Bulega, Conrad's grandfather. Ruth was laughing loudly and she seemed to be happy.

"This is my granddaughter, Nakato," Ruth said, introducing her to Cornelius. "She is a pediatrician."

"Yes, of course, I recognize her," Cornelius said as he tried to get up with the help of his walking stick to shake hands with Nakato.

Realizing the effort Cornelius was making to get up, Nakato moved closer to shake his hand.

"You are beautiful," Cornelius said in English as he shook Nakato's hand. "Just like your grandmother."

"Thank you, sir," Nakato said and sat down.

Cornelius asked Nakato a few questions about her work before she went out of the living room to let Ruth and Cornelius continue their conversation.

"That young woman has a twin sister," Ruth said. "She is also a doctor, a gynecologist."

"I know your entire family well, Ruth," Cornelius answered.

※　※　※

"Grandma, I am here to ask you some questions to supplement and clarify some of the things in your diaries," Nakato said fifteen minutes later, after Cornelius had left, when she and Ruth sat down to chat. "By the way, you seemed to be enjoying that old man's company."

Ruth laughed loudly and Nakato looked at her, amused. Ruth didn't notice that Nakato was recording the conversation.

"Of course I enjoy his company. Why wouldn't I?" Ruth asked and laughed again.

"Do you find him interesting?" Nakato asked.

"Interesting? Yes. But there is something else," Ruth said, with a serious look. "This is a man who I know loves me—and I have known for decades—with a love so strong that it didn't diminish even with the passage of time. So I have been wondering, if I had married Cornelius instead of your grandfather, how my life would have turned out."

"Tell me more about it."

"I know you are the interviewer and you should be the one asking questions. But let me ask you just one question so you can put yourself in my shoes. What's your love story? Did more than one man show interest in you?"

"Of course, Grandma. Many men have asked me to be their girlfriend," Nakato said, smiling. "They still ask, even when they know that I am married."

"That's what they've always done. But I am asking about men or another man you considered as a potential husband."

"Yes, there were three suitors but I chose Roland," Nakato said and paused. "But sometimes I regret my choice." Her eyes glistened with tears.

"Sorry, that's not where I wanted to go with my question," Ruth said and touched Nakato's hand. "I wanted to tell you that Cornelius was one man I would have wanted to marry. However, because he did not tell me what he felt about me, I didn't know that he loved me. I am sorry to say, but Cornelius was a more successful man than my husband. For sure, if I had married him, my life would have turned out differently. Don't get me wrong, I loved my husband very much but that's how we are as human beings. We always have 'what ifs.'"

"Do you sometimes regret—"

"No, I don't regret but my parents chose my husband for me. Well, they suggested. They did not force me to marry your grandfather, but you get the point," Ruth said.

"What is your biggest regret in life?"

"Oh, has the interview begun? Ruth asked and shifted to sit up straight on the sofa. "I had been intending to write my autobiography but somehow I didn't get to do it. That has been one of my biggest regrets, so I am so glad that you, my granddaughters, have decided to write my biography. I think there would be a lot for young women and women in general, to learn from my life."

"To what one thing do you attribute your success in life and in business?"

Ruth kept quiet, her hand on the chin, to think. "Decisions. Firm decisions. I made my decisions quickly—and, fortunately, they turned out to be good ones. And by the way, I rarely changed my decisions. Especially in business."

"What was the hardest thing you've had to deal with in life?"

"Men," Ruth said without hesitation. "Relationships with men were hard, and I think that was the case for all the women in my generation. Do you know what your grandmother Merab went through in a polygamous—"

"I will ask her the same question," Nakato said. "But today I'd like to hear your perspective."

"From the men in our neighbourhood while I was growing up, the men I worked with while I was an education officer, the men I met on business trips, to the men who came to buy merchandise from the boutique, they all seemed to want a relationship," Ruth said and laughed. "They always made unwanted sexual advances and things like that. Oh, dear."

"You quit your boutique abruptly. In fact, during the first few weeks after you quit, Daddy and Mummy talked about nothing else. Daddy even worried about your health. Can you tell me why you quit?"

"I thought deeply about the way I was living my life after Clotilda died so suddenly, visiting her farm, hard at work. It was during her funeral service that I asked myself whether I had my priorities in life right. True, I loved my business. I worked hard to build it but I wondered whether I wanted to go on working for money at this old age. Honestly, the answer was no. That's not how I wanted to live the rest of my life."

"But you loved your business and enjoyed your work."

"Absolutely. But I had spent decades working, always on the move, traveling, attending one meeting after another, and always focusing on making more money. Don't get me wrong, it is good to earn money but at some point, you've got to realize that you need to slow down, to set aside time for loved ones and friends. Hey, now I am happy to host people here and to serve them a cup of tea and biscuits. I didn't have time to do that before," Ruth said and laughed.

The interview went on for about an hour. Ruth spoke frankly about the history of her business and answered Nakato's questions concerning her professional life, but when questioned about the early years of her marriage, she seemed not to want to talk about that period in her life, only saying, "You will find all the interesting details in the diaries."

"Okay, I have no more questions for now," Nakato said, and she joined her grandmother for lunch.

❋ ❋ ❋

Nakato went to see Merab later that afternoon and told her about the planned book.

"Oh, would people be interested in reading about me, an uneducated woman?" her grandmother asked. "Will you write the book in Luganda?"

"No, it will be in English," Nakato answered. "Grandma, don't underestimate yourself. You have lived an extraordinary life. You not only built a successful business—a difficult thing to do—but you also gave a lot to others. And not just to members of your family—"

"Thank you for saying that, Nakato. I've never thought about my life that way."

"I'll need to ask you a few things first, though, to gather information. What time of day do you think you would be most ready to answer my questions?"

"Oh, I have to answer questions?" Merab asked, alarmed.

"You can just try to recall events as well as you can," Nakato answered, laughing. "They won't be tough questions—we'll just have a conversation about your life, family and work."

❋ ❋ ❋

Nakato returned to Merab's home the following Saturday, and she wanted to start the interview right away. But Merab insisted they have lunch first. "Grandma, it's almost two o'clock! I eat my lunch at around noon, when I am not working at the clinic," Nakato said.

But she knew she could never successfully turn down Merab's offer of food, and Merab's only response to her objection was to open the cupboard where she kept the special plates and cutlery for visitors. Nakato perused a photo album while Merab served lunch, placing the plates of food on a mat on the floor before she and Nakato sat down to eat.

After lunch, Merab, a mat in her hand, asked Nakato to follow her outside. "Please bring a chair for yourself," she said, adding, "Whenever I see you girls wearing trousers, I recall your grandmother Ruth when I first saw her. What a sight that was!"

Nakato laughed loudly. "No, we will share the mat," she said.

When they sat down, Nakato placed her handbag next to Merab, the recorder inside already running. She didn't tell the old woman she was being recorded for fear that she wouldn't speak freely if she knew. "So, Grandma, tell me a little bit about your early life," Nakato said as she turned a page in her notebook.

"My name is Merab Gladys Nantamu. I was born in Senge in 1930. I was the youngest daughter of Levi Bukulu and Dolosi Nakasi. I had one brother and two sisters." She paused and resumed after about ten seconds. "That all sounds unreal to me now because I am the only surviving member of that family."

"What was the hardest period of your life?"

Merab kept quiet for a while, to think. "It was the time before your mother was born. I was married and tried to conceive but remained childless. I often worried that I would never have children. It was a very bad thing back then for a woman not to have children. If you didn't have children, people looked at you as if you had a very big problem. My aunt Namagembe—may her soul rest in peace—tried all sorts of remedies but it took me nearly ten agonizing years to conceive."

"What inner power helped you to succeed in the midst of adversity?"

"Intense focus. I have always had this habit and it sometimes annoyed my late husband," Merab said. "Whenever I want to learn something, I focus on it day and night until I master it. For example, when I opened the restaurant, I wanted to know what kind of food our customers would love—you know, the kind of food to which people would almost become addicted. I tried and tested different methods of cooking until I noticed that men—who were the majority of our diners—loved smoked meat. Smoked beef, goat meat, fish, you name it. We gave them that. I didn't know the impact our restaurant had in the city until when, during one of the meetings of *Omukyala Omugunjufu*.... Have you heard about *Omukyala Omugunjufu*—OO?"

"Yes, Mummy mentioned it during one of your birthday parties."

"Anyway, in one OO meeting, a woman said that she knew some women in the city who were complaining that their men did not want to eat their food again after they'd eaten at Kyatelekera Restaurant."

Nakato laughed.

"We smoked everything. The bananas that we served for dessert were ripened over a wood fireplace in Senge before they were delivered to the restaurant. They had a wonderful smoky flavour. We smoked the pots in which we cooled our drinking water too. Our water had a smoky flavour. By the way, water came free of charge with the meal. Back then we could never have imagined that there would ever be a time when people would buy drinking water!"

Nakato laughed again. "That's the order of the day now. I have heard that when you first met, you and Grandma Ruth were not friendly to each other. Is that true?"

Merab kept quiet and looked at Nakato for a few seconds. She lowered her voice. "Nakato, I hope you are not going to include this in the book. It's true. I did not like Ruth at all. I found her clothes inappropriate. Actually, I thought everything about her was wrong. I thought she had bad manners. For example, when she and her husband visited our home for the first time, she sat beside him on the sofa and started chatting with the men. That was very unusual in those days. But, in a way, I understood why she behaved that way. She was a very highly educated woman."

"Did your opinion of her change later on?"

"Yes, it changed a bit when I found out years later that she did what she did not because she felt superior to us uneducated women, but because she knew that she deserved the same treatment and the same good things out of life as men."

"You and Grandma Ruth have known each other for a long time. Is there anything important that you learnt from her?"

"Yes," Merab said and paused for a moment, thoughtful. "There are probably many things I've learned from her, but I think there is one thing I admire about her, something that I have failed to do myself. Ruth says what she thinks whether the person she is speaking to would like to hear it or not. I can't tell you how many times I have said yes to people simply because I didn't have the courage to say no to them. And I have regretted it numerous times. That's not the case with Ruth—and I think you know what I am talking about. If Ruth does not agree with you, she will say so. If the answer to your request is a no, she will say no even before you complete your sentence. That's a very admirable trait."

Both Merab and Nakato laughed.

The conversation continued for a while, and when Nakato thought she had recorded enough material for the biography, she stopped the recorder which she had hid in her bag. She told Merab that she would ask her a few more questions later if necessary.

When Nakato was leaving, Merab handed her a bag that was loaded with cooked food. Nakato was surprised and said that she did not need the food.

"No, take the food and serve it for dinner," Merab said. "You hardly touched your lunch."

# 11

# January 2014

RUTH HAD JUST finished lunch when her cellphone rang. *Cornelius? What's going on? He never calls me.*

"Ruth, I will be coming to see you this afternoon if you are home," Cornelius said when she answered the call. He sounded unusually upbeat.

As usual, Cornelius's driver walked him to Ruth's living room and then left them alone, going out to wait in the car.

"Ruth, I bring good news this afternoon," Cornelius said after the greetings, as he tried to sit up straight on the sofa.

"Oh, I am all ears," Ruth said, stood up to straighten her skirt and sat back down.

"Ruth, you know that I have been in love with you for a long time," Cornelius said and held Ruth's hand. He paused and remained silent for almost thirty seconds. He seemed to be uneasy. Ruth was about to ask what was going on when he continued. "Marrying you would fulfill one of my biggest dreams in life. So, will you marry me?"

Ruth stared at him speechlessly for a few seconds, obviously shocked.

"Should I repeat the question?" Cornelius asked, looking lovingly at Ruth.

"No need," she said. "I didn't expect that at all."

"You didn't expect what?"

"I didn't expect you to ask me to marry you. Will that be necessary? What's the purpose of getting married at this age? We are too old to get married now."

"We are not too old—"

"Yes we are. I know I am old. And of course we both know that you are older than I am. How old are you?"

"I am ninety," Cornelius answered. His hands were shaking.

Ruth laughed uneasily. "Cornelius, I care about you but I don't want to marry a ninety-year-old man."

"I am not any man."

"I know that but sorry, no."

Cornelius sat back and dropped his head thoughtfully. His mood had changed. Ruth noticed his disappointment and gently rubbed his right shoulder. They remained silent in the sofa, he thinking about her and she trying to make him comfortable.

"Would you like something to drink?" Ruth asked after a while.

Cornelius did not answer. When she took a closer look, Ruth realized that he was already asleep. She gently pushed him back and let him sleep on the sofa. He started snoring. He slept there for about ten minutes. When he woke up, he said he'd better be going.

❄ ❄ ❄

Brandon and Delilah returned home soon after Cornelius had left. Ruth was still in the living room when they walked in. Delilah went to their bedroom and Brandon stayed with Ruth to chat.

"Something interesting has just happened, my grandson," Ruth said. "Cornelius has asked me to marry him."

"What?" Brandon asked and laughed.

"Yes, you should laugh because it is funny."

"What did he say?"

"Exactly what I have told you. He said that he wanted me to marry him."

"Really?"

"Yes. It was awkward. I turned down his proposal and of course, he felt bad."

"That's not fair, Grandma. You should have said yes," Brandon said, teasingly.

Ruth laughed. "The poor man slept on the sofa after I turned him down. Brandon, what would be there for me—or for him—to gain from marriage at this very old age?" She laughed.

Brandon laughed out loud and was still laughing when he walked out of the living room to his bedroom.

\* \* \*

Cornelius died in hospital just a week after Ruth had turned down his marriage proposal.

"Did I break his heart?" Ruth asked when Brandon told her the sad news and showed her the notice with his photo in the newspaper.

"Yes, Grandma, it seems you broke the old man's heart," Brandon said, laughing.

"Please don't laugh, Brandon. I cared about Cornelius even though I refused to marry him. Of course, you know how the story would have ended up if I'd married him—in the newspapers! The very old widower and very old widow who couldn't resist each other. Who wants that sort of publicity?"

But even though she did not want the publicity, Ruth got it. Three days after Cornelius died, a long obituary for the former headmaster of the prestigious Musasa High School in *Informed Pages* mentioned that Cornelius had apparently had a long-lasting crush on Ruth.

"Is it true, Grandma? Were you aware of this?" Brandon asked as he and Ruth perused the article.

"Yes, I knew it. But who leaked that information to the newspapers?" Ruth asked.

"I guess we will never know," Brandon said, but he soon recalled that when Nakato had mentioned her grandmother's comments to Brandon following her interview with Ruth, his friend Zoe had been with them. Brandon now suspected that Zoe must have told someone.

\* \* \*

Three weeks later, Nakato had gathered most of the information that she and her sisters would need to start writing their grandmothers' biography. She sent a text message to Hellen, asking her to call about the biography. She and Babirye met in Babirye's home that afternoon to wait for Hellen's call.

"Who is going to lead the meeting?" Hellen asked after the greetings.

"You, of course," Babirye answered. The twins seemed to have a tacit agreement that their younger sister was their leader.

"Okay, I am ready. Thanks for your confidence in me! So what are we talking about?" Hellen said.

"What are we talking about?" Babirye asked and laughed. "We are going to discuss how to write both our grandmothers' biography. Hellen, don't tell me that you didn't know why you called!"

"Of course I knew why we are having this meeting but everything must be clear in our minds, every step of the way. And I'll be taking notes on my computer as we go along. Okay, so step one is done," Hellen said, slowing down to type. "We have stated the reason for the meeting. It is to discuss how we will write both our grandmothers' biography."

"I like your approach," Nakato said.

"Thanks. Next, why are we writing the biography? I hope we have a strong reason because that is what will keep us going when the task becomes hard," Hellen said.

"We are writing the biography in order to share our two extraordinary grandmothers' remarkable life stories with our readers," Nakato said.

"That sounds good, Nakato," Hellen said. "Did you memorize it?"

"Yes," Nakato and Babirye said in unison, and laughed.

"Okay, good," Hellen said, and the twins could hear her typing. "Next—how long will the writing take and when should the book be ready?"

"We'll need one year," Nakato answered.

"That's rather ambitious for a co-writing project for first-time authors," Hellen said. "Let's say one year for the first draft."

"One year is too short, in my opinion," Babirye said. "Why not three years?"

"We don't have so much time," Nakato said. "Grandma Merab is sick, and we don't know how much longer she will be with us. It would be nice to have both of our grandmothers present to listen to their written stories during a book launch party."

"That's very important. So, one year for the first draft. Nakato—" Hellen began.

"Where does a busy doctor find time to write? Babirye asked and laughed.

"A busy doctor who wants to give the world the gift of her grandmothers' written story creates the time," Hellen answered.

The three of them were laughing now.

"Nakato, send your notes to each of us this afternoon. Have you assigned who is writing which section of the book?" Hellen asked.

"Yes, I have," Nakato answered. "Hellen, you are writing about Grandma Ruth's life and career. I am writing about Grandma Merab's life and career. Babirye, you are writing about the interaction of the two grandmothers in a joint family story. I have contacted my friend Professor Zedekiah Kamau, who's the executive editor of the *East African Journal of Medicine*, and he has agreed to edit the book. He tells me he'll need a couple of months to do that."

"Cool. So, for accountability, to keep things on track, I will be calling both of you every Monday evening, your time, to check on progress," Hellen said. "Deal?"

"Every week?" Babirye asked, alarmed.

"Yeah, I'll check on you every week. I have a friend who's a writer—she says that if you want to succeed at writing, you've got to write something every day, even if it's as few as five hundred words."

"Don't worry, Babirye," Nakato said. "I'll give you some writing tips. Actually, we can work together sometimes."

"Nakato, did you do the recordings?" Hellen asked.

"Yes I did," Nakato told her. "I will e-mail them to you right away."

"Okay, sisters. Talk to you on Monday, eight days from today. I will e-mail today's meeting notes to you this afternoon. Now, I'm going out for brunch," Hellen said, and rung off.

✻ ✻ ✻

That evening, Babirye sat in her home office, planning to start writing. She switched on her laptop and opened a Word file. Or maybe she should write on paper? She opened a notebook and selected a suitable pen from a pencil-holder on her desk. She thought for a few minutes but couldn't find the words to write. *Oh, this is harder than I thought. Where do I start?*

Her cellphone rang and she answered it. Her new secretary told her that cleaning supplies were running low at the clinic and would need to be replenished the following day.

"What!" *But I shouldn't yell at the poor woman. She's still learning.* She calmed down. "Nadia, I've told you this twice already but I will repeat it. We use the petty cash in the upper drawer at the reception to purchase cleaning supplies." She almost added "and that is your job" but restrained herself. Then Brian walked into the office, complaining about the nanny, so Babirye ended the call abruptly. Brian's rant lasted more than five minutes.

*No. Forget writing. I can't do anything this evening,* Babirye thought, deciding to listen to Nakato's interview with Merab instead. Although she laughed hard at some points, the interview was mostly boring and a little depressing. At the end of the hour she went right to bed.

✻ ✻ ✻

"I have a confession to make. Hellen will be calling in three days' time but I haven't written anything as yet," Babirye said to Nakato while they were having lunch at their clinic at the end of the week.

"Oh."

"I know. It is kind of disappointing but I haven't found any free time to write," Babirye said.

"I understand, but you won't find free time to write. You'll have to create time," Nakato answered.

"I hope I can do it."

"Yes, you can. Let me tell you how I do it. I've set up a specific time. When I return home, I take a bath, prepare a cup of tea and dive into writing for one hour. I do that however tired I may be. Fortunately, Roland has been cooperating so far. He takes Collin out for the hour that I am writing. By the time they return, I am done."

"That sounds like a good strategy. I will try it," Babirye said and for the first time felt enthusiastic about the writing project.

# 12

# February 2014

WHILE SHE WAS reading Ruth's diaries in her home office, Nakato was sometimes amused by the things that Ruth had written about, especially the events and incidents concerning her children. But some of Ruth's entries made Nakato sad because she noticed some similarities between Jude, her late grandfather, and her own husband Roland.

An entry from 1971, which Ruth had written during the weeks following her resignation from the civil service, stood out.

> *"I opened Ruth's Boutique three weeks ago. I am optimistic about the future of the shop but there are no signs of success yet. My mother and my husband are asking me to look for another job. So far I have refused to do so. Because of that, my husband quarrels every night. Tonight he has said that I am eating his food for free, and that I am not contributing anything to the family."*

Nakato put the diary down and cried. She realized that in some cases she was living a life similar to Ruth's. Having returned home late, drunk, the previous evening, Roland had said that Nakato left all the housework to the nanny and that she was worthless as a wife and a mother.

*If my grandmother survived an abusive relationship, I will too.* She consoled herself but after she had regained her composure, she decided not to continue reading the 1971 diary. She put it back in the bag and drew out a few of the later diaries. Nakato read some entries from 1977 and learned about Ruth's triumphs as a netball coach.

*"This evening, we have beaten East Mengo for the first time in our club's history. Obviously, my coaching has led to victory."*

Nakato laughed out loud. *That's so typical of my grandmother! She wants all the credit for herself.* She turned the page.

*"Mitego continues to be silly. He hugged me excitedly inside the stadium's office and pretended to have accidentally touched my buttocks. I slapped his hand very hard."*

Nakato laughed again. She read the entry again and called Babirye while still laughing.

"What's so funny?" Babirye asked.

"I am reading Grandma's diaries. In 1977 she wrote about a time when she was a netball coach. Someone grabbed her bum after a victorious match and she slapped him!" Nakato read the entry out loud to Babirye.

Babirye joined in the laughter and said she would ask Ruth about Mitego. Nakato said that she shouldn't because it would embarrass Ruth.

"I don't think so. Few things embarrass Grandma," Babirye said and laughed again.

\* \* \*

"I noticed that you mention Grandpa's verbal abuse several times in some of your earliest diaries. Can you tell me about it?" Nakato asked Ruth while they chatted three days later.

"Your grandfather Jude had a habit—which he started while I was away studying in England—of going out to drink at a bar every evening after work. In most cases he returned home, sober, before dinner. But on some occasions, especially on Friday evenings, he would return home late, drunk. Then he would wake me up at midnight or even as late as one o'clock in the morning, demanding that I serve him dinner or just to talk. Whenever I refused to get out of bed, he would quarrel, sometimes till daybreak."

"Somewhere you wrote about him telling you that you were eating his food for free—"

Ruth laughed. "Yes, that was when my business was still in its infancy and I was not earning any money. When he said that I was eating his food for free, I asked him whether he cooked it. He said that anyone can cook. Oh dear, my husband was nasty in those days! The following day, for dinner, I didn't serve his meal. I let the maid serve him while I was watching TV. One of the things he hated most was me letting the helper serve him dinner while, according to him, I sat there doing nothing. He told my father that I was neglecting some of my duties as a wife," Ruth said. "But he improved his behaviour a bit afterwards." She noticed that the interviewer was crying. "What's wrong?" she asked Nakato.

"There are some similarities between my grandfather and my husband. My husband abuses me in much the same way as Grandfather abused you. But I don't know why he does it. I treat him well and respect him."

Ruth listened to Nakato and thanked her for confiding in her about the abuse. "Don't be ashamed," she told the young woman. "You are a good person who deserves respect from your husband."

Hearing these kind words, Nakato calmed down and was able to resume the interview.

＊ ＊ ＊

As soon as Nakato left, Ruth called Babirye and asked her for Roland's telephone number and called Roland mid-morning the following day. "Please come see me at home any time this weekend," she told him.

Roland was surprised that Ruth had called him, and even more surprised that she had asked him to come see her. He wondered what it was about but he was a successful businessman, he thought, so maybe it had to do with her boutique.

When Roland arrived, Ruth opened the front door and asked him to sit on a sofa in the living room. He was still wondering what she wanted to talk to him about, alone. He didn't have to wait long to find out.

After the greetings, Ruth began. "Your dear wife tells me that she is not happy with the way you treat her, Roland," she said calmly, her neutral tone suggesting that she did not judge him.

"Oh, really? When and why did she say that?" Roland asked, surprised.

"She came here to interview me for the biography that she and her sisters are writing. Do you know about the biography?"

"Yes, I do."

"Part of the conversation was about marriage, so she mentioned that you treat her badly. What do have you say about that?"

Roland did not answer. He was now gazing at the carpet.

"Are you proud of the way you treat your wife?" Ruth asked, trying to lighten her tone so it didn't sound like an interrogation.

"Sometimes yes, sometimes no. Just like any other man," Roland answered, looking up.

"Oh dear, we are not talking about other men. We are talking about you, Roland."

"Sometimes, when I am angry, I yell at her. When my business is not doing well, I sometimes take out my frustrations on her. Of course it is a bad thing and I regret whenever I do it."

"But your wife should be your best friend."

"That's true and I love her very much."

"Roland, you should express your love through your actions too, not just your words."

"I understand, Grandma. Thank you for your advice. I'll take it to heart and make the necessary changes."

"Unfortunately, for a long time, my husband behaved in the same way you are behaving and I am wondering whether you are doing the same things that he was doing," Ruth said and paused. "Are you keeping any secrets from your wife?"

Roland hesitated. He avoided Ruth's gaze for a few seconds. "No, I am not."

"That's good. Otherwise, secret things like cheating kill marriages."

Roland's heart beat faster. *Does she know anything else? What else did Nakato say?*

He was relieved when the conversation turned to his and Nakato's son Collin, whom Ruth loved a lot, especially since he had been named after her own late father. Roland had lunch with Ruth, and when he left he felt better than when he had arrived.

# 13

# February 2014

TO HELLEN, THE six months after her wedding had seemed to be the longest ones in her life. When she traveled back to Kampala, she was so eager to see Conrad that the flight seemed to take even longer than usual.

When she walked out of the airport, Conrad and his brother Nathan were outside, waiting for her. She let go of the cart on which she had been pushing her suitcases and rushed to embrace Conrad. She attempted twice to kiss him on the mouth but he turned away.

"Hey, what's going on?" she asked. "Aren't you happy to see me?"

"Let's wait, dear. It's not appropriate to kiss in public," Conrad answered.

"Whatever," Hellen said as she planted a quick kiss on his mouth.

Nathan laughed. "It's okay. Enjoy each other while you are still young."

Later that evening, Hellen called her parents from Conrad's and said she'd see them the next day and bring Gwen's report.

❄ ❄ ❄

After lunch at her parents' place the next day, Hellen, her father and mother sat in the living room, ready to discuss Gwen's report. Leah gave a bottle of beer and a newspaper to Conrad, who went to wait in the backyard.

"I'll present the report in English for two reasons," Hellen said, speaking more formally than usual to her parents. "One, my Luganda is not that great." She laughed. "Two, the report itself is in English, of course, and it's fairly technical. So it will be easier for me to present it as it's written, rather than trying to translate it."

"Fair enough," Herbert said.

"I've made each of you a copy," Hellen said as she pointed to the reports she had placed on the coffee table. "I'll go through the most important points and you can read the rest later."

Herbert and Leah opened their spiral-bound copies of the report, and both commented on its professional look and asked Hellen to thank Gwen for producing it. "Gwen is a wonderful young woman," Leah added. "Everyone she met here is saying good things about her."

"Thanks for the kind comments—I'll let her know. By the way, she sends her warm regards to you and I have some chocolates she gave me to give you. But we will talk about all that later," Hellen said and rose to straighten her miniskirt. "I would like both of you to check out the statement on page 34 and tell me if it's true or not," she said, now all business. "'If Leah were not donating funds to pay the restaurant's rent and Sam's wages, the business would not be able to meet its operating costs.'" She placed her report down on the coffee table, crossed her legs and asked, "Mom, is that statement true or false?"

Leah remained silent for about ten seconds. Hellen looked at her intensely. "I don't know if it's true or false but I have been paying the rent for the last—let me see—about nine months."

Hellen gazed at Herbert and then at Leah. "You get money from elsewhere to pay the restaurant's rent?"

"Yes," Leah answered and laughed.

"Dad, are you stunned by that?"

"I am surprised but I am not stunned," Herbert said as he lovingly rubbed Leah's shoulder.

"That's strange," Hellen said, feigning laughter. "You didn't show surprise."

"But I am surprised."

"Mom and Dad, I think you are not managing your wealth well," Hellen said. "Now let me ask this as a concerned daughter. Where does the money come from to pay the restaurant's rent and Uncle Sam's wages?"

Neither parent responded.

"I guess I have to repeat the question. Where does the money come from to pay the restaurant's rent and Uncle Sam's wages?"

"I don't know," Herbert said. "Your mother should answer. She manages the income from our rental properties."

"Mom, where does the money that pays the restaurant's rent and Uncle Sam's wages come from?"

"Your father has just solved the puzzle for you—it comes from our rental properties," Leah answered.

"Dad, you are an economist! You allow that?"

Herbert leaned back on the sofa. "Hellen, dear, like I said, your mother manages the income. The last time I was involved in that stream of our income was when we were still paying your university tuition."

"Okay, enough already! Dad, I will need an inventory of all the family's sources of income. And I'll get to that in a separate meeting before I leave."

"Hellen, you can complain about the restaurant's rent. That's okay. But as far as Sam is concerned, I can't abandon him in his time of need," Leah said. "Sam is like a brother to me. We grew up together and his father cared a lot for my mother."

"Okay, but our recommendation is to close down the restaurant, because right now you're throwing good money after bad," Hellen said as she reviewed the report.

"Let's give the restaurant a chance, at least six months. I know I can turn it around. I'll be more involved in its day-to-day operations as soon as I retire," Leah said.

"How do you plan to do that?" Herbert asked his wife. "I don't picture you working there."

"You don't picture me working there? Where did you meet me?" Leah asked.

That question made Hellen laugh out loud.

"That was a much younger Leah, decades ago," Herbert said, smiling. "My dear wife, today, can't work in a restaurant."

"You will be surprised. I will work there and I will turn the restaurant around," Leah said.

"Okay. I'll check in with you in six months but please update me on how the restaurant is doing between now and then," Hellen said. "Now let's discuss the boutique."

Herbert sat up straight, ready to hear Gwen's verdict about the boutique. He hoped she had recommended closing it down too.

"According to the report, the boutique is doing well," Hellen said when each one of them had opened the section of the report that covered the boutique. "However, it has two major problems. The first one is that it is understaffed. The second one is that there is no general manager. Elsie told Gwen that she feels that her salary does not match the level of responsibility she has taken on."

"But Clement has been helping out," Herbert said. "Elsie shouldn't be complaining."

"Can you please turn with me to page 65?" Hellen said. They all turned to page 65. Hellen read out loud. "'Clement has no clue how to manage a business. All he does here is sit in the managing director's office for most of the day, just pretending to be busy. And then he demands cash.'" She paused and asked, "Dad, is that the kind of person you want to have as the general manager for your boutique?"

For about five minutes they argued about Clement, with Herbert defending him and Hellen insisting that Gwen's report had demonstrated how incompetent Clement was. Leah listened without commenting. "It is okay," Herbert finally said when he noticed that Hellen was getting angry. "Let's hire a general manager."

"Cool, then. Nakato is ready to contact a recruiting firm to help with the hiring," Hellen said. "She was only waiting for your instructions." She paused as Leah left the room to prepare tea. "Dad, I am serious," Hellen now said more quietly. "I will need an inventory of all the family's sources of income. Please compile a list of all your properties and investments so we know everything."

"Everything? What do you want to do with the properties?" Herbert asked.

"Dad, I thought what I said was clear—I think that you and Mom are not managing the family's wealth well."

"Fair enough. Now let me ask you a question. Let's say we want to sell one of our properties. Shall we need to get permission to do so first from you, our beloved daughters?"

"No, but I don't think you get it. All we want is for you guys to pay more attention to the family's wealth. We are not taking over control of any of your stuff," Hellen said, plainly upset. "You know what? Let me chill out with my hubby," she said. Not waiting for tea, she rose and walked out to the backyard to join Conrad, leaving her copy of the report on the table.

\* \* \*

Babirye, Nakato and their aunt Kate and Ruth joined the family for dinner that evening, and afterwards the three sisters stayed chatting at the dinner table. "You know what I discovered by reading Gwen's report? Mom is throwing away too much money," Hellen told the others. "We need to step up and help the family even beyond our grandmothers' businesses."

"Mummy is too generous," Nakato said.

"And a lot of money is being wasted. She pays the restaurant's rent and she pays Uncle Sam a salary. But Gwen's report indicates in clear terms that Uncle Sam does next to nothing at the restaurant," Hellen said. "I want us to help the family by stepping up to manage our wealth."

"How do you suggest we do that? Wouldn't we be taking on too much responsibility?" Babirye asked.

"But we can do it," Hellen said. "I've asked Dad to give me a complete inventory of the family's properties and investments. But I will be returning to Boston in two weeks' time. Can either of you ensure that he gives it to you?"

"I know who can help," Nakato said and rose to go to the living room. She returned two minutes later with Ruth.

"Hellen, please ask your husband to join you here," Ruth said, walking into the dining room. "The poor man is not comfortable where he is seated with his loud-mouthed in-laws."

"He'll be fine for a few more minutes, Grandma. He doesn't talk much," Hellen said. "Grandma, can you please tell us everything you know about our family's wealth? We have realized that our parents are not managing the family's wealth well, and we want to do something to help. We would like to take over from Mom and Dad."

"Good. I am glad to hear that," Ruth answered, smiling as she pulled out a chair and sat down with her granddaughters. "I can't tell you how much I am proud of you three girls—your parents did a better job raising you than we did raising them," Ruth said, taking a sip of juice. "I am sorry to say it but I realized too late that Merab and I spoiled our children. Your parents are too passive for the family's good. So, what do you want to know about the family's wealth? Do you want your inheritance now?"

Everybody laughed.

"Great idea, but no. We want to take over just so we manage the family's wealth better than our parents are managing it now," Hellen said.

"Here is a bit of history," Ruth said. "Your great-great-grandfather Boaz was a labourer during the construction of the Uganda railway. Later, he started a small business that your great-grandfather eventually grew into a group of companies, Kiyaga Holdings. When your great-grandfather passed away, your grand-aunt Catherine—she herself passed away about seven years ago—took over from him as managing director. Your father and I were also directors in the company. Are you following me?"

"Yes," the sisters answered in unison.

"But your grandfather, my husband Jude, was not directly in-volved in the business. Oh, dear, Jude was even lazier and more carefree than your father is."

The granddaughters laughed.

"Catherine and I disagreed so much during the company meetings that I resigned from the directorship after only two years. I think she had planned to make it hard for me to continue as a director. Anyway, to cut a long story short, Catherine and her family took over the company. Presently her sons and grandchildren are much richer than we are."

"Grandma, we will need your help. Can you please ensure that we get a list of all the family's properties and investments?" Hellen said.

Ruth laughed. "Your parents are grown and independent now. And I don't know what they own. Wouldn't it be strange if I sat them down and said, 'Oh, give me a list of all your properties and investments; your daughters want it'? Oh, dear, of course that would be strange, even for a crazy old woman like me."

The granddaughters laughed.

"But I am glad you are taking an interest in the family's wealth because honestly, your parents don't seem to be diligent about it. You should take over because right now, even though we worked hard to accumulate our wealth, Merab and I are now irrelevant."

The granddaughters laughed again.

"What's so funny?" Herbert asked, walking into the dining room, but Ruth said nothing more, and went back to the living room with him a few minutes later.

"That was an interesting story that Grandma just told us," Nakato said.

"Interesting? I think it's sad," Hellen said. "So this is where we come in. Let's think of a way to play a more active role to save the family's wealth."

"I am in. Let's do it," Babirye said.

"I am in too," Nakato said.

# 14

# February 2014

HELLEN FELT BAD that the last time she had been in Kampala, for her wedding, she hadn't gone to visit her grandmother Merab's home. She decided to surprise her. When she knocked on the front door, it didn't open for close to three minutes, but Hellen knew that Merab was sickly and slow. She waited.

When Merab opened the door and saw Hellen, a wide smile lit up her face. "Hellen, I am glad to see you. I wasn't expecting you! When did you arrive in the country?"

"I've been in town for a few days now, Grandma. I felt bad that I didn't pay you a visit the last time I was in Kampala, so I've decided to come spend the day here, to chat with you," Hellen said as she walked into the living room.

"Oh, I am happy to hear that. Since you will be here the whole day, I will be able to prepare a big meal for you," Merab said.

Hellen went to the dining room, placed her laptop and handbag on the table, and then returned to greet her grandmother in the proper customary manner. Merab picked a mat from a corner in the living room and sat down.

"Come, sit here," Merab said, gesturing for Hellen to sit on her lap. "I want to see if you are feeding yourself properly."

"No, Grandma. I am too heavy to sit on your lap," Hellen answered.

"Oh, you fear that you might break the old bones?" Merab said, laughing. "But you are so thin! Come sit for just one minute, like you used to when you were little. Do you remember any of the many stories I told you when you were little?"

Hellen laughed and sat briefly on Merab's lap. She then rose and sat back on the sofa.

"How is your life now that you are a married woman?" Merab asked after she, her stepson Kulumba and several other people who lived in the home had greeted Hellen.

"Grandma, it's not been easy to be in a long-distance relationship. It's hard to be far away from the one I love. You know, my husband and I are at that stage where we want to sit and talk and stare in each other's eyes all the time. You know that stage, Grandma, don't you?" Hellen said, gesturing and moving on the sofa.

"No, I don't!" Merab laughed, amused by Hellen's gestures and her funny Luganda accent. "Do you remember what I told you about your grandfather and me? I didn't love him at first. And just around the time that I really fell in love with him, he brought home another woman! The rivalry that started between us women was a very different feeling than the one you are describing."

"Oh, let me tell you, Grandma, there is a sweet stage of love. Conrad and I talk on the phone every day, and chat via video on the computer—"

"What? You can see each other on the computer? There is technology that enables you to do that? That's so interesting!" Merab said, shaking her head. "How much will this world keep changing?"

"But even though we talk and see each other on the computer whenever we want, it's not the same as being physically together. It is even harder for me since I live alone," Hellen continued.

"So you have challenges too," Merab said, her look somber. "You know, we old folks think that we lived the hardest lives that could be and that things are much easier for younger generations. But now I can imagine that alone in your house on a cold day over there in America, you feel as bad as I felt when I was a young girl, trapped in an older man's house."

"Exactly, Grandma," Hellen said. "So my husband and I spend hours and hours on the phone, talking and exchanging loving, reassuring words."

"Your grandmother Ruth told me that you and your sisters want to put some order in the family because your parents are losing a lot of money."

"Yes, but so far it's not been easy to get them to trust us," Hellen said. "But we will get there."

"To me you sound like a woman who is fully in control of your life."

"How could I not be?" Hellen said, smiling. "I am your grand-daughter. No doubt I inherited your genes."

"You think so? I don't think I was ever in control of my life."

"Yes, you were—believe me, Grandma. I listened to the recording of your interview with Nakato. You *are* a strong woman," Hellen said and laughed. "By the way, can I have the Wi-Fi password, Grandma? I've got some work to do."

Merab laughed and pointed to the modem and the TV. "Your mother installed those things there but I don't know how to use them. I never touch them."

She rose and went out to get Kulumba, who came in, retrieved a scrap of paper from under the modem, handed it to Hellen and then after she'd connected to the internet placed it back under the modem and walked out. Merab watched in silence.

Hellen's cellphone beeped for an e-mail message. After reading the message, she rose and went to switch on her laptop on the dining room table, then joined Merab again back in the living room. Five minutes later, her phone beeped again and Hellen responded by going back to her laptop in the dining room.

"Do you have to do that whenever you hear a sound on your telephone?" Merab asked her granddaughter when she'd returned to the living room a few minutes later.

Hellen laughed. "No, Grandma, not every sound. There are several types of beeping sounds on the phone. The one you just heard alerts me when there is urgent work."

"Oh, you are working now?"

"Yes, I am working. Even though I am here, out of the office and very far away, my clients still expect a response to their questions. They can't wait simply because I am away from the office."

"Oh, but I know that when we wake up in the morning here, you people are sleeping, over there in America."

"You are very clever, Grandma. That's true. People in Boston, where I live, are sleeping now. But the clients whose messages I am responding to now have an office in London, in England. I know it all sounds crazy to you," Hellen said and laughed.

"Your life is complicated," Merab said, shaking her head.

"It is complicated sometimes but I enjoy myself. I love my work."

It started raining hard. Merab excused herself and went out to the back of the house while Hellen sat at the dining table, working on her laptop. She put on her headphones to listen to music while she worked and to mute the noise of the heavy rain falling on the iron roof.

Twenty-five minutes later, Hellen saw Merab opening the back door, with a steaming kettle and a plastic bag in her hands. "Grandma, you are dripping wet! Where have you been?" Hellen asked.

"I was preparing tea. Let me change and then I will have the tea ready in a few minutes," Merab answered.

"You didn't have to do that, Grandma!" Hellen exclaimed. "The tea could have waited. I am not even hungry."

"You've been here for more than an hour and I haven't given you anything to eat. Isn't that shameful?" Merab said as she placed the kettle on the bare cement floor and went to her bedroom to change.

Hellen rose to see what was in the plastic bag, and when she saw the buns and packet of tea, she realized that Merab had boiled water on the outdoor kitchen's charcoal stove and gone in the pouring rain to a nearby shop to buy the tea and the buns. Hellen sat back and cried.

"What's wrong, my dear?" Merab asked, coming into the room.

"Grandma, you went through all the trouble for me? You could have waited for the rain to stop or sent somebody else instead," Hellen said.

"Don't worry about it," Merab said, smiling. "This is my way of caring for you during the short time that I have left with you. I am tired and sickly. You know, these are the things that will create good memories for you when I am gone."

Hellen rose, hugged her grandmother, and cried again.

"Please call your husband and ask him join us for lunch. We are preparing a big meal," Merab said.

"Oh yes, I will call him. He is not working today. He took two weeks off so we can maximize our time together," Hellen said and laughed.

Soon after Merab and Hellen had enjoyed their cups of tea and fresh buns, the rain stopped. They continued their conversation in the living room while they waited for Conrad to come for lunch. "I've heard that you are successful and rich," Merab said.

Hellen laughed. "Who told you that? It's true, I am successful—my partner and I run a successful business—but we are not rich."

"There was a reason why I said that," Merab continued. "I wanted to ask you a question. Do you give enough time to the people in your life or do you spend all your energy working and looking for money?"

"No. Grandma, have you heard any rumours about me?" Hellen asked and laughed again.

"No, but when I saw you working here, I remembered something that I usually share with young people. Having run a business for many years, I know that money is sweet but I wanted to tell you that people are more important than money."

"I care about people and that's why I made it a point to come to see you today. In my business too, I have a good relationship with my clients," Hellen said.

"People matter and I have an example. I spent many years working at the restaurant but all that is in the past. All I have left are people; good relationships with people. A married couple who met me at the restaurant many years ago and became friends came to see me here yesterday." She paused. "Oh, I hear that you and your sisters want to close it down."

"Yes. It was my recommendation," Hellen said. "But what do you think?"

"If the restaurant is failing, go ahead and close it down!" Merab answered without any hesitation.

❋ ❋ ❋

Gwen picked Hellen up at Logan Airport, and they talked about Conrad and Hellen's visit to Kampala all the way back into town. Only later, back in her apartment, did they discuss Hellen's parents' reaction to Gwen's report.

"As expected, my mom rejected our recommendation to close down the restaurant. She was, like, 'I will start working at the restaurant when I retire soon.' And in my mind I was, like, good luck with that."

"Oh, well. What about the boutique?" Gwen asked.

"My dad and I argued about Uncle Clement but he finally agreed to hire a general manager. I think they will hire one soon."

"Oh, great," Gwen said. "By the way, I had a date with someone while you were away."

"Who? And how did it go?" Hellen asked, excited, as she rose to prepare some coffee.

"Actually, it's someone you know. I met Miguel."

"Miguel? The VA?" Hellen asked. She had already noticed when he e-mailed whenever Gwen was away from the office that their Virtual Assistant cared a lot about Gwen and would ask about her.

"Yeah. He sent me some messages in the past few months and wanted to meet me. When I told him that I had a boyfriend he sort of gave up, but he asked again after I had broken up with Lorenzo. He invited me to dinner."

"Up until now you didn't like online dating," Hellen said, laughing. "What made you change your mind?"

"I don't really consider that online dating. Miguel wasn't, like, some creepy stranger. And when we finally met, I thought he was amazing," Gwen said. "And you know what? I think I'm into him. And we are meeting again tonight."

"That's awesome. I'm glad for you, Gwen," Hellen said, turning to face her. "Wait a minute.... Isn't Miguel based in San Diego? He lives in San Diego, right?"

"Yeah. He's come all the way up here for me—twice in two weeks! It's actually freaking me out a bit, you know what I'm saying? It kind of reminds me of Lorenzo, during those early days of our relationship."

"You know what? Why don't you forget Lorenzo and focus on your new guy?"

"Yeah, that's what I've decided to do. And I can't wait for tonight's date."

❋ ❋ ❋

Shortly after Hellen had returned to Boston, Nakato and Babirye took some time after their clinic closed to stay and discuss their mother's upcoming retirement. "Mummy has planned so many things to do in retirement that I doubt she will do anything at all," Nakato said.

Babirye laughed. "Listening to her, you would think she has an unlimited amount of money to spend. One thing is certain—she loves people and I think she will be hosting dinners every week. Can we try to control her spending?"

Nakato laughed. "No, we can't. We are not signatories to her bank accounts. The best thing we can do for her is to advise her to plan her activities, especially now that she won't be working in an office."

They discussed their father, too. Herbert would be retiring in two years' time but his daughters did not worry about him. He would be busy attending international conferences and could continue working as a consultant. And he was a member of the boards of three corporations. "I trust him to keep himself busy," Babirye said.

They both laughed as they walked out of the clinic.

❋ ❋ ❋

After rising through many ranks to finally become a principal administrative secretary, Leah retired from the Ministry of Commerce, the only place she had ever worked. She was retiring one year earlier than she would normally have done, but she wanted to concentrate on her other responsibilities. Leah gave a speech at her farewell party, saying that she wanted to spend more time with her aging mother and also wanted to help turn Kyatelekera Restaurant around. Several of her colleagues spoke, too, and said that they would miss her.

Brandon, Nakato and Babirye attended the party, too. On their way home they asked Leah what her plans were now that she had retired. She was seated in the back of the car with Nakato, unwrapping the presents from her former colleagues. "You heard my plans when I was speaking at the Ministry," Leah said. "I thought you were listening!"

"Be honest, Mummy," Babirye said. "You made a speech and I think you impressed your colleagues. But do you really believe that you can work in the restaurant?"

Leah handed the picture frame she was holding to Nakato for her to admire. "Your father said that I can't work in the restaurant, too, but I wonder why you all think that I can't."

"Go work hard, Mummy. Turn the restaurant around and amaze the doubters!" Brandon said and he and his sisters laughed.

*** *** ***

Leah had looked forward to her new life in retirement, but after only two weeks of driving over to her mother's home every day and spending the entire day there for two weekends, she was getting bored, so she decided to work full time in Kyatelekera Restaurant. The restaurant immediately regained some of its momentum.

"Hagar, what kind of work did my mother do here?" Leah asked the restaurant's manager on her third full day of work there. She was impressed by the young woman's demeanour and intelligence.

"Most days she was the first to arrive," Hagar said. "She wanted to make sure that she knew everything that took place here throughout the day."

Leah laughed. "Okay, although I'll never be the first to arrive, I think I am already doing well as far as timekeeping is concerned."

"She would inspect all areas for cleanliness," Hagar continued. "Many times, she would clean the toilets again, even though the cleaners had done so the evening before, after closing."

"That's how my mother behaves," Leah said, nodding. "She doesn't trust anybody to do things as well as she does."

"She would then supervise food preparation. She was very strict about the quantity of water that was added to the milk. Actually, as far as I remember, she always did that job herself." Leah was writing notes on a napkin. "She would also inspect the food that was delivered. I can't tell you how many times she rejected leafy vegetables for being limp. Anyway, Mama Merab did everything, but her most important duties were to greet the customers and to control the cash."

"I think I will do well with the cash, but not so well with the customers. I am a bit shy," Leah said.

Three times every week after the restaurant's busy lunch hour, Leah would drive to Kalasa to deliver various items to the farm, including fertilizers and chicken feed, then return to resume work before the restaurant closed. She was proud of herself for the work she did. When Nakato visited the restaurant one evening, Leah told her how much she was investing in the farm, paying the workers and donating money to her relatives.

❄ ❄ ❄

Now, three weeks since she'd retired, Leah was exhausted. "Mummy, you are working in a haphazard way and you will wear yourself out quickly," Nakato said when she and Babirye visited that evening.

"I can't help it. I've got a lot to do," Leah answered.

"I know you have a lot to do and I am not suggesting that you shouldn't do whatever you want to do. But you've got to write down all your projects and then prioritize them. You can't do everything at a go."

"I appreciate your advice but you shouldn't just advise me—you girls should help me with some of the work. I need your help with the farm in Kalasa and renovating Mother's house."

"I can help you with the farm," Babirye said.

"And I can help you with the renovations," Nakato said.

When they left, the twins congratulated themselves. Maybe, since their mother had asked for their help, they'd also be able to take over some control from her and reduce her spending.

❄ ❄ ❄

When Leah and Nakato went to Kawempe to inspect the house, Leah told Merab that renovations would begin the following month, and asked if there were any free rooms to store the construction materials in.

"I don't think there are any free rooms," Merab answered. "I think all the rooms in the compound in the back are occupied."

"Grandma, you don't know what's going on at home? How many people live here?" Nakato asked.

"I don't know the exact number—remember, 'He who has no people is poor however much money he has.'"

"Really?" Nakato said, gazing through the window at the row of rooms at the back of the main house.

"That's how your grandmother has lived all her life," Leah said. "I learned to love people from her."

Nakato rose from her chair and walked out to the back of the house to see how many rooms there were. The rows of rooms had all been built at the back of the house to form an enclosure, and several women cooked on charcoal stoves there while their children played around them.

Nakato greeted them and continued to inspect the area. It badly needed renovation. And as she walked around she thought of Merab's generosity, and wondered whether any of the families paid rent.

* * *

The following week, during a visit to the farm in Kalasa after she and Babirye had toured the farm, Leah stayed behind so that she could chat with the workers for a few minutes while Babirye went to her uncle Jonah's nearby home to deliver some groceries she'd brought for him.

Jonah—one of Leah's half-brothers—welcomed Babirye warmly, and one of his grandchildren brought a mat for Babirye to sit on so they could chat. Babirye soon told her uncle that Merab wanted to move back to Kalasa.

"Let her stay in the city. Our life is very hard here. Most of the time my grandchildren are sick. There is a lot of witchcraft in this village. There has always been," Jonah said, shaking his head.

Leah, now walking toward Jonah's house, saw her daughter in conversation with him and cringed. She hoped Babirye would not say anything that would displease her uncle.

"Is it witchcraft or poor feeding?" Babirye asked. She signaled one of the little girls to come to where she was seated.

*Stop it, Babirye.* Leah walked faster into the front yard.

"You are a doctor. What do you think?" Jonah asked.

"Uncle, the problem is not witchcraft. Your grandchildren are sick because of poor feeding. Some of you think that you have to have a lot of money to feed children properly, which is not true."

"You wouldn't understand. You have always lived in the city," Jonah said.

"Mummy, can you have Nakato examine these children one of these days? They are sick and malnourished," Babirye said as she examined the little girl's eyes.

"Yes, it would be good if you could help us," Jonah said, and asked Leah to sit on the mat with Babirye.

※ ※ ※

"I don't think you will need my help on the farm," Babirye said to her mother while they were driving back home. "Everything seems to be working well there."

"What a coincidence—I was thinking the same thing, and you're right," Leah said. "I won't need any help. And I think we should keep your interactions with my family in Kalasa at a minimum."

"Why do you say that?" Babirye asked, taking her eyes off the bumpy road for a few seconds to look at her mother.

"Babirye, you are too blunt. You shouldn't tell a man who is struggling to feed his grandchildren that he is not feeding them properly."

"Did you hear him blaming their sickness on witchcraft? I can't believe that people, in this day and age, still—"

"You won't understand. Let's talk about something else," Leah said.

# 15

# March 2014

CONRAD FINALLY DECIDED to take a year's sabbatical leave to go to live in Boston with Hellen. It had been hard for him to decide to leave but he missed his wife.

On the eve of his departure Conrad met up with seven buddies at the Sunset Pub like he'd done most evenings for the past eight years, for beer, roasted *matooke* plantain and ribs. They had a noisy evening as they both teased and counseled Conrad.

"Go have a good time with your wife but don't forget us. And remember to come back home," one of his friends said. "East or west, home is best."

"Hear, hear," the rest of the group said, raising their beer bottles to toast him.

When they were about to part, one of his friends gave him an envelope. "What's this?" Conrad asked, as he started to open the envelope.

"Hey, don't open it here," his friend said. "Open it at home."

Conrad returned home at midnight. He had already packed his suitcases, but couldn't sleep. On one hand, he was excited about reuniting with Hellen, but on the other, he was a little scared by the uncertainty of his new life in America. And he was already starting to miss his friends. It was only a half an hour later, still lying awake, that he remembered the envelope that his friends had given him. He rose, took the envelope out of his jacket pocket and opened it. It was full of cash—a thousand US dollars. *What a kind gesture! They didn't have to give me money.* It made Conrad miss his friends even more.

He slept little that night.

✳ ✳ ✳

Hellen was shopping when she met her aunt Victoria in the aisles of a Boston grocery store. After the greetings, she told Victoria that Conrad would be arriving later in the day.

"Good. What kind of arrangements have you made for him?" Victoria asked. "He will need a job, won't he?"

"Yeah. I contacted the Massachusetts Society of Chartered Accountants and they sent me some useful information."

"Good. You will also need to make some adjustments, my dear. For example, you might need to cook more frequently than when you are alone," Victoria said, glancing at Hellen's grocery cart. You might also need to cook different foodstuffs for him in addition to what you usually cook for yourself. Let me see what you have," Victoria said and rummaged through her niece's grocery cart. "Oh, that's all? You aren't buying any foodstuffs that your husband can eat?"

"I'm too busy to cook every day," Hellen answered, annoyed. "And what do you mean? He can eat everything I've bought," Hellen said, trying not let her irritation show. *When will she stop controlling me?*

"No. Check out my groceries," Victoria said, pointing to the sweet potatoes, cassava and yams in her grocery cart. "You know, the kind of foodstuffs that your uncle and I eat sometimes."

"I don't think I need to prepare any special foods for Conrad."

"Okay, I'll prepare some food for him and I'll drop it off for his lunch and dinner tomorrow. Another thing, I don't know what your aunt Kate told you before the wedding, so I might repeat some things that she has already told you," Victoria said, lowering her voice. She had noticed a couple of shoppers looking at them. "You have forgotten some aspects of our culture. Or should I say, you don't know certain aspects of our culture. Please bear that fact in mind in your day-to-day life with your husband."

"Yeah, I already know that," Hellen said.

"Knowing is one thing. Doing is another. Be patient with Conrad and give him time to adjust to his new life. By the way, what's the plan? Is he planning to live here?"

"The plan is for him to spend a year here. He has a year off work in Kampala. And if he gets a suitable job here, he will stay. Otherwise, he'll go back."

"You know what? After the newlyweds' bliss wears off, he will go through tough moments. Sitting around doing nothing affects a person's ego, especially a man's. Be patient and kind. Keep reassuring him."

"I will," Hellen said, but she'd had enough. "Aunt, I am pissed— stop trying to control me! I don't know whether you will one day realize it, but I am a grown woman," she said, and pushed her cart towards the check-out.

Victoria shook her head and continued shopping.

❋ ❋ ❋

Right after she got back from the grocery store, Hellen went to the airport to pick Conrad up. They were happy to reunite. "Welcome home," she said, opening the door to her apartment, and Conrad pulled his two suitcases in.

Conrad sat on the couch and had a quick look around the room. "Your apartment is beautiful—and I can see that it's expensive, too. Did your father pay for it?"

Hellen laughed. "That's an interesting question. And you know what's funny? When my dad came here the first time, he asked the same question! He was like, 'This is an expensive apartment, Hellen. Did your boyfriend pay for it?' I didn't even have a boyfriend then! And I was like, 'Come on, Dad, I am a big girl! I make my own money.'"

"It is really beautiful," Conrad said, unzipping his winter coat.

"Thank you. I'll give you a tour," Hellen said, but they cuddled on the couch for about ten minutes before she got up to show him the place, starting with the kitchen.

"It is obvious that you live alone. Everything is neatly arranged in its place," Conrad said.

"Yeah, I love clean environments and I don't want to look for stuff. I just grab and go," Hellen said. "And since I am busy during the week and I don't want to eat out, I cook all my meals on Sunday afternoon and toss them in the freezer. So when it's time to eat, I simply reheat the food."

"What? You eat frozen food?" Conrad asked.

"No, I don't eat frozen food—it's fresh food that I cook and freeze, especially veggies. I am huge on veggies. It's easy to cook and freeze in portions. It also helps me to preplan my weekly meals."

Next, they went to Hellen's office. "This is meant to be a solarium but I use it as my office. You can check it out after I've cleaned up," Hellen said. There was a stack of box folders on the table.

"This is a hardworking woman's office and it shows," Conrad said.

Hellen laughed, and led him to a small bedroom. "Gwen sleeps here sometimes when we work till late and she doesn't want to drive back home, but this room is mostly empty. She has another room in her apartment for me, as well, that I sleep in sometimes. You know we work like crazy." She laughed again.

"That's good. You are not just business partners—you are friends, too," Conrad said.

Hellen ended the tour in her own bedroom, and they lingered there for a half hour. "You can sleep off your jetlag here after lunch," she said as they walked out of the room.

"I am too excited to sleep," Conrad said as they returned to the kitchen for lunch.

\* \* \*

The following day, when Hellen woke up, she realized that Conrad was not in bed. After a shower she looked into the second bedroom and saw that he was there, chatting on the phone. He carried on his conversation while she dressed.

"Hey, you woke up early. What's going on? Are you homesick already?" Hellen asked when Conrad ended his call.

Conrad laughed. "I had an important phone call to make to the office in Kampala. Where are you going?"

"I am going to work," Hellen said, laughing.

"You dress up like that even when you work from home?"

"Yeah, I know, it sounds kind of silly, but I dress up in this room and head to the office a few steps away. My morale is high when I look and feel good," she said.

Conrad went back to sleep until noon and Hellen was working in her office when the condo security man called just as she was reheating some leftover food for lunch. She and Conrad had a visitor.

Hellen's aunt Victoria came upstairs, carrying a reusable grocery bag full of cooked food, chatted with them for about fifteen minutes and then rose to leave. Conrad tried to persuade her to join them for lunch but she refused. So Hellen enjoyed her reheated lasagna while Conrad enjoyed some beans with two medium-sized Jamaican sweet potatoes.

In the middle of the meal, Conrad opened the bottle of wine that was on the table. "I don't drink wine during working hours but I will drink a bit since you've opened the bottle," Hellen said.

They chatted at the dining table until Hellen realized that she had taken a longer break than usual. "Will you please excuse me? Back to work," she said as she kissed him and rose. "I had actually planned to take this week off to hang out with you but some urgent work came up."

When Hellen went off to the gym early in the evening, before dinner, Conrad went into her office and looked around. He read her schedule for the day written on a whiteboard, and saw her annual calendar on the wall with events and meetings marked throughout. He sat on her office chair, admiring the neatly decorated office and saw her monthly schedule set out on the table, written out on a large manila sheet. He even saw the notebook with its detailed daily meal list next to the computer. *What? Her life is very structured, a complete contrast with mine.*

＊ ＊ ＊

"I checked out your office while you were out, dear," Conrad told Hellen after dinner. "It is impressive. Everything is so well organized, and it is evident that there is no chaos in your life."

Hellen laughed. "There is a nuance in what you've just said. What do you mean?"

"Your life is very organized. I noticed that you have a list of daily activities, weekly activities and so on. I mean, who lives like that?"

"You are right," Hellen said as she rose to clear the dishes. "My physical space is organized but my work is unpredictable—you should see Gwen and me at work! It seems we are putting out fires all the time."

\* \* \*

"I will do a bit of work this afternoon and if you want, we can go grocery shopping," Hellen said to Conrad after lunch two weeks later, but he did not answer. "And you know what I have noticed?" she added, teasingly. "You don't seem to be fully living here. What's going on?"

"Your life is very structured and organized, so I am trying to fit in without disrupting it," Conrad answered.

"What do you mean?"

"Look," Conrad said as he opened the refrigerator. "This is one example. The eggs have their specific place, the juice containers have their place—"

"I thought that was a good thing. You don't have to look for anything." *He is probably bored here. What should I do to cheer him up?*

But Hellen's afternoon didn't go as planned. Gwen called and came to the apartment a half-hour later. "It's time for some work, buddy," Gwen told Conrad. "I am sorry to interrupt your plans for the afternoon, but it won't take long."

Conrad went to the kitchen to find something to do. He over-heard Gwen explaining the situation to Hellen—apparently, one of their clients was experiencing a crisis. From where he sat at the kitchen table he watched as Hellen and Gwen paced around the small living room, talking nonstop. Hellen looked stressed and Gwen kept throwing her hair back, but she seemed calmer. Conrad almost asked them why they didn't sit down to talk until he realized that they were in a walking meeting. Gwen was talking to the client on the speakerphone and Hellen was writing notes on a legal pad.

"What was that about?" Conrad asked an hour and a half later after Gwen had finally left. "You both looked stressed."

"Welcome to our work world," Hellen said. "But it's all good now. We were talking to one of our clients, an online store. We'd advised them to test their order-taking app before it went live but I think they got too excited and granted their customers access to it too quickly. They've been panicking because when they launched their new products this morning the app had glitches and everything didn't go according to plan."

"Is that an example of the fires you put out?" Conrad asked.

"That's right," Hellen said and slapped him gently on the cheek.

Hellen's gesture made Conrad laugh. "How often do you deal with such crises?"

"Once in a while, but we do it quite well because we are used to working hard ever since we started our company. We started it when we were still undergrads, working on it full time while we pursued our MBAs."

"Congratulations, but that's hard work!" Conrad said, shaking his head.

"It is hard but it is doable. Now, honey, what about you? You should have used the time Gwen and I were working to do stuff. Like writing down your list of things to do this month," Hellen said, smiling, as she collapsed on Conrad's lap.

Conrad laughed. "I don't think I will ever be as organized as you are. I don't write anything down."

"You should. It will make your work easier."

❋ ❋ ❋

Conrad soon got bored. He had nothing to do. After working out in the gym for an hour, he'd return to the apartment and watch TV while Hellen worked in her home office. He felt lazy and unproductive.

When Hellen called her parents one evening, they told her that her aunt Kate was visiting. Hellen asked to talk to her. "Aunt Kate, now that Conrad is living here with me, I will be asking you for advice once in a while," Hellen said towards the end of their conversation, laughing.

"Yes. Don't hesitate to call me whenever you have a question. Remember I am here to support you," Kate said.

"Thanks, Aunt. Conrad has been here for a couple of months now and I think he is no longer excited to be here. Sometimes he sits around watching TV while I am working in my office but anyone can see that he is really bored. Like, while I am working, he seems to be missing me, you know what I mean? But you know I put in long hours," Hellen said.

"That's okay. I guess he understands that his presence shouldn't interfere with your professional life. Do you give him enough time when you are not working?"

"Yes. A lot," Hellen answered, and giggled.

"That's all that matters. And please, whenever you see that he seems to be bored or that he is bothered, give him your full attention. You should have a special place in the house just for the two of you, where—"

"Yes, we have a love seat."

"A love what?" Kate asked, laughing. "Anyway, sit in your special place, ask him how he's doing, ask him what's going on. Tell him that you love him, tell him that you care—and do that now, early in your marriage. Then teach him to show you the same affection, the same caring. Men sometimes need to be reminded to show their women some love." This time, it was Kate who giggled.

❄ ❄ ❄

The following week, Conrad and Hellen went to Victoria's home to attend her husband's sixty-fifth birthday party. As soon as they arrived, Conrad went into the family room, sat quietly on the couch, and started watching a football match on TV. Hellen asked what he wanted to drink and brought him a bottle of soda water, placing it on the table beside him. She then went to the kitchen to help her aunt and the friends who were there preparing the dinner. Several people who walked in tried to engage Conrad in conversation but he didn't talk much. While the visitors proceeded to the large basement, where tables were set up and the dinner was to take place, he remained in the family room.

"You won't drink alcohol tonight?" Hellen asked Conrad when she returned to the family room and noticed he was still alone.

"No, just a bit of soda water. I don't want to drink and end up talking too much at my in-laws' home."

Hellen laughed and went back to the kitchen.

A quarter an hour later three men arrived, and one of them was Kawozamasiga, who'd been Conrad's classmate in Musasa High School. Happy to see each other again, the two men began chatting and before Conrad knew it, he was finishing a second beer before dinner had been served.

The dinner went well and so did the speeches, when several speakers congratulated Bugembe on his sixty-fifth birthday and thanked him for his long service as a physician. Conrad and Kawozamasiga, meanwhile, sat up in the family room, retelling each other stories from their years in Musasa High School.

❊ ❊ ❊

After Conrad reunited with Kawozamasiga he was no longer bored in Boston. Kawozamasiga had a truck which he and Conrad used during the day for business, and in the evenings, they would park it, shower in Kawozamasiga's apartment and then go out to drink.

For a while, Hellen was happy that Conrad had company other than her. On most evenings, he'd return home late, drunk. On one hand, Hellen liked that because when Conrad was drunk he would loosen up, talk more and eat more, including the foods that normally he would not eat, like lasagna and perogies. On the other hand, she didn't like it because when he returned late, she would have already had dinner.

"Honey, it's okay to go out but every evening is not cool," Hellen said to Conrad one evening when she felt she had had enough.

"Dear, if you are tired of me going out to do some useful work, buy me an air ticket so I go back home. Or if you don't want to, my parents can send me one. You can come to see me in Kampala whenever you feel like you want to see me," Conrad said and collapsed on the couch. He was snoring within three minutes.

Hellen lost her temper. She went to the bedroom and cried for a few minutes, then she called her aunt Victoria. "Aunt, I am disappointed with Conrad. Can you please help? Since he reunited with Kawoza-something, whatever his name is—who is a real loser—Conrad is becoming a loser too. I don't see him much these days and that makes me mad."

Victoria listened and let Hellen vent, then she said, "I gave you some advice before Conrad came. Wasn't it helpful? I think he is trying to adjust to his new life. You need to remember that disappointments are common in marriage but they don't last forever—that's what real marriage is about. But the problem with you young people is that you watch too many soap operas on daytime TV, which distorts your opinion of marriage."

"Are you serious, Aunt?" Hellen couldn't believe what she was hearing. "You think I watch soaps? When I am home, I am busy working, not watching TV. I thought you knew that!"

"What's the progress with his certification?" Victoria asked.

"He submitted his academic transcripts to the Massachusetts Society of Chartered Accountants and he is still waiting. In the meantime, I think he is getting frustrated and I am becoming impatient. Oh, this is so hard."

"Hellen, be patient. The tough times won't last. A few months from now you will look back at this time and laugh about it."

"I hope so, Aunt. This is hard," Hellen said, and said goodbye. She returned to the living room to wake Conrad up, try to speak more kindly to him and to serve him his dinner.

\* \* \*

The following morning, Conrad apologized to Hellen for his behaviour. He stopped meeting with Kawozamasiga for a few days and instead stayed home to watch TV until Hellen finished her work day.

However, she didn't like the fact that he reverted to his old self. She called her aunt Kate for advice.

"Aunt, I have a problem that is kind of serious. Conrad is so much of an introvert that sometimes it seems like I am inconveniencing him when I talk to him. You know what I mean?"

"I know the people in his family well. Most of them are like that," Kate answered. "They don't talk much. Actually, some people here accuse them of being too proud simply because three or four generations of men in their family studied in Musasa High School."

"And oh, another problem," Hellen said. "He's gaining a lot of weight! I think he eats too much and—"

"Does he eat too much or is it the foods he eats that are making him gain weight?"

"I think it is the food. He hates the stuff I cook, like pasta, lasagna and stuff like that. And then he goes out to eat burgers or pizza. Can you talk to him?"

"You want me to talk to him? It's not my duty to talk to him. It should be a member of his family who talks to him," Kate said, laughing. "I talk to you because you are my niece but I can't talk to him. That's how it works."

"I just don't get it."

"Are your problems already too big for the two of you to handle? Can't you try and find some simple solutions?"

"I will try but it's not easy."

"But I must say something to you, Hellen. To me it sounds like everything is about you, and I think that is selfish," Kate said. "Have you tried to find out if Conrad has complaints, too?"

"What do you mean?"

"You are complaining about him. Now I want to know, does he have any complaints about you?"

"I don't know."

"Find out. While you two are seated on your love chair, ask him—"

"Love seat," Hellen said and laughed.

"Yes, sit down on your love seat and ask him gently and lovingly whether he has any complaints. You will be surprised by what he will say."

"He is likely to say nothing. Oh, my gosh—he is like totally an introvert."

"Okay, if he says nothing, I want you to put yourself in his shoes and imagine what you would find annoying or what you wouldn't like about Hellen. Then go ahead and change those things."

"I will try."

\* \* \*

Realizing that it was better for Conrad to go out to do some work instead of sitting at home idle, Hellen encouraged him to rejoin Kawozamasiga.

About two weeks later, she had a busy day in her office and news for Conrad. She popped in and out of the office several times during the afternoon to check if Conrad had returned home. He hadn't.

A conference call with Gwen and one of their clients was the last activity of the day. When the call ended, although Hellen wanted to relax on the couch in front of the TV, she had her routine, and if she watched TV she'd have to force herself to ignore the gym clothes and running shoes neatly arranged in an open closet across from the office door. So she resisted the urge to sit on the sofa, changed into her gym clothes, drove to the gym, and exercised for an hour before she returned home, showered and went to the kitchen to prepare dinner.

She had gotten halfway through preparing dinner when she realized that she did not have the mozzarella cheese the recipe called for. *Too bad—I will use ricotta.*

Conrad returned a half an hour later. Dinner was ready.

"How was your day, honey?" Hellen asked when they started eating.

"It was both busy and exhausting. How was yours?" Conrad answered.

"Good. Exhausting, too. After work I went to the gym and returned to prepare dinner. Do you like the food?"

"Yes. It tastes good. Thanks."

"You know what, dear?" Hellen said, borrowing Conrad's word 'dear.' "I've noticed that you are kind of unhappy. You know what I'm saying? Am I stressing you out?"

"No, it's not you, dear. Life in the States is becoming too hard for me. Take today, for example. I am tired and hopeless after a day of hard work."

"What did you do today?"

"Kawozamasiga and I moved a certain lady's stuff into her new house. We made several trips and I am exhausted."

"I am sorry. Did you earn any money?"

"Yes. But only a hundred bucks. It is awful."

"You know what? Why don't you, like, do just the bare minimum for now? Just to keep yourself occupied—we don't have any financial worries."

"I think you are right, dear," Conrad said as he rose and poured some wine, first for Hellen, then for himself.

"Thank you but I will drink water instead," Hellen said.

Conrad sat back down. "I was seriously thinking this morning whether it would be better for me to return to Kampala for now. Of course I would miss you a lot but I would probably be better off there."

Hellen looked at him, quiet for a while. "That's probably not gonna work now, honey," she said, smiling. "I did a test this morning. I am pregnant."

Conrad smiled and rose without saying a word. He held her tightly and kissed her, first on both cheeks and then on the mouth. "That's wonderful news, dear! That changes everything. I will have a more meaningful purpose here and I am not going to think of returning home again." He lifted her up and carried her out of the dining room.

"Honey, it's exciting news but we are still having dinner," Hellen protested.

A half-hour later they reheated the food and sat back at the dining table.

# 16

# June 2014

IN TORONTO, CANADA, two blocks away from her apartment, Veronica Kiwuka boarded a half-empty bus and sat down at the back. She pulled her iPad out of her handbag and began to peruse her e-mail messages, deleting several messages announcing ongoing sales before she saw the message from her cousin Lugard in Kampala.

For the past year and a half, Veronica had been sending money to Lugard in installments so he could buy her a plot of land. This morning's e-mail bore good news—Lugard had finally bought the land, and he'd attached a photo of it. Veronica opened the attachment and smiled.

The bus stopped and more people boarded. Veronica glanced up to greet the girl who sat next to her, then looked back at the picture on her iPad—a bare plot of land, fenced with barbed wire, with a large beautiful house, still under construction, in the background. The house reassured Veronica that Lugard had chosen a good spot for her although just a few days earlier Veronica's friend Tammy had told her that Lugard could not be trusted with money. Tammy also lived in Kampala, and she'd said that Lugard could have conned Veronica out of thousands of dollars.

Now, on one hand, Veronica felt happy and energized. If she saved a few thousand dollars more, she could start building her dream home in Kampala. On the other hand, she felt scared. *What if Lugard has conned me of my money, like Tammy is claiming? Maybe he has taken pictures of somebody else's property and is duping me? Such occurrences are common these days. But Lugard is like a brother to me.* Lugard and Veronica had been brought up together. While Veronica was still on the bus, and still thinking about him and the land, she saw that Lugard had sent another message: "We will need $2,500 to start building the foundation for your home." *No, I don't have that kind of money!* Veronica almost screamed, barely restraining herself.

The bus finally arrived at her stop. She exited and walked into Fresh Melodies, the convenience store where she worked as a sales clerk, greeting the young man who worked the night shift. After he left, she put several stands outside on the sidewalk and began to place various fresh fruits and vegetables on the stands. At the same time, she called her friend Tammy in Kampala.

"Thanks for warning me about Lugard but I don't believe you," Veronica said towards the end of their conversation. "He has e-mailed a photo of the plot of land. I think the land is in a good neighbourhood, and I am glad about it."

"You don't believe me?" Tammy asked.

"No, I don't. I don't think Lugard would steal from me," Veronica said.

"Maybe you are right, but judging from his current lifestyle I think he has more money than he can earn as a bus conductor," Tammy said.

"Sorry, I'll call you back, Tammy," Veronica said and ended the call when she noticed the store's owner, Melody, walking in.

"Hey, hi Veronica. I can't wait. Three more sleeps and we are off to Vegas. Devante is so excited he barely sleeps these days," Melody said as she handed a cup of coffee to Veronica.

"Thanks, Mel," Veronica said.

"It's going be a lot of fun. Our neighbour has agreed to take care of our dog for us while we are away," Melody said as she walked to the counter.

Veronica did not respond. *Could Tammy be right? Did Lugard steal my money?*

❊ ❊ ❊

During the day, Veronica tried not to think about the possible loss of the money she had sent to Lugard to buy her land. But however much she tried to avoid thinking about the money, she couldn't completely get the thought out of her mind. It had been twelve thousand dollars.

"My perennials by the driveway look miserable this season," Melody said as she arranged some lottery tickets on the counter. "I think I will leave early this afternoon to go take care of them."

*Lugard can't steal my money. Surely he knows that I work very hard to earn it.* "What did you say? Sorry, I wasn't paying attention," Veronica said as a customer placed some merchandise on the counter.

"I was telling you about my perennials," Melody said as she processed the customer's purchases at the cash register.

Veronica did not respond.

"Vegas, oh yeah, baby. I can't wait," Melody said after the customer left.

*I won't let him get away with it. I will confront him. Twelve thousand dollars is too much money for me to lose!* "You are too excited, Mel. You'd think that this was going to be the first time for you to visit Las Vegas," Veronica said.

"I know, eh? That's how excited I am whenever I'm about to go there," Melody said as she cashed out another customer's purchases.

"Lucky you! You are going to Vegas?" the customer said.

"Oh, yeah—I can't wait," Melody answered.

❋ ❋ ❋

Veronica's husband, Kyle Mitego, had been born and raised in Toronto. He'd met Veronica in Kyatelekera Restaurant, where she was the manager, when he'd visited Kampala to meet his father's family. They had married during his third visit to the city, six months after they had met. Now, when she returned home, Veronica was upset the entire evening but she couldn't tell Kyle why. He did not know that she'd been sending money to Kampala to buy land.

❋ ❋ ❋

Gwen had promised to help advise Sam for nine months but eight months passed without Sam seeing any success. "I can't tell you how disappointed I am," Sam said to Gwen during the second-last phone call. "I am a man of great faith but nothing has worked so far."

"Stay positive and don't give up," Gwen said. "I don't know whether you will get exactly what you want but I have a feeling that you will succeed."

❋ ❋ ❋

After three more disappointing weeks, Sam was at home one evening when he received a phone call from a man called Kavulu, an acquaintance and owner of Enviro Assessments Limited. Sam sat back on the sofa as he listened to the verbose man. Kavulu explained that hundreds of families would be displaced by a new road whose construction was scheduled to begin in two years' time, and that his company would subcontract Sam to help assess and prepare their compensation.

"Thank you—you know how much experience I have in that job, Mr. Kavulu," Sam said when he was finally able to squeeze in a few words in Kavulu's monologue.

"Of course I know it. That's why I called you. It's guys like you who know what you are doing who will take all jobs in the long run. You can't trust young people these days," Kavulu said. "Oh, I have another call. Come to our office tomorrow morning and I will walk you through the paperwork. If you agree to all the terms, you will walk out of our office with a signed contract, my friend."

"I can't thank you enough for remembering me, Mr. Kavulu," Sam said. He placed his cellphone on the coffee table and cried. *Hallelujah!*

❋ ❋ ❋

The following day, Sam was overjoyed when he left Kavulu's office with a signed contract in his handbag. He walked the two kilometres back to Kyatelekera Restaurant, singing and whistling all the way.

He spent the weekend in a jovial mood and when he returned home on Monday evening, he paced around the room as he waited for Gwen's final phone call.

"You are a very clever girl, Gwen," Sam yelled as soon as he answered the call. "I signed a contract last Friday."

"Cool, that's great! Congratulations, buddy! I am happy for you. What kind of work are you going to do?" Gwen asked, and Sam told her. "That's great. See? That's a strong reason to go to work. Not only are you going to make money, you will also help the families by calculating fair compensation for them."

"Thank you. Yes, I got a contract but the terms are not so favourable. But I signed it all the same," Sam said. "It is better than nothing."

"So, what's not favourable about the terms?"

"They want me to complete the job in six months. But a more realistic timeline would have been about nine months. I tried to negotiate for an extension but I wasn't able to get it. The pay is quite good, though."

"So, you have six months to do the job."

"That's right. Six months. But I am not sure it can be done in six months. We'll see."

"Okay, here is the deal. I would like you to under-promise and over-deliver. This is—"

"What does that mean?"

"You agreed to do the job in six months, right?"

"Yes, but—"

"Okay, so here is what I'm gonna suggest you do. Find a way to complete the job in half the time—three months. Actually, do the job in two and a half months, without compromising quality."

"My friend, what are you talking about? I am telling you that I am not sure I can complete the job in six months and you are suggesting I do it in two and a half months?"

"I am not suggesting you do the job alone. What I am suggesting is put together an excellent team, get to work right away and wow your client by doing the job in two and a half months. Do you know any good workers you can employ?"

"Yes, but that will mean that I will share the money with others; then I will earn less."

"I get it but for this first contract, let's not focus on your bottom line. Let's focus on value for the client. And let's kick butt and get that job done in less than half the time."

"I will certainly set up a formidable team," Sam said. "Thanks for all your help, Gwen. I am very grateful."

❋ ❋ ❋

Having secured a contract, Sam was ready and eager to start work. *Gwen is right—if I put a strong team together I can actually complete the project in five months.*

He contacted three of his former workmates and had a team in place by the end of the week. But three weeks in, the project hadn't started—it had hit a snag right from the beginning, and so Sam and his team couldn't start work as scheduled. Even after daily meetings with his team, they realized they weren't ready to start.

Sam called Gwen early one morning. She did not answer. He then realized his mistake, *Oh, we are eight hours ahead; she is still sleeping.* He called again four hours later. Still, she did not answer. He called again one hour later and she finally picked up. When they'd spoken on previous occasions she'd recognized his voice right away, but this time she didn't. *Oh, wait a minute. This is not Gwen.* Sam identified himself.

"Good morning, Uncle Sam. Sorry, I hadn't realized it was you," Hellen said in Luganda.

Sam wanted to excuse himself. *I shouldn't waste my time with Kiyaga's daughter.* "Yes, it's me," he said, instantly changing his mind. "I wanted to speak to Gwen."

"Sorry," Hellen said, switching to English. "Gwen is not available. Can I help you?"

"No, thanks. It's for business," Sam said.

"Uncle Sam, Gwen has already told me about your ongoing project. Actually, the number you called is her office phone number," Hellen said.

"Oh, sorry—I hadn't realized that. She used the same phone to call me a few times."

"No problem. How can I help you?"

"I'll tell you, since you insist. Gwen has been advising me in business," Sam said, and Hellen waited while he paused for a while, looking for a way to state his facts. "But now I am stuck. That's why I really wanted to talk to her."

"What's going on?"

"You see, I signed a contract several weeks ago and she is aware..."

*Come on now. Get to the point.* Hellen coughed.

"... However, even though I should have started work, the contractor has not advanced any funds as yet," Sam said and paused again.

"So, what's the problem?"

Sam wanted to end the call at that moment. *Kiyaga's daughters are curt and unfriendly.* Then he continued. "They told me that the funds have not yet been disbursed."

"So you need to borrow money to start?"

"Yes. That's where I needed Gwen—"

"I can help you with that. How much money do you need?"

Sam's spirits rose. "Thank you very much, Hellen. I tell you, I didn't expect that. Thank you. Thanks—"

"How much money do you need?"

Sam hesitated. "My colleagues have each put down the equivalent in shillings of a few thousand dollars. But I don't have any money to contribute. That's where the snag is—I will need a few thousand dollars."

"Uncle Sam, please state a specific amount."

"Ten thousand. I will need ten thousand dollars."

"Yeah, I can lend you the money. Let me text Nakato. Oh, wait," Hellen said. "Are you willing to go to a law office to sign a loan agreement?"

"Yes, of course. It's for business," Sam said.

"Cool. You can get the money as early as tomorrow. Look forward to my call in a bit. Bye, Uncle, and please send my regards to your family."

Sam sat back on the sofa. He put the phone down and cried. *Hallelujah!*

# 17

# July - October 2014

IN TORONTO, VERONICA woke up early one morning to prepare bagged lunches for her husband and her five-year-old stepson. Shortly after she entered the kitchen, her cellphone rang but she ignored it. She was running late. The phone rang four more times and when she finally checked, she noticed it was her mother who had been calling from Kampala.

"Mummy, you've called so many times this morning. Is there a problem?" Veronica said as soon as she called her mother, a few minutes after her husband and stepson had left.

"There is no problem. Don't I have a right to call you however many times I want?" Petua asked. "I have been thinking a lot about you these days. When are you coming home?"

*Oh, I hate this. Why doesn't she leave me alone?* "I've asked Kyle about it and he says that we'll visit later this year," Veronica answered.

"When is that? Give me a specific date so we can arrange your wedding."

"Mummy, we are not getting married again."

"But you are *not* married! To me, you just eloped. And I know you went overseas simply because you wanted to make money. I won't consider you married until my family, friends and I have met your so-called husband."

"I am serious, Mummy. Kyle and I *are* married. Besides, a big wedding would cost a lot of money, which we don't have."

"Don't worry about money. Friends and family will donate money. Veronica, I'll have no peace of mind until you've returned home and married properly," Petua said, her voice rising.

Veronica had married Kyle in Kampala in a ceremony that was attended by just five other people. But she knew why her mother insisted that her family and friends should meet her husband. Petua wanted a big church wedding, probably one as big as Hellen Kiyaga's wedding, so she could show off. As long as Veronica could remember, her mother had seemed to be competing with the family of the much wealthier Herbert Kiyaga, the son of her longtime employer Ruth, but she did not know why.

Veronica did not enjoy her day off. She knew that her mother would pester her to go to Kampala until she did. When Kyle returned that evening, she told him about her conversation with her mother. "I am tired of her nagging me. Why don't we go to Kampala, organize a wedding and get it over with?"

"You know what?" Kyle answered. "I love you so much, I am ready to go meet your mother and her family. Let's go to Kampala already!" Together they chose a date a few months in the future for the wedding ceremony.

Veronica called Petua the following morning to inform her. "Good!" Petua said. "Let me start making arrangements—and don't worry about the cost."

Veronica almost laughed out loud, but did not want to annoy her mother. *Where is she expecting to get the money from to fund a big wedding?*

\* \* \*

"You know what, Mel?" Veronica said to her boss Melody, the following day, "I am sick and tired of my mother attacking me for living with a man who, according to her, I am not properly married to!"

"Properly married to? What does that mean?" Melody asked as she placed bottles of water into the refrigerator.

"I married Kyle in a small ceremony with just five guests in attendance, and my mother wasn't among them. And that's not the kind of wedding that she wanted for me. She would have liked me to marry in a big church wedding, with all her family and friends there so she could show off."

"I wouldn't blame her for wanting to show off," Melody said, laughing, turning to face Veronica. "If I were her, I would love to attend my daughter's wedding. In fact, I think it's kind of weird that you didn't invite her...."

"So, I have decided to take Kyle to meet my mother and the family," Veronica said, ignoring Melody's comment. "Possibly that will help get her off my back."

"I totally get it, do what you've got to do. When are you going?"

"In two months' time." *And when I go to Kampala, I will confront Lugard about my money. I work hard for it and I won't let him steal it.* Lugard was no longer responding to her e-mails or answering her phone calls, and Veronica no longer doubted that he'd stolen her money.

Lost in thought, she did not notice that Melody had placed a sandwich near her cellphone on the counter where she was standing. "Do you like the sandwich?" Melody asked, interrupting her thoughts.

"Yes, good timing, I didn't have breakfast—thank you," Veronica said and unwrapped the sandwich.

"You are welcome," Melody said as she walked out with a box of apples to add to the outside display.

"This sandwich is good!" Veronica told Melody when she returned inside. "Did you make it this morning?"

"No. Devante made it. He does all the cooking—he is better at it than I am," Melody said, laughing as she went to the cash register to serve a customer.

❋ ❋ ❋

"Guess what, Veronica! I told Devante that you are going to get married. And he was, like, 'Let's go and attend the wedding,'" Melody told Veronica the following day.

"But the wedding will be back home in Uganda, not here," Veronica said.

"Yep, we will still attend the wedding. Give me the name of the city and the airport. Devante is going to start searching for flights, hotels and stuff," Melody said. "I can't wait to see Africa!"

Veronica laughed. "Mel, you are a diva. I don't picture you in Kampala."

"Why not? I think it's going to be fun for Devante and me to visit Africa—our ancestors were taken from Africa ages ago and we can't miss this chance to visit," Melody said, excited. "I can't wait."

❋ ❋ ❋

Kyle and Veronica argued about their arrangements for accommodation in Kampala. They'd be taking a six-week vacation, and while Veronica suggested they spend it in her mother's home, Kyle wanted them to spend the first four weeks in a cheap hotel and the last two weeks, after their wedding, touring the country. "But why spend money on a hotel when my mother's house is available for us to stay free of charge?" Veronica asked.

"I wouldn't mind spending a little money for some freedom," Kyle said.

"What do you mean?"

"Living in a hotel, we wouldn't inconvenience anybody if we returned late from a party."

"No, let's save the money. For your information, I have a bedroom in my mother's house."

"I've never met your mom, but she seems to be pretty controlling," Kyle said.

They finally agreed that they would spend the first two weeks in a hotel, go out dancing and visiting relatives, and move to Petua's home afterwards.

"But I'm warning you in advance—if I don't feel free in your mother's home I will check back into the hotel," Kyle said, and Veronica agreed.

It had been during his second visit to the country of his father's birth that Kyle Mitego had first met his future wife Veronica at Kyatelekera Restaurant. That visit had turned out to be special. But now, Kyle's upcoming visit, his fifth, was going to be even more special—one, he was going to marry Veronica "properly," and two, his father, Adrian, would be returning to Uganda for the first time in thirty-five years, travelling to Kampala two weeks before the wedding.

※ ※ ※

Veronica and Kyle checked into a hotel in downtown Kampala late in the afternoon. Veronica went to see her mother at her home the next morning. Petua thanked Veronica for coming home and told her that the wedding preparations were progressing well, and that it was important for Kyle to meet the family.

"Couldn't he meet the family without a wedding?" Veronica said. "After all, we are already married."

"We've already had that conversation and I don't want to repeat myself," Petua said. "What I want now is for you and me to meet Mr. Kiyaga so you can thank him for his help with the wedding."

"I will be glad to see Uncle Herbert again," Veronica replied.

*Sorry, but he is* not *your uncle,* Petua thought, her heart racing. "Herbert has been very helpful with the wedding arrangements," she said. "I'll call him this afternoon."

"Is Lugard aware that I am visiting?" Veronica asked.

"I haven't seen him for the past two weeks but I think he knew that you were going to be visiting," Petua answered.

Veronica didn't ask any more questions about Lugard and she did not tell her mother about the money she had been sending to him to buy land. She called him twice that afternoon but he did not answer the calls. *He is probably avoiding me.* She decided that if he did not come home, she would look for him after the wedding.

# 18

# October 2014

HERBERT KIYAGA WAS getting ready to leave his office when his cellphone rang. It was Petua. *Petua? Why doesn't she leave me alone?* He had given her a lot of money during the past two months to help organize Veronica's wedding and was now worried that she was calling to ask for more. He sat back in his chair and answered the call.

"Veronica and her fiancé are in town. They arrived yesterday," Petua said without greeting Herbert or engaging him in small talk.

"Oh, that's great," Herbert answered and kept quiet.

"Oh, that's all you have to say?"

"What did you want me to say? And if you want more money, I'm sorry. I don't have it," Herbert said.

Petua did not respond. She ended the call, annoyed.

Herbert sat in his office to think. *How much longer am I going to keep this secret? It's killing me! It's high time I informed the family.*

When he arrived home, Leah was not home and he was still worried. He opened a bottle of beer, picked up a glass from the kitchen and went to sit in the backyard. Then he decided to call Petua back.

"Can I meet with you and Veronica tomorrow? Let's meet at the William Street Grill at ten o'clock. And please be prepared to finally tell her who I am," he said.

"Are you ready for it this time?" Petua asked.

"Yes, I am."

"You aren't afraid anymore to face your mother and your wife with the facts?"

"I don't know," Herbert said, "but let's do it."

Herbert had left the house early the following morning after their usual Saturday breakfast, telling Leah that he would be away in the city for a few hours. Now, sitting at a table on the balcony of the restaurant he'd suggested, distractedly perusing the headlines of a newspaper he'd just bought, he was nervous about meeting Petua and Veronica.

When Petua and Veronica came in soon after, Veronica knelt to greet him. Herbert took a close look at the young woman and noticed, again, that she resembled his twin daughters in more ways than one.

"Would you like some coffee?" Herbert asked.

"Yes please," Petua answered. *Now is the time to tell Veronica the truth but how do I do it?*

"I am very glad to see you again, Veronica," Herbert said.

"I am glad to see you too, Uncle Herbert," Veronica answered.

In the awkward silence that followed, Herbert realized that Petua was nervous, too.

"Veronica, this is not Uncle Herbert," Petua finally said and paused, not sure how to proceed.

Veronica was puzzled. She had always known the gentleman as Uncle Herbert, and she knew that his mother, Ruth, Petua's longtime employer, had paid for most of her education. She waited for the explanation, noticing that her mother was struggling to find the right words.

"Mr. Herbert Kiyaga is your father—I am sorry I couldn't tell you earlier," Petua said finally, her voice breaking. "When I conceived you, we were not in a long-term relationship. And as you know, he already had a family." Petua attempted to take Veronica's hand.

Veronica moved her hand away. She glanced at Herbert, and then at her mother, before starting to fidget with her cellphone. Herbert watched her reaction.

"Please kneel and greet your father again," Petua said.

Veronica knelt.

"Veronica, I am very glad to meet you for the first time as your father," Herbert said after Veronica had returned to her chair. "Like your mother said, the circumstances of your birth were less than ideal.

Nonetheless, you should not doubt our love for you. I hope you will forgive us."

Veronica was a calm well-mannered young woman, and she kept her cool, but Herbert was bothered by her silence.

"Do you think that it was a good idea for us to meet as father and daughter?" he asked.

"Yes," Veronica answered, and then turned to her mother. "Mummy, is this why you insisted so much on my coming to Kampala?"

"No. I wanted you to honour us by marrying properly. But it's also good that you have met your father. And I am sorry that I didn't tell you the truth for years, that Tucker Kabanda was not your father," Petua said. There was a second detail in the lie she still wasn't disclosing—Petua had never been in a relationship with Tucker, her former workmate. She had only used Tucker's name when he died, when Veronica was seven years old, as a cover-up for Herbert.

❋ ❋ ❋

"What the hell happened? Wherever have you've been?" Kyle asked Veronica. She'd returned to the hotel that afternoon and gone straight to bed.

"I've just received shocking news," Veronica said. "I have told you several times about the interesting lady that my mother worked for. Do you remember her?"

"Ruth? Yes, I remember her. Has she died?" Kyle said.

"No, I've just found out that she is my grandmother. Her son, the man my mother took me to meet this morning, is my father."

"But you told me that your father died long ago."

"That was a lie—my mother lied to me," Veronica said and started to cry.

"You are just finding out now who your real father is? What the hell?" Kyle said as he sat on the bed and gently massaged Veronica's shoulders.

"'What the hell?' That's exactly what I had wanted to say when my mother broke the news!"

"So what's next? Does that affect our wedding plans?"

"I don't know. I will wait for my mother to call me. In the meantime, let's head out somewhere and have fun this evening," Veronica said, soothed a bit by Kyle's gentle touch.

"That's exactly what I was talking about! That's an example of why it would be difficult for us to stay in your mother's house. Why don't we stay—"

"You know what? Where we stay is not important to me for now," Veronica said. "I have a lot to think about."

"Okay, take a nap if it will help," Kyle said and rose to go take a shower.

❋ ❋ ❋

Petua called Veronica two hours later, again apologizing for not having told her sooner that Herbert was her father.

Veronica said that she was angry. "And I actually don't want to hear about the wedding you were planning anymore," she said.

"I am sorry, but preparations for the wedding are in full gear, and almost everything has already been paid for," Petua said. "Calm down, because whether you like it or not it will go on as planned—and when you get an opportunity, thank your father for his enormous contribution, too. It's he who has covered most of the wedding's expenses."

Veronica did not respond as Petua read out Herbert's telephone number, but she wrote it down on a piece of paper. Then she ended the call and lay on the bed, fuming.

❋ ❋ ❋

That evening, when Herbert, Leah and Ruth finished their weekly Saturday dinner in Ruth's home, Herbert rose from the dining table and went to the living room before the dishes had been cleared. That was unusual. Since his father had died he'd taken his place at the table and was always the last to leave, as had been his father's custom.

While Leah and Ruth's maid Nabakka cleared the dishes and chatted in the kitchen, Ruth put three glasses and a jug of fruit juice on a tray, switched off the light in the dining room and went to the living room to join Herbert.

*Tell them. Don't waste a minute.* Herbert was nervous. His straight-talking mother had trained him to say whatever it was he wanted to say but his long marriage to Leah—the daughter of the ever-thoughtful Merab—had taught him the virtue of caution.

"Veronica and her husband are in town," Herbert began, as Leah sat down on the sofa next to him a few minutes later. "I met her this morning."

"Oh, that's good. How is she?" Leah asked.

"Veronica is married?" Ruth asked.

"Yes—a little more than two years ago. But it was a ceremony that was attended by just a handful of people, and then she went to Canada to join her husband," Herbert answered.

"Really?" Ruth said. "I didn't know that. Petua often talks to me about Veronica but she never told me that she was married."

"Yes. You would know before anybody else because you are close to Petua." *Tell them. Say it.* Herbert knew he had to say it before Ruth changed the topic, but still he hesitated. Now. He took a breath. "But I knew, because Veronica is my daughter."

Although Leah hadn't paid attention to what Herbert had just said, Ruth was sitting across from Herbert and she did. "Say that again," Ruth said.

"Veronica is my daughter," Herbert repeated, looking down on the carpet in front of him, trying to hide his nervousness. This time Leah had noticed the seriousness in her husband's voice and had heard what he was telling them.

"That is an inappropriate joke, Herbert," Ruth said, looking sternly at her son as her daughter-in-law got up and walked into the unlit dining room and sat on a mat.

"It's not a joke, Mummy. Petua conceived at around the time when you reopened the boutique," Herbert said, feeling all over again like he was six years old. "It was so many years ago."

"I thought I knew you well, Herbert, but obviously I don't. And you know what I am thinking? You are disgracing the family, your wife and your children," Ruth said.

"I am sorry, Mummy."

"Go tell that to your wife," Ruth said, but Herbert remained speechless, his face buried in his hands, not moving from where he was seated. They could hear Leah sobbing in the next room and he felt awful about it. *What should I say to her? Will she listen to me?*

"Does anybody know about your illegitimate daughter?" Ruth asked. Herbert did not answer. "Did you hear my question?" she asked again.

"Yes, Clement knows about Veronica," Herbert answered.

"Clement knows and your dear wife doesn't?"

"I am very sorry, Leah," Herbert said from where he was seated.

"Hey, do what I taught you to do!," Ruth yelled, pointing in the direction of the dining room. "*Show* her that you care."

Herbert got up and went into the dark dining room, where Leah now lay face down on the mat, sobbing. Herbert touched her on both shoulders, massaging them. "I am very sorry, darling. I am sorry that you have to suffer because of my stupidity," he said and paused, shaking, "... and my selfishness."

Leah did not respond.

Ruth couldn't hide her irritation. "I didn't know that Petua was that bad—I should have fired her when I found out that she was associated with Clotilda! But it's not surprising that she did that. Birds of a feather..."

Herbert went back to the living room and saw that his mother was angry. "I am very sorry, Mummy."

"Please come talk to me, Leah," Ruth said, not responding to her son. "I am very saddened by this. I still can't believe it."

"Can we talk later, Mummy? Tomorrow, maybe?" Leah said as she rose and walked to the front door. It was locked.

"Nabakka, can you please come unlock the front door?" Ruth called out to her maid.

"I guess we should be leaving now. Good night, Mummy," Herbert said as he too rose.

"No. Stay here to chat with Mummy. I will walk home," Leah said, waiting for Nabakka to open the door.

"You want to walk home? It's already dark," Herbert said, still shaking.

"It's all right. I will walk."

Herbert was speechless.

At that moment a key rattled in the lock. It was Brandon and his girlfriend just coming in. "Good evening, Delilah," Leah said, walking up to the couple in the doorway. "Brandon, can you please drive me home?"

Brandon noticed right away that his mother was not her usual cheerful self. As he drove her home, he tried to start a conversation. "What's wrong, Mummy?"

"I don't want to discuss anything now, Brandon."

Brandon could see that surely something was wrong. His parents enjoyed each other's company and spent most of their time together, but now his father had stayed behind at his grandmother's home. When they arrived at his parents' home he honked for the night security guard to open the gate, then drove through the large front yard to the door. He left as soon as his mother had entered the house.

Before Herbert returned, Leah had already packed her suitcase and driven to Kawempe.

✳ ✳ ✳

Merab was preparing to go to bed when Leah arrived. When she saw the suitcase, Merab knew there was a problem.

"What is wrong with you?" Merab said when Leah sat down. "You look so unhappy."

"Yes, I am unhappy, but I need to rest. Can we talk tomorrow?" Leah answered.

Merab understood. She sat on a chair, something she rarely did. She looked on as Leah dragged her suitcase into the bedroom and closed the door.

✳ ✳ ✳

"Mother, I found out last evening that Veronica is Herbert's daughter," Leah told Merab while they were having breakfast the following morning.

"Veronica who?"

"That girl who was a manager at your restaurant a few years ago. Herbert himself told me and his mother that she is his daughter, after dinner last evening."

Merab didn't say anything.

"Mother, you don't seem to be surprised," Leah said.

"No. I am not surprised," Merab said and paused. "When Herbert brought that girl to the restaurant, I noticed an unsettling resemblance to the twins right away."

"Oh, but you didn't tell me anything."

"I am an old woman. What would I say about a situation that I knew nothing about?"

"Mother, you could have said something."

"Like what? My child, it would be foolish of me to start rumours about my son-in-law. Men! I didn't think Herbert—"

"I didn't notice anything," Leah said, her eyes glistening with tears.

"When Veronica started working at the restaurant, the more I observed her, the more I realized how much she resembled my granddaughters."

"Mother, I am either not observant or I'm stupid. How come I didn't notice her resemblance to my daughters?" Leah said as she blew her nose.

"I probably wouldn't have noticed, either, but I had a sudden gut feeling. Remember, I interacted with Veronica on a daily basis."

"I feel awful about it."

"That's understandable," Merab said. "But you grew up in a polygamous family, and you also know that some of our men cheat."

"I didn't think Herbert could do that to me. I'd like to stay away from him for a few weeks."

"A few weeks? A few days, maybe, but you need to go back home soon," Merab said. "I'll never forget what my aunt told me when my husband got himself a second wife. And I am going to tell you the same thing. It is things like a husband's messing up that make us stronger as women."

"Don't tell me that, Mother," Leah said, annoyed. "How can I trust him now? How can I sit down and chat with him, knowing he has been keeping a big secret for all these years?"

"But he has told you now. Everyone has secrets—most probably you, too, Leah. There are probably things that you wouldn't tell even me, your dear mother."

"Mother, I am very angry with him and I don't think I will ever forgive him."

"Please don't say that. You've just received the news—that's why you are feeling bad," Merab said. "But I know you will forgive him."

Leah rose and went to the bedroom in tears.

❋ ❋ ❋

That afternoon Petua called Herbert three times but he did not answer. When she called a fourth time, he told her that he had told his wife and his mother about Veronica.

"What did they say?" Petua said, interrupting.

"Mummy got very angry. And Leah left home, so don't expect me to be involved in Veronica's wedding preparations any more than I have done up until this point."

"But the reception venue isn't fully paid for. We only paid a deposit."

"I am sorry but that's not my problem. I've already given you more than enough money," Herbert said and ended the call.

❋ ❋ ❋

Nakato and Babirye went to Merab's home to talk to their mother the following day. When they knocked on the door, Leah rose and welcomed them in. After she had greeted her granddaughters, Merab left the room to go prepare some tea for them.

"Mummy, what is going on?" Babirye asked. "Brandon called us all to tell us that you are not home."

"I am angry with your father," Leah said and sat quietly back in the sofa.

"Why?" Babirye asked.

"He has an illegitimate daughter—Veronica, the girl who used to work at the restaurant."

"So the rumours were true?" Babirye said. "You know, people talk. A couple of my patients told me about that girl."

"Of course people talk. That's not surprising," Nakato said.

"You two knew about it and—"

"Mummy, when I heard the rumour I went to see Veronica at the restaurant," Babirye said, "and I noticed right away how much she resembles us."

"Yes, she is some sort of cross between Hellen and us," Nakato said.

Leah laughed. "I guess I am stupid. How come I didn't notice anything? But now that you—and Mother—have said it, I've tried to recall Veronica's face, and I think it's true. That girl resembles you."

"And she is a good girl," Merab said from the kitchen where she was preparing the teacups. "She was one of the best employees I ever had at the restaurant. Girls, please accept her. She is your sister."

"We have no problem with Veronica. She is innocent," Babirye said. "But Daddy is stupid. How could he do that?"

"Babirye," Merab said as she walked back into the living room, "you are only a daughter. Don't meddle into your parents' affairs."

"Leave me alone, Grandma," Babirye said as she pulled her cell-phone out of her handbag. "I will blast Daddy. And Petua—*both* of them are stupid."

"Who are you calling?" Merab asked.

"Daddy," Babirye answered.

"No. Don't call him. Wait until you get a chance to meet him in person and after you've cooled down. If you talk to him when you are angry, you might say things that you will live to regret," Merab said and walked out of the room.

"I need a break from your father," Leah said to her daughters. "He and I were planning to go see Hellen later this year. I already have the US visa. Can one of you book an air ticket for me?"

"Yes, I will book your ticket and call Hellen this afternoon," Babirye said.

# 19

# October 2014

TWO DAYS AFTER Herbert had told her and Leah about Veronica, Ruth called Petua, who was awakened by the sound of her cellphone ringing in the living room. She knew who was calling—the only person who had called her at the same hour for years. But for the very first time in all those years she did not rush out of her bed to answer the call.

Ruth called Petua again after lunch, and when she still did not answer Ruth lost her temper. *Of course I know why she won't answer! She is aware that I know about Veronica now.* She left a message. "Petua, it's Ruth, and I need to talk to you urgently. Please come see me at home, any time."

\* \* \*

Herbert went to Merab's home after work two days after Leah had left home. Leah was in the living room and when she saw him parking his car in the front yard, she quickly went to the bedroom she'd been sleeping in. She started to cry.

Merab was slow in opening the front door after Herbert knocked. He'd brought her three plastic bags full of groceries and when he came in, he placed them on the floor by the entrance. Merab asked him to sit down and after the greetings thanked him for the groceries. But after that Herbert did not know where to start the conversation. He talked about the weather and Merab responded politely. An awkward silence followed.

As had been the case since he had first met Merab, Herbert appreciated his mother-in-law's personality and emotional intelligence. He was sure that she now knew about the problems in his marriage but Merab was as calm as always. He couldn't help but think how his own mother would have behaved if she'd learned that one of her sons-in-law had fathered an illegitimate child and he was right there in the room with her.

Merab had rarely been alone with her son-in-law, and didn't know what to say to him either. "Thanks again for our groceries," she said as she struggled to rise and to pick up the bags. "I'll have Leah come talk to you."

When Leah walked into the living room, Herbert noticed that she had been crying. "I am very sorry for what I did to you, darling," he said.

Leah did not answer. She sat on the mat on which her mother had been seated and politely greeted her husband.

"I wish I could undo the events of that evening twenty-seven years ago that are now causing this stress in our marriage."

Leah did not respond.

"I was drunk at a party shortly before Mummy's boutique reopened. And I did things that I now regret."

"I notice that you are remorseful. But do you think I can trust you anymore?" Leah said.

"Yes, trust me. Other than that one time which, unfortunately, resulted in the conception of a child, I have never cheated on you."

"Don't say 'unfortunate' because Veronica is a good girl. Let me stay here with my mother for a few more days. I'll return home if I feel better," Leah said and rose. She went back to the bedroom.

Herbert sat quietly by himself for a few minutes, thinking. *She is a very understanding wife. Why have I put her through this?* He then rose, walked out, closed the door behind him and drove home, where he went straight to bed. But he slept little that night.

✳ ✳ ✳

When Ruth called for "an urgent meeting" with her children neither Kate nor Victoria had any idea of what it could possibly be about. Now

Kate was sitting with Herbert in Ruth's living room and Victoria had joined them by phone.

"I will let you tell your sisters what this meeting is about," Ruth said to Herbert after the greetings.

"How do I begin? I don't know how to begin because I have kept this secret for a long time," Herbert said, looking at his sister Kate. "Anyway, we are going to discuss the fact that I have another daughter," he said, and paused.

"Tell them the whole story, Herbert. You have a grown illegitimate daughter," Ruth said, and she could see that Kate was surprised.

"Yes, I am the father of Petua's daughter, Veronica," Herbert said.

"Say that again, Herby?" Victoria said over the phone. "What?"

"I am the father of Petua's daughter, Veronica," Herbert repeated.

"For years, I have been proud of myself for having raised three trustworthy children but it turns out that that's not the case. I failed," Ruth said.

"Mummy, please, don't criticize yourself! It's not you that failed—it's me," Herbert said.

"Herbert, it turns out that you are not any better than your father was," Ruth said.

"Mummy, let Daddy rest in peace! If you go on like that, I will end the call," Victoria yelled.

"Do you have other secrets?" Ruth asked, placing her glass of water back on the table without sipping on the water. "And I'll ask your sisters the same question."

"Mummy, everyone, including you, has secrets," Kate said. "Now that Herbert has voluntarily decided to reveal his secret, why don't you forgive him and leave him alone?"

"That's a good suggestion, Kate, and I thank you for it. But if there is anything else that any of you would like to share with me, now is the right time," Ruth said, annoyed. "Before I pass away."

"Mummy, please!" Herbert said.

"Mummy, don't make this whole matter about you because it is not," Victoria said. "Herby, does Leah know about Veronica?"

"Yes, I told her and Mummy together last Saturday evening. She was so angry with me that she left home."

"What? Where is she?" Kate asked.

"She is at her mother's home. I went to see her there yesterday and it's clear that she has not forgiven me. I don't know how to tell you all how sorry I am."

"Herby, I don't know what you feel about Petua but I am sorry to say that I have never liked her," Kate said.

"Neither have I," Victoria said. "She is pretentious."

"But what should we do about Veronica?" Kate asked.

"Veronica is innocent. Let her meet the family and get a chance to know everybody else," Victoria said.

At the end of the meeting, both sisters agreed to call Leah to console her and to beg her to accept Veronica. But Herbert still did not tell his mother and his sisters about Veronica's upcoming wedding. He was too afraid that they'd accuse him of having made the wedding preparations without their knowledge, which was so contrary to the close-knit family's usual way of doing things.

\* \* \*

Ruth waited for Petua's call for two days but when Petua did not call back Ruth decided to go to her home. She was going to blast her, but there was just one problem—she didn't know where Petua lived, not exactly. When Nakato had come to visit Ruth at home that morning Ruth had asked her to take her to Ruth's Classic Boutique. She was sure that Petua's friend Katana, a manager at the boutique, would know where Petua lived.

When Nakato drove into the boutique's staff parking lot, Ruth's memories flooded back. Her parking spot, clearly marked "Managing Director," was still there, unoccupied. Nakato parked there and when they went into the boutique, activity momentarily came to a standstill as several employees who were working on the floor rushed to greet Ruth.

When Elsie saw Ruth, she welcomed her with a smile and a firm handshake. "I am very glad to see you, Aunt Ruth," she said. "Shall we go to the office?"

"Yes, sure," Ruth answered.

"Do you know where Petua lives?" Ruth finally asked after she and Elsie had chatted for a few minutes.

"No, but I think Katana does," Elsie answered, and called Katana to her office.

Katana came in and gave Ruth and Nakato the directions to Petua's home.

※ ※ ※

Ruth could see Petua's house from a distance, long before they arrived. Her thoughts were still racing as Nakato pulled into the front yard. *Does this house belong to her? The salary she earned at the boutique wouldn't have been enough for her to build such a house.*

Petua had just locked her front door, ready to go out, when Nakato stopped the car a few metres away. She did not recognize the car but when she took a close look inside and saw Ruth she wished the ground could open to swallow her. *I am in trouble. Who directed her to my home?* She knelt even before Ruth stepped out of the car.

"Thanks so much for giving me your precious time, Nakato. I'll call Brandon to come take me home, so please just go attend to your duties," Ruth said to Nakato as she opened the car's door.

"It's my pleasure, Grandma. I have the day off today. Call me when you are ready for me to pick you up," Nakato said as she drove away.

"I am very glad to see you, Aunt Ruth," Petua said, still kneeling down.

"You haven't answered my phone calls. That's why I came looking for you," Ruth said, ignoring Petua's stretched hand.

"You are welcome to my modest home, Aunt," Petua said as she rose, opened the door and led Ruth inside.

"You had a child with my son and didn't tell me about it all those years?" Ruth said as soon as she had sat down on the sofa.

"I was too ashamed to mention it to anyone. It was a mistake that I still regret," Petua answered. She was shaking on the mat where she was seated, facing Ruth.

"And can I tell you something?" Ruth said. "The first time I saw your daughter—I think she was two—I noticed right away that she resembled my granddaughters, the twins. But I didn't think anything about it because it didn't cross my mind that you could be stupid enough to fall in love with a married man."

*I didn't seduce him. He came voluntarily, to beg for my love.* "I am very sorry."

"I know it is bad to speak ill of dead people but do you know what I am thinking? You are as untrustworthy as your friend Clotilda."

"I am sorry, Aunt. I can't tell you how much I regret my actions, to this—"

"Don't make excuses, because you are talking nonsense! Are you still seeing my son?"

"No. It was a short-lived relationship."

The conversation went on for about twenty minutes more, with Petua apologizing profusely and Ruth telling her how untrustworthy she was. When Petua asked Ruth if she would drink or eat something, Ruth refused.

"It would be a great honour to me, Aunt, if you ate something," Petua said, trying her hardest to placate her old employer. "This is your first visit to my home."

"No, and please don't insist," Ruth said, and called Nakato.

"I am sorry, Aunt," Petua said again as Ruth walked out about fifteen minutes later, after Nakato arrived.

"I forgive you, even though I won't forget your wrongdoing, Petua," Ruth said. "Please tell my granddaughter Veronica that I love her—and tell her to come pay me a visit before she returns home."

❋ ❋ ❋

"Nakato, if you don't mind, will you please take me to Kalerwe Market?" Ruth said when she sat in the car.

"Sure, Grandma. What are you going to buy there?" Nakato asked.

"I am not buying anything. There is a group of women traders there who I check on every Wednesday afternoon, advising them on business matters, but I missed the meeting this week," Ruth said.

"I don't think it's a good idea for you to visit them now, when you are still angry."

"No, it's okay. I am not angry with them."

Nakato dropped her grandmother off at the market and continued to drive around looking for a parking spot. Only five minutes later, when she returned, she found Ruth almost yelling at the women. "You've got to pull up your socks!" she heard her say to the women. "I provided the startup capital for your businesses, and now you expect me to do everything for you?"

"Ladies, please excuse me—my grandmother is not well today. She'll come to talk to you next week," Nakato said as she led Ruth away by the hand.

✳ ✳ ✳

Brandon took Ruth to the boutique the following day. When Elsie saw her she assumed she was there to discuss business, so she started talking about the boutique's sales figures and current challenges when they were seated in her office. But Ruth was not listening. She seemed to be preoccupied and impatient.

"Elsie, I am here to talk to Katana. Can you please let me chat with her in my former office?" Ruth said and rose to go there.

Katana walked into the managing director's office and closed the door, excited. It was plain that she was expecting good news, maybe a promotion. "Can I ask you something, Katana? Ruth said after they'd chatted for a few minutes. "What do you know about Petua and my son?"

"Other than the fact that they have a daughter?" Katana asked, looking nervous.

"Oh, so you know about the girl? For how long have you known that Veronica is Herbert's daughter?"

"About four years," the young woman said.

"What else do you know about Petua and Herbert?"

"Won't I get in trouble if—"

"No, whatever you tell me is between me and you," Ruth said.

"It's Herbert who bought the house where Petua lives."

"What? I suspected so. She wouldn't have the means to pay for that house on her own. "Thanks for the information," Ruth said, rising. She and Katana walked out of the office together.

❋ ❋ ❋

Ruth was sitting in her living room, thinking about the events of the past week. Ever since Herbert had told the family that he was Veronica's father, everything had changed—Leah had left her home, bitter, Herbert seemed changed and hadn't returned to his mother's home since the meeting with his sisters. The granddaughters were unhappy. Brandon was the only person who didn't seem to be bothered by the news.

Ruth picked up her cellphone and called Herbert. "I would like to talk to you today," she said. "It's urgent." When Herbert came, he found his mother seated in the living room. There were two cups and a thermos on a tray on the coffee table in front of her.

"Would you like a cup of tea?" Ruth asked after the greetings.

"No, thanks. I'll have a beer," Herbert answered as he walked to the fridge.

"Herbert, you have disappointed me," Ruth said as he sat down on the sofa, facing her. "I thought you lived your life with integrity but you have not."

"I am very sorry that I disappointed you, Mummy," Herbert said.

"Does Leah know about the house you bought for Petua?"

Herbert's heart skipped a beat. *How did she find that out?* "No, she doesn't."

"Will you tell her about it?"

"Yes, I will," he said, "at the right moment."

"Better do so soon," she said, "because if you don't, I will tell her myself. But I haven't called you to discuss you and Petua again. I called you so we find a way to move forward."

Herbert remained silent. *Oh, great. The grilling is over.*

"You are the head of the Kiyaga family and you have a lot of responsibilities on your shoulders."

"I know that, Mummy, and I take my responsibilities seriously."

"I hope so. Do you know what is bothering me now? I don't know how seriously you took what I told you about Brandon. I think you have neglected your only son. My advice to you is, get closer to him and be more involved in his life. You'll see good changes in him."

"Yes, I will do that as soon as Leah returns home."

"Another thing, can you please make arrangements for Veronica to meet the rest of the family?"

"Yes, I will do so, Mummy, but I think it would also be better if Veronica came after Leah has returned home."

"It's all up to you," Ruth said. "But Veronica shouldn't feel that we don't care about her."

# 20

# October 2014

"MOM, I HOPE you have enough time to tour Boston this time around. There is a lot for you to see and I have planned to take you places," Hellen said as she drove her mother from the airport.

"I am very happy to visit but I would have liked to visit in happier circumstances," Leah answered.

"Happier circumstances? What's going on? Are you sick or something?"

"No, I am not sick. When Babirye called you about my visit didn't she tell you what's been going on at home? Your father has a grown illegitimate daughter—and I am now taking a break away from him."

"What? What are you talking about?" Hellen asked as she made a lane change, cutting off another driver, who honked at her. "Oh, sorry! I screwed up."

"Your father has another daughter. And it is both sad and strange, because I have known the girl since she was little. Her mother worked in the boutique for a long time, but I didn't know that her girl was your father's daughter."

"What?"

"The girl's name is Veronica."

"What? How did that happen? How old is she?"

"I don't know her exact age but know she's less than thirty years old, younger than you. So, my dear, you are not Daddy's youngest daughter anymore."

"Oh no," Hellen said, obviously shocked.

"Throughout our marriage, I have never doubted my husband's faithfulness, so the news was totally unexpected. He told me himself, Hellen. I need a break away from your father, even for a few weeks. I am so angry with him!"

They drove in silence for a few more minutes, each lost in her own thoughts.

"Mom, I guess this is an example of a good person who did a bad thing. What can I say? Please forgive Dad," Hellen said, breaking the silence. "I wish I had something better to say to make you feel better."

"We'll see, but now I am still angry with him," Leah answered.

❊ ❊ ❊

Leah could not sleep that night, thinking about her mother. She wondered how Merab would react after finding out that Leah, instead of returning to her home, had decided to go to Boston. *She is old and sickly. She needs my care but I selfishly abandoned her*, she thought, starting to cry. After a while, she called her mother, but Merab did not answer the phone. Leah finally fell asleep.

She called Merab again after breakfast the following day. "Leah, I found out only this morning that you are in America," Merab said. "Why didn't you return home?"

"Mother, I am still angry with Herbert. And, actually, if it were not for you, I would stay here indefinitely."

"Don't say that! It is not me that you should be worrying about. You should be concerned about your home and how your husband is doing. You can't abandon him—he needs your care," Merab said. "You can't let anybody else cook his meals because it is your responsibility to do so. I know he made a mistake but you should forgive him and return home."

"I know, but I need his care and caring too. And I don't trust him anymore."

"I understand that and I am sorry for you but you should forgive him."

"Mother, I will return in two weeks' time," Leah said, "but only because I miss you."

❋ ❋ ❋

While Leah was talking to Merab in the second bedroom, Hellen and Conrad were seated at the kitchen table, chatting. "You are so quiet and you don't seem to be interested in anything since my mom arrived," Hellen said. "Aren't you happy that she is here?"

"Your impression is false, dear. I am happy that your mother is here but she is my mother-in-law. How did you expect me to behave in her presence? I have to keep some distance between my mother-in-law and me," Conrad answered.

"But that's not the way I would behave if your mom were here."

"That's a different story. Anyway, it's a cultural thing."

"Whatever," Hellen said, impatient. "But my mom is a wonderful loving lady, so you should feel relaxed with her."

"I will try," Conrad said, getting up to load the dishwasher while Hellen switched on her laptop to watch music videos.

Leah came to the kitchen when she ended her call. When saw Conrad loading the dishwasher, she asked him to stop, saying she would load the dishwasher herself.

"No, no, Mummy," Conrad answered. "Just sit around and enjoy your vacation. I am just dropping the dishes in here, pressing a button, and the machine will do the rest."

"Hellen, you shouldn't let Conrad do so many chores. There are certain things that a husband shouldn't do. Have you ever seen your father washing dishes?" Leah said, laughing, a little more cheerful after talking to her mother.

"Mom, what age are you living in? I didn't know you were so old-fashioned," Hellen answered, her eyes still glued to her laptop.

Leah laughed. "What? Did you call me old-fashioned?"

"Yes, and you are old-fashioned if you think that there are still separate roles for men and women. But you know what? If you have any spare money you can hire somebody to help me so Conrad won't have to do chores at all," Hellen said, laughing.

"It's true, you are old-fashioned, Mummy—I like to do chores," Conrad said. "Besides, I have been doing household chores for a long time. I lived alone for years."

"I understand, and the circumstances are different," Leah said. "but it's still surprising to me to see Hellen sitting at the kitchen table watching videos while you are busy washing dishes."

"So, how is Grandma?" Hellen asked, happy to change the subject.

"She is well but she wasn't happy about the fact that I traveled to America instead of returning home. But I don't care—I will stay here as long as I want because now it is clear to me that your father doesn't care about me," Leah said as she sat down at the table facing Hellen.

"Of course he cares about you," Hellen said.

"If he did, he would have already called to ask how I am."

"How would he call when your cellphone has been switched off since you arrived here?"

A phone call from Babirye to Hellen interrupted the conversation. After the greetings, Babirye asked her sister about their mother. Hellen said that Leah was well but still angry with their father, and then she asked Babirye about their father.

"I don't know," Babirye said. "I haven't spoken to him since I learned about his infidelity, and I don't think I will talk to him ever again!"

"Babirye please! Instead of helping our parents to reconcile, I think you are getting sucked into their drama," Hellen said. "And you know what? Mom says that she is angry with Dad because he has not taken the trouble to call her. Why don't you ask Dad to step up and do something about this situation?"

"Okay, I will talk to him, then. I hope he *will* do something about it," Babirye said.

"How are you progressing with the biography?" Hellen asked.

"Honestly, I haven't made any progress since the family problems began…"

"That's not acceptable, Babirye. We made a commitment to our grandmothers. We must honour that commitment."

✳ ✳ ✳

Babirye called Nakato after her conversation with Hellen and told her what she'd said about getting sucked into their parents' drama.

"I have been thinking the same thing and agree with Hellen. Let's not avoid Daddy—he needs our support. Let's talk to him and ask him to do something to correct the situation," Nakato said. "I can call him to tell him that we would like to talk to him."

"No. Don't call him—Let's surprise him," Babirye said and sighed. "This is so annoying."

❋ ❋ ❋

The following morning, Herbert had just opened the front door, ready to leave for work, when he saw Nakato's car pulling into the front yard. He took a close look and noticed that both of the twins were in the car. *Oh, why are they here so early in the morning? And they didn't call first. Is there a problem?* He stood at the veranda to wait for them.

"Good morning Daddy," Babirye said as soon as she exited the car. "We are here to talk to you. There is a problem that we need to discuss." She walked up the three steps to the veranda.

Herbert frowned. "At this time? I am going to work. Why don't we talk in the evening when we have—"

"No. Let's talk now. I had a sleepless night, and I think we've waited too long to discuss our family's problems," Babirye said.

"I had a sleepless night, too," Nakato said as both twins stood in front of their father.

*They were babies only a few years ago, and now they are giving me orders?* "I am sorry that you both had sleepless nights. Is that why you've ambushed me?"

Herbert stepped aside so they could enter the house. He closed the door and followed them inside, where the twins then knelt to greet their father.

"Daddy, we are concerned that the family is falling apart, just because of your being inconsiderate," Babirye said after they had sat down.

"I understand your frustration, but—"

"Daddy, we are angry with you. Mummy is angry with you, too, and your behaviour has forced her to abandon her home," Nakato said.

"You are right to be angry," Herbert said calmly. "And I am sorry for my actions."

"Instead, you should be sorry for your *in*action," Babirye said. "You've done nothing to reunite the family."

"What should I do? I went to see your mother but it seems she did not really want to talk to me. And I have called her several times since then but her phone is off. It seems she doesn't want to talk to me."

"Call Hellen—she will get Mummy to talk to you," Babirye said.

"Why should I call Hellen who is in Boston to talk to your mother who is in Kawempe?"

"Mummy is in Boston," Babirye said. "She flew there two days ago."

"What?" Herbert said and paused, shaking his head. "She is in Boston? She went to the U.S. without informing me?"

"Yes, things are that bad, Daddy," Babirye said.

"Call her, then we will chat again," Nakato said as she rose. "Have a good day, Daddy."

"Daddy, by the beginning of next week we should have a concrete plan of action to reconcile the family," Babirye said.

Herbert remained seated for about ten minutes, thinking about Leah, and admitting that his daughters were right. He had to take action.

# 21

# October 2014

THREE DAYS LATER in Boston, as Victoria opened her car door, empty grocery bags in hand, a cab pulled into her driveway. When she saw who the passenger was, she rushed over to open the cab's back door. "Hey, big brother!" she shouted. "Herby, I'm so glad to see you!"

She led him into her house, still smiling broadly.

"Please call Leah," Herbert said to his sister after the greetings. "I am here to speak to her, apologize to her and solve our problems once and for all. I hope she will accept to meet me. I've booked a room at the Boston Shore Hotel for one week—we'll sleep and talk there."

"Thus says the rich man," Victoria said, laughing, as she rose to call Hellen with the news.

\* \* \*

Two hours later, when she dropped her mother at the reception of the Boston Shore Hotel, Hellen looked on, amused, as her parents hugged and laughed in between deep emotionally-charged breaths.

Leah started crying. "I am very happy to see you, darling," Hellen heard her whispering in Luganda into Herbert's ear.

"You guys, I'm so impressed," Hellen said in English. "And you've set an amazing example for me."

Her parents turned to look at her as if she had woken them from a deep sleep—for the last moments, while they'd been hugging and laughing, it had been like she hadn't been there at all. "What do you mean, Baby?" Leah asked now.

"I mean, like, I'd been expecting a fight. Like, you've been so mad at Dad all these days but now here you are hugging and stuff!"

Leah laughed, and Herbert let go of her to hug Hellen, and to congratulate her about her pregnancy.

"Now I'll let you guys enjoy your second honeymoon," Hellen said, laughing. The young woman working at the reception tried not to giggle. "Call me if you need anything," Hellen said, and left.

✳ ✳ ✳

In the week that followed, Herbert and Leah did enjoy a sort of second honeymoon.

They talked about Petua and Veronica the following day, but only for a few minutes, when Herbert confessed what had happened. "When Mummy hired Petua to work in the boutique, I was still a student in Musasa. We started seeing each other a couple of years after she'd begun working there, but kept the relationship secret, since Petua would have lost her job if Mummy had learned about it. Especially because Petua was about seven years older than me."

*So you rekindled the romance when she conceived? Uh, it's no use saying that.* "No wonder the first time I visited the boutique to meet your mother, Petua gave me that dirty look!" Leah said.

"But the relationship had ended long before I met you," Herbert said, laughing uneasily. Anyway, when Veronica was born, I bought Petua a small house so she could raise her daughter in a decent home." Herbert also told Leah that Veronica had recently returned to Kampala to get married and that he had contributed a substantial amount of money for the wedding. "I am sorry for not having told you all these things sooner," he said.

Leah said that it was all fine, that it was right that Veronica should marry properly and be accepted as a full member of the family. She then changed the topic to Hellen's pregnancy. She told Herbert that their daughter was expecting a girl.

They spent the rest of the week rediscovering each other and touring Boston before flying back to Kampala together, in love once again. On the same day they got home they attended a party where Brandon and his friend Zoe launched their new album, *Muddabirize.*

At the party, they ate, drank and danced to Brandon and Zoe's new music, celebrating their reconciliation.

❊ ❊ ❊

On the day after he and Leah returned from Boston, Herbert called Veronica, inviting her to meet the rest of the family at his home.

While they were waiting for Veronica, Leah felt nervous because she was going to meet her for the first time as her stepmother.

Veronica was nervous, too. When the taxi dropped her outside the perimeter wall of the Kiyagas' house for the first visit there, she was awed by the home's beauty and its size. As she rang the bell at the gate she wished that Kyle had come along to keep her company. She watched the departing taxi turn the corner as she waited for the gate to be opened. *It's not my fault that I was born out of wedlock. I have to be strong.*

Then Brandon opened the gate. "Veronica," Brandon said excitedly as he stretched his hand to shake hers. "Welcome back to Kampala— I'm glad to see you again!"

"I am glad to see you again, too, Brandon," Veronica said as she shook his hand.

Brandon closed the gate behind them. "I heard the news, that you are my sister," he said, smiling. "Isn't that interesting?"

Distracted, Veronica, did not respond. She'd noticed that Leah was watching her through one of the bedroom windows and was now feeling even more nervous. She didn't know how Leah was going to receive her. She'd only known Leah as her employer's daughter—and now she was her stepmother.

When Brandon opened the front door and Herbert stepped forward to welcome Veronica, it was obvious that he was nervous, too.

"Welcome home, Veronica," Brandon said again.

"Thank you," Veronica answered. Then she knelt on the rug to greet her father.

While Veronica was still kneeling, Leah walked past her to sit on a chair near the entrance to the dining room, greeting the young woman only once she was seated. "I am glad to see you again, Veronica," she said.

I am glad to see you too," Veronica said. *Is she really glad to see me? How should I address her now?* She had always called Leah by her name before.

For about five minutes while Veronica conversed with Herbert and Brandon, Leah sat quietly. Then she rose and went to the kitchen.

❄ ❄ ❄

When the bell rang a few minutes later, Brandon got up and went outside to open the gate. Veronica was about to meet more members of the family. Soon Ruth and her daughter Kate walked into the living room.

Previously Veronica had only known Ruth as the kind, generous woman who had paid for most of her education. *It all makes so much more sense now. The old woman knew I was her granddaughter.* But Veronica had never met Ruth's daughter Kate. While Ruth hugged Veronica, she could see Kate on a sofa from the corner of her eye, and noticed that Kate was watching her so closely it made her a bit uneasy. *Why is she looking at me like that?*

"This is your aunt Kate," Herbert said. "She is a professor of sociology."

"Hello, Veronica. I'm glad to meet you," Kate said finally as Veronica knelt to greet her, but her look belied her words.

"Brandon, please bring me a chair. These sofas are too soft for my back," Ruth said as she turned and walked closer to where Veronica was now seated.

"So, you live in Canada," Ruth said to Veronica while Brandon placed a chair in front of where Veronica was seated.

"Get ready for an interrogation, Veronica," Brandon said, laughing, as he walked away to help Leah set up the dining table for brunch.

"Yes, I live in Toronto," Veronica answered her grandmother.

"What do you do there? I mean, what do you do for money?"

"I work in a retail store."

"Oh, I see. But if I remember correctly, you studied zoology."

"Yes, I studied zoology but—"

"And you got married in Canada?"

"No. I got married here in Kampala before I went to live in Toronto with my husband."

"I've heard that your husband is the late Mitego's grandson. How come I didn't hear about your wedding?" Ruth asked. "Veronica, I thought you and I were friends, and it turns out we were not just friends—you are my granddaughter! Give me a hug one more time."

Veronica rose to hug Ruth. "I am glad to see you again, Grandma," Veronica said, sitting down again.

"You are not yet off the hook," Ruth said as Kate and Herbert looked on, amused. "How come I was not invited to this wedding?"

*It was a small wedding. I wish I could tell her that I wasn't even sure I loved Kyle when I married him.* "It was a small wedding, attended by only five other people," Veronica said. She noticed that Leah was now looking straight at her with an interested expression.

"My grandchildren must marry *properly*," Ruth said. "They marry in church, in the presence of the entire family. When you go back, please tell your husband that you are going to marry again—in a church this time. Herbert, please start making arrangements for Veronica to marry properly."

"Yes, I will," Herbert answered. He did not tell her that the wedding arrangements had been going on for months and a date had already been set.

"By the way, Veronica, that's not a joke. Our grandma rarely jokes around," Brandon said, laughing, from where he was standing in the dining room.

When Ruth asked Veronica where she and Kyle were staying at the moment and learned they were in a hotel, she told her to tell Kyle that they should check out and move to her home for the rest of their visit. Veronica thanked Ruth for her hospitality. She knew Ruth's home and thought that Kyle would be more at ease there than in Petua's much smaller home.

"The twins are at work now but they wondered if you and your husband can join them for dinner tomorrow," Herbert said to Veronica while they were having brunch.

"Yes, we are available for dinner tomorrow," Veronica said. "I will be glad to meet them."

\* \* \*

Veronica and Kyle checked out of the hotel the following day and moved into Ruth's home. In the evening, Brandon took them for dinner at Nakato's home.

As soon as Brandon parked the car in the front yard of the large house, Veronica panicked. *My shoes are cheap. My hair doesn't look good. I am an illegitimate daughter and probably the girls won't accept me as their sister. Why did I accept the invitation to dinner?*

"Are you okay?" Kyle asked. He was standing outside and had opened the door on Veronica's side of the car.

So lost in thought, Veronica hadn't even realized that Kyle had already exited the car. "Yeah, I'm fine," she said and came out of the car.

Babirye and Nakato were already waiting on the veranda. They cheered and Veronica noticed that they seemed genuinely happy to see her.

\* \* \*

After dinner, while Kyle remained at the dining table with Brian, Brandon and Roland to continue their conversation about English Premier League soccer, Veronica went to sit in the living room and chat with Babirye.

"We are glad to meet you, Veronica," Babirye said. "Even though Nakato and I are identical twins we have different personalities, and I am the chatty one. Mummy says that I am rude—I am not rude, though," she said, laughing. "I am just a straight talker."

"I understand. I think you need to be blunt with some people to get them to behave," Veronica said and laughed too.

"Nakato is the reserved one," Babirye continued.

"Am I reserved? I don't think so," Nakato said, walking into the room with three glasses and a bottle of wine.

"It's funny, but Daddy says that the two of us have our grandmothers' personalities. Nakato is more like Grandma Merab while I am more like Grandma Ruth," Babirye said.

"And he says that Hellen is like a cross between the two grand-mothers," Nakato said. "Veronica, you worked for Grandma Merab, so you know her quite well," she said, sitting down beside Veronica on the sofa. "Are you like her in some ways?"

"But don't forget—Veronica doesn't have Grandma Merab's blood. So we'll have to see if she is like Grandma Ruth," Babirye said, and she, Nakato and Veronica started laughing again.

The three of them continued their conversation and by the end of the evening, Veronica felt at ease with her new half-sisters.

❋ ❋ ❋

Adrian and Wendy Mitego arrived in Kampala for their son's wedding the following week, and they brought their little grandson Chase, Kyle's five-year-old son. Back in the country for the first time in thirty-five years, Adrian was overwhelmed by the number of people he was meeting—most of them hadn't even been born when he left.

In honour of Adrian and Wendy's visit, a big lunch was served in the home of Adrian's older brother Albert, and Veronica and Kyle attended as well.

During lunch, one of Kyle's cousins, Mugula, told Kyle that he would need to write a letter to Herbert, asking to pay a formal visit to Herbert's family before the wedding.

"Why do I need to do that?" Kyle asked. "Veronica and I are already married."

"That's what you think, but her family doesn't know you. We can write the letter together, then one of Veronica's aunts will hand-deliver it to Mr. Kiyaga," Mugula said.

"But do we really need to go through all that trouble?" Kyle asked, laughing. "We didn't meet through some kind of matchmaker!"

"It doesn't matter if you met in a bar, at school, in a discotheque, at a funeral or on the bus," Mugula said. "Culture is culture, and it has to be respected."

"Okay," Kyle said and laughed. "Go ahead and write the letter for me, if you can."

Mugula wrote the letter that evening and gave it to Kyle.

❊ ❊ ❊

Merab was one of the people that Veronica had been looking forward to seeing again in Kampala, so the following day she took a taxi and went to see her. When Veronica arrived at Merab's home, she saw the old woman seated on the veranda, weaving a mat. As soon as she'd exited the car, she greeted her at the top of her voice. "I am glad to see you again, Mama Merab!"

Merab did not recognize Veronica immediately.

"I am not your mama anymore," Merab said, laughing when she realized who it was. "Now I am your grandmother!"

Veronica laughed, too, as she sat down on the mat to greet Merab.

"When you quit your job at the restaurant, I didn't know that you had married," Merab said a few minutes into their conversation.

"I am sorry. When I got the visa I had to travel right away to join my husband."

"And the wedding—*was* there a wedding?"

"Yes, there was, but only a few people attended. That's why my mother asked us to wed again, in church."

"I think we've got a lot to catch up on. What crossed your mind when you were told that Herbert was your father?"

"I was speechless. I couldn't find the words to respond."

"I understand. I heard that you met the family."

"Yes, I met the family. Everybody welcomed me and I am happy to be a member of the family."

"I am glad to hear that," Merab said as she struggled to rise to go prepare some tea for Veronica.

"Mama Merab, I would like you to attend my wedding. Do you think you will be able to?" Veronica said while they were having tea on the veranda twenty minutes later.

"Yes, thanks for the invitation, and I will be glad to attend," Merab answered. "I will ask Brandon or one of his sisters to take me to the church."

"Just the church? I would like you to attend the reception too."

"We'll see about that. These days I prefer not to attend ceremonies, especially ones where there are long speeches—I doze off so easily," Merab said, and she and Veronica laughed again.

"What kind of food do you cook for your husband?" Merab asked after a few minutes of silence. "Is there any decent food where you live?"

"Yes, there is plenty of food, but I don't cook," Veronica said, and laughed. "My husband is a great cook and he enjoys cooking," she tried to explain. "So he does all the cooking and I do other work, like washing the dishes or taking out the garbage."

Merab was looking at her in horror, as if she had said something sinful. *What kind of woman doesn't cook for her husband?* She shook her head. "So, tell me how you do that. You sit there and watch him cook?"

"Sometimes I sit in the kitchen and chat with him while he is cooking but in most cases I am elsewhere in the apartment, doing something else, like washing laundry or even napping. When the food is ready at the table he calls me to eat."

"What? But do you sometimes make a good meal for him? You should prepare a meal for him, just for him, to show him that you care. I don't know any better way that you can use to show your husband that you care," Merab said and paused. "Anyway, you should always do whatever you can to show your husband how special he is. You girls are now living in a different world—I don't even know whether what I am telling you makes any sense to you."

"Thank you for the advice but what you are saying wouldn't work for my husband and me. He was raised differently from how I was raised, and he doesn't like the food I cook. Honestly, Mama Merab, I love *matooke*, sweet potatoes, yams and beans and I cook those foods once in a while but what can I prepare for a man who is a great cook himself? Nothing!"

Merab laughed out loud. She tried to persuade Veronica to stay for lunch. Veronica thanked her but said she had other errands.

# 22

# October 2014

HERBERT CALLED VERONICA two days later, at the beginning of the wedding week, asking her to meet him that morning at his office. After the greetings, when Herbert asked Veronica to go meet her new aunt Kate for some premarital advice, Veronica almost refused. The only time she had met Kate, she'd found her too serious and even a little intimidating. She thought Kate did not like her because she was an illegitimate daughter and had not felt comfortable around her.

She called her mother as soon as she left her father's office. "Uncle Herbert told me—"

"Get used to calling him 'Daddy,'" Petua interrupted. "He is your father."

"*Daddy* has asked me to go see Aunt Kate but I don't feel like meeting her," Veronica said. "I didn't feel comfortable around her when we met. I didn't like her attitude towards me."

"I understand. Kate is a difficult and unfriendly woman. But don't be afraid of her. Go, meet her and listen to what she has to tell you."

"I hear that these days there are ceremonial 'aunties' for hire. Can't I—"

"Why would you hire a ceremonial aunt when you have a real one?" Petua asked, her voice rising a little.

"I don't know. I just don't feel like meeting Aunt Kate."

"It's culture," Petua answered. "You have no choice."

❋ ❋ ❋

Veronica took a taxi to Kate's home shortly before noon. She felt apprehensive, but when she arrived there, she was surprised by her aunt's warm welcome. Kate placed a mat on the floor and she and Veronica sat down. After Kate and her husband Ham had greeted Veronica, Kate asked her to sit on a sofa.

Veronica hesitated. She remained seated on the mat. She thought that on such a culturally prescribed visit, she should sit on a mat. *Is she testing my manners?*

"Feel free to sit on the sofa. You are in your aunt's home," Kate said.

Veronica rose and sat on the sofa. Kate sat on another one, facing her.

"Your father asked me to give you some premarital advice. What's your future husband's name?" Kate asked.

"His name is Kyle, and actually, he already is my husband. We already were married, only now my mother insists that we must get married in church."

"Oh yes, I heard you telling my mother that you are already married. That means you are already experienced, and I don't need to give you a lot of advice," Kate said in English.

Veronica laughed, "You are already experienced" sounding funny to her, like "job experience."

Kate switched back to Luganda. "Since you don't have much time left before the wedding, we will try to squeeze everything into the short time available. I have prepared lunch, so please call your husband and ask him to join us for the meal. I will need to meet him before we introduce him to the family."

Kate went to the kitchen to check on the cooking food and Veronica called Kyle.

When Kate returned, they resumed their conversation. "How is your marriage? Is everything working well for you?" she asked.

"Kyle and I have been married for two and a half years, but—"

"Oh. That's a short while. Ideally everything should be still working well," Kate said and laughed.

"Yes, my marriage is great, but we argue a lot—Kyle finds me submissive and he doesn't like it. So sometimes he starts an argument just for its own sake. He might make a suggestion just to get me to say no, like going out to eat instead of cooking and eating at home. He doesn't like it when I agree and say yes," Veronica said and laughed. "He tells me, 'Can't you say no? Do you always have to agree with everything I say?' He gets frustrated with me."

"Why do you do that?" Kate asked. "Are you a yes-woman?"

"My mother trained me not to challenge her and I think it's the same attitude I have taken into my marriage and my work."

"It's good you are aware of that weakness. What have you done about it?"

The conversation with her aunt was feeling like a formal interview. "I have tried not to say yes all the time but differences of opinion usually just lead to unnecessary arguments," Veronica said. "For example, it took us a while to agree whether we should stay in a hotel here or spend our vacation in my mother's house."

Kate found Veronica intelligent and they continued their conversation for two hours, with Veronica answering all her questions until Kyle arrived for lunch. He and his cousin Mugula brought a basket of groceries which they handed to Kate before they ate. Kyle was silent through most of the meal. Mugula spoke on his behalf.

After lunch, Kyle handed the letter that Mugula had written to Kate. Kate accepted it and promised to deliver it to her brother that evening.

※ ※ ※

"Why does this process have to be as complicated as it is?" Kyle asked Brandon later the same evening when Brandon had delivered his father's reply, granting Kyle permission to marry his daughter.

"No, the process is not complicated," Brandon said and laughed. "Everything is now official. Now you can take Veronica knowing that nobody will bother you again."

Kyle burst out laughing.

Veronica was in the kitchen still telling Ruth about her visit to Kate's home when her phone rang. Apologizing, she answered it.

"That was my boss, Melody," Veronica explained after she'd ended the call. "She and her husband Devante have just arrived in Kampala. They've come to attend the wedding."

"Hey, that's wonderful news," Ruth said. "They've come all the way here for you?"

"Yes. My boss treats me like I were her sister," Veronica replied.

"Where are they now?"

"They are at the City View Hotel."

"Let them save their money. As you can see, there are two unoccupied rooms in this house and they are welcome to use one of them. All my children grew up and left home."

Veronica agreed and thanked Ruth for her kindness.

✳ ✳ ✳

Veronica and Brandon went to the hotel to pick up Melody and Devante. On the way back to Ruth's, Melody asked Brandon many questions. She was curious about Kampala's history, its people, and about the city's nightlife, and said that she couldn't wait to begin exploring the city.

"Wow, this is amazing," Melody exclaimed as they drove through Kololo, the Kiyagas' upscale Kampala neighbourhood. When they arrived outside the perimeter wall of Ruth's home, Brandon stopped the car and honked at the closed gate. "Wow, these people are rich! The images I had of Africa were totally different. Can you believe this, Devante?" Devante squeezed Melody's hand to signal her to shut up, but she couldn't help herself. "This is, like, totally unbelievable!"

# 23

# October 2014

HERBERT AND LEAH had called a meeting at their home to prepare for Veronica's introduction ceremony. Sengo, the hired spokesman, also attended. After speaking at all three of the Kiyaga girls' introduction ceremonies he had become a family friend.

When the meeting started, Herbert informed Sengo that he had another daughter, Veronica. "Mr. Sengo, you understand this well. You are also a man so you know that sometimes mistakes happen in a man's life," Herbert said. "The daughter I am talking about was born due to such a mistake."

"That's not what we are here to talk about," Leah said, frowning. "Let's plan for the ceremony."

Sengo, who said nothing, nodded his approval.

"For that reason, even though the ceremony will take place here at home, I will not be involved in the preparations," Herbert said. Then he turned to his daughters, formally asked them to organize the introduction ceremony on his behalf, they accepted, and Herbert thanked them for accepting the responsibility. "Out of respect for your mother, I will not be involved in the preparations for Veronica's wedding," he repeated.

"Daddy, do you think Veronica and her mother will be happy about that? Petua knows how much you were involved in our weddings," Nakato said.

"I'll give money but I will not participate in the arrangements. I trust you to do everything you can on my behalf. A date has already been set for the wedding. So please draft a moderate budget for the introduction ceremony and give it to us."

"Daddy, I've been wondering. Since a date has already been set for the wedding, why don't we leave out the introduction ceremony? It will save us a lot of headache," Babirye said.

"That's not how things are done," Sengo said, laughing. "There always has to be an introduction ceremony before a wedding."

Leah and Herbert kept quiet as Babirye and Sengo argued until they agreed that all the ceremonies would take place during that same weekend.

"Let me call Veronica right away to let her know our decisions," Nakato said as she rose and went to a bedroom to make the call.

"Please make sure that the visiting party's spokesman does not mention Veronica's mother during the introduction ceremony," Babirye said to Sengo, who nodded in approval. "I am emphasizing that because we won't let Veronica's mother attend the party," she said.

"You didn't need to say that, Babirye," Leah said.

Herbert was embarrassed.

"I understand that," Sengo said. "And I'll make it clear."

❊ ❊ ❊

Two days later, on the morning of the introduction ceremony, Veronica and several of her girlfriends, including her boss Melody, were gathered in a bedroom in Herbert and Leah's home. Nakato was helping the young women practise wearing their *gomesis*.

As they were dressing, Melody asked Nakato several questions about the ceremony and said that to support Veronica, she wanted to fully participate. "Since a *gomesi* is a dress that requires several layers and accessories, wearing it correctly is an art," Nakato told her as she helped her properly put on one of her own *gomesis*. "Young people rarely wear them."

Melody was the most excited of all to wear one. Tall and beautiful, she looked elegant in Nakato's *gomesi* and when Nakato asked them all to change back into their normal clothes she did not want to.

"Mel, if you wear the *gomesi* all day, you will be uncomfortable," Veronica told her. "Wear it only for the ceremony this afternoon."

Meanwhile, in the front yard, there was a lot of excitement and activity. A team of decorators hired for the occasion were setting up two large tents, one for Veronica's guests and the other for Kyle's, but now they'd stopped working because Petua's cousin Gillian had told them that the tents were facing in the wrong direction and that they should use more balloons and fresh flowers. The decorators were still standing there, wondering what to do, when Babirye arrived.

The team leader took Babirye aside. "Doctor, I am confused," she said. "I'm getting conflicting instructions. Can you please help sort things out?"

"Who else is giving you instructions?" Babirye asked as she turned around to face the people who were standing around, idle. She didn't know any of them. She assumed they were members of Petua's family.

The woman discreetly pointed to Gillian.

"It's I who hired you—you will take instructions only from me. Proceed as agreed," Babirye said, loud enough for everybody to hear, and went inside the house.

Gillian lost her temper. *These people are underrating us*, she thought, taking a plastic chair to the veranda and sitting quietly.

Meanwhile, in the backyard, where the hired caterers were cooking a variety of foods for the party, Kate prepared a special meal of chicken *luwombo* for Kyle. First she smoked a whole chicken on a charcoal stove, and when it had browned and was giving off a nice aroma she chopped it up and placed the pieces on a tray. Then she smoked a large young banana leaf, folded it, placed the chicken inside and added tomatoes, onions, salt, green pepper, water and a bit of curry powder. She then wrapped the whole mixture in the banana leaf and secured the bundle with banana fibre. She then peeled some *matooke* plantain and placed them in banana leaves and tied the bundle with banana fibre, like she'd done for the *luwombo*, and began steaming them.

❋ ❋ ❋

In the afternoon Kyle arrived with a large entourage, and Sengo met them outside the gate, wondering how it was that so many people had been able to find the time to come to the ceremony on a Thursday afternoon. It looked like Kyle had brought along more than two hundred people. "Are these only one hundred people?" Sengo asked Katantazi, who was Kyle's hired spokesman. "Doctor Babirye gave us strict instructions concerning the number of guests, and she expected a maximum of one hundred. That's the number of chairs that have been prepared for the visiting party."

Katantazi turned back to face his crowd. "Ladies and gentlemen, I would like only those who were officially invited to join this party to step forward."

There was a loud murmur. One woman stepped forward. "The Kiyagas have been friends of the Mitegos for generations. And they know how many we are. They can't exclude any of our people from our son's ceremony. If they don't have enough money to feed us, they should let us know and we will contribute some."

"Miss, I can't let you in; I have strict orders to follow," Katantazi answered.

The grumbling continued as Kyle and the guests who had been invited proceeded to walk into the compound, one by one, as Sengo counted. When the last of the one hundred had walked through the gate, the two security guards hired for the occasion closed the gate. Kyle's cousin Mugula remained outside for a while to calm down the irate members of his family, who calmed down briefly.

Mugula went inside, leaving them stranded at the gate. "We will make so much noise out here that the occasion will not proceed!" yelled the woman who had spoken earlier.

"Miss, we will be forced to call the police on you for being idle and disorderly," one of the security guards said. "Please just go home." The people walked back to their cars a few at a time, and they had all driven away by the end of the hour.

While most of Kyle's guests were served lunch in their tent, he and ten of his guests, including Devante, were greeted in the house and served lunch there. Eight of the guests sat at the dining table and Babirye and Nakato served them. Kyle invited Devante to come sit with him in the living room where Kate and one of her cousins were waiting to serve him his special meal. Sitting on a mat, Kate placed several plates of food and the chicken *luwombo* on the table in front of them. When she realized that they did not know what to do with the chicken *luwombo*, she untied it and served two pieces of chicken, the first to Kyle and then one to Devante.

At the dining table, while the rest of the visitors ate and chatted, Melody watched in silence what was going on in the living room. When Kate came to the dining room to get some drinks for Kyle and Devante, Melody asked her why Kyle had been served a separate dish from his guests.

"It's because he is special. It's a sign that we appreciate him for marrying our daughter," Kate said and laughed.

Melody laughed too. "Oh, Devante would love that kind of treatment! Look at him. He must be wishing he married an African girl. When he proposed marriage to me, my mom did not like him at all and we would have called off the engagement if I hadn't I been madly in love with him."

❋ ❋ ❋

After lunch, Kyle and the guests who'd been inside the house with him came out to the tent, and he sat for a moment on a chair at the back among his guests. Quite formally, as if he did not know already, Sengo asked Katantazi the purpose of their visit. After that, the greetings began.

Brandon came out of the house in the company of five other young men to greet the visitors. Sengo pointed him out of the group to the guests, informing them that he was Veronica's brother, and Katantazi gave Brandon a firm handshake.

Next, Kate came out with three of her cousins and sat on mats in front of the visitors to greet them. After the greetings, with the women still seated, Sengo asked Kate what this group of "strangers" wanted. "Sir, they are here to ask for my niece's hand in marriage," Kate answered.

"The whole group?"

"No, I'll show you the suitor. I will be back in a moment," Kate said and she and her cousins rose.

As they waited, Sengo asked the DJ to play some music, and the DJ played a song from Brandon's album *Tobbanga Nkoko*.

Soon a group of ten young women walked out of the house, dressed in their elegant *gomesis*, dancing to the music. Melody was the first in line, Veronica was in the middle, and Kate was with them, too, at the back of the line. The guests cheered as the women slowly made their way to the space in between the two tents where mats had been placed for them to sit down.

When the women sat on the mats to greet the visitors, Sengo handed his microphone to Kate. But before she'd said anything Melody asked her to hand the microphone to her—she wanted to show off her newly-acquired skills in Luganda. Everyone cheered and laughed as they heard Melody confidently reciting the long greetings in her funny Luganda accent, and how she was exaggerating the humming that's characteristic of Luganda greetings.

After the greetings, Melody followed Kate as they made their way through the guests' tent to look for Kyle. When they found him, Kate pinned a carnation on his jacket and brought him dancing, hand in hand, to the sofa that had been reserved for him in front of the crowd.

The formal discussions and negotiations ensued. Katantazi narrated Kyle's family tree, tracing it back four generations. He also mentioned Kyle's mother Wendy, describing her as a beautiful Canadian woman that Kyle's father Adrian had met in the Canadian city of Saskatoon before they both moved to Toronto.

When Katantazi was done, Sengo narrated Veronica's family tree as well, tracing it back to four generations of Kiyagas. But unlike Katantazi, who had talked at length about Wendy, Sengo did not mention Petua.

Sengo declared that the Kiyagas wanted their daughter to "marry properly." Katantazi said that a wedding would take place in three days' time.

"Oh, why that fast?" Sengo asked.

"Sir, Kyle is a Canadian, and Canadians don't waste time. When they commit themselves to doing something, they do it right away."

The audience laughed.

Veronica and the other young women went back inside the house and came back out twenty minutes later dressed in different, even more expensive *gomesis*.

Katantazi then presented the gifts that Kyle had brought for Veronica's family. Sengo thanked him for the gifts and said that Kyle had Herbert's blessings to marry his daughter. Kyle's guests clapped and cheered.

The DJ played more music and several people from both tents rose to dance. After twenty minutes the music was paused and Kyle gave an engagement ring to Veronica and placed it on her finger, and then the dancing and drinking resumed.

"It's funny that these guys are getting engaged again," Melody said to Devante, "but this is a lot of fun."

"I know, eh?" Devante said.

❋ ❋ ❋

Even before the ceremony had ended, Petua's cousin Gillian went to report everything to her. She said that the party had been poorly organized and that she and the other members of Petua's family had been made to feel excluded. "Your name wasn't even mentioned," Gillian said. "You could think that Veronica has no mother at all!"

"I know those people well and I didn't expect my name to be mentioned. Herbert's daughters are controlling everything and I don't think they will ever accept my daughter," Petua answered, losing her temper. *How dare Herbert disrespect me! I will blast him!*

Petua got Gillian and her boyfriend to take her to Herbert's home, where they waited in the car, discreetly drinking and chatting until the party ended. But when Kyle and Veronica walked out of the gate, late in the evening, Gillian brought Veronica to the car to talk to her mother, who told her that she was not happy with the Kiyagas.

Veronica denied Gillian's story. "There wasn't any problem at all. Everything went well and Melody can't stop talking how well organized the event was."

"Don't defend them!" Petua yelled.

"Everyone was happy. In fact, Nakato and Babirye spent a lot more money than Uncle Herbert had budgeted. Including their own money," Veronica added.

"You are saying that because you've never attended any parties in this home," Gillian said. "They always spend way more than they did this time."

As they continued to argue, Veronica noticed that both her mother and her aunt were drunk. And when she realized that they seemed to enjoy feeling bad, she walked away to rejoin Kyle.

"If they treat us in the same way at the wedding we will cause a scene," Gillian said as she opened her tenth beer of the evening. "We will disrupt the ceremony."

❋ ❋ ❋

The following day Babirye and Nakato held a meeting with the team of volunteers from both the Kiyaga and the Mitego families who'd agreed to take on duties, to go through the wedding program. They met on the balcony of a Kampala restaurant.

"Looking at this mix of people, I'm guessing there is going to be a lot of arguing in this meeting," Brandon said to Kyle and Veronica as soon as they had walked up the stairs and onto the balcony. "I would advise you to sit inside at the bar to enjoy some drinks and conversation. I will call you outside if you are needed."

"It's their wedding program we'll be discussing. Let them stay," Nakato said.

"No, Brandon is right," Babirye said to Veronica and Kyle. "You two and your guests should enjoy your evening. Stay inside the restaurant while we sort things out."

Melody and Devante were the first to go to the bar. Kyle and Veronica followed them there a few minutes later.

❋ ❋ ❋

"Many members of our family are not happy because they were barred from participating in the introduction ceremony," said Aida, one of Kyle's cousins, when the meeting started.

"Miss, we are not here to review the introduction ceremony. We are here to assign duties and to finalize the program for the wedding," Babirye answered.

"But how can we plan for the wedding when the groom's family still has grievances?" Aida asked.

Babirye, ignoring her, asked Brandon to distribute copies of the program.

The discussions continued and seemed to progress smoothly until Namuleme, another of Kyle's many cousins present there, looked unhappy and raised her hand. Babirye ignored her, but Namuleme kept her hand up until Nakato whispered in her sister's ear. Babirye gave Namuleme permission to speak.

"It seems that the bride's family is underrating us," Namuleme said. "Members of the bridegroom's family haven't been assigned to any of the important roles. For example, shouldn't the Master of Ceremonies come from the groom's family?"

"We go by capabilities, not by rules," Babirye answered . Both Aida and Namuleme rose and stormed out of the meeting. "Good riddance," Babirye said. "Are there any other questions about the program?"

There were no questions but there was a lot of grumbling, and by the time the meeting ended one hour later, a quarter of Kyle's relatives had already stormed out, accusing the Kiyagas of underrating them. By the next afternoon Herbert had heard that both Petua and Kyle's relatives were angry with his daughters. *I caused the problem in the first place when I fathered an illegitimate daughter.* He decided not to intervene.

❄ ❄ ❄

That evening, many members of Veronica and Kyle's families and their friends attended a joint bachelor and bachelorette party in the dance hall of the beautiful Turquoise Club. Babirye, Nakato and their husbands were there. So were Brandon and his girlfriend. Veronica, Kyle and their bridal entourage sat at a large high table next to the DJ.

"Veronica, you shouldn't drink a lot this evening. You need to wake up energetic and fresh," Melody said as the party went on. "I've got my eyes on you," she said, smiling as she gestured, pointing to and from her eyes.

Melody was enjoying the party. She danced to one song after another, and when Zoe and Brandon's title duet *Muddabirize* from their newly launched album ended, she asked the DJ to play it again.

Devante went to the high table to talk to Veronica. "I can't tell you how happy I am," he said as he watched his wife dancing to *Muddabirize.* "Melody is having a lot of fun in Kampala. And you know what? I'm happy when she's happy."

"Yes, but she would be mad if she understood the lyrics of this song," Veronica said, laughing.

"Oh, what is it about?" Devante asked, moving closer to hear Veronica better in the noisy hall.

"It is encouraging women to take care of their tired husbands at the end of the work day. Can you hear the chorus? *Muwe ka chai. Mubuuze kyanaalya.* That means 'Give him a cup of tea, ask him what kind of food he wants for dinner.'"

Devante laughed heartily as he ran to the dance floor to join Melody. "Oh, yeah, I love this song!" he said as he tried to sing along to the chorus. "Mu-way the chai. Moo-booze the nalia."

When the song ended, Melody and Devante went to the high table and sat down on a couple of empty chairs next to Veronica. "That song is awesome!" Melody said.

When Devante glanced knowingly at Veronica and sang the chorus again, "Mu-way the chai. Moo-booze the nalia," Veronica just laughed.

"What?" Melody asked.

✻ ✻ ✻

"Wow, Veronica, you look fabulous," Melody said the following morning when Veronica walked out of the dressing room of the bridal salon.

"Thanks, Mel," Veronica said as she hugged Melody. "I am very pleased that you and Devante are here for me."

"But please remember to smile," Melody said. "This is your special day."

"I know, but I am kind of freaking out. There will be lots of people from my father's family whom I've never met and they will be talking—"

"Come on, now—shut off the negativity! Devante and I will be right there cheering you on."

Two hours later, while Herbert and his daughters waited at the back of the church for the bride and her entourage to walk in and the service to begin, he suddenly shook his head. "Out of respect for your mother, I don't want to walk Veronica down the aisle," he said.

"But that's a detail that you and Mummy should have already discussed," Babirye said. "Now you have to get ready, Daddy. There is no more time to waste. They are coming in."

"Daddy, Mummy has already forgiven you," Nakato added.

Still, Herbert hesitated, and as he and Veronica walked he kept his eyes glued in the direction of the altar where Kyle was waiting for his bride.

* * *

When it was time to exchange their vows, Kyle pulled a sheet of paper from his jacket pocket. He was emotional as he read.

Vero, the first time I saw you I realized how truly beautiful and amazing you are. When I saw you working so quickly and methodically at the cash register in Kia-te-lekira Restaurant while remaining alert to the needs of the diners I said to myself, 'I would like to one day talk to this girl and share a meal with her.' And when we spoke I wasn't disappointed. I realized how intelligent you are and I knew right away that I wanted to spend the rest of my life with you. Vero, you are my rock. You complete me as a man and you complement me as a friend. Even when I'm away at work or anywhere else I look forward to returning home to be with you, my love. I could never live without you. And Chase is happy, too—what a wonderful mother you are to him.

"Great job, Daddy!" Chase said, and the congregation laughed at the adorable little pageboy's enthusiastic words.

Decades earlier another man had met a beautiful girl in Kyatelekera Restaurant. Tears formed in Herbert's eyes as history seemed to repeat itself. He could have used Kyle's exact words when he wed Leah. Now he squeezed her hand. Leah smiled.

Veronica felt just a bit ashamed—she hadn't thought of writing her vows. But she repeated after the reverend with sincere emotion, "I Veronica Kiwuka, take thee, Kyle, to be my wedded husband, to have and to hold, from this day forward, for better, for worse, for richer, for poorer, in sickness and in health, to love and to cherish, till death do us apart, according to God's holy ordinance and therefore I pledge myself to you."

"How come we didn't have our first kiss?" Kyle whispered as he and Veronica walked to the vestry to sign their marriage certificate. He had been eagerly waiting to be asked to kiss his bride, and when the request didn't come he'd been disappointed.

Veronica laughed. "We are in Kampala, remember? We don't kiss in public."

"Whatever," Kyle said, pulled Veronica closer and kissed her on the cheek.

❉ ❉ ❉

During the reception, Herbert sat quietly while Leah and the other members of the family who were seated at their table chatted. "Cheer up," Leah whispered to her husband. "You are giving a bad impression, sulking at your daughter's wedding. By the way, have you prepared your speech?"

"No. Clement will speak on my behalf. I am not ready to do it."

"You want Clement to speak on your behalf when you are present?" Leah said, surprised, but said nothing else about it.

The guests enjoyed a copious dinner and when dessert was being served, the music stopped.

Sengo, the Master of Ceremonies, thanked the guests for coming on behalf of Veronica, Kyle and their parents, and then introduced first the bridegroom's parents and then the bride's, calling out Mr. and Mrs. Kiyaga. Herbert stood up, but Leah hesitated for a few seconds. *I am not the bride's mother.* Then she stood up.

Sengo froze. For almost twenty seconds he stood there with the microphone in his hand, the guests looking at him, puzzled. Sengo never ran out of words but he was standing there, speechless. He looked at Babirye, seeking her approval for what he was about to say. She smiled.

*How should I put it? Oh well,* he thought, *best to just go for it.* "And, let me introduce the mother of the bride," Sengo said, and Petua stood up.

Her cousin Gillian cheered loudly, then the rest of the members of her family joined in.

Leah squeezed Herbert's hand, and that reassured him.

When he rose to speak, Clement thanked the guests for coming and added, "The Kiyagas and the Mitegos have been friends for generations. We are glad that our longtime friendship has today been further reinforced by your son's marriage to our daughter." He then addressed the newlyweds. "Our daughter Veronica and your husband Kayile…"

Some of the guests laughed at the mispronunciation of Kyle. "It's Kyle," Brandon yelled.

"Yes, thanks Brandon," Clement said. "Our daughter Veronica and your husband Kyle, thanks for honouring us by returning home to wed. What you have done is noteworthy because young people do as they please these days—others would have just wed over there in Canada, forgetting that their parents, family and friends would be glad to share their joy. We wish you a long, happy marriage. May you prosper and may you have children. Teach your children our good manners and, please, keep our culture alive by teaching them our language, Luganda."

Wendy glanced at Adrian and Adrian knew right away what she must be thinking. *But you didn't teach Kyle your language. It's your fault.*

"He spoke very well," Leah whispered to Herbert after Clement had ended his speech. "You couldn't have made a better speech."

"Yes, he spoke well. I am proud of him," Herbert answered.

Then one of Kyle's uncles rose to speak on behalf of the Mitegos. "Ladies and gentlemen, I am glad to see you this evening. My name is Albert Mitego. I am the chairman and managing director of Mitego Group of Companies, which many of you here will know, and an older brother of Kyle's father, Adrian. We are gathered here this evening to celebrate with both Kyle and Veronica, not to talk about Adrian," he said. "However, as a family, we can't fail to mention the return of my brother Adrian. For more than thirty years we believed that he was dead, until, a few years ago, a brown, handsome young man stood in my secretary's office one day, introducing himself as a son of my dear younger brother. I could not hold back tears of joy! His father was hesitant, but Kyle looked for and found us in Kampala—and this month we got the chance to see Adrian again, after so many years. And it turned out that for years both Adrian and my sister Robin lived in the same province in Canada but had never met."

Like Clement had before him, Albert thanked Kyle and Veronica for honouring their families and friends by returning home to wed.

*I forced them to return home to marry properly and now they are basking in the glory, smiling like morons.* Petua thought, waving discreetly to Veronica, who laughed.

# 24

# November 2014

TWO DAYS AFTER Veronica's wedding, after the day at their clinic, Nakato told Babirye that it was a shame that Gwen had worked so hard to prepare her report when nothing was being done to follow it up. "Why don't we visit the boutique tomorrow, talk to Elsie and see what's going on there?" Babirye said.

Before work the following day the twins went to Ruth's Classic Boutique, and an employee there told them that Elsie was in a meeting with Clement. "Okay, we will wait for her," Nakato said as she turned around to admire a beautiful vase.

"No, we'll interrupt the meeting," Babirye said as she started walking towards Elsie's office, with Nakato following behind. "Uncle Clement has no business here." She knocked twice on the door and waited a few seconds. Inside, she could hear Elsie and Clement arguing.

"Come in," Elsie said.

Clement was surprised to see, first Babirye, then Nakato right behind her.

"There you are, my favourite twins. How are you?" Clement said as he shook both women's hands.

"Uncle, will you please excuse us? We would like to talk to Elsie alone," Babirye said, walking back to the door and opening it wider, nodding in the direction of the corridor to signal Clement to walk out.

"Let them finish their conversation," Nakato said. "We can wait."

"Uncle, please excuse us," Babirye said again without responding to Nakato.

"Babirye, I am in the middle of an important discussion with the manager," Clement said.

"As who?" Babirye asked.

"Are you aware that your father entrusted me with the responsibility of overseeing this shop?"

"Show me your appointment letter," Babirye said as she approached Clement with her outstretched hand.

"What are you talking about?"

"Show me your appointment letter," she repeated. "And if you don't have one, please leave now."

Clement picked up his jacket from the back of the chair he'd been sitting on and walked out without another word.

As soon as he was outside the building he called Herbert to tell him what had happened. Herbert said that he was sorry for Babirye's actions, and thanked Clement for his "enormous help" with the boutique. He promised to talk to his daughters.

\* \* \*

The twins spent another hour talking to Elsie, who told them that Clement was making it hard for her to run the boutique efficiently. "It seems he wants me to get fed up and quit my job so his friend Katana can take over. Let me tell you one thing, though—if I were no longer working here this boutique would fail. Clement and Katana would steal money from it."

"Elsie, you have our support. Uncle Clement has no job here and from now on you should never take orders from him. Call me if he bothers you again," Babirye said and rose.

When the twins left the boutique to go to their clinic, Nakato drove while Babirye called her father, annoyed. "Daddy, we want to talk to you this evening about the boutique."

"Oh, yes, Babirye. You've called at the right time. I want to talk to you too," Herbert answered. "Your uncle called me about an hour ago…"

"…to tell you what I did to him, no doubt! I sent him away from the boutique—and he should never set foot there again."

"Babirye!"

"Daddy, let's discuss that this evening," Babirye said and ended the call.

\* \* \*

"It's my daughters," Herbert said, laughing, to a colleague who was chatting with him in his office. "They want to run my affairs for me, even when I am still able."

"But don't you think it is a good thing that the girls are stepping up?" Herbert's colleague said. "Girls are more involved in family matters these days than boys. I tell you, my sons don't even think of coming home to see us. It's the girl who cares about us."

\* \* \*

The meeting started after dinner that evening. Brandon was there, too. "What have you done since Hellen presented Gwen's report to you, what have you done about it?" Nakato asked her parents, getting right to the point.

"Nothing much as yet," Leah said, laughing.

"What's so funny, Mummy?" Babirye asked.

"It's just that we haven't implemented Gwen's recommendations as yet. But don't worry about the restaurant—it is doing fine."

"Daddy, please ask Uncle Clement to stop going to the boutique. We no longer want him to be involved in its management," Babirye said.

"But Clement has been very helpful. And he now considers managing the boutique his job. Do you have alternative employment for him?" Herbert asked.

"No, I don't. And, actually, it's not my job to find him a job, Daddy. What we intend to do is to protect the family's wealth. Do you think our intention is good?"

"Yes, it is."

"Will you cooperate fully with us?"

"Yes, I will."

"Then you should ensure that Uncle Clement stops going to the boutique."

"Babirye, it's not as simple as that," Leah said. "Your father wouldn't have the courage to ask his brother, who is unemployed, to stop—"

"Mummy, listen. Do you support what we are trying to do?"

"Yes, but—"

"Good, then I'll fire Uncle Clement myself. I will write a letter firing him, even though he didn't get one when he was 'hired,' and then we'll go through the process of finding a qualified general manager."

"But Clement has been very helpful since your grandmother abandoned the boutique," Herbert said.

"No, not at all," Babirye answered. "We talked to Elsie this morning and she said that Uncle Clement is making it hard for her to run the boutique."

"Your uncle told me that he felt insulted by the way you talked to him, Babirye, that you ordered him around like a little boy."

"Babirye, you are rude," Leah said. "And I wonder whether that's how you treat your patients."

"Babirye is not rude, Mummy—she is just strict," Brandon said.

"Okay, she is strict … but a little rude, too," Leah answered.

"I had to place Uncle Clement where he belongs," Babirye said. "He has no business whatsoever at the boutique."

"So, what do you suggest we should do?" Herbert asked.

"We use Executive Staffing Solutions to hire for our clinics," Nakato said. "Let's use them to hire a general manager. If you agree, you can authorize me to contact them, and the search can begin as early as next week."

※ ※ ※

When the twins left after dinner, Herbert called Kate and told her how embarrassed he was that his daughters had thrown Clement out of the boutique.

"I think they did the right thing," Kate said.

"How dare you support them?" Herbert asked. "You've disappointed me, Kate. I thought you'd advise your nieces to behave better."

"It's because I've never liked Clement and his late mother. And I don't think I know him well. Actually, I doubt that you know him well either."

\* \* \*

While they were chatting at a bar the following day, Brandon told his friend Zoe that the family would be hiring a new general manager for the boutique. Zoe was neither interested in applying for, nor qualified for the job but she knew someone who she thought might be. Her aunt Brittany.

\* \* \*

Two days after Herbert had told her about Clement's encounter with the twins at the boutique, Kate and her husband Ham had run into Jairus at the Premier Golf Club, where they were all members. Kate knew that Jairus had been Clement's former business partner and told him what had happened. "Herbert put Clement in charge of my mother's boutique but now my nieces are pushing him out," she told him.

"Your nieces are doing the right thing," Jairus answered. "You can't trust Clement with any business. He is a troubled man who is always short of money. Kate, there is a lot I could tell you about Clement, even if he were here now."

"Yes, of course, no doubt about that," Kate said. "You know him better than I do."

"Herbert loves Clement like any good big brother would, but I doubt he knows Clement well. For example, I think Herbert—and probably everyone in your family—thinks that Clement is a qualified pharmacist," Jairus said, pausing to sip his beer.

Kate's eyes widened and she shifted in her chair.

"But he's not," Jairus said. "Clement never completed his degree. While we were in the university in Calcutta, he spent most of his time out having fun. He didn't graduate."

"What?"

"He did not graduate," Jairus repeated. "And I don't think his mother knew that. When we returned she convinced your father to help us to start a pharmacy. He did, and, as you know, we ran the pharmacy together for years. But Clement didn't have any active role in the business. And then one day he stopped coming to work."

"What?" Kate asked, shaking her head as she looked at Ham and again at Jairus.

"But his mother was not any better," Jairus said and paused again to sip his beer. "During her funeral service, Clement told the assembled mourners that she graduated from Landsborough College in Nairobi—but that college does not even exist! Google it and tell me if you find it."

"What?"

"But Clement's mother is the one to blame for his troubles. On one hand, she spoiled him by doing everything for him. On the other hand, she abused him. For example, I was shocked, on the eve of our departure for India, when she slapped him—"

"What?" Kate gasped, almost speechless.

"She slapped him, right there, in front of me, because he'd said no when she told him to pack a few more trousers."

"Don't you think it would be good for Herbert to know these things about his brother?" Ham asked.

"Absolutely it would be good for Herbert to know," Jairus answered, "but whenever Clement realizes that someone wants to intervene to help him with his behavioural problems, he cuts off communication. He has been avoiding me for months now. But he still goes to the pharmacy to ask for money when he knows that I am not there."

# 25

# November 2014

TWO WEEKS AFTER the wedding, while Veronica, Kyle, Wendy and Chase were preparing to return to Toronto, Adrian was preparing to visit a place he had dreaded for more than three decades.

On the night before the visit he slept little. Even though he knew that he wouldn't recognize or be recognized in the place where he had almost been killed, he felt anxious and uneasy. As he tossed and turned in bed, he tried to replay in his mind the day when a mob of villagers had tried to lynch him during the Ugandan-Tanzanian war of 1978 and 1979.

While he and his comrades had been fleeing from the advancing Tanzanian army, he had tried to forcibly take some civilian clothes from a young man so he could throw away his military uniform and go into hiding. The young man had sounded an alarm and several villagers had quickly gathered to help him, and had almost killed Adrian. The memory of the incident had barely faded after thirty-five years. Now, he was anxious but also eager to meet a son of the village elder, now long dead, who had rescued him from the mob.

By the morning Adrian felt ready. He was setting off in the company of his half-brother Job Mitego, who was a cashier at J & C Pharmacy, their former boss, Clement, and his colleague Eliezar, who hailed from the town they were visiting and had been the one who connected Adrian to his rescuer's family.

"This is the place—this is Kalisizo," Eliezar said when they stopped at a market to buy some groceries for their host. Adrian could not believe it—he even felt a bit of shame. He could not recognize the place he had been dreading for close to thirty-five years.

For several years, he'd had nightmares about this place. A crowd of people chasing him. A man trying to choke him. A mob beating him. Old women about to lynch him.

But now when he looked around, it dawned upon him that nobody knew him. Nobody looked at him. None of the town's activities stopped because he was there. It was business as usual. "I was almost killed here in 1979," he said, almost to himself. "I would have been dead by now if Mr. Kakembo had not intervened to save me."

"Try to forget that. You are safe now," Clement said. He didn't want Adrian repeating the story he had already retold dozens of times in the weeks since he'd arrived in Kampala.

After they had bought the groceries Adrian and his companions drove to their host's shop, and the man, seeing them arrive, brought stools out to the veranda for the visitors to sit on.

"Adrian, meet Zadok," Eliezar said, introducing the host after the greetings. "Zadok, meet Adrian—and let him tell you his story."

Adrian cleared his throat and shifted on the stool to face Zadok, who was visibly puzzled. "Sir, when I was a young soldier, in 1979, your father saved my life," Adrian said. "That's why I am here, to meet you and your family and to honour the memory of your father."

"1979?" Zadok asked. "I see. Actually, my father died that same year, 1979, shortly after the war."

"I'm sorry for your loss," Adrian said in a genuinely sad tone. "What I remember was that it was apparent that your father was ill. Someone had called him out of his home to tell him that a young soldier was about to be killed."

"My father was a kind man. And he was respected in this area. Earlier, he had been a chief."

Adrian continued. "When he came, he pleaded with the people to be merciful and to stop hitting me. Then he and two men took me to his home. I tried to explain how I had got into trouble but I could hardly talk. I was bleeding all over. Your father and the two men washed me, changed my clothes, brought a car and took me to a place I don't remember now, for treatment. Then, two weeks later, the two men helped me to escape."

They chatted for a while, then Zadok excused himself, went to another shop a few metres away, and returned with a young man who would look after the shop for the afternoon. "Gentlemen, I will take you home to meet the rest of the family," he said. "And we will have lunch there together."

The visitors rose and, following Zadok on his motorcycle, drove to his home.

* * *

When they arrived at Zadok's home, Adrian and Clement were surprised to see about thirty people walking around and chatting in the front yard of the large home—it was obviously going to be a big lunch. But Job and Eliezar were not surprised. They'd sent Zadok money to prepare the lunch after they'd told him they would be bringing a visitor to his home.

Now Adrian and his companions sat on the chairs that had been prepared for them in the living room, and all the people present came to greet them one by one.

While a table was being laid for the visitors, Adrian continued chatting with Zadok. "So when I got well I eventually escaped to Nairobi, where I lived in a refugee camp. When it was time to choose a safe country, I chose to go to Canada. I met my wife, Wendy, in 1981 and we married in January the following year. Our son Kyle was born in 1983. He wedded last weekend in Kampala."

"What a story!" Zadok said. "I am glad you are alive and everything ended well for you."

"A psychologist suggested I visit the town where I had been traumatized, and the home of the man who saved me. So, I hope this can be part of my healing, and I will always cherish this meeting with you," Adrian said.

After lunch, when he and his companions returned to Zadok's shop, something was still bothering Clement. An old man had been looking intently at him while they'd been having lunch. What did he want?

* * *

"Thanks for the hospitality," Adrian said to Zadok when they sat down again at the shop's veranda.

"It was my pleasure to host you and to know that you are alive, thanks to my father's intervention," Zadok answered.

As the conversation continued, Clement tried to ignore his thoughts about the old man at Zadok's house. But the more he tried, the more he thought about him. "Zadok, there was an old man in your house, who was wearing a *kanzu*," he said. "Who is—"

"Oh, that old man? He's my uncle. His name is Kyotera. Incidentally he lives in Kyotera, not far from here," Zadok answered and laughed at his own comments.

Clement's heart started racing. *Kyotera? That might be my father!*

Clement wanted to know more about the old man but he hesitated to ask Zadok more questions that would make him curious. He kept quiet while Zadok chatted with Adrian, but he couldn't get Kyotera off his mind. He finally thought of a tactful way to ask just one more question. "I found Mr. Kyotera polite and personable," he began.

"Yes, he is a kind man," Zadok answered.

"By the way, his face looked familiar," Clement said, his tone casual. "Has he ever worked in Kampala?"

"Kampala? I'm not sure, but I don't think so. He has always lived here. Perhaps he worked there in the past. You never know."

Before they left, Adrian thanked Zadok for his hospitality once again, and he and Clement both exchanged telephone numbers with him.

❊ ❊ ❊

Clement thought about Kyotera for most of the night. He estimated that the man was old enough to be his father, and tried to remember the details of his face, trying to identify any features that suggested a resemblance, but as the night wore on, he found he couldn't remember the old man's face at all. He thought about the late Jude Kiyaga, and knew without a doubt that Jude was not his father. Jude had always been distant, and as far as Clement could remember Clotilda had always said unkind things about Jude, throughout her long on-and-off relationship with him.

# 26

# November 2014

CLEMENT CALLED LAWYER Sekitto's office early the next morning, but it took three calls before he was able to speak to the lawyer later in the day. After a brief conversation, Clement told Sekitto that he wanted to meet him for a private conversation the following day.

"Clement, I am fully booked tomorrow. Can your matter wait till the end of the week?" Sekitto said.

"No. It's urgent, Mr. Sekitto, but it won't take a lot of your time. We can chat for fifteen minutes during your lunch break."

"All right, then. See you at noon in my office tomorrow for a brief chat."

\* \* \*

"I met a man the other day who might be my father," Clement said after about two minutes of small talk with Sekitto the following day.

"Kyotera?" Sekitto said, the man's name coming readily to his lips as he shifted uncomfortably on his chair. "Where did you meet him?"

"I accompanied the father of Herbert's new son-in-law to Kalisizo. Our host treated us to a lunch, which might sound strange to you—because, honestly, it was. While we were eating, one of the old men there made me uneasy. He kept looking at me, but when our eyes met, twice, he looked away. He seemed to show a little too much interest in me and I can't help wondering why." Sekitto frowned and jotted a few words in the notebook on his table. "After we left the home where we'd had lunch, I asked the man who had hosted us about the curious old man. He told me that his name is Kyotera. I asked whether Kyotera had ever worked in Kampala but our host did not know."

"That's interesting. How old do you think that man is?"

"I don't know. Seventy-five? Eighty? It's difficult to guess."

"We can talk to him directly," Sekitto said.

"What? How?" Clement asked.

"We would just ask the man who hosted you to introduce us to Kyotera. Then we would ask Kyotera about his history. Perhaps he and I might even recognize each other."

"We could do that?"

"Yes. I have a question for you, though. Would you want to meet him, to introduce yourself, and to get to know him, if he is your father?"

"Yes, I would love to meet him if he is my father," Clement answered, aware that meeting the old man could greatly change his life.

"Did you get your host's telephone number?"

"Yes I did," Clement said, and pulled one of his cellphones out of his pocket to give the telephone number to Sekitto. "Our host's name was Zadok," he added.

"Thank you. I will contact him," Sekitto said.

* * *

The following week, when Clement and Sekitto arrived at his modest home, Kyotera was sitting on a wooden chair under a tree in the front yard. Clement parked the car in the yard, a few metres from the dirt road. "I can't tell you how nervous I am," Clement said.

"I understand," Sekitto answered. "It is a very important meeting for you."

When Clement and Sekitto exited the car, Kyotera rose and walked towards them to greet them. He, too, was nervous, wondering what the visit was about. At first, when Zadok had told him about a lawyer and a younger man from Kampala who wanted to pay him a visit, he had become excited. The following day, however, the excitement had turned to worry.

One of the two young men who lived in Kyotera's home brought two chairs and placed them under the tree where Kyotera had been seated, before going back to the outdoor kitchen where he'd been cooking lunch.

"Sirs, I am glad to see you," Kyotera said, and as he shook first Sekitto's hand and then Clement's. It was clear to Sekitto that Kyotera did not recognize him. That did not surprise him. Sekitto had been a young boy when they had last seen each other. However, he recognized Kyotera right away. His heart raced.

Kyotera then led his visitors to where he had been seated and invited them to sit down. After the greetings and some brief small talk, with Kyotera's eyes fixed inquisitively on Clement, Sekitto broached the subject of their visit. "Sir, my name is Joseph Sekitto. I am a son of the late Constantine Sekitto of Lungujja."

"Oh!" Kyotera exclaimed, and he rose to hug Sekitto. "I am sorry I did not recognize you! I remember Mr. Constantine Sekitto, and I have thought about him many times during the past several decades."

"And my companion here," Sekitto said, pointing at Clement, "is Clement Musasizi. His mother was Clotilda. She passed away a few years ago." Sekitto then paused for a few moments. He could see that Kyotera was listening attentively. "I have brought Clement to meet you because he is your son."

For about twenty seconds Kyotera looked at Clement, whose heart had skipped a beat at the mention of his late mother and was struggling with his emotions. "I am glad to meet you, Clement," Kyotera finally said and rose to hug him, before sitting back down and silently facing Sekitto.

"The lady I just mentioned, Clement's mother, Clotilda," Sekitto continued, choosing each word carefully, as if he were in court, "was your girlfriend. Unfortunately, she got you fired from your job after she conceived this young man. I am sorry to say it but she probably found you unsuitable as a partner at that time. And of course, you were still young."

Kyotera looked closely at Clement again, silent for about ten seconds. "I have been thinking about Clotilda throughout the last fifty years and I have been wondering why the hatred—why a woman I loved had turned against me all of a sudden," Kyotera said, and tears sprung into his eyes.

Clement and Sekitto watched in silence as he wept.

"But now, as I look at you, I have no doubt at all that you are my son, Clement," Kyotera continued, now sobbing, as he rose to hug Clement again.

Kyotera and Clement hugged tightly for close to a minute. "When I saw you at Zadok's home last week, I felt that there was something about you," Kyotera told his son. "I had a weird feeling of familiarity that I couldn't explain. But you resemble my late brother Segujja."

"Yes, I saw you looking at me a few times and I left wondering why and decided to ask Zadok about you," Clement answered.

"My name is Kayiga, by the way, and I am of the elephant clan. Actually, I will tell you more about me after I have known a bit more about you. I am really glad to meet you, Clement," Kyotera said, warmly shaking Clement's hand.

"Do you remember Jude Kiyaga?" Sekitto asked. "After you left, it seems that Clotilda told him she was pregnant with his child."

"No, I don't remember him," Kyotera said.

"Anyway, when the child—Clement—was born, Clotilda got Kiyaga to pay for his education, and your son is now a highly educated man. However, at some point, Kiyaga found out that the boy was not his son. But he was a gentleman, and he did not tell Clement this fact. It was I, in my capacity as the late Kiyaga's lawyer, who broke the news to Clement when Mr. Kiyaga passed away a few years ago. I also told him that you were his father—I had heard Clotilda with my own ears, plotting with another woman to get you fired from your job." While Kyotera listened attentively, Clement stared on the ground, head between his hands, obviously reliving his pain at first hearing that news. "So," Sekitto continued, "when Clement told me last week that he might have found his father, I didn't hesitate to bring him to meet you."

Kyotera shook his head, incredulous. "Mr. Sekitto, thank you for bringing my son to me. I am very glad to hear that story. It answers a lot of questions that I have had for the past fifty years. I've tried to forget it but I couldn't, unaware that there was an important detail therein."

"I am glad that I've been able to help," Sekitto answered. He asked Clement for the car keys and went to wait in the car.

"I am very glad to finally meet you, Father," Clement said.

Kyotera shook Clement's hand again, and began to tell him about himself. "After Mr. Sekitto's father fired me, two other families employed me," he said, "but after those three years I returned home to Kyotera and never set foot in Kampala again. I met a woman soon after I returned and we got married. We had one daughter, the mother of the young man who is preparing lunch in the kitchen. My wife died two years ago. However, my daughter—your sister—lives in Kampala," he said, now smiling at his son. "Clement, please tell me more about you."

"I live in the home that belonged to my mother. It is near the school that she built. I have five children, three sons and two daughters. They all live with their mothers," Clement said.

"Their mothers?" Kyotera asked.

"Yes, unfortunately—I've not led an exemplary life. Each one of the five children has a different mother. And I am single. Father, I must confess that I haven't been good in my relationships."

"What is the problem?"

"It is not easy to judge oneself, but the truth is, I have been a difficult partner in all my relationships. And I've sometimes hit my girlfriends out of jealousy."

*Oh, nobody in my family has that personality. We don't hit women.* Kyotera frowned.

"I know that as a grown man I shouldn't look for excuses, but I think that my behavioural problems are due to a lack of true love from my mother. She was never kind to me," Clement said, and he started to cry.

"I can't tell you how glad I am to meet you," Kyotera said uneasily, changing the subject.

When the lunch was ready, Kyotera and his guests ate and chatted at a small table under a tree, and after lunch he brought out an envelope that contained family photos.

Clement was glad to find this missing piece in his life, and glad to see the picture of his late uncle Segujja, whom Kyotera had mentioned. "You could think this is me in this picture," he exclaimed, showing the photo to Sekitto.

"Yes, absolutely," Sekitto answered.

While Clement and Sekitto were looking at the photos, Kyotera sent his grandson to call two of his neighbours to greet the visitors.

Clement was happy to have met his father. And when he and Sekitto left to return to Kampala that evening, the car's trunk was full of food items, including two live roosters and three hens.

\* \* \*

A month later, Clement went back to see his father and to bring him to the city. Whe they arrived in Kampala they went first to the school, and Kyotera followed Clement in silence as they walked around the buildings and grounds, trying to keep the memory of Clotilda out of his mind. Then they went to Clement's home.

Clement told his father that he wanted him to move permanently into his home, but Kyotera refused. "I am old and sickly and I don't want to become a burden to you. Let me stay in my home—you can see me there whenever you want," he answered. "But this is a large house. You live here alone?"

"I am rarely alone here. Most of the time there are members of my late mother's family who come to visit," Clement answered.

As they continued chatting, Kyotera finally found the courage to ask a question he had hesitated to ask since he'd arrived at the school. "I remember that your mother was an ordinary young woman. How was she able to accumulate all this property?"

When Clement answered, "Oh, she received a lot of help from my father, Mr. Kiyaga," Kyotera didn't ask any more questions.

An hour later, Herbert came to meet Kyotera and Clement introduced them, saying how lucky he's always been to have Herbert as a big brother. They chatted for a few minutes, then Herbert rose, went to his car and returned with a copious fast-food dinner he'd bought to share with Clement and Kyotera. Soon after they'd started eating, Anastasia and Brittany came, too, with their sons, so the boys could meet their grandfather. Brittany's son, Clement's oldest child, was fourteen and Anastasia's son, the youngest of Clement's children, was five. Herbert asked the women and their children to join them for dinner, but the women refused. Only the boys ate.

Brittany did not mention that she was interested in applying for the position of general manager at Ruth's Classic Boutique, but she complimented Herbert for having brought up Brandon so well, praising his son for mentoring her niece Zoe, a previously "troubled teenager," in music.

Herbert thanked her, noting that Brandon and Zoe's new album was so popular that if they continued collaborating, their musical career would rise to new heights. He left soon after dinner.

While Anastasia chatted with Kyotera in the living room, and the boys played in the front yard, Brittany argued with Clement in the dining room, accusing him of being an irresponsible father, and then the women and the children left.

"The older woman gave me a bad first impression," Kyotera said. *And it's rather strange that she reminded me of Clotilda.*

"Brittany? She is the most difficult and uncooperative of all. In fact, of all my children's mothers, she is the only one who makes my life difficult," Clement said.

"But the other one seems to be well-behaved," Kyotera said.

"Anastasia? Yes, she is well-behaved. In fact, even though she is many years younger than I am Anastasia was ready to marry me, but I let her down by my unwillingness to commit."

"Why don't you talk to her—and if she is still available, marry her? I am worried that you will get older and continue to live in this large home alone. It is neither good nor fun to live alone," Kyotera said.

Kyotera spent a month in Clement's home. Several times he noticed that Clement quietly snuck women into the house in the wee hours of the night, thinking that he was asleep, and then, before dawn, would drive them back to wherever they came from.

# 27

# **January 2015**

CLEMENT ARRIVED HOME tired one afternoon a few days after Kyotera had returned to Kyotera. He was opening the front door when Brittany parked her car beside his.

*How come I didn't see her along the way? Has she been hiding somewhere, waiting for me?* Clement feared Brittany. He even thought of rushing into the house and locking her out, but it was too late—within seconds she was standing in the doorway. Brittany was a big woman, about five inches taller than he was. When she wore high heels, like she was now, she was even taller.

"I need money to feed your son," Brittany yelled as soon as she and Clement walked into the living room. Clement closed the door.

"Is that the way your mother taught you to greet people?" Clement asked.

"Shut up! I need money to feed your son."

"You don't need money from me. The fact that you can afford such an expensive car—"

"Don't be silly! I want money now, to feed your son, and if you don't give it to me I will bring your son here so *you* can take care of him full time."

Clement pulled two fifty-thousand-shilling notes out of his pocket and gave them to Brittany.

"This is not enough to feed your son even for one week," Brittany said as she dropped the money in her handbag and grabbed Clement's tie as if to strangle him.

He pulled one more fifty-thousand-shilling note out of his pocket and gave it to her. "Take that, dear, and let's meet the day after tomorrow. I'll give you more money."

"Shut up. I am tired of your empty promises," Brittany said as she let go of his tie. "And don't call me dear ever again!"

"Listen to me, Brittany. Like I said, we will be hiring a general manager soon for the boutique. And I will make sure you are hired. Please give me some time to work things out."

"You are a liar," Brittany said, raising her voice. "How much longer shall I wait?"

"Sit down and calm down. Let me explain the situation to you," Clement said, touching Brittany's shoulder.

"Don't touch me ever again," Brittany yelled, and stormed out of the house.

Clement rose to close the door. He sat down to think about Brittany—he both loved and feared her, and was never sure how their encounters would go. Sometimes she was friendly, sleeping over at his house and doing chores for him. Other times she was hostile and uncompromising, like today. *What can I do to get rid of Brittany?* But he had no answer.

He went to the refrigerator and got a bottle of beer and then sat back down in the living room, still worried. He knew his financial situation was dire.

When he mentally calculated how much it was costing him to pay for his children's needs, from schooling to feeding, he had the momentary idea of hiring an old woman to help him raise them here, in his home, to save some money. But he doubted the mothers would accept that arrangement, and quickly dropped the idea.

Then he thought about the situation at the school he'd inherited from his mother. The standards were declining; more and more parents were abandoning the school, taking their children elsewhere. Adding to his worries, he needed money to pay salary arrears—just the previous week the headmaster had warned him that the teachers would soon walk off the job if they were not paid in full. Last year the auditors had advised him to stop withdrawing money from the school's accounts for personal expenses, but he was still doing it. He had used a chunk of the bank loan he'd obtained to renovate the school's oldest classroom blocks and to pay for his children's education and upkeep, and the loan's repayment period was fast approaching. That worried him too.

After his mother had died, Clement had walked away from the pharmacy that he and his business partner Jairus had operated for years. Could he return there? He doubted Jairus would let him do so.

Clement realized that he was drinking on an empty stomach. He had not eaten since dinner the previous evening. He warmed up some leftover chicken and rice and began to eat. The food didn't taste good but he ate it anyway, then started washing the dishes, feeling sorry for himself the whole time. He began to cry. *How did I end up in this situation? Where did I go wrong?*

He left the dishes half-washed in the sink and went back to the living room to drink some more. His phone rang several times but he did not answer it. Three hours later, too drunk to walk to his bedroom, he fell asleep on the sofa.

# 28

# January 2015

"I THOUGHT IT would be easy for me to work in the restaurant, but it is not. Actually, it's harder than I thought," Leah said, exhausted when she returned home one evening.

"What's going on?" Herbert asked.

"First of all, I don't want to have to wake up early anymore—I am retired but it's like I am not, and I'm busy working for a little money, which I don't need," Leah answered. "Secondly, I hate how unpredictable the work days are—sometimes we are busier during the lunch hours, other days in the evenings, but no two days are alike! After working in an office for decades, I got used to routines, but there are no routines in the restaurant business." She collapsed on the sofa next to Herbert.

"Be patient, darling. I think you will get used to it," Herbert said as he gently massaged Leah's shoulders.

"And the income varies from week to week. It is difficult to plan for the business—I don't know how Mother managed to run that restaurant for so many decades. I hate to admit it, but I am failing."

"Darling, now that you realize that you are failing, wouldn't it be better if you closed down the business altogether?" Herbert said, seizing the opportunity to speak his mind.

"Unfortunately, I think that is what I am going to do. Let's close it down," she said. "And I won't be going back there tomorrow. In fact, I don't want to work in that restaurant ever again!"

"Now, don't follow Mummy's example," Herbert said and laughed. "You have to wind up the business in a proper manner. You can go in later than usual—call the manager to let her know. And if you've decided to close down the restaurant you should respectfully inform the staff. Remember that your decision is going to affect them and their families. And after the restaurant has been closed down, we will need to contact Mr. Sekitto, to see what is expected of us as far as liquidating the business is concerned."

"Thanks for the advice, dear," Leah said and lay on Herbert's lap. "This *is* the end of Kyatelekera Restaurant ... I've made up my mind."

They continued the conversation and agreed to host a closing dinner at the restaurant, and then Leah called her daughters and asked them to come home the following evening after work. She did not tell them the reason she wanted to meet them.

❋ ❋ ❋

Babirye and Nakato went to their parents' home together and the family sat in the living room. "I have called you here this evening," Leah said to her daughters, while sobbing, "to tell you that I have finally made the difficult decision to close down Kyatelekera Restaurant."

Nakato opened her bag, pulled out a tissue and wiped her nose, and Herbert squeezed Leah's hand, but Babirye just looked up the ceiling, not feeling it should be an emotional moment. *Why did it take you so long to make that decision? You could have saved time and money.*

"Let me tell you that it hasn't been an easy decision for your mother to make," Herbert said after nearly a half a minute of silence. "But I am glad she did—working at the restaurant these past few weeks had taken away all her joy."

"Now, I would like you to help us to plan a final dinner," Leah said, "in honour of five decades of Kyatelekera Restaurant and in honour of my mother, a woman who..." She burst into tears and couldn't complete the sentence.

"Yes, we'll need your help to organize, should I say, a farewell dinner," Herbert said. "We're thinking in three weeks' time, on the

28$^{th}$, a big dinner during which we will host our friends and family as we celebrate the end of an era in our family."

"How many people are you looking at, how many sittings, and how much per person?" Nakato asked.

Both Leah and Herbert knew where the question was leading. They remained quiet for a few seconds. Herbert finally answered. "No, the dinner will be free of charge, in honour—"

"What?" Babirye and Nakato said in unison.

"You are closing down the restaurant due to poor performance and you are planning to give away food for free?" Babirye said.

"On that day alone, you can make months' worth of business!" Nakato said. "I'd actually suggest to stretch the restaurant's final closing over an entire weekend, if not an entire month—a closing month."

"Yes, that's a good idea," Herbert said, nodding in agreement.

"It would be a good idea but I don't have any more energy left to spend on that restaurant," Leah said, regaining her composure.

"Okay, let's plan just one dinner. We too will invite our friends and acquaintances," Babirye said as she typed some notes on her phone.

They agreed to host the dinner—which all guests would pay for—during the last five hours of the restaurant's business day.

❇ ❇ ❇

As the news that Kyatelekera Restaurant was closing quickly spread, that week the number of diners increased, and the manager, Hagar, noticed the bizarre occurrence with joy. "Let's hire a few more temporary employees to cope with the surge," she suggested to Leah.

"No. It doesn't make sense," Leah answered. "We can't hire people when we are closing down."

"But look," Hagar said, pointing at the people who were waiting outside for tables to become free, "there are too many customers to serve this evening."

"Hagar, I have decided to close down the restaurant and I am not ready to reverse that decision," Leah said.

❇ ❇ ❇

Early in the morning of the day of the restaurant's closing, Leah received a call from her brother, Kulumba. Merab was critically ill. Leah abandoned her to-do list and she and Herbert drove right away to go see her mother. They took her to hospital and she was admitted with high blood pressure—her heart seemed to be failing and her whole body ached. Later, Herbert went back home but Leah stayed in the hospital to care for her mother. When the twins visited them there, they reassured Leah by telling her Merab would recover.

That evening, the restaurant hosted the largest number of guests in its history. Nakato joined the kitchen staff to oversee meal service while Babirye took over as the greeter. When Herbert and Leah arrived at the restaurant, they were surprised to see their daughters in charge, with Babirye escorting guests in and out of the restaurant. "I didn't know you could do this job," Leah whispered to Babirye at the entrance. "Maybe we don't need to close down the restaurant after all."

"Mummy, are you suggesting that I should abandon the clinic and my patients to become a greeter here?" Babirye asked, laughing.

Leah laughed, and Herbert, too, as they walked over to the table where Conrad's parents were seated, and Herbert sat down.

But Leah couldn't. Instead, while the guests were enjoying their dinner, she stood in a corner in the corridor that led to the kitchen and quietly wiped away tears with a handkerchief.

"Leah, I see that you are very emotional. Why did you decide to organize a dinner at the restaurant?" her friend Phoebe Mbogo asked shortly after she had arrived. "You could have closed the restaurant without a ceremony."

"Phoebe, it was not my choice to close this restaurant, but that's a long story. Tonight I wanted to honour my mother publicly. I thought she would be here so we could recognize her and give her a deserving standing ovation. But she couldn't be here. My daughters are reassuring me that she will be well but she is very sick. I don't think she will live much longer."

"Leah, that's the painful reality of life. We should always remember that our loved ones will not be here forever. But you should be grateful for your mother's long life. You should cherish her love, and everything else she has done to make you the person you are, because that's what matters," Phoebe said and held Leah's hand.

"Thank you."

"But, even though the restaurant has been important in your life, it is a business, like any other. Once it is no longer serving its major purpose, making a profit, it is the wise thing to close it down."

While Leah was chatting with Phoebe, Brandon and his girlfriend Delilah were seated at a table near the entrance to the kitchen, watching her. "Mummy is very emotional but I don't know why, really," Brandon said.

"Of course she'd be emotional!" Delilah said. "Didn't you say that she and your father met in this restaurant?"

"I know they met in the restaurant," Brandon said, "but not in this building—this isn't the original location. It's moved a few times."

"Then maybe it's because of your grandmother's illness," Delilah said.

❆ ❆ ❆

"Do you think it was a good decision to close down this historical restaurant?" Clement asked Sam. They were seated at the table beside Brandon's.

"Certainly not, but it must have been her daughters' decision," Sam answered. "I doubt it was Leah's."

"The girls have taken over everything—I really don't know where this family is heading," Clement said.

"My friend, I think they are right to take control of everything from us because, let's be honest, Clement, our generation has wasted wealth. And I think we don't feel we fully own our fortunes because we did not build them."

"What do you mean?"

"We have mismanaged our parents' wealth. Let's consider my case, for example—since I took over control of my father's property, what do I have to show? Not much. How about you? How is your mother's school doing?"

"Oh, so you think the school's performance is declining because of me?" Clement asked seriously.

"That question is for you to answer, but you get my point," Sam said. "Nothing is working as well as before we took over from our parents."

"Seriously, Sam, do you think the school's performance is declining—"

"Clement, the school's performance *has* to decline when you hire and fire headmaster after headmaster, when—"

"You've changed the topic of our discussion, Sam," Clement said. "Do you think it was a good decision to close down this historical restaurant?"

"Can I tell you the truth, my friend? Restaurants are businesses, and this business was failing," Sam answered.

"Leah could have tried harder but I think her daughters twisted her arm and won."

"Clement, here is my advice to you. Befriend those girls. Get to know them better and—"

"No" Clement said. "They are all arrogant."

"That's what I thought but I can't praise them enough. Hellen and her friend helped me turn my life around," said Sam, who was already negotiating another contract with Enviro Assessments.

Herbert rose and interrupted the conversation. "Everyone, can I please have your attention? I would like us to make a final toast in honour of Kyatelekera Restaurant and its founder, my wonderful mother-in-law, Merab, who unfortunately, hasn't been able to be with us here tonight."

As the guests rose to toast, Leah burst into tears.

# 29

# January 2015

THE FAMILY REMAINED at the restaurant to clean up after the guests had left, and it was late before everything was in order and they all returned to their homes.

"Why are you so late?" Roland yelled at Nakato as soon as she came through the door of their home. "Where have you been?"

"Please calm down. I sent you a text message. Today—"

"Where have you been?" He was slurring his words.

"That's what I am trying to tell you. Kyatelekera Restaurant was closed for good today and a dinner was served. The entire family was—"

Roland rose and stormed out of the living room before Nakato had finished her explanation, his drink still in his hand. He went to their bedroom and slammed the door and Nakato heard the glass shattering on the floor.

She lay down on the sofa, exhausted after all the emotions and sheer physical labour of the day. *Let me stay away from him; he is very drunk tonight.* She dozed for a while before rousing herself to go the kitchen and get a broom so that she could sweep the shards of glass off the bedroom floor. Roland would be asleep.

She opened the door gently and quietly switched on the light, but as soon as she had started sweeping, Roland jumped up from the bed. "Get out of my sight now!" he yelled.

"Why are you so angry? I think you drank too much tonight," Nakato said.

"I drank too much? Did you buy me the liquor?" Roland asked, pushing her towards the door so abruptly that she stumbled and fell onto the floor, and a piece of glass cut her cheek.

"Oh, no! Are you hurt? I am very sorry," he said as he helped her off the floor. He was too drunk to stand still. He only noticed the blood dripping from Nakato's face when she turned to him, silent. "Oh, what have I done to you? I am very sorry—please forgive me!" He reached for one of his shirts to wipe the wound.

"No, don't bother. I'll take care of myself," Nakato said and went to check herself in the dressing-room mirror.

\* \* \*

"What happened to you?" Babirye whispered when she saw the bandage on Nakato's cheek the following day in Merab's hospital room.

"There was an incident at home last night," Nakato answered. "Let's talk outside."

"What kind of incident?" Babirye asked, once they were in the corridor.

"Roland was so furious that I was late coming home last night that he smashed his whisky glass on the bedroom floor. Unfortunately, when I went to clean the floor, he pushed me. I slipped and fell and the glass cut my cheek," Nakato said.

"That's not acceptable," Babirye answered. "You should have called the police."

"It is okay."

"No. It is not okay and don't even try to defend him! He has started assaulting you physically? What will he do to you next? Strangle you? You have to throw him out of the home before he does something worse."

"I have been thinking about kicking him out but I wouldn't want my son—"

"No. Throw him out! I can help you. Let him go find somewhere else to live."

"Let's give him one chance," Nakato said. "I will have a frank talk with him this evening."

"Okay—talk to him and let me know," Babirye said. "But I won't let him mistreat you any longer."

* * *

Babirye was too angry to wait until Nakato had spoken to Roland. When she returned home, she called Roland. He tried to deny the facts, but when she questioned him further, he admitted that he had pushed Nakato and she had fallen on to the floor.

"I don't have any respect left for you," Babirye told Roland.

"I am sorry," he answered.

"Saying sorry is not enough. I am not going to let you mistreat my sister any longer. Go find another place to live. If not, I will call the police."

* * *

"So, my dear wife, you are going around publicizing how bad I am to you. First, it was your grandmother who blasted me and now, your sister. What do you gain by doing that?" Roland asked after dinner that evening.

"My grandmother? What do you mean?" Nakato asked.

"Your grandmother Ruth summoned me to her home last year and when I went there, she told me that you had complained about my behaviour."

"My grandmother, my sister and my whole family should know. Roland, you are not only mistreating me, you are also keeping secrets," Nakato said, pointing a finger at Roland.

Roland's heart raced. *What does she know about?* "What do you mean?" he asked.

"Collin was playing at the office table last month and he accidentally knocked your bag over. The contents spilled—and do you know what I saw in there?" Nakato asked. "An architect's drawing of a multi-storey apartment building."

"Oh, you saw that?" Roland said, feigning laughter. "I wanted to surprise you on our upcoming anniversary by taking you to see the building. It's our building and it's now complete."

Nakato did not respond. She rose and went to the bedroom.

The fact that he owned an apartment building and that it was complete was all that Roland was confessing to. But there was more.

✳ ✳ ✳

*What should I do now that she knows about the building? Can I hide anything now? She will surely find out.* Roland had not found any answers to his questions by the time he went to bed, and he spent all night and the following day wondering what to do. Finally, after two days of worry, he woke up early with a solution. He decided to make changes, even though it would be costly for him. *I will move her out of there and rent a place for her elsewhere.*

He drove to the apartment building. When Kibalama the custodian, who was also his relative, saw him, he wondered why he had come so early. Roland greeted Kibalama and proceeded to climb the stairs.

*Oh, no. He is going to that musician girl's apartment.* Kibalama thought of stopping him but he knew he couldn't, and it was none of his business, anyway.

Roland knocked twice on a door on the third floor. There was no answer, but no problem. He had the key. He opened the door, locked it behind him and proceeded to the bedroom, where Zoe was already awake. But she was not alone.

"Who is this?" Roland yelled, pointing to the young man who lay beside Zoe on the bed, shaking.

Zoe did not answer. She stood up and looked fearlessly straight at Roland.

"Who is this?" Roland asked again.

"This is my boyfriend."

"What? How many boyfriends do you have?"

"As many as I want."

"And you are stupid enough to bring this dog into my apartment?" Roland said, pointing to the man, then pulling Zoe towards him by the hand.

"Don't touch me! I can do whatever I want—I am not your wife!" she yelled as she pointed a finger at him.

He slapped her twice, once on each cheek.

Zoe sat back on the bed and cried.

"Take whatever you want for yourself and vacate my apartment!" Roland yelled and walked out of the bedroom.

Zoe followed him to the door, still crying.

"I want you out of here by the end of the day tomorrow," Roland said, thinking that she was going to plead for mercy.

"For your information, I have somewhere else to live. This is the worst-looking of my three residences," Zoe said, slamming the door behind him.

"I want Zoe out of my apartment by the weekend," Roland said to the custodian as he rushed down the stairs in a rage. "Change the lock if she is still there by Monday."

"But do I have the authority to do that?" Kibalama asked, shaking.

"Yes, *I* am authorizing you to do it! And if she is still there by Tuesday morning, go find yourself a job somewhere else!" Roland yelled before getting into his car and speeding away.

※ ※ ※

Merab remained in the hospital for a week, and after she was discharged Leah spent three days taking care of her at her mother's home. When she felt confident that her mother was well, Leah returned home to enjoy some free time, something she had not done since the restaurant had been closed down.

However, that freedom lasted for only one week. Various people started visiting her home every day, especially members of her mother's family. Whenever her daughters called, Leah said that she had visitors.

"Mummy, you shouldn't be hosting people every day; you need some time for yourself," Babirye said one evening after Leah told her that just that day five people had visited at various times.

"That's true, but don't think I will change overnight," Leah answered. "Remember what your grandmother says: 'He who has no people, however rich he may be, is poor.' I believe that fully."

"That's all good but you need some kind of schedule for your—"

"What are you talking about? I don't invite all those people—they come uninvited! So I don't understand what you mean by having a schedule."

"Oh, dear, they come because they know that you are happy to host them, Mummy! Don't get me wrong—it is good to welcome people into your home but it shouldn't cost you all your free time. Besides, it is expensive to host people on a daily basis."

"You are right. I think I will have to make some changes," Leah said, lying on the sofa as she spoke to her daughter, exhausted.

✳ ✳ ✳

The following week, when Nakato went to see her mother at home, she found seven visitors there—two men and five women. When she returned to the clinic, she told Babirye about the visitors. "And they were still there when I left an hour ago," she said. Babirye decided to go to talk to the visitors at her parents' home after work that evening.

When she arrived, Leah was in the kitchen preparing dinner, and the visitors were all still there, in the living room watching TV. Babirye greeted them, only recognizing the two men, whose names she'd forgotten.

"Ladies, I am glad to see you," Babirye said to the five women after the greetings. "Please introduce yourselves."

Before the women answered, one man introduced one of the women as his friend. The other man introduced the remaining four women—his wife and three daughters. The first man explained that they were all members of Merab's family and that they were there to visit Leah.

"My mother is tired. She receives too many visitors these days," Babirye said, "so I kindly beg you to reduce the frequency of your visits here." All seven looked at her, stunned, but said nothing. "I am serious. My mother is tired. I am sorry to say but some of you visit this home too frequently. "Sir," she said, pointing to one of the men, "weren't you here only last week?"

"Yes, I was," the man answered, shaking his head.

Leah walked into the living room at that moment. She had over-heard the last bit of the conversation. "Babirye, what is going on?" she asked.

"I am asking your visitors to try to come here less frequently because you are tired," Babirye answered.

"Hey, don't speak for me," Leah said laughing, trying to lessen the tension. "I am not tired, Babirye," she said, turning to the visitors. "Don't be bothered by what my daughter said. I am glad to see you and you are always welcome here." She returned to the kitchen, but Babirye followed her.

"Mummy, I didn't say that you are not glad to see them. What I said was that you are tired. They can still visit but less frequently."

One of the men rose and asked his lady friend to follow him outside. "Leah, we are sorry for being a burden to you. Rest assured that we will never set foot here again," he said loudly.

"I am sorry. Please stay," Leah said as she and Babirye walked back into the living room but the man and the woman were already out of the door. The other man and the four women followed them outside.

"Babirye, do you realize what you've just done? You've sent my mother's people away, and I am sure they will tell her about the way you have treated them. And that will worsen her illness. Please go and ask them to come back inside and apologize to them," Leah said, panicking. "I can't stand the shame your behaviour will bring on me!" By now, the visitors were already in the front yard, walking towards the gate. "I blame myself—I should have introduced those people to you before you talked to them. The taller man is my cousin Lwere, my late uncle Absalom's—"

"Mummy, don't tell me who people are after they've left!"

"You've annoyed them."

"I am sorry but I think they understand," Babirye said, picking up her handbag and getting ready to leave. "The rate at which you host people these days is not healthy—it is exhausting you. You will realize what I mean and you will thank me when you regain your freedom and enjoy your retirement. I know it is hard for you to do, but whenever you get unwanted visitors call me. I will politely send them away for you."

\* \* \*

However, Leah reconciled with her mother's relatives quickly, before Merab had been told about what had happened. The following week she went to Senge, her mother's birthplace, with a big load of groceries on her pickup truck, and spent the day there, visiting homes and donating a kilogram of sugar here, a bar of soap there. By the time she returned home that evening, she had more friends than enemies. And in the next couple of weeks during trips to Senge, the pickup truck transported people to two funerals, ferried some building materials and transported gifts to an introduction ceremony, among other duties.

Leah was rarely at home during the day now, and Herbert liked it because she was happier living that way than spending the days alone at home. But her daughters did not like it. They tried to stop her but they couldn't.

"I have a few things to deliver to Senge. I will be back in time for the dinner," Leah told Babirye one weekend, when Babirye was organizing her twin sons' birthday dinner. And she showed up at the party that evening, but only just before midnight, when the children had already gone to sleep. She felt so guilty; she rose early the next morning and was at Babirye's home by 10 a.m., offering to take her grandchildren out for the day. "We will go for some ice cream and to the amusement park," she told the excited kids. Collin, Nakato's son, also tagged along, and their fun day out ended with a tour of the farm in Kalasa.

✳ ✳ ✳

Soon, Leah was even more exhausted. "This lifestyle is not sustainable," she told Nakato one afternoon at the clinic.

Nakato checked her mother's blood pressure. "It's good you've realized it yourself. Your blood pressure is a little higher than normal," Nakato said. "You had no issues before."

"Oh, I was talking mainly in terms of money. I've realized that I am spending too much."

"Do you have a budget?"

*But can I call a list I hardly stick to a budget?* "Yes I do, but even that is not helping—I go over each month."

"I have a solution for you. You should let us manage your finances for you," Nakato said, and when Leah protested she just shook her head. "Mummy, let's talk about it when you feel ready. I don't think you've got into enough trouble yet to need our help. But don't think we'll bail you out if you do get into trouble. We won't."

Leah was not used to Nakato talking to her in such a manner, but her words seemed to make more sense to her than if Babirye had said them. "What do you suggest then?" she asked her daughter, softening her voice.

"Give me your budget, including your minimum essential expenses. Then give me your ATM cards and cheque books. I will manage your money for you. You will be home more, you will rest and you will be happier."

"That sounds good in theory—"

"I promise."

＊ ＊ ＊

Leah tried to prepare a budget during the following weeks but she did not complete it. She procrastinated, and her activities did not stop. However, when Herbert became concerned about her exhaustion one evening, she told him about Nakato's plan.

"That's the sensible thing to do," Herbert said. "You will make yourself sick if you go on working like you are doing." He called Nakato and asked her to come to the house to examine her mother. Nakato said that she'd had a busy day herself and had just arrived home, hoping for a well-deserved rest, but Herbert insisted.

When Nakato examined her mother later that evening Leah noticed that she was angry, but that she didn't bring up their earlier conversation. "Please help me now to make a budget," Leah said, and she opened her bag and handed her cheque books and ATM cards to her daughter.

Nakato sat at the computer to make a budget and was done at the end of the hour.

"But now that you have my cheque books and ATM cards, I am afraid I will be like a child, begging you to allow me access to my own money. Is there any other way—"

"No, no, my intention is not to grant you or deny you access to your money. My having your cheque books and ATM cards will only serve as an extra step in protecting your money. Let's say you've used up your budget for a particular month, you will think 'Do I really need to make this purchase?' or 'Should I give away this amount?' before you ask me to give you more money. In many cases, you will find that the answer will be no."

"Oh, I see. That's a clever idea," Leah said.

"And, Mummy, I am going to give your cheque books and ATM cards to Babirye."

"No, please don't. It will be difficult for me to get money from Babirye."

"But having her managing your money is a good thing *because* she is strict, and all she will be doing is to help protect your money. It will still be yours."

Leah accepted grudgingly, and the next day Nakato handed her cheque books and ATM cards over to Babirye.

# 30

# **March 2015**

LEAH'S COUSIN LWERE hadn't visited her home since the evening Babirye had sent him and the other visitors away. However, he needed money to start a business, and Leah was the only hope he had to get the initial capital. One evening he gathered the courage to go there.

Shortly after he arrived, Lwere told Leah he needed 500,000 shillings to start a business selling firewood. "I don't have the money now but come back on Sunday afternoon. I will see what I can do for you," Leah answered. She did not tell Lwere that her daughters now managed her money.

When Lwere left, she called Babirye and told her about his request. "Where does he intend to start the business?" Babirye asked.

"I don't know. I didn't ask him the details. Do you think we can help him?" Leah asked.

"Yes, I can give him my own money," Babirye said, pausing to think. "Yes, we will help him, but only this one time. Call me when he returns and I will give him the money myself. Alternatively, I will join you for lunch so that when he comes, he will meet me there," Babirye said.

Leah was happy with the arrangement.

❋ ❋ ❋

On Sunday afternoon, when Lwere went to Leah's, he was disappointed to see Babirye sitting in the living room chatting with her mother. *So Leah decided to call her daughter to send me away again instead of helping to fund my business?* So he was surprised, when as soon as he sat down, Babirye knelt and greeted him warmly, even for a moment doubting her sincerity. *How can she, a distinguished doctor, kneel down to greet me, a poor peasant? But she is probably sincere. After all, I am her uncle.*

Leah introduced them before Babirye walked out of the living room to her old childhood bedroom, leaving her mother and her cousin to chat.

"I have returned, hoping that you can help me like you promised," Lwere finally got to the point after half an hour, as he sipped tea and dug into the loaf of bread that had been placed on the coffee table in front of him.

"Yes, we will help you," Leah said and rose to get Babirye, who came back into the living room and sat down, asking Lwere about his business. He told them he was planning to sell firewood to traders, who bought plenty of it wholesale in Senge to supply to retail businesses elsewhere in the country.

"That sounds like a good business," Babirye said. "You have a ready market."

"Yes, it is a good business—in fact, the buyers are already lining up. One of my friends has been in this business for the last two years and he tells me that he cannot satisfy the demand," Lwere answered. "What I lack is the initial capital. I need 500,000 shillings for a great start."

"Good," Babirye said, and opened her handbag, pulling out a bundle of new notes held together by a rubber band. Lwere could see right away that it was a million shillings and got excited just thinking that Babirye was going to count off 500,000 shillings and hand it over to him. But he was astonished when Babirye rose, walked across the large room and handed the whole bundle of notes to him before she went and sat back down.

"Oh! Is the whole amount for me? Thank you very much! Thanks again!" He put down his cup of tea and with both hands raised the bundle of notes in the air. He was shaking.

"If I were you, I would invest only half the money in the firewood business, to gauge its performance, and only invest the rest after I was sure the business was viable. And I am sure that's what you will do. We are helping you this one time only. You should handle that money well," Babirye said, rose and went back to her bedroom.

Lwere quickly counted the money. Leah watched him in silence. "Leah, how do I begin to thank you and your daughter?" Lwere said, still shaking.

"It's a donation from Babirye, not me. She gave you her own money," Leah said.

*I will never judge people again before I get to know them well.* "What? It's like I am in a dream. Me? Holding a million shillings in my two hands? I have never handled a million shillings, let alone owning so much money. I have never had a million shillings in my life and never thought I ever would."

"Leave now and go get to work," Leah said, smiling. She was now getting used to not having visitors all the time at home and wanted to resume her Sunday afternoon downtime.

When Lwere left, Leah called Babirye out of the bedroom. "Lwere is very happy. The million shillings left him almost speechless."

"I suggest you follow up with him and advise him to invest it wisely. As you heard me telling him, we won't give him more money," Babirye said.

"He is a grown man and I guess he knows that he should handle his money well."

"We'll see."

❊ ❊ ❊

On a phone call the following week, Nakato and Babirye told Hellen about their initial success in controlling their mother's money. They also said that the family was now peaceful.

"Congratulations. Let's celebrate that," Hellen said. "What a year it's been for us. Now we can finally relax."

# 31

# March 2015

HERBERT HAD SUCCEEDED in rebuilding his relationship with his wife. He decided that his next task, like his mother had suggested, would be to improve his relationship with Brandon, and he planned to start by sitting down with his son for a long meaningful conversation.

When Herbert called Brandon one Saturday at Ruth's, asking to see him that evening and his son said he already had plans to go out with his girlfriend, it was the kind of answer that Herbert usually gave up on. But this time he didn't—he told Brandon that he had been thinking a lot about him lately and that he would really like to talk to him, and that afternoon would be fine.

His father's statement pleased Brandon. As far as he could remember Herbert had always criticized him, sometimes comparing his intellectual abilities to his sisters'. But now the tone of his father's voice suggested that they would have a friendly conversation. He postponed his date with Delilah to the following day.

Herbert walked to his mother's home with several bottles of beer in a bag. He and Brandon sat in the dining room. Brandon was surprised and pleased when his father opened a bottle of Club Pilsener without asking what kind of beer he preferred. Since he had become a musician, one-on-one interactions with his father were rare. And he'd often heard Herbert say that he'd disappointed him by not choosing a normal career. Now they chatted briefly at the dining table, and then Herbert asked Brandon to follow him to the backyard, where they began a friendly conversation that left Brandon wondering what had happened to his perpetually critical father.

Herbert asked about Brandon's next musical project, and about his aspirations beyond music. Brandon said that he wanted to start a business. When Herbert asked what kind of business he wanted to start, Brandon was embarrassed, saying that he did not know for sure.

"It's okay to not be sure of what one wants to do," Herbert said. "Keep trying and experimenting with various businesses on a small scale until you find what works for you."

Ruth watched them through the window. *I love the new Herbert. His marital problems seem to have woken him up from his slumber.*

Herbert and Brandon talked for hours. "Your grandmother tells me that you and your girlfriend are preparing to get married," Herbert said finally, when Ruth called them in for dinner.

"Yes, we are planning to get married in a few months' time," Brandon answered.

"How are the arrangements going?"

"We have not yet begun preparations."

"Oh, are you waiting to organize a wedding that's befitting of a superstar?" Herbert asked, laughing.

Brandon laughed too. "Not really," he answered.

"You will let me know when you are ready. I will help you in whatever way I can," Herbert said, patting Brandon on the back.

By the time they parted that evening, both Herbert and Brandon were happy about the conversation they'd had.

＊ ＊ ＊

Brandon called his sisters the following week. "Please come home at 6 p.m. on Saturday," he told them. "I've got some exciting news to share concerning Delilah and me."

Babirye and Nakato spent Saturday looking forward to Brandon's news and made sure that they and their children arrived at Ruth's home by six o'clock. When they got there, Brandon and Delilah had already prepared dinner. As usual whenever her great-grandchildren visited, Ruth gave them a few "rules for the evening," then let them watch TV and play in her library. The twins chatted with Ruth while Brandon and Delilah set the table.

When the table was ready, Brandon asked everyone to sit down. "Let me share the news before we have dinner," he said, touching Delilah's shoulder. "There are two pieces of news. One, Delilah is two months pregnant—"

"Hey, congratulations!" Babirye and Nakato said in unison, jumping up to hug Delilah.

"What's the second piece of news?" Nakato asked before they sat back down.

"Delilah and I have set a date for our wedding. We will marry in three months' time."

Babirye and Nakato cheered and hugged Delilah again. Ruth sat there just smiling, without making any comments. It was obvious that she'd already heard the news.

After dinner, Brandon and his sisters remained at the dining table to chat. He asked them for advice about how to proceed with the introduction and wedding ceremonies. Nakato said that the first step would be to write a letter to Delilah's father to request his permission to marry his daughter.

"A letter?" Brandon asked. "What do I say in the letter?"

"Bring a sheet of paper," Nakato said. "I will draft the letter for you."

While Nakato was writing the letter, Babirye, Delilah and Brandon discussed some details concerning the wedding. When the letter was ready, Brandon thanked Nakato and said he would type it out before sending it.

"No. Don't type the letter," Ruth said from the living room, where she was telling stories to her great-grandsons. "Get a neat sheet of paper and rewrite the letter by hand. Actually, I suggest you add your own words to your sister's draft, sign the letter and then send it."

Brandon laughed. He folded the letter and put it in his shirt pocket.

Ruth knew what he was planning to do—he'd simply sign the letter, put it in an envelope and send it. She rose and went to the library, her great-grandsons following behind her. She returned a few minutes later with two sheets of paper, an envelope and a pen. "Brandon, I want you to sit down and write that letter now. Please write neatly."

Brandon rewrote the letter and gave it to Delilah to deliver to her aunt Dorcas the following day. He and his sisters agreed to meet again the following week to discuss further plans, for the introduction ceremony and the wedding.

✳ ✳ ✳

Four days later, a letter from Delilah's father was delivered to Herbert's office. Herbert gave it to Brandon that evening. Delilah was not home.

Brandon eagerly opened the letter. In the first paragraph, he was happy to note that his future father-in-law had given him permission to marry his daughter. However, further down, Brandon didn't like what he read. The letter enumerated the things that Delilah's family required him to donate to them before the wedding. Brandon shook his head in disbelief and placed it on the dining table.

Herbert was in the living room chatting with Ruth. He noticed that Brandon seemed to be less enthusiastic. "Is everything okay?" he asked. Brandon did not answer. He walked to his father and handed him the letter. "This is good news," Herbert said, reading the first paragraph. "The problem with you young people these days is that you don't understand written Luganda."

"Read the entire letter, Daddy," Brandon said.

"What?" Herbert said after he had read the entire letter. He then placed it on the sofa beside him in distaste. "What's this about? Are they selling their daughter?" He picked up the letter again and handed it to Ruth, pointing at a passage. "Have a look at this, Mummy."

Ruth put on her reading glasses and read the list of demands. Among other things, Delilah's family wanted Brandon to give them a plot of land. "Are these people joking?" She laughed.

"No, they are serious," Brandon answered.

*Mummy has been accusing me of not taking any interest in my son's affairs. Let me step up now.* "Where does this gentleman live?" Herbert asked when Ruth handed the letter back to him.

"He lives in Janda, about forty-five minutes from here," Brandon answered.

"What does he do?"

"I am not sure. I think he is a farmer of some sort."

Ruth laughed at Brandon's answer.

"Okay, I'll think about this and I will let you know what to do," Herbert said.

Brandon went to his bedroom, not knowing what his father intended to do to follow up.

Herbert, meanwhile, folded the letter, put it in his shirt's pocket and resumed the conversation with his mother.

* * *

Herbert arrived at Delilah's parents' home shortly after lunch the following day. He was surprised when Delilah's father Bukko welcomed him warmly and ushered him into his house without asking who he was.

After the greetings, Bukko told Herbert how he knew him, telling him that one of his neighbours was a cleaner in the Ministry of Finance, where Herbert worked.

When he found out that Bukko knew him, Herbert momentarily thought of changing his plans for the visit. *No—it's too late now.* "Sir, we received your letter granting permission to my son to marry your daughter. Thank you very much for that," he said after he had declined Bukko's offer of a cup of tea.

"Yes, I am very glad that my daughter is marrying into the family of the late Dawson Kiyaga," Bukko answered.

Herbert was pleased to learn that Bukko also knew his late grandfather. "Thank you for honouring my family," he said and paused for a few seconds. "There is a problem, though. Your list of demands is excessive. Remember, these are young people who are just starting out in life."

"I am sorry that you feel that way. However, there is nothing extraordinary in—"

"Sir, my son has other things to take care of. Besides, do you think it's fair for you to demand things worth millions of shillings from your future son-in-law? Be reasonable."

"I understand your concern. However, we were told that some people ask for these things in the city these days," Bukko answered.

"Some people might be doing so but it's inappropriate. Do you want to make money off your daughter? Are you selling her off?"

"No, certainly not," Bukko answered angrily, raising his voice. "Sir, you may be rich but I beg you to not insult me in my own home."

"My intention is not to insult you. I came to talk to you respectfully and I think that's what I have done up to this point," Herbert said, unfolding his arms to appear more friendly.

The negotiations continued for about ten minutes with Bukko raising his voice at times. Herbert remained calm. "Our list is not written in stone. It can be amended," Bukko said, finally softening.

"Then I beg you to revise your demands," Herbert said.

Bukko agreed to drop the plot of land from his list of demands. Herbert then requested him to rewrite the letter.

"That would be all right. Unfortunately, I don't remember all the contents of the first letter," Bukko said, not mentioning his problem. He could not write.

Herbert opened his bag and handed the letter to Bukko.

Bukko thanked him and went to see his neighbour Sengonzi, who had written the first letter. Sengonzi came, greeted Herbert and rewrote the letter in the dining room while Herbert and Bukko continued chatting in the living room. Fifteen minutes later, Herbert shook hands with both Bukko and Sengonzi and before he drove away with the new letter gave a fifty-thousand-shilling note to each of them.

❊ ❊ ❊

"I don't know about you but with the problems that have been going on in the family, I couldn't make any progress on the biography," Babirye said on a phone call with Hellen.

"You are not alone. I don't even think I know where my notebook is," Nakato said.

"You know what? I have actually made progress and I am almost done writing," Hellen said. "Nakato, do you handwrite your work?"

"Yes. I write by hand, type out everything on the computer, and then I edit. It's easier that way."

"I think we should resume writing. Shall we extend the deadline for the first draft so we catch up?" Babirye asked.

"Let's extend the deadline and double our efforts. I also suggest we share our work on a weekly basis," Hellen said, although she was not sure how she would do it in the last term of her pregnancy. "We can e-mail our week's work to each other every Sunday afternoon. That will keep us accountable."

The sisters resumed writing the biography with renewed enthusiasm. Hellen was the first to submit her final manuscript.

❋ ❋ ❋

Early one morning, a week later, as soon as Hellen felt the first labour pains, she asked Conrad to call Gwen—she'd agreed to drive them to the hospital. Their daughter Mary, named after Conrad's mother, was born six hours later, an alert healthy child weighing seven pounds and six ounces. Conrad was overjoyed. He stopped his job search and decided to stay at home to take care of his daughter.

# 32

# March - May 2015

DELILAH, BRANDON AND his sisters met in Babirye's home to discuss his introduction ceremony. When Nakato suggested that they should send money to renovate Delilah's parents' house before the ceremony, Delilah was pleased—she knew the house badly needed renovating. But when her future sister-in-law didn't ask her why she thought so, Nakato was relieved. She didn't want to inform the group that she'd found directions to Delilah's parents' neighbourhood without Brandon or Delilah's knowledge and had driven there to discreetly see the home's condition. A renovated house would impress Brandon's companions.

Babirye suggested that no more than fifty people accompany Brandon to the introduction ceremony. Brandon disagreed, saying that as a musician he had many friends. He wanted one hundred and fifty, triple that number, and after a few minutes of arguing, they compromised on one hundred and twenty. When Delilah called her father to report the number, Bukko said that he was agreeable to it, as long as the Kiyagas paid for "their people."

In the next meeting Brandon and his sisters put money together to pay for the food and gave it to Delilah, as well as the money to rent tents and chairs, to pay for decorations, and to renovate the exterior of her parents' home.

❋ ❋ ❋

Bukko's renovated house, the huge tents, the decorations and the fact that Brandon was a popular musician all created an atmosphere of glamour and a colourful ceremony. Many curious children and young people stood by the side of the road to watch Brandon and his entourage making a grand entry into the village.

Brandon, his sisters and three of his friends were served lunch inside the house. The rest of his entourage was served their lunch in the tent.

When it was time to hand Brandon's presents to Delilah's family, his spokesman, Sengo, asked the people who were standing in the front yard near the tents to move away. "We bought every expensive item there was on the market. Can you please let the truck carrying the goodies back up here so we don't have to fetch them by hand, and to save time?" he asked proudly.

"Yes, you are free to do so," said Delilah's family's spokesman, Sengozi. The truck backed up into the front yard and several young men, members of Delilah's extended family, offloaded the items as Sengo named them one by one and handed them to Sengozi.

"Please have a seat and enjoy the European upholstery. This is the latest make," Sengo said to Sengozi when a brand-new sofa set was placed in front of him.

Sengozi sat on the sofa and thanked Brandon through Sengo. Brandon smiled and nodded.

"I tell you, we left the shops in Kampala empty. You won't need to buy anything for the rest of the year. I suggest you let the young men continue offloading the truck as we proceed with the rest of the ceremony," Sengo said and sat down.

The audience laughed and clapped as they admired the hundreds of neatly gift-wrapped packages.

"Please stand up," Sengozi said to Sengo once the clapping stopped. Sengo rose. "Drink some water before I ask you one tough question." Sengo opened a bottle of mineral water, sipped some water and faced Sengozi, ready for the question. "Before you came here today, the man you are representing was a stranger to our family, wasn't he?" Sengozi said.

"Yes he was," Sengo answered.

Brandon shifted on the sofa on which he was seated between his identical twin sisters, wondering where Sengozi was going with the conversation.

"A stranger who stole things from us," Sengozi added and looked sternly at Sengo. Sengo looked puzzled. "Do you admit that your friend stole things from us?" When Sengo remained silent Sengozi realized that the man did not know what he was talking about. "You were probably not told about it, so take a moment, consult your friend and get ready to pay a fine," he said and sat down.

Sengo turned around, still puzzled. Babirye discreetly signaled him to move close to her. In a whisper, she told him that Delilah was pregnant. She opened her bag, discreetly took out four fifty-thousand-shilling notes and handed them to Sengo. Sengo searched for an envelope in his jacket pocket, slid the money into it and returned to face Sengozi.

Sengozi stood up. "So, you do admit that your friend stole something from us and you are ready to pay a fine," he said, a smirk on his face.

"Yes, sir," Sengo said and handed the envelope to Sengozi.

"All is well now. Please sit down," Sengozi said, and nodded in the direction of the DJ, who began to play an instrumental version of Brandon and Zoe's hit, *Muddabirize*.

Brandon and Zoe rose to sing. The crowd cheered and clapped as Delilah, her aunt Dorcas and Brandon's sisters danced in a circle around Brandon and Zoe.

✳ ✳ ✳

Hellen, Conrad and their baby arrived in Kampala a month later, at the beginning of the week of Brandon's wedding, and when they went for dinner at Hellen's parents' home, baby Mary was overwhelmed by the number of people who took turns to hold her. By the time the thirtieth person tried, she was fed up and just held tightly on to her father's shirt, the nipple of her bottle firmly in her mouth.

After dinner, the family argued over whether Merab should attend the wedding—she was now almost always sick. Nakato and Herbert were the most opposed, saying that Merab should stay at home to rest, while Leah, Hellen and Babirye most wanted her to attend. "Grandma can still sit, talk, and eat. I don't see why we should exclude her from such an important gathering," Hellen said.

"Let her rest," Herbert said. "She can watch the video of the wedding afterwards, in the comfort of her home."

"Dad, I don't mind that we spent thousands of dollars to travel here for the wedding, but if Grandma is staying home I would rather go there, to keep her company," Hellen said.

"You win," Herbert said. "We will have her attend."

❋ ❋ ❋

Two days before the wedding, Brandon sat in the living room after lunch, waiting for Zoe. They were going to do one final rehearsal of the songs they'd selected to sing during the wedding reception. But after an hour she still hadn't turned up. He called her several times, and texted her, but she did not answer. He was getting concerned.

He called one of her friends, who said that she had seen Zoe that morning and she'd been all right. "She must have gotten busy with something," she added.

That evening, while he was preparing to go out for his bachelor's party, Brandon told Ruth that he'd like her to speak at the wedding reception, now only two days away.

"I will be honoured to speak at your wedding, Brandon, but you should have given me more time to prepare my speech," Ruth answered.

"You don't need to prepare, Grandma. You have a way with words."

Ruth laughed. "But there are things I can't say to you in public. If you have time, I can tell you those things now so you understand that men need to be prepared too before they get married."

"Oh, I have time," Brandon said and sat on the sofa.

"Brandon, you might find this a waste of time, thinking 'Oh, what's this old woman going to tell me?' But I have to talk to you because since you've spent a few years of your life living under my roof, I will be judged for some of your actions, whether we want that or not."

"Grandma, I am happy to listen to you. It's not a waste of time," Brandon said.

"You are a good man and I have been observing your relationship with Delilah. You will make a good husband."

"Thanks for the confidence, Grandma."

"And you are lucky because you are wealthy, unlike millions of other young men who are beginning their marriages. In addition to your own money, everything that I own—well, almost everything—will be yours the moment I check out…"

Brandon laughed out loud. Although the conversation was in Luganda, Ruth had said part of the sentence in English, including "check out."

"… And so you will not know the challenges of struggling to make ends meet while raising a family. Unless you squander that wealth." Brandon nodded. "Oh, there is something else," Ruth continued. "I have observed you for a few years. You are prone to cheating." She paused.

Brandon was shocked. "Why do you say so, Grandma?"

"When you became famous you enjoyed the company of other young women, ignoring Delilah for some time. Is that true?"

"Yes, it is true," Brandon said, avoiding Ruth's gaze.

"And sometimes even now you go out alone and return late, sometimes drunk. You may not know that I see you but I actually do." Brandon did not respond. "Now tell me truth. Do you cheat on Delilah?"

"No, I don't," Brandon said, looking at Ruth without blinking.

"I won't tell her whatever you will tell me but I want to know the truth. I am suspicious. Do you cheat on Delilah?" Ruth said, realizing that Brandon was trying to hide something.

"I used to but I stopped when she agreed to marry me."

"Oh, that's very recent! You've got to ensure that you honour your commitment to yourself—and above all, your commitment to Delilah." Brandon's cellphone rang but he ignored it. "Answer your phone call," Ruth said.

"I can't, Grandma. We are still talking."

"Answer it. I have told you the most important things I wanted to tell you. And I hope you will take them to heart," Ruth said.

"Yes I will," Brandon said, and answered the call. It was his best man, Will, telling him he'd sent a car to take Brandon to his bachelor's party.

Brandon waited for twenty minutes, still thinking about Zoe and wondering why she had abandoned him at the last minute. And when she didn't show up at the party, Brandon talked to Will about her.

"I know it's upsetting that she hasn't called to say why she can't join you, but try to forget her and enjoy this once-in-a-lifetime party," Will said.

"I can't forget her—she and I are supposed to sing at the reception."

"Oh—then you should prepare to sing alone. Zoe can join you if she decides to show up at the last minute," Will said.

"But I can't sing the duet alone!"

"I know that. Choose another song or don't sing at all. Come on now, let's enjoy the party," Will said as he grabbed Brandon's hand and led him to the dance floor.

✳ ✳ ✳

The speeches started in the middle of the reception dinner, and Ruth was the first to speak. She was still praising her grandson when Brandon saw Brittany and her son walk into the hall. He whispered to Will, asking him if he could find a way of getting a message to Brittany, to ask her where her niece Zoe was.

"Forget Zoe, man. Pay attention to the speeches," Will whispered back.

Brandon listened to Will's advice. After the speeches, he and Delilah cut the cake, and then he sang one song, solo. The guests cheered and applauded him, and Delilah shed a few tears of joy. Will congratulated Brandon, reassuring him that he'd done well, even without Zoe. Then Brandon and Delilah went out of the hall to change, returning twenty-five minutes later to open the dance.

While Mary sat peacefully on her father's lap, eyeing her great-grandmother Merab who was next to them, dozing in her wheelchair,

Hellen and her sisters joined Brandon and Delilah on the dance floor. A half an hour later, as the dancing continued, Hellen came to feed Mary so Conrad could dance, too. The baby tried to cling to her father as he got up to join the dancers and Hellen took her.

"She seems to be looking around for her daddy," Babirye said a few minutes later as Mary sucked on her bottle.

"Yeah, she spends most of the time with him and they've become kind of inseparable," Hellen said and laughed. "Conrad is so devoted to caring for his daughter that I actually wonder whether he will still know how to do his job when he returns to work."

✻ ✻ ✻

After his wedding, Brandon called Zoe again, trying to find out why she had abandoned him, but she didn't pick up and she didn't call him back. When one of their friends had a small congratulatory party that Zoe usually wouldn't have missed, she didn't come. Brandon decided to go to her apartment to ask her what was wrong.

It was Brandon's first time visiting Zoe's new apartment, and he was surprised by how expensively furnished and decorated it was. Two young women were already there when he arrived, playing cards and drinking with Zoe. Brandon joined their conversation, but he noticed that Zoe did not want to talk to him. After a while, he commented on the change in her attitude towards him.

"You are now married; you no longer fit in the singles' club," Zoe said.

Her friends laughed.

"Zoe, can I talk to you outside?" Brandon said, getting up and walking out. Zoe followed him down the two flights of stairs silently.

"Brandon, I guess my actions are not loud enough for you," she said when they were outside the building. "I don't want to see you again. I don't want your friendship anymore."

"Why? What's wrong?" Brandon asked. "Zoe, you are one of my closest friends. Surely, something must have happened that made you behave like this. Can you tell me what it is?"

"I said I don't want your friendship anymore. Isn't that clear? I simply don't want to be your friend anymore. A friendship can start and a friendship can end," Zoe said and turned to leave. "You can't force me to be your friend."

"Okay," Brandon said, shaken. "That's true, but you have to repay all the money you owe me."

"How much money do I owe?" Zoe asked, angry.

"Twelve million shillings."

"Brandon, if you rub me the wrong way, I will ruin you."

"Don't threaten me. Repay my money and I'll leave you alone," Brandon said, trying to remain calm.

"Come for your money next week," Zoe said, turning and walking back up the stairs.

Brandon left, still wondering why Zoe had changed suddenly. He also wondered how she had been able to acquire such a beautiful apartment in such a short time. He knew that she was becoming more popular as a singer, but was sure that she had not made that much money yet by performing.

The following week she called him and told him to come get his money. Delilah accompanied him, but when they arrived at her apartment, Zoe did not greet them. She handed Brandon the 12,000,000 shillings in cash at the door and closed it without a word.

✻ ✻ ✻

For a few months, Clement had thought over Kyotera's advice to ask Anastasia to marry him. He did not want to give up the freedom he enjoyed, returning home however late he wanted and with whomever he pleased, but after a while he started to feel that his new-found father's advice was sensible. If he married Anastasia they could start a family together. She was still young and could produce a few more children, and she could also raise his other children in his home so that he'd no longer need to give money to their mothers. That thought pleased him the most because it would mean that he would no longer have to put up with their demands, especially Brittany's. So when Anastasia went to Clement's office at the school one afternoon to ask for money for her son, he asked her to marry him.

Anastasia could not believe it. She called Brittany as soon as she had walked out of Clement's office and was in her car. "Something unexpected has just happened. Clement wants me to marry him."

"That's good," Brittany said. "If you are free, let's meet at Nakivubo Lane Café at 3 p.m. to discuss it."

Anastasia agreed to meet Brittany. But after a while, considering Brittany's unfriendly relationship with Clement, she wondered whether Brittany had been the best person to tell about Clement's proposal.

※ ※ ※

When they met that afternoon at the café, Anastasia said that she could not marry Clement even though she loved him. "I am already committed to another man," she said.

"Marry him and we will milk him dry," Brittany said. "What exactly did Clement say to you?"

"He asked me to marry him, as I told you. At first I thought he was joking and I told him so. But he said he was serious. That put me in a dilemma. I love Clement and it would be good for Arnie to live with both his parents but I am already committed to Dominic and I have already agreed to marry him."

"Don't be a coward. Let's teach Clement a lesson," Brittany said, and laughed. "Let's take him through the whole range of pre-wedding ceremonies and then you will dump him at the end."

"How do you suggest we do that?" Anastasia said, suddenly feeling vengeful and warming up to the idea of teaching Clement a lesson. He had sometimes been cruel to her in the past.

"We'll introduce him to a fake aunt, let him prepare an introduction ceremony, let him buy expensive presents—remember, he likes to show off—and take him through the entire process, then dump him before the wedding. Actually, if you are courageous—and I know you can be when you want to—you can let him wait at the altar and not show up."

"What?"

"Yes, let's do it. And I would take him through worse things if he asked *me* to marry him," Brittany said. "But of course we know that he can't ask me to marry him."

"But I can't take him to meet my parents. I have already taken Dominic to meet them."

"No, you are not going to take him to meet your parents. They know how much he has mistreated you. So you will tell him that they don't want to meet him. We will instead host him in a home far from the city. I can even organize some media coverage—and of course his school's reputation will continue to slip after the scandal."

"But what if Dominic hears about it? Won't he dump *me*?"

"If Dominic dumps you, you can then marry Clement for real if you want."

❋ ❋ ❋

Three days later, Anastasia went to see Clement, and told him she had decided to accept his proposal. Clement was so happy that he asked her to bring her son to his home, and they spent the day together there.

While Anastasia prepared lunch, she and Clement chatted in the kitchen. The conversation went well, unlike in the past when he'd yelled at her whenever she asked him questions or said anything that displeased him. Now she noticed that he was more patient and thoughtful.

So should she call off the wedding to her fiancé Dominic and marry Clement instead? Maybe Clement was getting wiser as he grew older. On the one hand, there were some good things about Dominic. He was only two years older than her and he was both respectful and kind to her. On the other hand, he had no job. Clement was much older but he was already established, and now his behaviour seemed to have improved. When she and her son went back to the home she shared with Dominic that evening, Anastasia was still in a dilemma.

But Clement was glad that he had finally decided to marry Anastasia and start a family with her. When she and her son left, he called Herbert to give him the news. "I am finally going to settle down. Anastasia is a good girl and I think she will help me to organize my finances, which are currently in a mess," Clement said.

"That's a good thing, brother. I am happy for you and proud of you. You need to organize your life. Remember that you are getting older and you need someone to share your life and love with," Herbert said.

✳ ✳ ✳

One month later, Clement and his entourage of fifty people, including Herbert, Leah, Kate and her husband Ham, visited the home of Anastasia's "older brother." The introduction ceremony was colourful and Clement donated so many presents during the ceremony that Anastasia felt guilty about the ruse. It was only later at night when she couldn't fall asleep that she contemplated the magnitude of what Brittany had gotten her into. *The whole thing is stupid and my son will grow up and hear about how I duped his father. Besides, what is there for us to gain when our children's father's school and reputation collapse?* She was feeling angry with Brittany and hoped that neither Clement nor Dominic would somehow find out what she had done.

✳ ✳ ✳

Two weeks after the fake introduction ceremony, while walking to the bank on her lunch hour, Anastasia met Gilda, who used to work at J & C Pharmacy, where Clement was a director. Gilda said that she had heard that Anastasia was finally going to marry Clement, her son's father.

"Yes, I am, and he has already started making preparations for the wedding," Anastasia replied, her heart racing, regretting again what a mess Brittany had put her into. Not wanting to discuss Clement any further, she pretended to be in a hurry, but Gilda kept chatting.

"Anastasia, are you really ready to marry Clement?" she asked.

"I am not sure, but I said yes to him," Anastasia said. "And now that he has given many presents to my family I don't think I can change my mind."

"Oh, yes. You *can* still change your mind. Why proceed to marry him when deep down you still have doubts?"

"It's true…. I still have doubts and it is an uncomfortable situation to be in," Anastasia said. "Furthermore, Clement is so old that—"

"No. His age shouldn't be an issue. He is only fifty-one, isn't he?"

"Yes, he is fifty-one but I am thirty-two. He is very old."

"To me, the issue is not how old he is. The issue is his behaviour. How sure are you that he will never hit you again? Or that he will never try to strangle you again?"

"I am not sure. Actually, I fear him. He used to have a very short temper but he seems to have changed—and he is now older."

"If I were you," Gilda said, "I would ask him to call off the wedding now, before it is too late. Call or text him and tell him that you have changed your mind."

"Thanks for the advice," Anastasia said when they parted. She couldn't help wondering whether Gilda herself was interested in Clement and was trying to persuade her to dump him so *she* could get him. But Anastasia did not care. She had already made up her mind.

❄ ❄ ❄

Gilda went to visit Brittany that evening and told her that Clement was preparing to get married to Anastasia. "I've heard about that but it's not true. Anastasia is getting married to another man," she said—and she had proof, she said, showing her invitation card to Gilda. Gilda took note of the details of the wedding venues.

❄ ❄ ❄

Anastasia looked beautiful in her wedding gown, and smiled and waved to friends and family as her father Desmond walked her down the aisle two weeks later. As they approached the altar, Dominic turned to look at his bride. He smiled. Anastasia smiled back.

The wedding photographers took photos, including one that Brittany had hired for the occasion. Two hours later, while the bridal party was out taking some pictures in a park, several freelance photographers stood outside the reception hall, selling the bridal couple's pictures they had taken at the church to the incoming guests. Gilda, who hadn't been invited, bought herself five photographs and walked quickly away.

Meanwhile, Clement was at home waiting for Anastasia to come over so they could discuss their wedding arrangements. He had called her several times that afternoon but she hadn't picked up. Maybe her cellphone was off. He got up several times to pace around the living room as he glanced at the clock on the wall. Anastasia was already an hour and a half late, and hadn't called to tell him why she was late, either. That was unusual. She'd always kept time.

There was still no sign of Anastasia by nightfall. Clement thought of calling Brittany to ask about Anastasia but knew the two friends were no longer talking, or so he thought. He called Zoe but her cellphone was off, too. *Anastasia will call if she thinks I am worth her time*, he thought, furious, and went to bed.

The following evening, Gilda went to visit Clement at home. After dinner, they sat in the living room to drink. Only when they were getting ready to go to bed did Clement tell her that this was going to be her last visit. He was getting married soon to Anastasia.

"I don't think so," Gilda said, smiling as she reached for her bag and took out the photos of Anastasia and Dominic's wedding. "You might want to reconsider after you've seen these."

❋ ❋ ❋

After checking to make sure that she, Babirye and Hellen had all written as many pages as they'd committed to, Nakato combined all three sub-sections of their grandmothers' biography into one manuscript and decided to read the book through before handing it to the editor. For the next three weeks she woke up an hour and a half earlier than usual and went to bed one hour later, reviewing the book and rewriting some of the sections.

When she noticed that there weren't sufficient details about Ruth's career she called Hellen. "I think you omitted a lot of details in Grandma's business life, but I think those are the things that the readers will be most interested in," she told her sister. "Can you rewrite your section to add some details? There is a lot of information you can use in the recordings."

Hellen laughed. "Nakato, those recordings are boring—I can't listen to them again! And, you know what? I am busy right now. I'm finding I don't have as much time as I used to before my daughter was born."

So Nakato decided to listen to the recordings again and add details to the manuscript herself. And later, when she started working with the editor to polish the manuscript, she decided to sleep even fewer hours each night so that she could concentrate on the rewrites.

# 33

# June - October 2015

WHEN THE MANUSCRIPT was ready, Hellen wrote to twenty literary agents, both in Massachusetts and even further afield, to inquire about finding a publisher but all of them rejected it. Her co-authors were disappointed each time she called them to share the news. "Don't lose hope," Hellen told her sisters. "Did you expect that publishers would be lining up, eager to get their hands onto our manuscript as soon as it was ready? No, reality is less rosy than that."

And so an intensive search for a publisher in Kampala and in Nairobi almost became Babirye's second job until, after two months, her husband, Brian was able to persuade Pebble Books, a small new publisher in Kampala, to publish the biography.

\* \* \*

Ruth was thrilled to hold an advance copy of the biography that Brandon had delivered straight from the publishers' offices. She thanked him and read the title and the subtitle out loud. "*GRITTY WOMEN: The biography of two budding entrepreneurs.* Won't it be interesting for me to read about my life?" she said, smiling.

That evening she took a bath, changed into her pajamas, had an early dinner and settled onto her reading sofa in a corner in her bedroom.

She was flattered by the good comments that Conrad's father, Doctor Gilead Bulega, who was the executive director of the East and Central Africa Centre for Clinical Research, had written about her in the foreword. And, as she read on, she was surprised to find out that her brother Mark had been interviewed for the book. The details about her life in Buweela High School, some of which she'd forgotten, made her feel nostalgic. She laughed out loud when she read that she had wanted to be the school's top netball player and had been jubilant when her arch-nemesis, Clotilda, had been expelled from the school. *That's not true! Mark must have told them that.*

Ruth read the book until shortly after midnight and resumed reading it after she had done her physical exercises and had breakfast the following morning. She put the book down and cried for a few moments when she read an excerpt from the interview that her daughters had had with Mark.

> Whenever Ruth was away on her business trips, my brother-in-law would come to my office. He would tell me that he was worried she would have an affair with the rich businessmen she met on her trips. "I know my sister well," I would tell him. "She would never do such a thing." And Jude would reply, "You never know. She is not angel." It was several years later that I found out that while he was telling me he was worried that Ruth would cheat on him, Jude himself was spending nights in Clotilda's house. But Ruth had never told me about her marital troubles.

Ruth picked up the book and reread the paragraph, then wiped her tears and continued reading.

*Daisy? Who told them about Daisy?* How had her grandchildren gotten to know about her oldest friend? She turned the page.

> I think it was Ruth's ability to not waver from her decisions that set her apart from the rest of us, her friends. I first noticed that trait in her when we were still high school students. If she felt that she was right, Ruth proceeded with her decision, even if it meant challenging authority. Then I noticed it again in the early days of her boutique when she opened it every day, even if she sold nothing, and she remained positive until the business took off.

Ruth laughed. *Oh, well! If the readers knew how scared I was back then, they would find out that I am not the fearless businesswoman my granddaughters are portraying in the book.*

She continued reading the excerpt from the interview with Daisy.

> But I think Ruth's ability to not waver from her decisions caused trouble for her in some areas of her life. For example, while we were in Buweela High School, she was almost expelled from school when she stood up to Clotilda, who had been bullying us right from junior school.

Ruth laughed, paused and tried to remember the details of the incident that Daisy had mentioned. She continued reading.

> But I thought Ruth's decision to marry the arrogant, self-absorbed Jude Kiyaga was the worst decision she had ever made. We were both single young teachers when she introduced him to me at the house we shared. He was arrogant, asking me where I came from—all while showing me how insignificant I was. I actually didn't think the marriage would last, but it did, and I think it lasted only due to the efforts Ruth made to make it work. In the end, though, it was all worth it because Ruth raised a wonderful family and well-behaved, respectful children.

*Sorry, no.* Ruth laughed again. *She* didn't *tell me that she had noticed how arrogant Jude was.*

As she read, she was most surprised to find out that her children had been interviewed for the biography—none of them had told her they had been. She read an excerpt from the interview with Herbert twice.

> My mother is a very caring woman, and she has always been. I am who I am today mainly because of her. She was very strict and she monitored our behaviour closely but she took very good care of us. I don't remember a single morning whenever she was home that Mummy did not prepare our breakfast or sit with each of the three of us to ask how we were doing, if we were happy or if there was anything bothering us. She made us the centre of her life and that way she made us feel special to her every single day. And unlike most parents at that time, who did not expect their children to talk back to them, she encouraged us—and even

demanded—that we speak our minds. To me, she is not only a mother; she is a close friend too.

*Oh. That's so kind of him.* She turned the page.

Unfortunately, for a long time, my father abused my mother. As a young boy, I often heard him yelling at her and calling her names. That annoyed me greatly. And years later, although I was glad to learn that I had a half-brother when we learned that Daddy had fathered an illegitimate son, as a family we were very upset. But my mother was very committed to my father. She really loved him. I sometimes overheard her lovingly advising him to put his life together—you know, like a mother would advise her son. She was there for him and I was glad when he finally settled down, and they enjoyed a happier marriage.

*My son is wiser and more thoughtful that I knew*, she thought, put the book down for a moment before she picked it up again and continued reading.

She found herself laughing at Kate's comments.

There are a lot of noteworthy things about my mother. She is an exceptional woman; she took good care of us and she is entirely responsible for our success. But I think Mummy did a disservice to us in some ways. My mother basically ran our lives—let me give you an example. She kept and filed all the family's official documents, but she did that so well that I doubt any of us learned to organize our documents and records. It was only after my father's death a few years ago that Mummy gave me my academic files, including report forms from all my primary and secondary-school years. And until recently, she has been completing our passport renewal applications, including my children's. And I think, Nakato, you know what I am talking about because, most likely, she has been completing your passport renewal applications, too!

Ruth continued reading and felt grateful for her children. She was eager to read what her "baby," Victoria, thought about her.

Mummy wanted to control everything that my sister, my brother and I did and she seemed to have succeeded. However, I became a source of frustration for her when, instead of going to university, I decided to get married. She got very angry with me and I felt guilty about what she had called my disobedience. I lived with the guilt for years until, when my boys were in middle school, I decided to go back to school. My parents didn't know that I had returned to school until we sent them an invitation to come to Boston to celebrate my graduation.

I don't think it had ever occurred to Mummy that of all her children, it would be me who would follow in her footsteps as an entrepreneur. But five years ago, when at the annual convention of the Ugandan North American Association I was awarded the prize for most industrious entrepreneur of the year for my interior design company, Mummy was in the audience, crying tears of joy.

Ruth had read the entire biography twice by the end of the week, and called all three authors individually to congratulate them.

✳ ✳ ✳

When Leah received her advance copy of the biography, she looked right away for the section that had been written about her mother. After she had read a few pages, she decided that she'd read the book aloud to Merab.

There was one problem though—Merab would not understand the English. Leah would need to translate the passages into Luganda.

She called Nakato. "I'd like my mother to hear the wonderful things you wrote about her. Can you get someone to translate the book into Luganda?"

"No, Mummy. Translating the book would be a long and costly project," Nakato answered.

"How do we ensure that my mother gets to know the contents of the book?"

"I don't know. And may I tell you something, Mummy? After toiling for more than a year on that book, I am fed up with it! And I don't want to look at it again for the remainder of this month."

❉ ❉ ❉

The following day, Leah took the biography to Merab's home to show it to her, but was disappointed when she got there. Even though it was only six o'clock in the evening, Merab was already in bed. When Leah showed her the book Merab sat up in the bed, and she looked at the pictures, but she had trouble recognizing even her late husband.

Leah went out of the bedroom and called Nakato, but she did not answer, so she called Babirye. "I wish you had written this book five or even three years ago. My mother would have been very happy about it. But now she can't appreciate it," she told her daughter. "Can you imagine? This early in the evening she is already in bed—and she is not at all excited about the book."

Leah was so upset she cried for a few moments after the call before returning to her mother's bedroom. She'd brought a chair which she placed by the bed. "Mother, let me read a few interesting passages for you."

"Can you read them another time?" Merab said. "This backache wouldn't allow me to pay attention to what you are reading."

❉ ❉ ❉

Later, when she returned home, Leah continued reading the biography, and when she read the detailed account of how Merab's desire to secure her future had motivated her to work and to succeed in business, she cried again. When she regained her composure, she decided not to continue reading.

But she couldn't resist skimming through the pages, and was happy to read a few of the excerpts from her half-brothers Kulumba and Roger's interviews. Kulumba had said that he'd had two mothers, "the first one was Mufuzi and the second one, my biological mother. Mufuzi raised me, disciplined me and made me what I am today." Roger had praised Merab for having intervened to convince his father to buy him a bicycle instead of having to walk twelve kilometres, each way, to and from his secondary school.

As she continued paging through the biography and read what Ruth had said when responding to the question, "What did you think about Merab when you first met her?" Leah lost her temper.

> What I thought about her? Nothing. Perhaps I was so self-absorbed but honestly, I didn't think anything about her. You know, she was a woman like many others I had met. Oh, one thing, though—I enjoyed the food in her restaurant once in a while. It was delicious. But I couldn't believe it when my son told me that he wanted to marry the restaurant owner's daughter. Oh, dear! Those people were not from within our social circles. Both my parents and my husband's parents had been very rich people. But Merab and her husband were not rich or prominent and I had wondered how we would be able to interact with them.

*Oh, oh. What else did the girls write?* Leah read Ruth's statement again. *I should have read through their manuscript and censored it before they published it.*

# 34

# November 2015

A BOOK LAUNCH at a Kampala hotel was organized, and although Merab was sick, Leah insisted that her mother must attend the party. So Babirye went to her grandmother's home and examined her, telling her mother that yes, Merab could attend the event, but that she would keep an eye on her during the party. That afternoon Leah cried as Brandon pushed Merab in her wheelchair into the hall.

The whole family, including "the Americans"—that is, Victoria, her husband Dan and their sons Sidney and Rodney, from Boston— attended the biography's launch party. And except for Hellen, who had not been able to travel to Kampala, the only member of the family who was missing was Kate.

"Where is Mummy?" Simon, the older of her two sons, asked his father when he and his brother Spencer arrived for the cocktail hour at the beginning of the party and noticed Ham standing alone.

"Oh, you didn't know?" Ham asked. "She's boycotting the book launch because your cousins didn't involve you in writing the biography."

"What?" the young men asked in unison and laughed.

"Did Mummy really think that I could find the time and the stamina to sit down to write a book?" Spencer said, still laughing. "It's a shame that she is missing such an important occasion in our family. Is she at home? Let's send a *boda-boda* to bring her here now."

"I will send her a taxi," Simon said, and stepped out of the hall to go call his mother. When he reached her she told him that she was already on her way—she'd felt bad for Ruth, and after thinking long and hard she had reconsidered, realizing she didn't want to miss the occasion during which her mother would be honoured.

Herbert came to greet both Spencer and Ham. While the three of them were chatting, Brandon saw Zoe walk into the room and go to join her aunt Brittany, who was standing in a corner. *What does she want here? Who invited her anyway?* he wondered. He told Delilah that he needed some fresh air and walked out of the hall to join Simon outside.

✳ ✳ ✳

Kate had just arrived when the Master of Ceremonies Sam Mukuye called the audience to order. He thanked them for coming and called Nakato to speak.

When she rose to speak, Nakato too thanked the audience for coming. She then read the "Author's Note."

> Dear reader, we thought you'd be interested to learn more about the lives of two extraordinary and interesting women. Although it was improbable at the beginning of their careers, both our grandmothers were very successful in business.
>
> We must confess that we found it challenging to write our grandmothers' biography because we found it difficult to detach ourselves from their story, and to forget that we were granddaughters. But we knew that we had to assume the role of impartial authors, and that we had an important job to do.
>
> We not only owe it to our grandmothers to tell their stories, we also owe it to generations of young women, both present and future, to tell a story that will teach, inspire and encourage them to strive to pursue their dreams. If there is just one thing for you to take away from our grandmothers' biography, we hope it will be to learn the value of resilience.

The audience clapped.

Nakato then read a passage that was an excerpt from her interview with Merab which she said would serve to illustrate the evolution of the status of women in the country.

> Other than the first few months after I married Lutalo, the period when I lived alone in Kawempe was the most difficult time in my life. Those days, society believed that a woman was not complete if she did not have a man. So here I was, a young woman without a man, living by myself, with no job and unsure about my future. Other times, I worried that my husband would one day come looking for me and force me to return to Kalasa. Sometimes I worried that he no longer cared for me. I didn't have enough money and I didn't know how much longer I could sustain my-self. It was the desire to improve my daughter's future that motivated me but at that time I doubted I could accomplish that goal.

While she was reading, Nakato looked into the audience. She had not realized that Zoe was at the party and she was now looking intently at her. Nakato's heart missed a beat and she was distracted for a few seconds. *Who invited that miserable creature to our book launch party?*

She turned a few pages and chose another excerpt to read from her interview with Merab.

> Like anyone can imagine, it was difficult to live with sister wives. Although I'd been raised a Christian, many times I failed to practise what I believed in. I did everything to retain our hus-band's favour and whenever any of the other wives made mistakes, deep inside I rejoiced.

The audience laughed. Leah looked at her mother, a little ashamed, but Merab was dozing in her wheelchair. Nakato continued reading.

> I was always on the lookout and found pleasure in their mistakes, and I learned a lot from their mistakes—it was like their mistakes were a classroom for me. At first, I had acted like a mother, always ready and willing to help them. But later, whenever they made mistakes, I did everything I could to avoid the same mistakes. My

husband loved me for that. Unaware of my strategies, the poor women accused me of being a witch, claiming that I put magic potions in our husband's food to gain his favour. Of course, that was not true.

The audience laughed again.

Nakato turned another few pages and chose another passage, an excerpt from an interview with Mark Wamala, Ruth's younger brother. "Ruth was ruthless in business..." she began, and the audience laughed.

Ruth turned to look at Mark. He smiled sheepishly.

Nakato continued.

Ruth is very ambitious. In fact, wherever she was, Ruth believed she was the smartest and the best at whatever she was doing. And, no one could stop her when she had her mind made up and had her sights set on something. Secondly, Ruth never stopped learning. Within a few months after she'd joined our father's construction company as the managing director, she had become an authority in many aspects of our projects. Yet she acquired all that knowledge through self-education, through the many books she read. Thirdly, Ruth was courageous. When she reopened her Classic Boutique, we thought she was crazy. However, I realized that she knew she was taking some risks by reopening the boutique. But she faced her fear and triumphed in the end.

Nakato answered two questions from the audience about Merab and sat down amid a lot of applause. Babirye then rose to read a passage in which Ruth had been asked to share the most important lesson of her life's experiences.

As a businesswoman, let me talk about opportunity. When I started out in business, I thought that opportunities would come to me. I did not look for them, or create them for myself. Fortunately, many curious people came to the shop every day. Months went by without me seizing the opportunity to sell. Then one day, I got out of my chair and started talking to people, whether I thought they were there to buy or simply to admire merchandise. Soon, I was demonstrating products and giving advice, from how to keep their homes clean and neat to how frequently to wash their curtains. My business grew by leaps and bounds. At that time, we relied on word of mouth only to spread the news about our businesses. Now you have the Internet, you have smartphones, you have infinite information at your fingertips. There is no excuse for not creating your opportunities.

The audience clapped. Herbert sprang to his feet as he applauded, and Kate and Victoria followed suit. Ruth smiled at their standing ovation.

Babirye leafed through a few more pages and now read a passage in which Merab shared the most important lesson based on *her* life's experiences.

Cultivate good relationships with people. Remember that people matter. However rich you may be, if you have no people close to you, you are poor. I worked in the restaurant almost every day for nearly fifty years. And my most important memories from that time have to do with people—not the meals I served there and not the money I made there. Therefore, care for your loved ones, create memories for them and share good food. And above all, mend broken relationships.

The audience clapped. Herbert rose again, giving a standing ovation to his mother-in-law this time, and Leah stood and clapped as well.

After the readings, Babirye introduced Ruth, who walked onto the stage to make a speech.

"Good afternoon everyone, and thanks for being here. Although we are here to launch my and Merab's biography, this event is not about us. It is about the authors and it is the culmination of the hard work they did to write this book." She held the thick biography up with one hand and proudly showed it to the audience, who clapped enthusiastically.

"Now, let me take this opportunity to introduce the authors to you. The first is my granddaughter Nakato. Nakato is not only a distinguished pediatrician, she is also a member of the editorial board of the prestigious *East African Journal of Medicine*, and is a gifted writer, too. She has written numerous professional articles, but even though they deal with topics in medicine, I as a non-medical person find them easy to read and to understand. The second author, my granddaughter Babirye, is a distinguished gynecologist. When I heard that she would be co-writing the biography, I doubted she would succeed because Babirye seems to always be on the move, completing one project one day and pursuing another the following day. I didn't think that behaviour would work well with the kind of focus that one would need to write a book..."

The audience laughed.

"... but obviously I was wrong," Ruth continued. "And of course, Babirye had focused in medical school and had become a doctor. The third author is my granddaughter Hellen, a successful entrepreneur who holds an MBA from the Harvard Business School. Unfortunately, she couldn't be here today.

"I have been keeping diaries for more than fifty years. And my granddaughter Nakato conceived the idea for this biography one afternoon about two years ago while reading through several of my old diaries. When she said that she could write my biography basing on the material in the diaries, I doubted it. But here we are." She paused and sipped some water. "The authors wrote some very interesting things about Merab and me in the biography but I am not going to mention any of them. You will read the book and find them yourselves. Reading this book, I experienced a variety of emotions and it has changed me in many ways. And I am glad that the authors talked to the people who know me well. I am grateful for the gift I got through this biography— of getting to know what my loved ones think of me and what I mean to them." Ruth paused, smiling. "I have read the book twice already and have discovered some things I never knew about. But I also read things in there that I wish the authors had omitted," she said, and now she was laughing.

The audience laughed, too.

"Oh, there is one thing that is important to me that is not specifically mentioned in the biography. I am very grateful for the education I received and for the privileges and opportunities that I got. I encourage all you young women here, who like me are educated and privileged, to be grateful for what you are and for what you have, and to reach out to help those who are less fortunate than you are. I also encourage you to always demand more from yourselves and to never settle for the status quo. I know it sounds contradictory but it's possible to be both grateful and to strive for more."

The audience clapped.

"Before I end my speech, allow me to address my five grandsons for a moment." Ruth paused and looked at her grandsons, who were all seated together. "Young men, the girls have challenged you by writing this biography. I urge you to do something, too. But you don't have to write a book. Brandon, you can compose a song with your cousins or even record a CD. I will be the first one to buy a copy. Thank you, everyone," Ruth said, and walked off the stage.

While the audience was clapping for Ruth, the DJ realized that that was a perfect opportunity for him to play the song that Brandon had chosen for his surprise performance. A few seconds before the applause ended, the DJ played the instrumental version of Brandon's hit song *Tobbanga nkoko* for him to sing along. The audience was pleasantly surprised when Brandon jumped onto the stage, and they clapped and cheered as the DJ handed him the microphone. Brandon was surprised, too, when as if on cue his cousins Rodney and Sidney jumped onto the stage right after him, and then the other cousins, Spencer and Simon, followed suit.

As the song progressed, Rodney, standing next to Brandon now and sharing the microphone, sang along with his cousin even though he didn't know Luganda and couldn't sing the song perfectly in that language. And while they sang, the others danced, and when Brandon sang "...*tukitegeera tolina wadde ekuba ennyonyi*," and Rodney repeated after him, "*Tukitegra tolina a day Cuba onion*," the crowd jumped and cheered.

Zoe felt so jealous that she stormed out of the hall. Delilah watched her and laughed.

The grandsons' singing and dancing were so good that some in the audience thought that they had rehearsed their performance. Kate and Victoria shed some tears of joy as they filmed their sons with their iPhones and iPads. When the song ended there was a loud, long round of applause for Brandon and his cousins. Kate was so glad that she had finally come.

Then, after some last-minute reassurances from Herbert, Leah rose to speak on behalf of Merab. "Ladies and gentlemen, my name is Leah Nalutalo Kiyaga. I am the only daughter of Merab Nantamu Lutalo…"

Merab awoke when she heard her daughter mentioning her name and looked up for a few moments.

"…and the mother of our three authors," Leah continued. "I would like to thank all of you for coming this afternoon, not only to honour the authors but also to join our family in celebrating, once again, the lives of these two amazing and extraordinary women."

The audience clapped. Herbert rose and clapped louder and longer than the rest, overjoyed by his often-shy wife's confidence.

"It is indeed a great honour to my mother that her granddaughters found it fitting to write her biography alongside that of their other grandmother, the incomparable Ruth Kiyaga. My mother is a woman worth celebrating because she did not let the many obstacles she faced—from having been given little formal education, to having married very young in a rural area—get in the way of achieving great things. In addition to raising many children, she built the most enduring restaurant in the city. And as the book's authors have demonstrated, if there is one thing readers should emulate from my mother, it should be her perseverance. Everyone, get a copy of the biography, and please don't let it sit unopened on your shelves—read it! I promise that you will get some important life lessons out of it. I thank you." Leah walked off the stage amid applause and cheering.

❋ ❋ ❋

"Hellen should have been around to savour this moment with us," Babirye said to Nakato shortly after they had signed the book of the last of the three hundred and twenty readers who'd been standing in line.

"Yes, it would have been even more inspiring if Hellen had been here," Nakato agreed.

❋ ❋ ❋

Hellen had missed the biography's launch party for a reason. That afternoon in Boston, she was wiping away tears of joy as Gwen's maid of honour as Gwen and her boyfriend were exchanging their wedding vows. *You deserve this amazing man, Gwen. You've been through a lot. Go ahead, say "I do!" Kiss him!* Hellen thought. And the groom wasn't Lorenzo, or Miguel, either, who'd been quickly dumped as soon as Gwen discovered that he was more interested in her money than in her. It was Devon.

Devon, Hellen and Gwen had all been students at the Harvard Business School together and he had admired Gwen ever since, but hadn't had the courage to tell her what he felt, and then she met Lorenzo. But by chance they now lived in the same condo building, and one afternoon, meeting in the elevator shortly after Gwen had broken up with Miguel, Devon had gathered the courage to talk to her, and they had chatted happily until Devon got out on his floor. When they met that way a second time, he had asked her for her phone number. A few months later, using the opportunity to "help Gwen recover from the heartache," he had taken her on a Mediterranean cruise and proposed marriage to her on a gondola in Venice.

At the reception after the ceremony, Hellen was enjoying herself, and when Devon and Gwen opened the dance, she danced with Devon's older brother and best man, Todd. That reminded of her own wedding. She longed to dance with Conrad, but Conrad could not join in the dancing—she smiled at him as he walked past her and out of the hall, diaper bag and baby Mary in his arms, on his way to the restroom to go change her.

# 35

# November 2015

TWO DAYS LATER, Hellen called her sisters to congratulate them for having successfully organized the launch party. Babirye and Nakato said that they had missed her at the party and filled her in on the highlights. Hellen laughed when they mentioned that their cousins Sidney and Rodney, both dentists, had danced at the party and that Rodney had even sung. The conversation then turned to Gwen's wedding and then to Hellen's baby before, towards the end of the call, Hellen asked about their parents' finances.

Babirye said that she had been successful in controlling their mother's spending, and Hellen congratulated both her sisters for that. "And what about the boutique? How is it performing now?" Hellen asked.

"There are still challenges at the boutique," Nakato said, "and Elsie is getting fed up. I think one of these days we should start looking for a general manager."

"Here is my advice," Hellen said. "Don't wait any longer. Please, do it now—go ahead and hire a general manager. We will reorganize the business after that."

The following day, to start the process, Nakato called Executive Staffing Solutions to help with the search. After the contract had been signed, she called the managers at the boutique to communicate the news.

Two days later, while she was chatting with Petua, Katana, the other manager at the boutique, told Petua that a general manager was about to be hired. Petua advised Katana to apply for the position. Katana laughed and said that "they" would hire Elsie instead of her.

Ever since Veronica's wedding, Petua had been wondering what material benefit her daughter could get from Kiyaga's family. Now, when she returned home that evening, she got an idea—Veronica could become the general manager of Ruth's Classic Boutique! She could take over its ownership from her father eventually.

She called Veronica the following day. "They are hiring a general manager soon for your father's boutique and I would like you to apply for the job," Petua said after the greetings.

"What? Are you serious? That's a big position. I can't apply for it, Mummy," Veronica answered, laughing. "I am not qualified for it, and I don't even live in Kampala anymore!"

"I know what I am talking about," Petua answered. "I worked in that shop for decades and I know the demands of the job well. You can do it. And getting involved in the family's business is one sure way for you to get closer to the other members of your family. And for your information, now that your father owns the boutique, if you manage it well, it could eventually be yours."

Veronica laughed. "How did you arrive at that conclusion?"

Petua ignored the question. "Let me tell you the truth. You are the only one of Herbert's children who is poor."

"I'm not poor, Mummy," Veronica said, amused.

"Yes, you are. And listen to me carefully. I want you to apply for the job. I have friends still working in the boutique and they tell me that there is total chaos there and your father doesn't seem to care. When you get the job, you will reorganize the boutique and you'll end up owning it because Herbert would be glad to hand over the boutique to his own daughter."

"But, Mummy—"

"Think about it. I want an answer tomorrow, and I strongly advise you to return to Kampala by next week. Let's talk again tomorrow," Petua said, ending the call.

❊ ❊ ❊

Veronica went to the kitchen where Kyle was preparing breakfast. "Mummy just called, this time to ask me to return to Kampala for work."

"For work?" Kyle asked as he tossed an omelette onto a plate.

"Yeah, she wants me to apply for the position of general manager in Uncle Herbert's boutique."

"Cool. Apply for the job. 'Hi, I'm Veronica Mitego. I am the GM of Ruth's Boutique,' or whatever the name is," Kyle said, laughing.

Veronica laughed too. "Mummy is serious, though. What do you think?"

"I don't know. Are you interested in the job and would like to move back to work in Kampala?" Kyle asked as he began to cut some yellow peppers.

"No, I'm not."

"Then tell her that."

"But it is not as simple as that for me to do."

"Hey, you've got to stand up to your mother. If you don't, she will go on running your life to satisfy her ego," Kyle said, sliding the pepper slivers onto their plates. "And we know that's not good."

❊ ❊ ❊

Veronica called Petua the following morning.

"Do you have an answer? Time is running out," Petua said after the greetings.

"Yes. I talked it over with my husband. I can't return to Kampala," Veronica said.

"What would stop you from returning?"

"Mummy, I have a job and an amazing life here and honestly, I don't think that I am qualified to become the boutique's general manager."

"Veronica, for years you wanted to go overseas to earn money, so you could get rich quickly. But then you did not know that you were a rich man's daughter. But now I am telling you that there is an opportunity for you to get rich. The boutique is very profitable."

"Mummy, I am not ready to return—"

"Vero, I know how much you want to get rich, and this is what I think. Instead of working as a clerk in a small store, in a foreign country, come back home to your father's flourishing business. You will make all the money you want."

"Is it as easy as that? Aren't they going through a hiring process with several other candidates for the job?"

"Probably, but I'll ensure that you get the job."

"What's there to guarantee that I will get the job?"

"It's your father's boutique. Leave everything to me. I will convince him."

❄ ❄ ❄

Petua, feeling confident that she had convinced Veronica to apply for the job, called Herbert right away, telling him that she wanted to discuss Veronica's future.

"I am busy right now," Herbert said. "I don't think—"

"Listen, sir. I am not asking to see you right now. Can we meet this weekend?"

Herbert kept quiet for a few seconds. "Why don't you tell me whatever you want to say over the phone?"

"No, it is an important matter. I want to discuss it in person."

"I am afraid you'll have to come to my home. I promised Leah—"

"No," Petua answered angrily. "It is a private matter between you and your daughter."

"Then why doesn't Veronica call me herself? Actually, she called me three days ago but she did not mention any pressing issues."

"Listen, Mr. Kiyaga, sir—your daughter is working as a clerk in a small store, in spite of her academic qualifications and experience. Yet you own a successful boutique. Why don't you let her manage it?"

"Is that what you wanted to tell me? Of course I would love to have my daughter managing my mother's business!"

"No, it is no longer your mother's business. It is your business. Don't think I am stupid."

"Yes," Herbert said, trying not to lose his temper. "I would love to have my daughter managing *my* business. But I didn't know that she was interested in the job. We are beginning the search for a general manager soon."

"Yes, I know that. That's why I am telling you, early enough, that your qualified and experienced daughter is available, ready and very interested in the position."

"Good—very good, I am happy to hear that. But I don't know if she is qualified to manage such a big shop."

"Yes, she is, and I want you to assure me now that Veronica will get the job."

"A formal process will begin soon but I will make sure that if she is qualified for the job she will get it."

"Can I count on you?"

"Yes."

# 36

# **November 2015**

HELLEN CALLED VERONICA that afternoon. She introduced herself and they chatted for a few minutes. Towards the end of the call, Hellen said that she would like to travel to Toronto to meet her, and Veronica said that she was excited to meet Hellen.

"But do you feel ready to host me? I have some free time next weekend and can book a flight," Hellen said, and then hesitated. "But I would totally understand if you were not ready."

"I would love to meet you! Yes, please come visit us," Veronica answered. "I work till late on Fridays, but I can probably take a day off."

"No, you don't need to do that—I'll fly into Toronto Friday evening and can take a cab from the airport straight to the hotel downtown. I'll join you guys for breakfast and lunch on Saturday and fly back here Saturday evening. Does that sound like a good plan?"

"Yes," Veronica answered.

❋ ❋ ❋

Hellen arrived at Kyle and Veronica's apartment the following Saturday morning with a bottle of wine, a bouquet of flowers and some toys for Kyle's son Chase. She and Veronica were glad to meet and while Kyle prepared the table for breakfast, they chatted like they had grown up together.

After breakfast, Hellen and Veronica sat in the living room and continued chatting while watching a slideshow of Kyle and Veronica's wedding. "That looks like it was an amazing wedding," Hellen said. "I feel bad that I missed it."

"Your wedding was amazing too," Veronica said. "I saw the pictures at Aunt Ruth's house. I mean Grandma Ruth's house," she said, laughing.

* * *

Later, while Hellen remained in the living room to play with Chase, Kyle and Veronica went into the kitchen to cook lunch. "It's true. She is your sister," Kyle whispered to Veronica.

"Why do you think so?"

"You look so much alike! I wonder why people failed to notice that for so long. Man, oh man, she is *hot*! Oh my gosh, those gorgeous eyes—"

"Will you stop that?"

"Sorry," Kyle said and gently poked Veronica in the ribs. "Are you jealous?"

* * *

While they were having lunch, Veronica told Hellen that her mother Petua wanted her to return to Kampala to become the general manager of Ruth's Classic Boutique. "Do you think it would be a good idea for me to go?" Veronica asked.

Hellen hesitated. "I think it would be a good idea for you to give it a shot," she said finally. "But it all depends. Would you like to work in a retail store?"

"She works in a retail store here, albeit a smaller one," Kyle answered before Veronica responded.

"Cool. I guess what matters is, like, for you guys to agree and then you go give it a shot. Would you want to move to Kampala, Kyle?"

"No," Chase answered, and everyone laughed.

"Hey, buddy, you are not Kyle," Kyle said to his son and turned to address Hellen. "I am not sure I would move to Kampala."

"I understand. Conrad had a hard time adjusting to life in Boston. I guess it would be hard for you, too, to adjust and to enjoy life in Kampala," Hellen said.

"Oh, well. But what I don't get is that Veronica can't say no to her mother's demands," Kyle answered.

"This is an important matter for you guys to agree on," Hellen said, sensing some tension between Kyle and Veronica.

"We will work it out," Veronica said, and asked Hellen about her baby, pointedly changing the topic.

※ ※ ※

After the biography had been launched, the twins bought several newspapers every day, and enjoyed reading about themselves and the positive reviews that the biography was receiving. And when she saw an article in the *East African Journal of Medicine* that mentioned that she had co-written a biography, Nakato photocopied it, framed it, and hung it in her home office.

One Saturday afternoon while perusing *The New Observer*, she saw another review, this one written by Phoebe Mbogo. She was Leah's friend, and also a daughter of Ruth's longtime friend Timothy Mbogo.

On one hand, Phoebe had praised the authors for having written their grandmothers' biography despite their busy lives. On the other hand, Phoebe wrote, she thought that as a person who had known Ruth personally for a long time, it had not covered her extraordinary career satisfactorily—that, for instance, she'd been surprised to note that the Women's Development Association, founded by Ruth, her late sister Hannah and a number of other women, had not been mentioned at all. She also felt that the section dedicated to Merab's career was shallow.

As Nakato read, she could feel herself losing her temper, and— contrary to what she'd told her nanny for years never to do—placed her coffee cup on the glass table and rose to go call Phoebe.

When Phoebe did not answer she immediately called Leah and asked her to talk to Phoebe, to express her disappointment. "Nakato, you didn't think you would get only positive reviews—or did you?" Leah asked, surprised by her daughter's unusually hot temper.

"I didn't expect only positive reviews, but Aunt Phoebe should have been more civil in her comments."

❄ ❄ ❄

Even though she did not want to, Veronica traveled to Kampala to be interviewed for the job. *What I am doing is stupid. I am not qualified for the job, and I am going to end up wasting a lot of time interviewing for a job that I don't want and can't get. Anyway, it is good to visit home and to see my people.* Petua was waiting for her at the airport, and they went directly to her home.

"Veronica is here," Petua told Herbert when she called him that afternoon. "She arrived this morning and she is ready for the job."

"Good, she is right on time. I'll let the recruiters know that she is here. They will contact her for the next steps," Herbert answered.

"Recruiters? What are you talking about?"

"We hired a company to interview the candidates for the position."

"You hired a company? But you promised me that my daughter will get the job."

"I think she will get the job, but there is a formal process. Unfortunately, I am not the one in charge of that process. My daughters are."

"Really? You promised—"

"Can I talk to Veronica?"

After Veronica had talked to Herbert, she told her mother that the conversation with her father had increased her doubt about her chances of getting the job. "He told me the kind of person they need for the job and it is clear that I don't have—"

"No! It is your father's boutique! Go for the interview and you will get the job," Petua said, but she sounded alarmed. Taking her cellphone back from Veronica, she went to the bedroom to call Clement.

Clement reassured her that Veronica could do the job. He also said that by becoming the boutique's general manager, Veronica could eventually own it. "That's what I thought," Petua said excitedly.

"I can help you throughout the process. Let's discuss the details tomorrow," Clement said, and gave Petua directions to the place where he'd meet her.

Petua had told Clement that she wanted his help as long as whatever he planned to do did not affect her relationship with Ruth and, by the end of the call, she felt confident that Veronica would get the job—and, eventually, the boutique. She knew that Kiyaga's daughters had stopped Clement from working at the boutique, but she also knew that he could influence his brother.

After talking to Petua, Clement rejoiced—if he supported Veronica for the job, he'd have even more chances to make money! In fact, he'd be able to extract money from Ruth's Classic Boutique if either his former girlfriend Brittany *or* Veronica got the job. Whoever was hired would feel indebted to him and would let him become a middleman in the boutique's supply chain.

* * *

The following day Petua went to the address Clement had given her, and when she knocked on the door was shocked when Zoe opened it. Petua knew Zoe as a popular musician and Brandon's close friend, but not as Clement's girlfriend.

Petua told Clement that she did not feel comfortable discussing Veronica with Zoe. Clement assured her that she could trust Zoe and said that because she knew the Kiyaga family well she would be helpful in securing Veronica the job. "Please sit down and feel at home," he said. "Let's start the conversation right away. Petua, what do you have in mind?"

"My greatest desire is for my daughter to become the general manager and to eventually take over ownership of the boutique, but I am not sure it can happen," Petua answered.

"Oh, yes, it can happen," Clement said. "Herbert is not at all interested in the boutique. His daughters are not interested in it, either. So he would be happy to give it to your daughter."

"Are you sure about that?" Petua asked again.

"Yes I am," Clement said. "You only have to speak nicely to him and praise him for being a good father and things like that. Tell him that your daughter had been excluded from the family for too long and then demand compensation. In the meantime, Zoe will find and give us some useful information. The boutique will eventually be Veronica's, and the first step we will take is to ensure that she is hired as the general manager." He paused. "If down the road she doesn't get ownership of the boutique, she can take money out of it to start her own."

"What can you do to help us out?" Petua asked.

"This is where Zoe comes in—she will provide all the information you need, on the condition that she and I get twenty percent of the shares in the boutique."

"But Ruth has been nice to me all these years and she paid for Veronica's education. I can't steal from her," Petua said.

Clement laughed. "Don't say that again. She's been nice to you all these years? So what? You want to miss a chance to make money simply because you want to remain loyal? That's why some of you will die poor."

When she returned home, Petua did not tell Veronica that she had met with Clement.

❋ ❋ ❋

Three days later, as she climbed the stairs of the staffing agency on her way to the interview, Veronica felt unsure of herself, but her mother had convinced her that it would be good for her to manage her father's business. *But will it be good for me or will it just be good for my mother's ego? I am going to waste time trying to please my mother.*

She stood still for a few seconds at the closed door. *I should calm down. I am competent. I can do this.* She knocked on the door and entered a large room where the interviewers—two men and one woman—were already seated at a big table. About two metres away at the front of the room there was a smaller table and a chair for the candidate.

The smiles on the faces of the interviewers immediately made Veronica feel at ease and more confident. The interview started promptly, and was to last about forty-five minutes. Veronica felt she was answering the questions satisfactorily until a question caught her off guard.

"How did your education prepare you for this job?"

She started to answer the question but lost her train of thought mid-sentence. She paused and focused on the woman, as if seeking her sympathy. The woman smiled at her and nodded slightly to encourage her. But Veronica still couldn't find the right words. *Are they doubting that a zoologist can manage a home furnishings shop? Do they think that I am not qualified for the job? That I am here only because my father owns the shop?* She took a deep breath before answering. "While at the university I often led experiments and class projects. When leading a team on such a project, we simulated an animal sanctuary, from conception to launch. It was my biggest accomplishment and it earned praise and high marks from our professors. And as far as job experience is concerned, I managed a restaurant here in Kampala and I currently work in a store in Toronto." She paused before saying, "I work well with people."

The interviewers thanked Veronica for her time, and the woman reassured her that she thought her interview had gone well. "We will be in touch soon."

When Veronica left the room, the interviewers discussed her, and all three said that she had impressed them.

❉ ❉ ❉

When Veronica returned home, Petua asked how her interview had been. Veronica said that she thought it had gone well but that she would wait for the results. Petua served her a cup of tea before returning to the kitchen. Veronica sat quietly in the living room, her thoughts ranging from the interview to her life in Toronto and to the possibility of returning to live in Kampala, before she broke her silence.

"Mummy, I think Lugard is avoiding me," she said. "I have been here for four days now and it's strange that he has not come to see me."

"I realized that he was avoiding you when he missed your wedding," Petua said, walking back into the living room and sitting to face Veronica. "Is there a problem between you two?" Petua asked.

"No, no problem. But it bothers me that he is avoiding me," Veronica said.

"It bothers me, too. He came here three weeks after your wedding and when I asked him why he had missed the wedding, he said that he had been sick. But then I told him that you had been in Kampala for over a month, and that he couldn't have been sick for over a month and we didn't know about it. His answers to that were not convincing," Petua said, looking sternly at Veronica.

"Yes, well, then, Lugard and I do have a problem," Veronica said. She regretted mentioning her cousin at all. "I sent him $12,000 in installments to buy me a plot of land and now I suspect that he conned me out of my money."

"Really? Of all people, you trusted Lugard with your money? I thought you knew him well," Petua said, shaking her head.

"What? You knew that he can't be trusted with money?" Veronica exclaimed. Her eyes were glistening with tears.

"Yes," Petua said and rose, picking up her cellphone. "Let me call him to see if he will talk to you and can offer some explanation." Lugard did not answer the call. "Let's wait to see if he calls back," Petua said and sat back down, "but I hope you have learned a lesson."

But Lugard did not call back that day or the next. "Most likely he knows that you are visiting," Petua told her daughter. "He always calls me back promptly."

"Do you know where he lives?" Veronica asked.

"No, I don't," Petua answered.

✳ ✳ ✳

Veronica called her friend Tammy, who had first reported suspicions about Lugard. Tammy said that she did not know where Lugard lived but she knew where to find him. When Veronica and Tammy arrived in Kamapala two hours later, they found Lugard sitting on a bench with two friends on a shop veranda, having lunch and chatting noisily.

"Oh, Veronica, I didn't know you were in town," Lugard said when Veronica and Tammy stood before him. He rose to shake hands with both of them.

"What would you have done if you had known I was in town?" Veronica asked, looking at Lugard without blinking.

"Of course I would have come to chat with you. I am glad to see you," Lugard answered, laughing uneasily.

"Mummy called you the other day to tell you that I was home. Why didn't you call her back?"

"Oh, she called me? I didn't realize that I missed her call," Lugard said and pulled his cellphone out of his pocket and pretended to check his missed calls as his friends rose to let Veronica and Tammy sit on the bench. They then walked away with their food and drinks and left Lugard alone with his visitors.

"Stop checking the phone," Veronica said as she sat on the bench next to Lugard. "I want you to take me now to see my plot of land."

Lugard remained silent for about twenty seconds his eyes fixed on the floor. Both Veronica and Tammy watched him as they waited for his response.

"Yes, I can take you there, but first I have to call the broker who connected me to the seller," Lugard answered, avoiding Veronica's gaze.

"Why would you need to contact the broker? You told me you paid for the land in full and took possession of it."

Lugard did not answer. It was clear that he did not have an answer to that question. He rose after a short awkward silence. "Okay, I will take you there now. I'll be back in a moment," he said.

"No, sit. Finish your lunch before we go there. We are not in a hurry," Veronica said.

"It's okay. I am done," Lugard said, and he started to walk away into an alley at the end of the veranda. "I will be back in a minute."

Veronica and Tammy remained chatting there on the bench for close to an hour, with Tammy getting up every five minutes or so to check the alley for Lugard, but there was no sign of him. About the tenth time she checked, she saw one of the young men who had been with Lugard when she and Veronica arrived. She signaled him to come.

"Where is Lugard?" Tammy asked.

"He went home."

"What? How do you know that he went home?" Tammy asked.

"He came and told us shortly after we left you and him here. I didn't even know that you two were still here."

"Okay, thank you," Veronica said to the young man and she and Tammy started walking away.

"I think my suspicions are correct," Tammy said.

"You know what? Let me forget the whole thing. I have more urgent things to attend to now," Veronica answered.

"But that's very bad. You work hard for your money and surely Lugard knows that," Tammy said, and noticed that Veronica was starting to cry.

When Veronica finally returned home, Petua was not there, and she cried for her money and felt an urge to talk to Kyle. But Kyle did not know that she had been sending money to Lugard, and so she cried some more before deciding that she had to let it go and went to bed. *I will not talk to Lugard ever again. And he is fooling himself if he thinks that the $12,000 will make him rich; it will never make him rich. He will die poor and miserable.*

❊ ❊ ❊

Three days after Veronica's interview, another candidate impressed the interviewers more than Veronica and the other eleven candidates they had interviewed earlier. And it was Brittany.

The oldest of all the candidates, Brittany was more confident than all the rest and seemed to be the best qualified for the job. She was so eloquent and well-prepared that her interview took the shortest time, too.

"I will ask you two more questions," the same woman who'd interviewed Veronica told Brittany as the other interviewers started to gather their folders. "First, why should we hire you instead of another candidate?"

Brittany shifted on the chair and sat up straight. "I have ten years' experience in retail. For five of those ten years, I was the general manager of Nile Fabrics. Actually, we sold some merchandise to Ruth's Classic Boutique. Under my leadership, Nile Fabrics grew at an average rate of eight percent annually over the period of five years until it was acquired by Eastern Textiles."

"And what strategies would you put in place to help Ruth's Classic Boutique grow?" the woman asked.

"I have been shopping at the boutique for more than ten years and two of my friends have worked there in managerial positions. When I was at Nile Fabrics, like I said, we sold some merchandise to the boutique. I therefore know the boutique's successes and challenges. If I were hired, I would focus on certain key details that have, up until now, not been prioritized. For example, that shop is too big for its current staff to run efficiently. I would hire six more employees, and another assistant manager. And within one year, I would open a second shop north of the city where there is a higher concentration of rich people. Furthermore, I would ensure that the boutique stocks the kind of high-quality goods it was known for during the decades its founder and owner worked there."

Brittany noticed that the two men had reopened their folders and were taking notes, and her spirits rose. She continued, "And I would streamline the business's core values to enhance the relationships between management and the employees and between the employees themselves." She hoped that what she'd just said was clear. She paused. It seemed it was clear. Nobody asked her to clarify.

The interviewers were impressed by Brittany's eloquence and confidence. They all said that she would be contacted for a second interview.

❋ ❋ ❋

The last candidate to be interviewed was Japheth Obuku, a nephew of John Odur, Leah's former boss. When the interviewers asked him about his most recent job experience, Japheth informed them that he had just returned to Uganda from London, where he'd had a fifteen-year career as a manager at Harrods.

At first, Obuku didn't come off as experienced as Brittany but as the interview progressed, the interviewers realized that he had plenty of practical and innovative ideas that would boost the boutique. Towards the end of the interview, he said that if he were hired, he would bring Ruth back to work.

The interviewers laughed. "How would you do that?" the woman asked.

"Ruth's Classic Boutique is Ruth herself. She is a powerful brand. I would capitalize on that to use her in marketing. I would use her on TV, online, and print media. The possibilities are endless."

The interviewers took notes.

"Let me ask you one final question," one of the men said. "How did you prepare for today's interview?"

"I visited the boutique and spent one hour there—discreetly, of course—to analyze its opportunities and threats," Obuku said. He then opened his bag and took out three copies of a thin neatly spiral-bound document. He rose and handed a copy to each of the interviewers. He went back and sat down.

He took the interviewers through the document, mentioning his observations at the boutique. Among other things, he said that it had so many customers that it was often crowded. He said that if he was hired as the general manager, he would open another location near the Northern Highway, and named the actual building where he would open the new location. It was evident that he had done his home-work—he told the interviewers that he'd found out that the lease of one of the businesses in the building was about to expire, and that it wasn't being renewed. He showed the interviewers some key figures, including the number of potential customers for the new location and the time it would take for it to break even. He also told them about some competitors—three smaller boutiques—that had opened near Ruth's Classic Boutique—to attract some of the Boutique's customers who were growing tired of standing in long lines to wait to pay for merchandise.

"Congratulations. You prepared for your interview very well and it shows," the woman said after Obuku's presentation. "Gentlemen, do you have any more questions for Japheth?"

"No more questions from me," one of the men said, tapping his spiral-bound copy. "This document answers everything."

"No more questions from me, either," the second man said.

All three congratulated Obuku, thanked him for coming to the interview and said that he should expect a call back for a second interview.

# 37

# December 2015

VERONICA WAS AT home, still thinking about Lugard's betrayal, when Executive Staffing Solutions called to invite her for a second interview. She was so surprised by the call that her thanks to the woman who called her were half-hearted. She called Kyle right away to give him the news. "I'm actually beginning to think that I might have a shot at this job after all," Veronica said after Kyle had congratulated her.

"Be sure of yourself and your confidence will shine. Then you will ace the second interview," Kyle said. He'd decided not to discourage Veronica. "I'm proud of you!"

"Thank you—I can't believe it! Is it possible that Uncle Herbert, I mean, my father, influenced their decision?"

"Veronica, I don't think it's your father's influence that helped. You are a competent, confident woman. And that's what you should tell yourself going into the second interview."

"Thanks for the encouragement, hon. I need it."

"But you don't sound happy. Are you really interested in that job?"

"Yes, I am beginning to get interested in it," she said. "But my gut feeling tells me that I will not get it, and I might be wasting my time here. A second interview means at least another week here, and I don't know how much longer Melody can wait for me. I might lose my job."

"Vero, I have been thinking about you and, seriously, I think you should stand up to your mother. Don't let her use you just to satisfy her ego. I am going to send you a link to a video—watch it, and you will understand what I mean."

Veronica ignored Kyle's comment. "How is Chase?"

"He's good. I will be picking him up in a bit."

\* \* \*

An hour later, in Toronto, Kyle picked up Chase from his mother's home to come spend the weekend with him. On the way to his place Chase asked about Veronica.

"Veronica is in Kampala—"

"She is in Kampala? I want to go back to Kampala, too," Chase said. "It's awesome!"

"Great. Actually, she is there to look for a job. If she gets it, we'll all move there," Kyle said, lightly.

"We will move there and live there, like *forever*?" Chase asked, now alarmed.

"Yes."

"No, I don't want to live there! Kampala sucks!"

"But you just said—"

"No, everyone in Kampala sucks. And I don't even speak Ugandan."

"You mean Luganda, not 'Ugandan,'" Kyle said, laughing.

"I don't speak it."

"Then you will stay here with your mom and I will go to Kampala with Veronica."

"No. Mom's apartment sucks, too! There are no toys!" Chase said, raising his voice.

\* \* \*

When she walked into the room for the second interview, Veronica noticed that there were three interviewers—the woman she had met during the first interview—and two men.

"Veronica, thanks for coming this morning. We would like to ask you a few more questions to understand your qualifications better," one of the men said after the greetings and some small talk about the weather in Canada. "Why do you want to work at Ruth's Classic Boutique?"

Veronica remained silent for a few seconds, thinking. "I would like to use my love for home furnishings meaningfully by leading a team of people in the best shop in the city. I shopped in the boutique several times in the past and I think it is a place where I would love to work."

"What are your two top strengths?" the same man asked.

"I am a good listener. I love people and I value the opinions of others. That quality has been appreciated in all the places where I have worked. Secondly, I am committed to my work. Whenever I am carrying out a task at work, I do it as if I were the business owner. The people I have worked for have all been pleasantly surprised by my level of dedication to my work."

"How do other people you work with help to make you a better leader?" the second man asked.

Veronica paused for about ten seconds to think about an answer. "I don't know everything. Because of that, I humbly accept the fact that even though I am the leader, there is a lot I can learn from my peers and my subordinates and I take the time to learn from them." She wondered whether her answer was satisfactory.

"Did you get a chance to visit the boutique recently?" the woman asked.

"Yes, I did."

"What did you observe there?"

"I went to the boutique at around noon last Tuesday and it was busy, with many people shopping and walking around the floor. I also noticed some customers walking around idly with merchandise in their shopping baskets while waiting to be served. I concluded that the store is understaffed."

"Those are good observations," the second man said. "What would you do to improve the business?"

"In addition to hiring more employees, I would expand the business by opening a bridal wear section inside the boutique. The boutique's customers are mainly rich young and middle-aged women— you know, women who have family members and friends who are about to get married, or even women who are preparing to get married themselves. I think bridal wear would be a great line of business that would have a direct, positive impact on sales of the other merchandise."

"I am a frequent shopper at Ruth's Classic Boutique myself," the woman said. "Please tell us how exactly you would position bridal wear in what you yourself acknowledge is a too-crowded home furnishings shop?"

Veronica hadn't prepared for that question. She paused for a while to think about an answer. "I would create low-hanging shelves in the furniture section in order to create room for the draperies. That would free up space for a small but cozy section for bridal wear." She doubted that her answer was convincing.

"Wouldn't bridal wear require lots of space, including a fitting room? You would probably need another area too where a team of tailors would sit to make some adjustments and touchups," the woman said.

"Yes," Veronica answered and kept quiet. She looked at the woman and smiled.

The second interview ended much earlier than Veronica had expected. The interviewers asked for her references and said that they would contact her.

❉ ❉ ❉

Veronica felt confident that she had done well in the second interview at first, but sitting in a taxi a half hour later, she began to feel doubtful. She wondered why she had had to go through all the trouble of taking time off work, leaving her husband behind and preparing for two interviews—all to apply for a job in her father's company that she was not guaranteed to get. Then she wondered whether she'd even been successful at faking her enthusiasm. *I neither want nor need this job— what a waste of time!*

Petua was not there when Veronica arrived home, so she lay on the couch and tried to nap while she waited for Kyle's call. But she couldn't.

"You know what?" she told her husband as soon as her phone rang. "I think I have just wasted a lot of time. I can't get that job."

"Then come back home, baby! I can't wait to see you back here," he said. "By the way, did you watch the video on the link I sent you?"

"No, I haven't checked my emails at all. I will watch the video later."

After the conversation with Kyle, Veronica quickly packed her suitcase. She was going to spend a few days in Nakato's home while she waited for the results of the second interview.

❋ ❋ ❋

On the day after her second interview, Brittany got a call from Executive Staffing Solutions asking for her academic transcripts, which made her hopeful about getting the job. She delivered them to the agency office that afternoon, and was pleasantly surprised when she got there, to note that the young woman she gave the transcripts to had been her niece Zoe's classmate, and she knew her. They chatted for a few minutes and the woman told Brittany that one of the shortlisted candidates was Kiyaga's daughter.

Brittany called Clement as soon as she left the agency, and she was fuming. "I've just found out that one of the candidates for the job is Kiyaga's daughter and I think she is the one they will hire for the job. The rest of us are there just as a formality. Clement, I can't believe that you managed to fool me!"

"I didn't fool you and I don't know why you doubt that you will get the job. The fact is, you *will* get the job," Clement said.

"How do you know?" Brittany asked, her voice rising.

"The fact that you were asked to submit your academic tran-scripts—"

"Shut up and stop fooling me. You are not at all involved in the hiring process. Actually, your nieces threw you out of the boutique because they don't need you there."

Clement was shocked—how did Brittany know about his encounter with the twins at the boutique?—but he did not respond.

"Clement, if I don't get that job, prepare to find me another one immediately or else I will ruin you!" Brittany yelled, and ended the call.

# 38

# January 2016

THE RELATIONSHIP BETWEEN Kate and Herbert's family did not improve even after the book launch party. Herbert often called his sister, but she hadn't answered or returned his phone calls for weeks, and he was getting concerned.

He called his brother-in-law about it and Ham confirmed that there was indeed a problem. Kate was bitter, he told Herbert, and asked Herbert to visit Kate at home to discuss the problem. But two days later, when Herbert did go to see Kate, nobody opened the gate for him to enter, even though he was certain she was home—her car was parked in the front yard. He told Leah and his children about it.

"I don't think the problem is just that we didn't involve Simon and Spencer in writing the biography," Babirye said to Nakato and Brandon while they were chatting in Ruth's home the following day.

"There is probably something else," Nakato agreed. "Aunt Kate has changed a lot."

Meanwhile, Brandon was thinking about Zoe. She had threatened to ruin him. *What could she mean?*

He decided to try to find out the cause of the problem. As soon as his sisters left he called Zoe and asked her to return the laptop they'd been using to write their music. She said that he should pick it up from her apartment.

When he went there, she brought the laptop to him outside the building and he took it, walking away without saying a word to her.

✳ ✳ ✳

It was plain that Kate felt a lot of resentment towards Herbert and his daughters. *They have taken over control of my mother's property. They are making themselves famous, first by organizing a party to celebrate Merab's and my mother's life. And then they published Merab's and my mother's unauthorized biography. Clement is up to something, too. I am sure he is not frequenting the boutique for nothing.*

But there was one member of Herbert's family for whom Kate only felt pity, and that was Veronica. *She is new to the family and she can't be part of the twins' schemes.* Kate decided to intervene to help Veronica, and she knew who could help her do so, Clement's former business partner, Jairus. So she called him. "I have been made aware that interviews are going on for a general manager for my mother's boutique. And I gather that my niece Veronica and Clement's ex-girlfriend Brittany are both candidates. Is Clement involved in or interfering with the process?"

"No, he is not involved in the process but he *is* trying to interfere with it," Jairus answered.

"I am concerned about Veronica. She is new to the family and I don't think she knows anything about the boutique," Kate said.

"You are right, Kate. Veronica should withdraw her candidacy," Jairus answered. "She stands no chance of becoming the boutique's general manager. I can talk to her if you want."

"Yes, please help."

"Okay. If you are available, you can introduce us at the club this evening. I will tell her everything I know."

Kate asked her son Spencer to find Veronica's phone number, and when he called Nakato for it, she also told him that Veronica was spending a few days in her home.

Kate called Veronica that afternoon.

※ ※ ※

When Kate and Veronica arrived at the club, Jairus was waiting for them. Kate introduced them and went to wait in another room.

"My mother is almost forcing me to work in the boutique," Veronica said just a few minutes into the conversation. "She actually seems to be interested in owning the boutique herself."

"I think that it is understandable that your mother would like you to get your share of some of Kiyaga's property, but the methods she is using are wrong. She is associating with Clement but he is not the right kind of person to help her," Jairus said and paused.

"What kind of help does she want from him?" Veronica asked.

"I think he convinced her that he can help you to get the job in the boutique but he can't—he has no influence in the process at all. Besides, tell me one thing, Veronica—do you really need that job?"

"No, I don't."

"Let me tell you this because you are a young woman, and you need to go on with your life with your family," Jairus said. "I know the owner of Executive Staffing Solutions. He tells me that you are still on the shortlist for the job just because your father put in a word for you."

"Thank you for telling me that," Veronica said, relief in her voice. "Actually, my mother doesn't know this but I have already decided to go back home."

"That's a wise decision because you can't get that job. I think your mother is hoping that your father will influence his daughters to give the job to you but the truth is, Herbert is more interested in saving his marriage than giving you the job. The real person who is going to decide who gets the job is his wife, Leah. And you are not Leah's favourite candidate."

* * *

Clement had called Petua early the next morning to tell her that he would call as soon as the new general manager of Ruth's Classic Boutique was announced later in the day, and she waited anxiously in her living room throughout the morning, too anxious to eat breakfast, waiting for the news. Whenever her cellphone rang, she thought it was going to be Clement, and when the phone rang towards noon, she rushed to pick it up. It wasn't Clement, but Herbert who was calling.

"Do you have any news for me?" Petua asked, ignoring Herbert's greetings.

"I have news but not for you. Can I please talk to Veronica?"

"She is not here. Did she get the job?"

"I said I want to talk to Veronica, not to you," Herbert said.

"Please tell me what it's about."

"No, I want to talk to her directly."

"Veronica went to Nakato's home to visit three days ago and she has not yet returned here."

"I've called her but her phone is not available."

"Are you sure about that? Okay, I'll call her and let her know that you wanted to talk to her." Petua hung up, now even more anxious. She called Veronica several times during the next two hours but the phone was off.

❋ ❋ ❋

Veronica woke up after four hours' sleep feeling tired and unrested, and needed to stretch her legs. She rose and went to the washroom, but when she returned and tried to watch a movie, she couldn't concentrate on it. Her thoughts kept wandering from her last interview to her family, around and around.

Then she switched on her iPad and saw the email from Kyle. When she opened it, there was the video link that Kyle had mentioned. *Oh, what's this about?* It was a short clip, a speech by a motivational speaker and author named Darren Brown. She leaned back and settled in to watch it.

Some of you are busy setting goals, day in and day out, year after year, but let me ask you this—are those goals your goals or your parents' goals? Are you pursuing your dreams or your parents' dreams?

Veronica shifted, interested. *That's an important question. I traveled to Kampala and wasted three weeks pursuing my mother's dream—who was I kidding?* she thought, becoming a little angry with herself. *Could I ever become a general manager of Ruth's Boutique? I've wasted a lot of time!* In the video, Brown was still speaking:

People waste precious years of their lives in jobs they don't like and working for bosses they hate, simply because they want to please their parents. But I say stop—don't do it any longer! Stop living somebody else's dreams. I know what most of you tell yourselves. "Oh, my parents want the best for me." That's true. But make no mistake—your parents don't know it all. They can choose the wrong school or the wrong course of study for you. Be the driver of your own life.

When the video ended Veronica watched it two more times, then sat back to think. *Oh, how I wish I had seen this video before I decided to go to Kampala! Oh, well.* But she felt better about herself. She was glad that she had decided to return to Toronto and not to wait for the news from Executive Staffing Solutions. *But what if I have been appointed general manager of the boutique? It's too late. I don't care.* She switched the movie back on that she had begun watching earlier, and dozed a little. Then the lights were switched on.

"Ladies and gentlemen, this is your captain. We will be starting our descent shortly. Make sure your seat backs are in an upright position and that your seat belts are securely fastened. Please double-check to make sure your carry-on luggage is stowed underneath the seat in front of you or in the overhead bins. The current temperature in Toronto is -14° Celsius. Please keep warm! I would like to thank you on behalf of the crew for choosing Atlantica Airlines. We hope that you've enjoyed your flight and do hope to see you again soon."

❋ ❋ ❋

Petua became more and more anxious as she waited for Clement's phone call but the phone did not ring. She called him while pacing in her living room, but Clement did not answer. She waited for close to an hour but there was still no phone call. She thought that Veronica would call with some news but she didn't call, either.

Petua decided to call Nakato. "I was expecting Veronica to return home this morning. Is she still at your home?"

"Oh, Veronica? She went back home to Toronto last evening," Nakato answered, surprised.

"Are you sure about that? She wouldn't leave without saying goodbye to me," Petua said, shaking.

"Yes, I am sure—Roland and I drove her to the airport and we did not leave until the plane had taken off."

"What? Why didn't she at least call me? Besides, I heard that the announcement will be made anytime today concerning the appointment of the Boutique's general manager," Petua said as she walked to Veronica's bedroom.

"The new general manager has already been announced. His name is Japheth Obuku."

"Thank you," Petua said, trying not to sound disappointed, and ended the call. Her heart raced when she saw that the bed was neatly made and Veronica's suitcase was not in the room. There was no doubt her daughter had planned to leave without informing her.

\* \* \*

"Clement has been lying to me and raising my hopes about the job at Ruth's Classic Boutique," Brittany said to Anastasia when they met at Nakivubo Lane café that evening. "I wasted a lot of time applying for the job and doing exhausting interviews, but in the end the job has been given to somebody else."

"Oh, I am sorry to hear that," Anastasia said, pretending to care.

"Now I am going to need your help. Clement must pay for his mischief. I want you to help me to get money—lots of money—from him."

"No, I am not going to get involved in your schemes anymore," Anastasia said, unable to hide her disgust.

"You will, because if you don't, I will tell Clement that you duped him, took lots of his gifts in a fake introduction ceremony and married another man instead. By the way, I have plenty of your wedding photos. I hired my own photographer to take them," Brittany said, opened her handbag and showed a few photographs to Anastasia.

Anastasia laughed loudly. "That's all right—if you tell Clement about my wedding to Dominic, I will tell him that you are an impersonator. I know that Brittany Bukirwa is not your real name, and that you never attended the university from which you claim to have graduated. You are actually using the academic papers of your cousin who died in an accident in Europe. You didn't take a single university course during the seven years that you spent in Europe—in fact, you worked as a hotel cleaner throughout your stay there, and I have proof of all that."

Brittany's heart started racing. She put her head in her hands, both elbows on the table, and remained in that position for a long time, speechless, before she gave Anastasia an angry look and started crying. Anastasia watched her in silence and for a moment felt pity for her.

Brittany rose after about five minutes. "You are very stupid, Anastasia, and you will get into a lot of trouble if you continue talking about things you know nothing about," she said and walked away quickly, fuming.

# 39

# January 2016

BRANDON'S SUSPICIONS ABOUT Zoe persisted. He felt that she had something to do with the misunderstandings in his family, but didn't know what, so he hired a private investigator. Two weeks later, Brandon and the investigator met in a restaurant.

They shook hands, and then the investigator placed a thick envelope on the table. "What's in here?" Brandon asked, pointing to the envelope without touching it.

"The information that you paid for," the investigator said and walked out.

Brandon drove home, and saw that Delilah had not yet returned home. He sat in the bedroom, opened the envelope, and slid out some of its contents, a stack of photographs. One answer they gave him was different from the one he had expected. *Spencer? This can't be true!* But there it was, the truth, staring at him—his cousin Spencer, enjoying time alone with Zoe, in a bar. *How could Spencer, a married man, do this?* He went through more of the stack, and when he saw Zoe also with Clement, he completely lost his temper. *What? Uncle Clement is dating Brittany and now her niece Zoe, at the same time? He is a sick man!* Placing the envelope in a drawer, he lay down on the bed, trying to calm himself. Ten minutes later, Ruth knocked on the door. It was time for dinner.

Brandon chatted with his grandmother for about twenty minutes after dinner before returning to his bedroom. He'd decided to see what was on the USB key in the envelope. It was an audio file, and on it he could make out what sounded like a quarrel between Zoe and Spencer. They seemed to be breaking up. "You are very stupid," Brandon heard Spencer saying. "Roland kicked you out of his apartment and I gave you an even better one. Is this how you pay me back? How dare you send untruthful email messages to my mother? Do you want to destroy my family?" *What does this mean? Roland, Zoe, an apartment. Untruthful email messages. Destroying Spencer's family. Had Roland been renting out an apartment to Zoe? Does Nakato know about the apartment?* Brandon paused the audio recording, now furious. *But what can I do with all this information?* He thought hard but couldn't find any answers.

Now, for the first time since Zoe had returned his laptop Brandon switched it on, and methodically began to open every file, examining each to look for any incriminating evidence. After opening about thirty files, just when he was about to quit, a file labelled "CZ_A" caught his eye. He opened it, and saw that it was an agreement between Clement and Zoe, which declared that Clement and Zoe would each own twenty percent of the shares in Ruth's Classic Boutique indefinitely if they helped Veronica to become its general manager and eventually to take over ownership of the boutique. Brandon was reading the agreement a second time when he heard Delilah talking to Ruth in the living room. He shut off the laptop and went to join them.

❊ ❊ ❊

"You are unhappy and you don't sleep well these days. What's going on?" Delilah asked Brandon in their bedroom later that evening.

"There are problems in the family—you've probably noticed something," Brandon answered.

"No, I am not aware of anything."

"We've been bothered by Aunt Kate's unusual attitude for several months now," he said, "and I suspected that Zoe has something to do with it. So I hired a private investigator to help find out what's going on. The investigation has unearthed more than I could imagine." Brandon took the photos out of the dresser drawer and showed them to Delilah.

Delilah was too stunned to say anything when she saw the pictures of Zoe with Spencer and with Clement, and when Brandon played her the audio recording on the USB key. "And that's not all," Brandon said, and showed his wife the agreement.

Delilah read the sentence twice. "'…twenty percent of the shares in Ruth's Classic Boutique'—but is this agreement authentic? Can your uncle betray the family?" Delilah asked.

"I don't know."

Delilah could see that her husband was crushed by his uncle and cousin's possible betrayals, and tried to put a positive spin on what she could see with her own eyes. "You've got to give some people the benefit of the doubt, Brandon. Spencer's meetings with Zoe were probably for business."

"You are right, but I've been asking myself many questions and finding no answers. What is the relationship between Zoe and Roland? What is the relationship between Zoe and Spencer? Do Petua and Veronica know about the agreement? If they do, what made them think that they could take over ownership of the boutique? Who do I tell about the things I have discovered?"

"You're telling me—that should make you feel better," Delilah said. "Besides, if you get answers to any of those questions, what are you going to do with them?"

"Probably nothing."

"Then let it go," Delilah said, and switched on some soft music.

❋ ❋ ❋

Brandon was not the only one who learned about Zoe's relationship with Clement. Brittany found out when Clement's on-and-off girlfriend Gilda told her. "So, instead of taking care of his children, Clement is wasting money on my good-for-nothing niece?" Brittany yelled when Gilda told her the news. "I will teach both of them a lesson!"

❋ ❋ ❋

Brandon went to his sisters' clinic the next afternoon to tell them what he'd discovered. Babirye was still working, so he met with Nakato in her office.

"I don't know why someone I considered a close friend turned against me all of a sudden. Zoe changed after I married Delilah," Brandon said, shaking his head.

"Tell me the truth, Brandon. Have you ever been in a relationship with Zoe?" Nakato asked, sitting down at her desk to face Brandon.

"Never."

"I've never liked Zoe," Nakato said. "I have never told anybody about this but I found out during the week before your wedding that she had been Roland's mistress until he found her in bed with another man, in *his* apartment!"

"Oh, who told you that?" Brandon asked.

"It was Kibalama, the custodian. He told me that Roland had given Zoe two days to vacate his apartment but she refused to leave, telling him that she couldn't before she found alternative accommodation. He heard that Roland threatened to throw her out but she told him she knew the law!" Nakato said. "Kibalama told me that Roland fired him a few days later because he refused to change the lock on the apartment's door. When he came to me during the week of your wedding, he was jobless and desperate, and asked me to intercede, but he didn't reveal the events that led to his firing until I interrogated him."

"So, did he confirm—" Brandon began.

"I actually went with Kibalama to Zoe's apartment and we confronted her with the facts."

"You did what?" Brandon asked, amazed at what she was telling him. "Babirye could do that, but not you, Nakato!"

"Yes, I did! I was fed up with Roland's lies. I blasted Zoe and that's probably why she has turned against you. When I confronted her, she denied everything. When the custodian persisted with his story, she threatened to call the police."

"What?"

"When I returned home, furious, I told Roland what I had found out. He denied that the incident I was talking about ever happened and he said that he would ensure that Kibalama was jailed. But when I said that I would divorce him, he admitted everything. That same evening, he called Kibalama—who's a relative of Roland's, by the way—and apologized to him and gave him his job back. And Roland is behaving much better these days, only drinking a little bit and returning home before dark every day."

"That's sad, but I am glad you know about Zoe and Roland's relationship. I have some sort of proof of it. Listen to this," Brandon said. He handed the USB key to Nakato, who plugged it into her computer and listened to the recording.

"This is further proof of what Kibalama told me," Nakato said, nodding her head.

"But what about Spencer and Zoe's relationship?" Brandon asked.

"Spencer sponsors Zoe's music career, that's all. She probably lives in his apartment as a part of the sponsorship."

"Oh, I didn't know anything about the sponsorship," Brandon replied, "but now that makes sense. I should never have trusted Zoe—she is a bad person."

Babirye joined Brandon and Nakato after her office closed twenty minutes later. They filled her in on what they'd been discussing, and Babirye said that she was shocked to know that Zoe had been Roland's girlfriend. Then Nakato retold her story about how she had confronted Zoe.

"But when did you and Kibalama go to Zoe's apartment? I didn't notice that you did anything unusual," Babirye said.

"It was on the evening of Brandon's last wedding meeting. Do you remember that you left the clinic early to go prepare for the meeting?" Nakato asked, and Babirye nodded. "I was walking out of the clinic when the custodian arrived. He asked to speak to me privately and we came back here, to my office. He told me everything about Roland and Zoe's breakup and when he said that he knew where Zoe lives now, I asked him to take me there."

"What?" Babirye said. "Nakato, I didn't know that you could do such a crazy thing!"

"I couldn't believe it either when she said it," Brandon said, smiling.

"So, I drove to Zoe's apartment, and I blasted her as soon as we got there," Nakato said.

"That makes sense now," Babirye said. "When the wedding meeting started, I remember I called you, and you said that you were held up some—"

"I was actually going to come to the meeting right after I had blasted Zoe, but the story takes an even stranger twist," Nakato said, and paused to drink some water. "When Zoe threatened to call the police on Kibalama, the poor man got afraid and rushed out of the apartment. Zoe started crying then, and saying how sorry she was for cheating with my husband. I took pity on her and sat next to her on the sofa to console her."

"What? You consoled the home-wrecker instead of slapping her?" Babirye said. She and Brandon laughed.

"Yes. She promised me that she was no longer seeing Roland, and we talked for several hours—that's how I found out that the apartment she lives in belongs to Spencer. By the time I left her apartment, it was too late for me to come to the meeting."

"The truth is, you are happier these days, and I am proud of you for having defended yourself and for saving your marriage," Babirye said.

Before they parted, Brandon and the twins agreed they would tell their parents about Zoe during a family meeting that Ruth had called for that weekend.

# 40

# January 2016

WHEN KATE AND HER son Spencer went to Ruth's home on Saturday evening for the family meeting and walked into the living room, Kate was surprised to see Herbert and his children there, and to learn that Hellen was phoning in, too. Only Leah was not there—she was at the hospital where Merab, eighty-five and seriously ill, had been admitted the previous day.

Kate wouldn't have wanted to meet any of them, but now it was too late. When Herbert warmly welcomed Kate and her son, Spencer responded well to his uncle's greetings, but Kate was cold.

"I am glad the entire family is here for this surprise meeting," Ruth said after the greetings. "Unfortunately Leah couldn't join us due to her mother's illness, but I knew that if I'd told Kate that Herbert and the rest of his family would be here, she probably wouldn't have come. I have been informed that there are some ongoing misunderstandings in the family—the reason I have brought you together this evening is to find out what is going on and to solve the problem. Please start talking."

Their mother's statement took Herbert and Kate back to their childhood when Ruth used to talk to them in the same room, in a similar manner. They knew she wanted answers and the conversation wouldn't end without them.

There was total silence.

*This is the right moment to share the investigator's findings, but how much of the findings do I share? Anyway, it's now or never.* Brandon rose and stood in the wide entrance to the dining room, where everybody could see him. "I think I know who is causing us all this misery. A few weeks ago, I took it upon myself to investigate the problems we are having in the family. And my investigations led me to a possible culprit. Unfortunately, it is my former friend, Zoe."

Kate, who didn't know that Brandon and Zoe were no longer friends, thought he had misspoken. "Now that you have mentioned Zoe, let me show you the emails she has been sending to me, which she said you sent her, Brandon," Kate said, opening her bag and taking out her iPad. She switched on the iPad, found the email messages and handed the device to Brandon.

Brandon perused the messages in silence, visibly shocked. "Read them out loud so we all get to hear what this is all about," Ruth said to Brandon.

The family listened, in disbelief, as Brandon read out a few passages from three of the many email messages that Zoe had sent to Kate over the last months, about Kiyaga's daughters wanting to control the family's wealth, their efforts to become their grandmothers' favourite grandchildren, Herbert's scheming to take ownership of Ruth's Classic Boutique by hiring Clement ...

"Brandon, please stop reading," Ruth said, raising one hand and picking her glasses off the table. "Kate, you believed that?"

"Yes, but I am sorry," Kate answered.

"When you were growing up in this home, what did I repeatedly say that we should do whenever we get unverified information?"

"I am sorry. Mummy, please don't interrogate me. Everyone, please accept my apologies. I didn't know that Zoe was a liar," Kate said and started crying.

Herbert rose and hugged his sister. "I forgive you," he said.

"Spencer, did you know about those emails before you came here this evening?" Ruth asked.

"Mummy, don't interrogate my son," Kate said before Spencer responded. "Please forgive me."

Nakato noticed that Babirye was boiling with anger, and when Babirye attempted to speak, she squeezed her hand to stop her, afraid that she might say something inappropriate to their aunt.

Kate had noticed, too. "Please forgive me," she said again, looking at the irate Babirye, who just sat back in the sofa without a word, her arms folded and her expression plainly revealing what she was thinking. *Shut up! I didn't know that you were so stupid.*

When Spencer rose and walked out of the living room Brandon followed him outside. "I have been sponsoring Zoe's music career and I know about her bad behaviour. I already knew about the emails you just read and I have already taken steps to end the sponsorship," Spencer said. "Actually, I am going to her apartment now to give her a piece of my mind."

Brandon said that he wanted to confront Zoe, too.

"If you want, we can talk to her together," Spencer said. He went back to the living room and asked Babirye to drop Kate off on her way back home. Meanwhile, Brandon went to fetch his laptop in his bedroom, and then he and his cousin drove to Zoe's apartment.

❋ ❋ ❋

When Spencer and Brandon arrived at Zoe's apartment, they found her drinking and chatting with Clement. Brandon was happy that Clement was there—it would give him the opportunity to confront them together. But Spencer was shocked to find Clement there. He did not know that Zoe was his girlfriend.

As for Clement, he was embarrassed and could not hide his uneasiness. He greeted the two young men nervously and as soon as they sat down, he rose and picked up his jacket, ready to leave. "Before you go, Uncle Clement, there is something I would like to show you," Brandon said, as he pulled his laptop out of its bag and switched it on.

Zoe's whole body started shaking.

Clement sat back down. "What is this?" he yelled after he had perused the document, attempting to fake indignation.

"Oh, you don't know what it is about?" Brandon asked. "I thought you knew about it."

"No, I don't. Who wrote this letter?" Clement asked, mustering an irritated tone.

"No, it is not a letter—it is an agreement. Zoe and I shared this laptop for years. Maybe she can tell us what this agreement is about,"

Brandon said and handed the computer to Zoe, who pretended to study the agreement. She looked up after a moment, declaring that she did not know anything about Ruth's Classic Boutique.

"But both you and Uncle Clement are named in this agreement," Brandon said.

"Yes, we are—so what? What is there to prove that you didn't type this document yourself?" Zoe asked.

"You are right. I have no proof because the document is not signed and I don't intend to follow up this matter," Brandon said. "But I wanted you and Uncle Clement to know that I came across it."

"My dear Brandon, do you believe that I could do what this so-called agreement alleges?" Clement asked in a soft tone, sitting back down.

"No, Uncle, I don't believe that you could do that but, like I said, I wanted you and Zoe—"

"Brandon, I will sue you!" Zoe yelled, dramatically pointing her finger at him.

"Before you think of suing Brandon, take a look at this letter for you. It's from my lawyers," Spencer said as he took a folded piece of paper from his pocket and rose to hand it to Zoe. "And let me warn both of you," he said, looking at Clement now, too. "We will likely sue *you*, or even have you charged, because some of your activities are criminal." Clement remained silent, his eyes fixed to the floor while Zoe gazed at Spencer and Brandon, the letter in her lap, her eyes glistening with tears.

Spencer and Brandon walked out.

As soon as the cousins had left, Zoe stood up and locked the door behind them, then opened and quickly read the letter before handing it to Clement so he could read it, too. Spencer's lawyers had written that because Zoe's actions were both unbecoming and regrettable their client had been forced to withdraw his sponsorship and the associated privileges she had been enjoying, demanding that she surrender the keys to their client's Range Rover immediately and vacate their client's apartment within ninety days. Zoe and Clement hugged on the sofa and started crying in each other's arms.

About five minutes later, when there was a knock on the door, Zoe's heart skipped a beat. *Have Brandon and Spencer come back?* She rose and gingerly opened the door. It was Brittany.

Zoe did not need to ask why her aunt had come to her apartment—she knew right away that she was looking for Clement. She tried to block Brittany in the doorway but her aunt was much stronger than Zoe was and pushed her so hard as she charged towards Clement that Zoe fell on the floor.

Brittany started attacking him even before Zoe rose. "You fool! Instead of caring for your children you are wasting money on this good-for-nothing girl?" Brittany said as she slapped and scratched Clement's face. Clement fought back but Brittany got hold of his shirt. She ripped it off. "You are pathetic!" Brittany yelled as she elbowed Clement in the stomach. "Herbert cares for you as if you were his real younger brother and you plot to steal from his business?"

"You are more pathetic than me," Clement yelled back, punching Brittany hard on the cheek. "You are an impersonator. You are using your dead cousin's academic—"

"Shut up!" Brittany yelled as she staggered back. She picked up a little side table and threw it at Clement, aiming for his face. Clement ducked, and the table flew across the room and smashed into the sideboard instead, narrowly missing the TV.

"Don't damage my property!" Zoe yelled, running out of the apartment to bang on her neighbour's door for help. The neighbour's boyfriend was there, a bouncer at Jupiter Night Club, and he rushed to Zoe's apartment and helped to end Brittany and Clement's fight.

❊ ❊ ❊

After dinner at Ruth's home, the twins had gone immediately to the hospital, where Merab was now in critical condition, to join their mother at her bedside. Herbert had driven Kate home and then returned home and was sitting in the living room, his cellphone on the table, waiting for Leah's call. But Leah did not call.

Herbert was beginning to doze on the sofa when he heard the security guard opening the gate. His heart skipped a beat. He wondered what kind of news Leah was bringing, and why she had not called him and had returned home instead. He rose and looked through the window.

But it was not Leah that drove into the front yard—it was Clement. *Why is he here so late, and why didn't he call first?* Herbert wondered. He rose, opened the door and went to the veranda to meet him. As Clement parked the car, got out and walked to where Herbert was waiting for him, Herbert noticed that Clement was crying, and that he was sober. Herbert's heart skipped a beat.

"What's wrong?" Herbert asked when Clement stood before him on the veranda, tears coursing down his cheeks.

"Herby, I met Brandon and Spencer this evening and I am sure they are going to tell you a number of bad things about me. Unfortunately, whatever they are going to tell you is true. I am a troubled man, Herby. And I have not been a good younger brother. I need help," Clement said, sinking down onto the veranda, still crying.

"What's going on?" Herbert asked, holding Clement's hand. For a moment he doubted Clement was sane. "Please come in and talk to me. You are in distress."

Herbert did not hear his cellphone ringing in the living room.

THE END

What is your impression of Frenemy Matriarchs and The Girls Take Control? Please post a review now at Amazon.com, Amazon.ca, Amazon.co.uk or Amazon.eu

www.geoffreykiggundu.com

www.facebook.com/geoffreykiggunduauthor

https://twitter.com/gkiggundu5

# About the Author

GEOFFREY KIGGUNDU was educated at Makerere University and Université de Rouen. He taught French in Makerere University before emigrating to Canada. He currently lives in Milton, Ontario with his wife and three children. His first novel The son of Kasaka was published in 2013.

www.ingramcontent.com/pod-product-compliance
Lightning Source LLC
Chambersburg PA
CBHW021331250626
47155CB00002B/677